Puppets of Chaos

Larry Arnold

iUniverse, Inc.
New York Bloomington

Puppets of Chaos

This is a work of fiction. All of the characters, names, incidents, organizations, and dialogue in this novel are either the products of the author's imagination or are used fictitiously.

iUniverse books may be ordered through booksellers or by contacting:

iUniverse
1663 Liberty Drive
Bloomington, IN 47403
www.iuniverse.com
1-800-Authors (1-800-288-4677)

ISBN: 978-1-4401-1687-2 (pbk)
ISBN: 978-1-4401-1689-6 (cloth)
ISBN: 978-1-4401-1688-9 (ebk)

Printed in the United States of America

iUniverse rev. date: 12/30/2008

PUPPETS OF CHAOS

Do my deeds tortured soul
I'm the one in control
I breed the life that you know,
I pull the strings--lead the way
Do just what I say
Suck up the pain and obey
You dedicate your whole life
Sacrificial knife
I'm the way you survive,
I make the way every day
Spreading pain and dismay
And with your life you repay,
I'm the shadow on the wall
You're the one I call
Someone to take the fall,
I know you well--where you dwell
In the darkness of hell
All alone in your cell
Time after time I betray
Silently you pray
But you don't know what to say,
Nothing more--nothing less
You're the puppet I test
Another chaotic mess,
I'm your anger in the night
The sole reason you fight
The one who takes all your light,
I bring the end--I descend
Onto your life and pretend
To be your only true friend,
But I disguise--tell you lies
Hide the truth from your eyes
Because it's you I despise,
Your twisted life is my game
I'm the one you can blame
Chaos is my wretched name . . .

PROLOGUE

Lil Joe stared out the window of the bus in an attempt to catch one last glimpse of the night's clear starry sky before entering the prison gates. He knew it would be a real long time, if ever, before he would set his sights on it again. Even if he could witness a beautiful night sky or a sunny day from within the prison walls, it wouldn't be the same as seeing it from the outside. The solitude of this particular prison had a way of stripping a man of his ability to enjoy the everyday miracles of life that were often taken for granted.

Upon entering the prison gates, Lil Joe immediately noticed the change of mood in all the prisoners on the bus. For some, it was the mixed emotions of excitement and nervousness from not knowing what to expect; for others it was just plain fear. But for returnees like Lil Joe, it was just the same old routine. A hovering cloud of darkness set in upon entering this particular prison known as California's notorious Pelican Bay, or "Skeleton Bay" as most convicts preferred to call it. For some, it was because of the hellish rumors that circulated about the place; for others it was the actual personal knowledge of life behind the walls of pain. Lil Joe was aware that the media often referred to the prison as the worst of the worst. However, whether the title referred to the convicts on the inside or the prison guards was a mystery to him.

After the bus entered the prison gate checkpoint, it was inspected inside and out by the gate guards on duty. Then it was driven down a short blacktop road past another gate into the pit of the Security Housing Unit (S.H.U.), where a large group of angry looking prison guards were waiting to welcome the new arrivals to what would be the beginning of their soul's decay. The bus came to a halt in front of the concrete loading dock and the rear gunner on the bus shouted out from behind his protective steel cage, "Everybody shut the fuck up!" Then with a wicked grin, he adds, "Welcome to Pelican Bay, the end of the road!"

That was a term Lil Joe had heard many times in his life. However, he had long ago come to the conclusion that there was no end of the road until you were dead.

A tall, burly, Caucasian guard with a familiar face stepped onto the front of the bus, opened the cage divider, and began calling out names from a crumpled list he held in his hand. As he called out the names, one at a time prisoners began to hobble to the front of the bus to be processed into the S.H.U. Halfway down the list, the guard hollered out Lil Joe's name. "Hernandez, Joseph, last two 76." Lil Joe slowly stood up and made his way to the front of the bus. Right away the guard recognized his face. "Aw sheet, Hernandez, you're back already?"

Lil Joe frowned. "Yeah, it appears so."

"For how long this time," the guard asked.

Lil Joe looked the guard in the eye with a hardened glare. "Until the fat lady sings," he replied.

"Damn," the guard frowned and said, "that's too bad. Well, welcome home."

Welcome home! thought Lil Joe. He decided not to take offense at the statement, figuring it more the truth than a disrespectful comment. After all, he was now a lifer, so the dark dungeon he was about to enter would more than likely be his home until the day he died.

A supervising sergeant standing on the pit dock yelled out, "Put all of these guys in holding cells!" Lil Joe knew the routine. He'd sit in a 4x4 holding cell until the prison medical staff evaluated him, and then he'd be taken to his assigned cellblock.

After the guards removed Lil Joe's leg irons, they placed him in a holding cell and removed his shackles through the metal slot in the holding cell door. Shortly afterwards, an elderly staff nurse pushing a small plastic cart stacked with prison medical supplies and prisoners' files approached Lil Joe's cell door. "Name and last two, please."

"Hernandez 76."

"Okay, good. I'm the nurse on duty tonight and I'm gonna need to ask you some questions regarding your health. Okay?"

Lil Joe smiled. "Sure, go ahead."

The nurse returned his smile. "Okay, do you have any medical conditions that we should be aware of?"

"No, I'm fine."

"Are you taking any medications at this time?"

"No."

"Well, okay then. I need to give you a tuberculosis skin test before we can release you to your cellblock."

Lil Joe nodded. "Okay, let's do it." He stuck his right arm through the metal door slot and the nurse administered the shot under the skin of his forearm.

"Okay." She smiled. "That's it. You have a good night."

"All right, I will. You too."

As soon as the nurse moved on to the next cell, a couple of escort guards walked up to the Lil Joe's cell. One of them yelled out, "Hernandez, you ready to go?"

"Yeah, I'm ready."

"All right, then, go ahead and strip out."

Lil Joe began to strip down. He knew the routine. Get naked, open your mouth, move your tongue around, lift up your arms, pick up your scrotum, and then turn around and squat and cough. Same old song and dance. Lil Joe grunted to himself, thinking that he could probably make a good living as a male stripper doing that same routine. After he redressed, one of the guards pulled out a pair of handcuffs. "All right, Hernandez, let's go." Lil Joe backed up to the door and stuck his arms through the slot to be handcuffed. After he was cuffed, the guards opened the door. "All right, back on out."

As he backed out, Lil Joe asked, "What block am I goin' to?"

"Nine Block," one of the guards replied. "C-9."

Lil Joe nodded in response and took a look around as he walked down the long corridor on his way to his housing unit. He observed that nothing had changed since he left. The place was still dark and dirty and smelled like wasted life. The gunner walking along the steel catwalk above the corridor floor stroked his mini 14 while sneering down at Lil Joe. The intimidation tactic made Lil Joe chuckle under his breath. Yeah, same old shit, he thought.

As he and the two escort guards reached the end of the corridor, they entered Nine Block through the open doorway and Lil Joe caught a glimpse of the wristwatch of a guard who passed by to talk to the tower guards. It was after 11 o'clock, pretty late to be arriving at the prison. The guards escorted Lil Joe all the way into his pod and his assigned cell on the bottom tier. The cell door was already open when he got there, so Lil Joe walked straight inside. Once inside, he was instantly reminded of the all too familiar sound of racking metal as the door slid shut behind him. Lil Joe backed up to the door and stuck his hands through the tray slot so the guards could remove the handcuffs.

Afterwards, the guards closed the slot and pointed to the lower bunk at the back of the cell where Lil Joe's bedding and other general necessities were. "There's your linen and fish kit. Everything's there," he said. Then he and his partner walked out of the pod.

Lil Joe looked around his cell as if sizing up an old adversary. "Well," he muttered, "here we are again. Just you and me." The cell was dirty, which came as no surprise. However, the 12x8 box of metal and concrete was now his home, so he decided to clean it. He grabbed a towel from his bunk and tossed it into the sink and pushed the hot water button. Though it was pretty late to be cleaning, he had to do it. There were too many health hazards in prison to let a dirty cell go unattended even for one night.

Lil Joe knew that most convicts in the S.H.U. were early risers and more than likely everyone in the pod was already asleep, so he would have to clean as quietly as possible. He grabbed a bar of soap from his fish kit and began soaping up the towel in the sink. It had been a long day and now all he wanted to do was clean the cell, take a bird bath, and try to get some sleep. Out of respect for the other convicts in the pod, he tried to keep from making any noise while he cleaned up. However, it wasn't exactly an easy tasks considering that the pods in the S.H.U. were so compact that a guy couldn't even fart without everyone else knowing about it.

While he was cleaning, Lil Joe wondered who else might be in the pod with him. Each S.H.U. pod has eight two-man cells, four upper-tier cells and four lower-tier cells, and each of the S.H.U.'s twenty-two cellblocks were made up of six pods. If Lil Joe had arrived earlier, one of the other convicts in the pod would have asked him who he was and where he was from, all common questions asked of new arrivals. He would have also found out who else was there in his surroundings. But it was too late and all that would have to wait until morning when everyone was awake.

As Lil Joe finished his cleaning, his stomach growled with hunger. He hadn't eaten all day. He had learned long ago not to eat anything on a transfer day. It was bad news. A guy could end up with an upset stomach and have to suffer through a long, uncomfortable bus ride. When he finished cleaning to his satisfaction, Lil Joe took a quick bird bath, made his bed, and lay down, attempting to sleep. But he couldn't. Instead, he lay on his bunk thinking about the events of his life that had led him to the present moment. His thoughts drifted all the way back to when he was thirteen, just before his life took a turn for the worse and took him on a journey through unimaginable chaos.

CHAPTER ONE

LIL JOE REMEMBERED HIS CHILDHOOD LIKE it was yesterday. He grew up in an old style housing project in the southern California city of San Bernardino. He came from a broken home and lived with his mother and younger brother, Marco, in a small, three-bedroom house on the west side of town. Marco was eight years old and had a different father, but that never mattered much to Lil Joe. He and Marco were real close and shared a tight brotherly bond.

Lil Joe's father, Joe Sr., lived out of state in a little town in Arizona where he moved after he and Lil Joe's mother were divorced in 1975. Lil Joe's parents maintained a respectable friendship for his sake and Lil Joe was able to visit with his father from time to time so that they could still be a part of each other's life. Their visits usually took place in the summer when school was out or sometimes during long holiday breaks. Lil Joe always enjoyed his visits with his old man. They shared a unique father/son relationship. They just seemed to understand each other and were actually good friends. Lil Joe always dreaded having to leave his old man's place when their short visits came to an end. Although he always looked forward to seeing his mother again, he hated the idea of having to leave one parent to be with the other. Nonetheless, divorce was a reality in his life and he learned to deal with it.

Lil Joe's mother was a very beautiful, intelligent young woman who just happened to be his whole world. He was a mama's boy, and he loved her without end. At a young age, he took it upon himself to be her protector, which he lived up to until, unfortunately, he became the one who caused her the most pain and heartache. She married Marco's dad when Lil Joe was just four years old, but their marriage didn't last and they were divorced by 1980, just three years after Marco was born. The divorce wasn't such a bad thing, though, because Marco's dad, Carlos, was an abusive alcoholic who liked to get drunk and make a sport out of beating women and kids. In Lil Joe's opinion, Marco was the only good thing that ever came from that marriage.

Lil Joe's mother was a strong woman who made the best of her situation, raising two kids on her own while living in a neighborhood infested with gang warfare, drugs, and prostitution. She worked ten to twelve hour shifts at a local drug treatment center in order to provide food and shelter for her two kids. She was Lil Joe's hero, but even his admiration for his mother wasn't enough to keep him from the temptation of his corrupt environment, where his invitation into the life of chaos was pretty much inevitable.

Late in 1985, Lil Joe was attending a local junior high school on the Westside with his two best friends, Franky Mu_oz and Jimmy Vasquez, both Westside kids that Lil Joe had known since the second grade. The three of them had a lot in common and came from very similar backgrounds, which was probably why they were practically inseparable. All of them were second generation Mexican-American kids who were born and raised in San Bernardino.

Jimmy was an only child who lived with his mother's parents. His mother had died of a drug overdose four years earlier and he never knew his father. Jimmy was the sly character of the trio, and he was also the oldest, but only by a couple of months. He looked much older than his thirteen years, mainly because he was tall and had already begun to grow facial hair on his sharp features. Jimmy was usually the one who came up with the ideas that landed the three of them in trouble.

Franky, on the other hand, was sort of the runt of the group. He was small with slick black hair and thick eyebrows. Both Lil Joe and Jimmy teased him and said he resembled Eddie Munster from the old "The Munsters" television show. Franky was a laid back kid who for the most part had a carefree attitude and just liked to have fun, one of the characteristics that made him easy to get along with.

As for Lil Joe, he was a good looking kid with strong, handsome facial features. He was tall for his age, which was something his mother told him he had inherited from his father's side of the family. At the age of thirteen, he had already begun developing a strong physical frame that he was learning to carry well. His mother often told him that he was beginning to look more like his father with every passing day. It was a comparison he took pride in. Besides being physically impressive for a kid his age, Lil Joe was a very intelligent young man who was extremely observant and quick to pick up on the lessons of life. However, Lil Joe was born with an old soul and overall he was complex in nature. He rarely cut loose and allowed himself to be a kid, which was more than likely attributable to his awareness of the harsh realities of life in his lower class surroundings. But he possessed a great sense of humor for a kid his age and was usually able to make light of his situation. However, he was cursed with the temper of a volcano, and when he became enraged, his anger would erupt and cause him to lose all self control, which usually got him into a lot of trouble. At a young age, Lil Joe had adopted violence as a way of expressing his anger, and by the time he was thirteen, violence was gradually becoming the answer to all his problems.

In one incident, during a school recess, he was hanging out with his two best friends, Franky and Jimmy, at their usual hangout behind the school's baseball diamond. It was a preferred hangout for kids who smoked because the area was heavily shaded by a huge maple tree that denied the teachers and school security a good view of the area. That day while Lil Joe and his two buddies were smoking under the big tree, the school tattletale, a porky, semi-retarded blond headed kid named Jake, caught them smoking and threatened to tell. "Ooh, I'm tellin'. You guys are busted!"

Jimmy attacked him with a vicious verbal assault. "Fuck you, you fat little piggy!"

Franky followed with a verbal attack of his own. "Yeah, fuck you, you fat ass rat!"

Lil Joe couldn't think of anything original to say, so he just picked up a rock and chucked it at Jake. The rock cracked the chunky kid right in the back of his head and Jake hit the ground instantly, clutching his head and bawling loudly. "Oh, shit," said Jimmy, who quickly ran over to the wounded kid. "Come on, Jake, don't be a baby. You don't wanna get anyone in trouble, do you?"

Obviously Jake did, because he began screaming as loud as he could in order to get the teacher's attention, and before they knew it, Lil Joe, Franky, and Jimmy were sitting in the principal's office awaiting punishment. The principal, Mrs. Tanner, was a wrinkled old lady with a thick European accent who stank of the rank mixture of cigarettes and feet. At first she attempted to get each of them to tell her who threw the rock, but when that turned out to be fruitless, she decided to suspend all three of them for three days. It was at that time that Lil Joe's conscience kicked in. He began thinking about Franky's situation at home with his alcoholic stepfather who liked to beat on him. He knew if Franky were suspended, he would be in for it when he got home. Jimmy, on the other hand, lived with his grandparents, who for the most part really didn't seem to care what kind of trouble he got into. More than likely, their lack of good parenting was because they were burnt out from all the heartache that Jimmy's mother had put them through when she was still alive and battling with her drug addiction. As for Lil Joe, his mother tried constantly to get through to him that violence wasn't the way to deal with problems, but a lot of the time she just didn't know what to do about his acting out in a violent manner. Nonetheless, Lil Joe always honored his mother's teachings to own up to his responsibilities, and since he was the one who threw the rock, he didn't want his two friends to be punished.

So he went to the principal and confessed in hopes she would lift Franky's and Jimmy's suspension. But the old lady was stubborn. "I appreciate your honesty, Mr. Hernandez," she said, "but it's too late for Mr. Mu_oz and Mr. Vasquez. They had their chance to come clean and they blew it, so now they'll have to suffer the consequences." Evidently the woman was a firm believer in the finger pointing process, and because Franky and Jimmy didn't play by her rules, she was going to punish them. Okay, thought Lil Joe, if that's how it's going to be, then Jake, the little fat rat, is going to have to suffer the consequences as well.

The school nurse's office where Jake was being treated just happened to be located behind the principal's office, so while Lil Joe was waiting to be sent home, he decided to sneak into her office and give Jake a good beating. He didn't care about any further consequences. He was already in trouble, so he figured What the hell? As it turned out, by the end of the day he had managed to turn his three-day suspension into a two-week vacation.

The week after Lil Joe returned from his suspension, a girl from school that he fancied, Melissa Ramos, a cute little chicana seventh grader with long black hair, bright green eyes, and a dimpled smile, invited him to a ditching party at her house that her older brother Paul was throwing that Friday. Lil Joe really liked Melissa, so of course he accepted. He didn't have a problem with ditching school; it was easy. All he had to do was ask one of the other kids in his classes to sign him up on the role list and he was good to go. Southern California schools were so overcrowded at that time that the teachers couldn't keep track of who attended class and who didn't. Besides, Lil Joe, Franky, and Jimmy weren't interested in school. They would often ditch just to hang out at the park or the mall with other Westside delinquents, so ditching was nothing new for them. Even though Melissa had only invited him, he wasn't about to go to any kind of party without Franky and Jimmy, so come Friday, the three of them showed up at Melissa's house around 10 A.M. She lived in the Waterman Gardens Housing Projects in an old colonial flat with a small front yard and a big concrete front porch.

When they first arrived, her front yard was crowded with people who had formed a large circle around a fight pit where one-on-one bare-knuckle boxing matches were taking place. Lil Joe spotted Melissa standing on the porch looking over the crowd, so he squeezed his way past the crowd toward her. As he approached, Melissa spotted him and yelled out, "Lil Joe!" greeting him with excitement and a sweet dimpled smile. As he stepped onto the porch, she embraced him and kissed him on the cheek. "I'm glad you came."

"Yeah, me too." he said as he stood there staring into her bright green eyes.

She rewarded him with another smile and then held out the palm of her hand revealing a rolled le o [joint] and a lighter. "You wanna get a buzz?" she asked.

Lil Joe hadn't yet experimented with any drugs, but he liked Melissa and figured it wouldn't hurt if he smoked a little weed with her. "Yeah, cool," he said, trying to sound relaxed.

Melissa smiled again and took him by the hand and led him inside the house into the compact living room where another small, mixed crowd was talking and listening to the Gap Band on the stereo. Melissa hurried off, pulling Lil Joe past the living room to a bedroom door at the end of a narrow hallway. Lil Joe looked behind him to see where Franky and Jimmy had ended up, but he didn't see either of them before Melissa pulled him inside the bedroom and closed the door. She led him across the room to a small bed in the corner, where they sat down.

Lil Joe took in his surroundings. With the exception of the small bed and an old dresser next to it, the room was empty. The walls were covered with posters of the Spanish singing group "Menudo." On top of the dresser was a boombox cassette player and several cassettes spread out in front of it. Melissa noticed him looking at it and asked, "You wanna listen to some music?"

Lil Joe wrinkled his brow. "Uh, yeah, sure. There's not a Menudo tape in there, is there?"

Melissa rolled her eyes and responded with an exaggerated, "Nooo--there's not a Menudo tape in it." She giggled and then got up and pushed the play button. The sounds of Zap's "More Bounce To The Ounce" came blaring out of the speaker. "See, no Menudo," she said, teasing him with a dimpled smile. She pulled the rollie and lighter from her pocket and held it in front of him. You wanna light it?

"Nah, go ahead, spark it up," he said, thinking his response sounded cool.

Melissa shrugged, lit the rollie, and puffed on it like she had done it many times before. Lil Joe watched her closely while making mental notes on how to smoke it right. He was quite amazed as he watched her. After a couple of long tokes, she passed the joint to him. "Here you go. It's good shit," she said with a smile.

With a smile, Lil Joe took a few tokes, inhaled, and held his breath like he had seen her do, except he choked and started coughing. It must have looked funny to Melissa because she started laughing at him. He was determined not to be shown up by a girl, so he took a few more tokes and passed it back to her. After a few minutes and a couple more tokes, Lil Joe began to feel pretty good and out of nowhere Melissa jumped on his lap and started kissing him, putting her tongue in his mouth. He was caught a little off guard by her aggressiveness but quickly got into the groove. They made out for a few minutes and then Melissa took it a step further and pulled her t-shirt over her head and tossed it to the side. She smiled at him mischievously and the first thing that popped into Lil Joe's mind was his grandmother saying "Cochina!" which made him laugh to himself because it was an expression he often heard her use when she saw a woman expose herself on television or when she saw a woman on the street wearing clothing that was too revealing.

So there he was with this girl he liked sitting on his lap bare chested with her little breasts in his face, and he had no idea what to do with them. But thankfully, before he could make a complete ass of himself fumbling all over her, someone in another room yelled out, "The cops! Vamanos hay vienen las placas!"

"Shit!" Melissa cursed. She hurried to put her t-shirt back on and turned to Lil Joe. "You can go out through the backyard. Just jump the fence." She kissed him again. "Hurry, go!"

Lil Joe left through her backyard and made it home without any hassle from the cops. It wasn't until later that afternoon that Franky and Jimmy stopped by his mom's house to see how things went with him and Melissa.

"So did you get any?" Franky asked.

"Nah, man," Lil Joe replied. "I came close, but the cops showed up and messed everything up. What happened with you guys?"

"Aw, man," Jimmy said, "we were checking out the fights when the juras [cops] showed up. So we took off towards Franky's house."

Franky cut in, "So what do you guys wanna do now?"

Jimmy looked at his wristwatch. "Aah, man, I gotta split. My abuela [grandma] wants me to go to the tienda [store] with her before dinner."

"Yeah," Franky said, "speaking of dinner, I better get home too."

"All right then, fellas," Lil Joe said, "I'll see you tomorrow."

Later that night while he lay in his bed thinking about Melissa, Lil Joe decided he was going to have to learn how to do the deed so the next time he was alone with Melissa he would be prepared to blow her little mind. Ha, he laughed at his thoughts. Here begins my never ending quest to get into some girl's panties.

The next day, Lil Joe and Franky met up with Jimmy at his grandparents' house to hang out. Jimmy's tio [uncle] Fred also lived there. Fred went by the nickname of Lobo [wolf], which fit him well. The guy was a big mean Mexican who looked like he could make a good living wrestling grizzly bears. But besides that, Lobo had spent most of his life in prison and was a little crazy. That was why the three of them didn't like to hang out at Jimmy's grandparents' house too often. However, they were aware that Lobo had an incredible collection of pornographic videos locked away in his bedroom, and now that Lil Joe was in the race for a piece of ass, he figured he should learn all he could from the pros. That weekend, Lobo was off visiting a friend who lived outside the county, so Lil Joe, Franky, and Jimmy decided to take advantage of his absence and get into his porn stash. They locked themselves in his bedroom and watched all his x-rated videos on his TV and brand new VCR.

Some time at the beginning of their porn-watching marathon, while rummaging through his uncle's things, Jimmy discovered a hidden baggy full of marijuana buds and rolling papers. He held up the baggy and with a wicked grin, said, "Look what I found!"

"Hell, yeah!" Franky said, "roll that shit up!"

So the three of them made a party of it and spent the entire weekend smoking weed, watching porn, and eating just about everything in the house. At some time during the weekend, they were all a little high and out of it and suddenly Franky jumped up and began dry humping the air while mimicking the porn sound effects. At the time they all thought it was the funniest thing they'd ever seen and they laughed about it for at least an hour. Later on, it would become an inside joke between them, and whenever they came across a girl who caught their eye, one of them would dry hump the air and mimic porn music while making funny faces.

After that weekend, Lil Joe was on a mission to get Melissa alone somewhere and pick up where they had left off. He thought he was a real stud now that he had picked up some moves from watching the fuck flicks, but as it turned out, his mission was cut short when the unexpected happened. One day after school, Franky called him on the phone to tell him to come over to his house; that the cops were at Melissa's place. Franky lived right down the street from Melissa.

When Lil Joe got there, Franky, along with the rest of the people on the block, was hanging out across the street from Melissa's house.

"What happened, Franky?" asked Lil Joe.

"I'm not sure, bro, but I overheard some lady say that Raul, Melissa's brother, killed their jefita's boyfriend."

"Damn," said Lil Joe, "that's crazy, man!"

"Yeah, I know," Franky said. "It might be true though, because the cops took Raul away right before you got here and when they brought him out of the house he was all covered in blood."

"Man!" said Lil Joe, absorbing all the information. "What about Melissa? Have you seen her?"

Franky shook his head. "Nah, bro, I haven't."

That day there was just too much going on at Melissa's house. Lil Joe knew he wouldn't be able to talk with her anytime soon. So he went back home about an hour later after failing to find out exactly what had happened. He figured after all the dust settled, he would see Melissa at school and talk to her. But he figured wrong. She never showed up at school and a week after the incident Lil Joe was hanging out with Franky in his front yard when he saw a moving truck pass by and drive into the driveway of Melissa's house. It caught him off guard. "What the fuck is that?" said Lil Joe, confused by what he had just seen. "Come on, Franky, let's go and check it out."

When he and Franky reached Melissa's house, Melissa's mother was standing on the front porch giving the movers instructions. She looked a mess and had obviously been going through a stressful time. Her clothes were raggedy and her hair was uncombed and wild looking. Her usually pretty face looked grief stricken and she had a distant look in her eyes. When Lil Joe approached and asked what was going on, she looked at him with a forced smile and said in a soft whisper, "We're moving, sweetheart."

Although it was obvious, Lil Joe was still shocked by her reply, and his heart dropped instantly. The only thing he managed to say was "Why?"

Melissa's mom fixed her eyes on him and sighed. "Things are just too crazy around here right now, mijo, so we're going to San Diego to live with my mother for a while."

San Diego! thought Lil Joe, what the hell? "Is Melissa home?" he asked.

"No, mijo, she's already in San Diego."

Damn! thought Lil Joe. I never even got the chance to say goodbye to her. Obviously Melissa's mom was busy, and he didn't want to take up any more of her time, so he started toward the curb where Franky was waiting for him. But then he turned around and said, "Can you do me a favor and tell Melissa that I said goodbye?"

Melissa's mother smiled at him and replied, "Sure I will, sweetie."

"Thanks," he said and walked away.

It wasn't until later that Lil Joe realized that Melissa's mom probably didn't even remember who he was, seeing that he had only been in her company on two prior occasions.

It wasn't until sometime later that year that Lil Joe found out what had happened that day at Melissa's house. Raul, Melissa's older brother, had come home early from his after school job to find his mom's boyfriend, Paul, having sex with Melissa on the living room couch. Raul went straight into the kitchen, grabbed a butcher knife from one of the drawers, and hacked the molester to death on the spot.

When Lil Joe first heard the news, he took it pretty hard. He couldn't understand what a grown man would want with a young girl Melissa's age, and not just any girl--his girl! Son of a bitch! he thought. Well, at least the piece of shit got what he had coming. Lil Joe only wished he could have killed Paul himself.

CHAPTER TWO

IT WAS CHRISTMAS TIME AND ALL the schools were out until the new year. Lil Joe, Franky, and Jimmy hung out every day in the mall or in the park. One day during the holidays the three of them were walking to the park when they came across a Z28 parked in the middle of the street with the engine running. Lil Joe stopped short. "Hey, fellas, check that out. No one's inside of it."

"Let's take it," said Jimmy.

Franky bypassed both of them and jumped right into the passenger seat. "Come on! What are you guys waiting for?"

Lil Joe and Jimmy shrugged at each other and quickly followed suit. Jimmy was the only one of them who had any driving experience, so he jumped into the driver's seat and Lil Joe jumped in back. "Hurry up. Take off!" yelled Franky.

Jimmy quickly put the car in gear and gunned it down the street. Just as they were driving off, some guy with a distorted look on his face ran out of the house in front of which the car had been parked yelling, "Hey, that's my car!"

Lil Joe stuck his head out the window and yelled back, "Not anymore, fucker!" Then he gave the guy the finger.

That was the first time any of them had done anything as serious as stealing a car, and it was quite an adrenaline rush for them. They were a couple of blocks away when Jimmy suggested that they go to the corner market and do a beer run. "It's 10 o'clock in the morning," Lil Joe said. "It'll be hard to pull it off."

"Nah, man," said Jimmy, "I'll stay in the car with the engine running while you and Franky go inside and grab the beer. It'll be a piece of cake."

Franky chimed in, "Yeah, a piece of cake."

Lil Joe thought about it for a second, then said, "Yeah, all right. Let's go!"

The market was crowded when they got there, probably because of the upcoming holidays. Jimmy parked the car right outside the exit door and left the engine running just like they'd planned. Lil Joe and Franky made their way to the beer aisle and Lil Joe grabbed a twelve pack of Budweiser and headed straight for the exit door with Franky right behind him. The second he stepped on the door pad, he heard a male voice yell, "Hey, get back here!" and out of the corner of his eye he saw a man running towards him and Franky. They wasted no time and bolted out the door and ran straight towards the car. Lil Joe looked back once to see Franky running for the car throwing beer cans over his shoulder at the man who was chasing him. Once they were inside the car, Jimmy hit the gas and they were off.

"What did you guys get?" he asked.

"I got a twelve pack of Bud," said Lil Joe.

Franky's face was flushed as he held up a six pack ring with only two cans of Coors Light left. "This is all I got away with." Lil Joe and Jimmy laughed so hard Jimmy had to pull the car over so they wouldn't get into a wreck. Franky was pissed. "Hey, fuck you guys!" he said. "That asshole was riding my ass. What was I suppose to do?"

"Yeah, I know," said Lil Joe, "but come on, bro. A six pack of Coors Light? Man, you should of just grabbed a gallon of milk." That made them all laugh, including Franky, who was now seeing the humor of the situation.

After Jimmy regained his composure, he drove to the neighborhood park, where they broke open the twelve pack and shared the beer. They spent the whole day drinking and shooting the shit with each other at their usual hangout behind the park pond. After it started to get dark and they had sobered up a little, Lil Joe asked Jimmy, "So hey, man, what do you wanna do with the car?"

Jimmy turned and looked towards the stolen Z28 that he had parked in the small parking lot behind them. "Shit, I don't know. Any ideas?"

Franky cut in with a suggestion. "Why don't we just drop it back off where we took it?"

Jimmy smiled and said, "Yeah, man, that sounds cool to me."

"Yeah," said Franky, "we just borrowed it for the day. Que no?"

Lil Joe laughed. "All right, man, fuck it. We'll take it back."

A few minutes later they hopped into the car and Jimmy drove it back, using only the side streets so they wouldn't attract any attention. They were still a little buzzed from the beer, but Jimmy seemed to know what he was doing behind the wheel. When they reached the street where they had stolen the car, Lil Joe said, "Hey, Jimmy, park the car a few houses down from the owner's place."

"All right," said Jimmy. He parked the Z28 along the curb just two houses down from where they stole it. Once Franky and Jimmy were out of the car, Lil Joe grabbed the keys and two warm cans of Coors Light and walked up to the car owner's front porch. He set the keys, along with the two cans of beer, on the doorstep, rang the doorbell, and took off running down the street to catch up with Franky and Jimmy. They then walked the rest of the way to Lil Joe's mom's house, horseplaying and laughing along the way.

When they got there, Lil Joe invited Franky and Jimmy inside, asking, "Are you guys hungry?"

"Hell, yeah," Franky replied, "I'm starving."

Jimmy laughed and pushed him on the shoulder. "Man, you're always hungry," he teased.

"So what!" Franky retorted. "You're always ugly, but you don't hear me complaining."

Lil Joe laughed. "Come on, let's go eat." They went in and made their way straight for the kitchen, where Lil Joe found a note from his mom on the refrigerator door explaining that she and Marco would be at their grandmother's house for a couple of hours and that there was food on the stove. His mom had left some frijoles [beans] and carne asada on the stove and some fresh tortillas and block cheese on the counter. He pointed to the food. "Dig in, fellas."

While they were eating, they talked about the events of the day. "So that was pretty crazy, huh?" Franky said, "Taking that car."

"Yeah," Jimmy replied. "Do you guys think anyone saw us drop it back off?"

Lil Joe shook his head. "Nah, I doubt it, bro," he said. "It was pretty dark already. But just in case, we should probably keep low key for a while. It would probably be a good idea not to tell anyone about it either." He frowned. "You guys know how people can get about stuff like that."

"Yeah," Jimmy agreed.

"You're right. Yeah, man, that's cool," Franky said.

Lil Joe nodded and said, "Cool. So hey, Franky, it's Elsa's birthday tomorrow, huh?"

Franky shrugged. "Yeah," he said with a raised brow. "I can't believe you remembered my sister's birthday, man. Anyway, there's gonna be a party at our house tomorrow afternoon. You guys can come if you want to."

"Count me in," Jimmy said.

"Yeah, me too," Lil Joe replied.

Of course they would be there. Franky's older sister was a fox. She reminded Lil Joe of the teenage version of the Wonderwoman, Lynda Carter, with her long, full body of black hair and the bright blue eyes she got from her half Irish mother. Besides being a looker, Elsa had the largest set of knockers either Lil Joe or Jimmy had ever seen. Elsa was going to be turning seventeen, and ever since Lil Joe and Jimmy had known Franky, they had had a crush on his older sister. But they never talked about it around Franky because he was real sensitive about the subject. And he had good reason to be.

Everyone liked Elsa. All of the guys at her high school were constantly trying to get up her skirt. Franky knew it too, so he was real protective of her. One of Lil Joe's fondest memories of Elsa was from earlier that year. During spring break, he, Franky, and Jimmy were all at Franky's house swimming in the pool in the backyard. Franky was the only one of them with a swimming pool, so they would often hang out there when the weather was nice. On that particular day, they were taking turns diving off the roof of Franky's house into the pool trying to see who could make the best dives. At one point Lil Joe went into the house to use the bathroom, and on his way back to the yard he heard some strange moaning noises coming from the direction of Elsa's bedroom. The noises sparked his curiosity, so he walked down the hall and peeked inside through the slightly open door.

Elsa must have thought she was home alone because what Lil Joe saw was Elsa lying on her bed on her back buck naked with her legs cocked masturbating vigorously. Lil Joe was caught off guard by what he saw and couldn't stop himself from standing there for a moment staring at her, caught in awe of the situation. But soon enough he decided to give her her privacy and went back out to the pool with that image of her forever burnt into his memory, and a good memory it was.

On the day of Elsa's birthday, everything started out fine. Quite a few people showed up to the party, mostly family but also some of her friends from school. Then there was Lil Joe, just a good ol' friend of the family. Everyone seemed to be having a good time until Robert, Franky and Elsa's stepfather, got piss drunk and ruined the whole thing by yelling at everyone and acting like an ass. After a couple of drunken outbursts accusing the party guests of freeloading and drinking all his beer, people started to leave, including Lil Joe. He saw no reason to stick around in an awkward situation so he walked over to Elsa, who by that time was sitting on the front porch with tears in her eyes.

"Hey, you all right?" he asked.

"Yeah, thanks," she said, wiping her tears away with her sleeve. "Thanks again for the jersey, Joe."

"No problem," said Lil Joe. He had given her a football jersey of her favorite team, the Miami Dolphins.

Just then Franky walked out onto the porch holding something under his t-shirt. "Here, Lil Joe," he said, pulling out a bottle of beer and handing it to him. "The asshole's accusing everyone of drinking his beer, so what the hell!"

Lil Joe laughed. "Thanks, bro. Well, I'm gonna split." He kissed Elsa on the cheek. "Feliz cumplea os [happy birthday]," and then turned to Franky. "See you tomorrow, Franky."

"All right, Lil Joe. Hasta ma ana [until tomorrow]."

Later that night, Lil Joe was awakened by the sound of someone knocking on his bedroom window and got up to see who it was. It was Franky. "Come on, bro, let me in; it's freezing out here."

Lil Joe opened the window and let Franky in. "What happened, man?" he asked although he already knew the answer.

Franky was worked up pretty good. "Fuck that asshole, man! I'm not goin' back this time, Lil Joe." He paused for a moment to regain his composure. "Man, after everyone left, Robert decided to end the night with a bang and kick my ass."

Lil Joe wasn't surprised. He knew the deal. He had been there himself a few times with Marcos's dad. "Don't worry about it. You can stay here. You know my mom won't mind."

"Yeah, thanks, bro."

The following day was Christmas Eve and Lil Joe awoke to the smell of <u>chorizo con huevos</u> cooking on the stove. He went into the kitchen and found Franky and his younger brother Marco helping his mom cook breakfast. "Good morning, <u>mijo</u>," his mom said, greeting him with a kiss on the forehead. "I didn't know that Franky was such a good cook," she said with a smile. "Here, <u>mijo</u>, grab a plate."

"Yeah," Franky teased, "grab a plate, <u>mijo</u>."

"Shut up," Lil Joe said as he playfully punched Franky on the shoulder.

While they sat at the kitchen table eating breakfast, the phone rang, and Lil Joe got up to answer it. "Yeah, what's up?" he said.

"Hey, it's me!" Jimmy said.

"Well, no shit, Sherlock!" Lil Joe said, which earned him a reproachful look from his mother. "Sorry, Mom," he apologized.

"So what do you wanna do today?" Jimmy asked.

"Man," Lil Joe sighed, "I don't know. Why don't you come over and we'll figure it out. Franky's here. He crashed here last night."

"Is that right?" Jimmy asked. "He had another run in with King Beer Gut, huh?"

"Yeah, man," Lil Joe replied in an exaggerated tone.

"Well, hey, man," Jimmy said, "tell Franky to take a dump before I get there so we don't have to wait on him once we're ready to go."

Lil Joe chuckled and looked across the kitchen at Franky, who had finished his breakfast and was eyeballing Lil Joe's plate. "All right, man, I will, but hey, I gotta go before he eats my breakfast."

Jimmy showed up half an hour later with a pocketful of rolled quarters. "Hey," he shrugged, "I figured we could go to the arcade."

"Sounds like a plan," Lil Joe said.

Jimmy looked around the living room. "Where's Franky?"

"He's on the toilet," Lil Joe said with a grin. "Come on, Franky, let's go!" he hollered.

Just then Franky walked out of the bathroom. "I'm done. Come on, let's go."

"All right, cool," said Lil Joe. He hollered out to his mom as they walked out the door. "Mom, we're going to the arcade on Highland."

"Okay, mijo, you be good," she hollered back from the kitchen.

On the walk to the arcade, Franky ran Jimmy down with what happened at Elsa's birthday party the night before. "That's messed up, man," Jimmy said. "Sorry I wasn't there. I had to help my abuela babysit Lobo. He was all doped up and slipped into a nod, so I had to stay home."

Franky shook his head. "Man, don't worry about it. It sounds like we both had a fucked up night."

Jimmy sighed. "Yeah, I hear you, bro."

On the way to the arcade, they took a shortcut through a field known as Hobo Lane. It was sort of a dangerous place to be, especially for kids, but they often cut through the area to get to places quicker and they had never run into any trouble. But on that day, things turned out for the worse. After walking underneath the crossing bridge of the railroad track, a filthy looking hobo who reeked of stale wine jumped out of a dark corner brandishing a knife.

"Give me your money, you little shits," he demanded.

They simultaneously backed away from him. "We don't have any money," Jimmy said.

"Bullshit!" yelled the hobo. "Empty your pockets before I cut ya!"

"Fuck you!" spat Franky. "You ain't gonna do shit with that knife!"

The hobo angrily stepped towards Franky, knife in hand. "Why you little smart mouth turd, I'll cut your balls off, you little bastard!"

Lil Joe was suddenly overcome by rage, and before he knew it he was holding a large rock in his hand. While the hobo was focused on Franky, Lil Joe quickly stepped closer and without hesitation slammed the rock as hard as he could into the side of the hobo's head. The blow knocked him face down into the gravel. Then they all jumped on him and kicked him repeatedly until Lil Joe suddenly stopped his assault and with a disgusted grimace, said, "Do you guys smell that? This fuckin' hobo shit on himself. Nasty bastard!"

Lil Joe and Franky began laughing at the situation, but they could tell that Jimmy was still worked up, and before they could stop him, he picked up the hobo's knife and cut the poor bastard's throat. Franky yelled out in shock, "Fuck, Jimmy, what did you do that for?"

"Fuck that, Franky," yelled Jimmy, "he was gonna do it to you."

"Shit, look at him, man!" Franky yelled. "Damn. Is he dead?"

Lil Joe's mind was racing. The hobo had to be dead; he was damn near decapitated. He had to think fast. "Come on, fellas, we can't stick around here. We gotta get out of here."

Jimmy's grandparents' house was the closest, so they ran off in that direction. Some of the hobo's blood had squirted onto Jimmy's face and arms, so when they got there they went straight to the backyard so Jimmy could wash up with water from the hose. After he finished rinsing the blood off, he pulled the hobo's bloody knife from his pocket and washed it off. Franky was struck with disbelief. "Aw, shit, Jimmy, you kept the knife? Come on, man, you gotta get rid of that thing."

"Nah, man," Jimmy said, holding the knife up to the sunlight to see if he'd gotten all the blood off. "I'm keeping it as a souvenir."

Franky shook his head. "You're crazy, man. Hey, Lil Joe, talk some sense into this guy."

At that moment, Lil Joe wasn't all that concerned about the knife. He was sitting on an old tire and leaning against the garage in deep thought. They had just killed somebody, and he wasn't sure what to think about it. His mind was racing with so many thoughts it made him dizzy. Everything had happened so fast. Although he wasn't the one who actually killed the hobo, he still felt responsible. Damn!, he thought. What is this shit? I'm a kid. I'm not suppose to be thinking about what to do after killing someone. "Hey, fellas," he said, "we need to talk about this shit." Both Franky and Jimmy turned their attention to him. "This is some heavy shit that went down, man. It's not like another beer run or stealing a car. That hobo's dead. The way I see it, we were just protecting ourselves, but I still think we should just keep what happened to ourselves. That way no one gets into trouble."

Jimmy was the first to respond. "Yeah, Lil Joe, that sounds like a good idea. Besides, the cops are always finding bodies on the lane, man. So as long as we keep quiet about it, everything should be cool."

Lil Joe looked at Franky. "What do you think, homeboy?"

Franky shrugged. "I'm with you guys. Whatever you wanna do."

"Cool, then," said Lil Joe. "We don't talk about it anymore."

Christmas and New Years came and went by fast. Franky spent the holidays with Lil Joe and his family. The holidays were a nice time that year with the exception of Elsa's birthday party and the incident with the hobo. But it would be the last holiday season Lil Joe would ever spend with his family.

Back in school, the trio went back to their regular program of being knuckleheads. Then about a week after they'd gone back, the cops showed up and arrested Jimmy. It was a big deal on the school grounds and everyone was talking about it except Lil Joe and Franky. Apparently Jimmy had run his mouth to a girl who lived next door to his grandparents and bragged about killing the hobo in an attempt to impress her. But he wound up scaring her instead, and she told her parents, who reported it to the police. And when the cops searched Jimmy, they found the knife he'd used to kill the hobo. Lil Joe never could figure out why Jimmy kept the knife, and especially why he carried it on him all the time.

After getting over the initial shock of Jimmy's arrest, Lil Joe thought for sure that the cops would come for him and Franky next, but fortunately for them Jimmy had told the girl that he killed the hobo by himself, and he stuck to that story when he was interrogated by the police. A couple of months later, Jimmy was committed to the California Youth Authority, where he would have to stay until his twenty-first birthday.

During that time, Franky went back home to live with his mother and stepfather. Franky's mother talked him into coming home after she explained that his stepfather had cut back on his drinking and wanted to make things up to him. Things were pretty smooth for a month or so and Lil Joe and Franky hung out every day. But as Lil Joe was quickly learning, things could, and often did, make a turn for the worse real fast.

CHAPTER THREE

LIL JOE'S GRANDMOTHER USED TO TELL him he had a magnet on his ass for trouble, and as it turned out, she was right. Late one night in February 1986, Lil Joe was awakened by the sound of the telephone ringing in the kitchen. Then a few minutes later, his mom walked into his bedroom.

"Mijo, are you awake?"

"Yeah, Ma, I'm up," he replied in a groggy voice. "What's goin' on?"

His mom sighed. "That was Elsa on the phone just now. She called from the hospital. Her mother has had some sort of an accident at home. She sounded real worried, so I want to go check on her. Okay? I'm going to go put your brother in the car, so meet me outside in a few minutes. Okay? And don't' forget to lock up."

Lil Joe yawned. "Okay, Mom, I won't." He got out of bed and dressed in a hurry, then made a quick stop in the bathroom before heading out to the car. When he got outside, his mom was already warming up the engine in her old Monte Carlo. As he made his way over to the car, Lil Joe wondered what kind of accident Franky's mother had been in, and he hoped it wasn't the kind he was thinking of. He figured his mom was probably thinking the same thing, which would explain why she was in such a hurry to get to the hospital. She and Claudia, Franky's mom, had known each other since junior high school and had always remained friends. They were always there for each other when needed.

As Lil Joe hopped into the car, he asked, "What hospital is she in, Mom?"

"The county medical center, mijo."

He should have known. The county medical center was where most residents on the Westside went. It was known as the poor man's hospital and had a bad reputation, which was common in many low-class neighborhoods. There were just too many poor people in need of medical attention and too few doctors.

When they arrived at the hospital, Marco was sound asleep on the back seat of the car, so Lil Joe's mom decided to leave him there. "He'll be okay, mijo. We won't be long."

As soon as they found out what room Mrs. Ortiz was in, they went straight there. When they walked into the small, dim room, Lil Joe noticed that she shared the room with an elderly woman who looked as if she were barely hanging onto life. Lil Joe tried not to stare at the lady as they walked past her to get to where Franky's mother was. She was half awake and recognized Lil Joe as soon as he walked past the dividing curtain. "Hi, mijo," she said, smiling at him as he approached. He tried not to appear upset when he saw that her entire head was bandaged in gauze wrap.

"Hello, Mrs. Ortiz. I hope you feel better soon," he managed to say before his mom joined him at her bedside and began speaking to her in Spanish.

"Claudia, como te sientes? Que paso?"

Lil Joe backed away and went over to where Elsa was sitting near the foot of her mother's bed. "Hey, Elsa, how you doin'?"

She didn't speak and only shook her head and looked up at him with tears in her eyes. He felt sorry for her, but he was anxious to know where Franky was and if he was all right. "Where's Franky?" he asked. But again she didn't speak. Instead she looked over his shoulder towards the other side of the room. When Lil Joe turned in that direction, he saw Robert stumbling towards them with an angry scowl on his face. As he got closer, Lil Joe could see he had been drinking. It was obvious. His eyes were bloodshot, he reeked of stale beer, and he looked a mess. His thinning hair was uncombed and his beer belly protruded from under his tight fitting t-shirt.

"Who the hell invited you people here?" he asked as he glared at Elsa with obvious contempt in his eyes.

Both Lil Joe and his mother ignored Robert's drunken comment, but there was a bad vibe in the room and Lil Joe could feel the tension thick in the air. He had a pretty good idea of how Franky's mom had ended up in the hospital, and it made him all the more anxious to know where Franky was. He knew that Elsa wouldn't talk in front of Robert, but luckily his mom created an opportunity for him to find out about Franky. "Joseph, mijo, why don't you take Elsa to get a soda or something from the vending machine. Here, here's some money." She handed him three dollar bills, but he was wary of leaving her in the room with Robert. She must have picked up on that because she added, "Don't worry. I'll be fine. I'll be out in a few minutes."

"Okay, Mam_," he said. He took the money, gave Robert a threatening look, and he and Elsa left the room.

When they were out of hearing distance, Elsa grabbed Lil Joe by the arm and pulled him to the side of the vending machine. She was hysterical. "Lil Joe, you have to find Franky. I'm afraid for him!"

"All right, I will." He tried to calm her. "What happened, Elsa?"

She put her head down in shame and in a soft whisper said, "Robert got drunk and he . . . he . . . he beat up my mom." She was crying. "Franky tried to stop him, but it was too late. She fell and hit her head on the coffee table." She stopped for a moment while a young couple got some snacks from the vending machine. After they walked away, she continued, "After I called the paramedics, Franky took off. You have to find him, Joe. Please!" she pleaded with tears streaming from her eyes.

Lil Joe hugged her and tried to comfort her the best he could. "I'll find him. I promise. Okay?"

"Okay," she said, lifting her head from his shoulder. "You know, she won't tell the hospital staff how she really got hurt. She'll just accept it like she always does and pretend it never happened."

Lil Joe had to put some space between himself and Elsa. It was totally inappropriate, but he couldn't help himself. Having her wrapped in his arms with her body pressed against his was just too much. He was beginning to get aroused and felt himself growing in his pants. So he pushed her back gently and tried to reassure her that everything would be fine. "I'll find Franky. Okay? So don't worry."

Just then Lil Joe's mom came out into the hall. "Come on, mijo, it's about time we get home." She turned to Elsa and with genuine concern said, "Elsa, if you need anything, mija, you can come to me. Okay?"

Elsa nodded her head. "Okay, I will. Thanks."

When Lil Joe and his mom reached the car, Marco was still sound asleep in the back seat. Lil Joe doubted that he would remember any of that night in the morning. On the drive home, Lil Joe asked his mom if he could skip school the next day because he was too tired, but his mom knew what time it was. "Yes, mijo, you can go look for Franky in the morning." She gave him an understanding smile and patted his forearm. He knew that his mother knew what had taken place with Franky's mom, but he also knew she wasn't the kind of person to get involved in other people's affairs without an invitation.

They got home about 1:30 A.M. and Lil Joe set his alarm clock radio for 6 A.M. and went straight to sleep. Come morning, he woke up half an hour before his alarm was due to go off, got out of bed, and jumped straight in the shower. After his morning wash-up ritual, he ate a bowl of cold cereal and made a couple of peanut butter and banana sandwiches (Franky's favorite). He knew were to find Franky. There was a little picnic area in the neighborhood park just behind the pond where they would often hang out and feed the ducks the breadcrumbs that people left behind for that purpose. It was a pretty peaceful spot for a person to hang out and gather their thoughts.

When Lil Joe arrived at the hangout, he spotted Franky right away. He was squatting down at the edge of the pond tossing breadcrumbs to a group of ducks that were swimming around in front of him. Lil Joe walked up and squatted on his heels next to Franky. "Hey, bro, how's it goin'?"

Franky tossed another handful of bread crumbs into the pond. "I knew you'd show up sooner or later."

"Yeah." Lil Joe pulled the sandwiches from his pocket and handed them to Franky. "Here, I brought you something to eat."

"Thanks, man," Franky said as he hurried to unwrap the sandwiches. "I was just about ready to eat these breadcrumbs." They both squatted there in silence for a few minutes while Franky devoured the sandwiches.

When he finished, he broke the silence. "That lush motherfucker hurt my mom bad, man!"

"I know," Lil Joe said with heartfelt sympathy.

"He could have killed her, bro," Franky said. "If I don't do somethin' about it, he'll kill one of us sooner or later."

Lil Joe shook his head and took a deep breath. "So what's on your mind?"

Franky sighed. "That's just it, man. I've been thinking about it all night, and I keep coming to the same conclusion." He turned to Lil Joe and looked him in the eye. "I'm gonna kill him, bro," he said in all seriousness. "There's no other way."

Lil Joe wasn't as surprised as he should have been. "Are you sure that's what you wanna do, Franky? That's some pretty serious shit, man, killin' someone. It's not somethin' you can take back later, bro. It's forever."

"Yeah, I know, but I can't let him get away with what he did to my mom, man. No way!"

Lil Joe's thoughts automatically drifted to the incident with the hobo, and that brought thoughts to the surface that he had tried to bury in the back of his mind. Well, he thought, maybe it's just meant to be. "So how are we gonna do this, bro?" he asked.

"What?" said Franky with surprise in his voice. "What do you mean, we?"

"Shit, you didn't think I would let you do this by yourself, did you?"

Franky shook his head in protest. "No, Lil Joe, I can't ask you to do somethin' like this with me."

"You don't have to ask," Lil Joe said stubbornly. "I'm there. Besides, something could go wrong. You might need me there."

"You can't, Lil Joe, it's my problem."

"Bullshit!"yelled Lil Joe. "If it was my jefita in this kind of situation, I know you wouldn't let me go it alone."

Franky stood quietly for a moment staring off towards the pond. "This is one big mess, all of it, man. The whole damn world. I just don't understand this shit, man. If my old man was still around, things wouldn't be like this. You know?"

Lil Joe nodded in agreement. He knew the story. Franky's real father, Frank Sr., died two years earlier in a shootout with the San Bernardino Police Department. He had just been paroled from Folsom State Prison after serving three years for robbery. Franky's mom and dad were never married, so while Frank Sr. was in prison, Franky's mom met Robert and they were married about a year later. So with Robert in the picture, Franky's hopes of his parents getting back together were ruined, and by the time Franky's dad was paroled, Robert had been living at his mother's house for a while.

Franky didn't take much of a liking to Robert from the beginning, mainly because Robert never passed up an opportunity to take a cheap shot at Franky's dad. If they were watching television and one of the segments on the news was about some idiot who had been apprehended after robbing a liquor store for some beer and licorice, or something ridiculously stupid like that, Robert would laugh and blurt out, "Hey, Franky, look, they caught your old man!" Franky would sometimes respond with a snide remark, which would usually earn him an ass kicking, but he didn't care. He despised Robert and viewed him as an alcoholic loser who freeloaded off his mom. It was true. Since Robert had moved in with them, he hadn't held a job for more than a month at a time, usually losing them because of his drunken behavior. Robert would often show up for work drunk or badly hung over, or sometimes he wouldn't show up at all because he would be passed out on the couch in a drunken stupor. One time Franky came home from school to find Robert in the bathroom passed out on the can.

Franky hated Robert and could hardly wait for his real dad to parole from the joint. He just knew that things would get better then. He had it all worked out in his mind. His dad was going to get back on his feet and get a job and a place to stay. Then once he was all settled in, Franky was going to live with him. Unfortunately, that wasn't how things worked out. When Franky's old man first got out of the joint, he seemed to be focused and level headed. He got out clean and stayed away from the booze and dope. However, after several months went by and he still hadn't landed a steady job, things went downhill for him real fast. It was as if he had just given up. He began hitting the bottle again, and in time he was strung out on heroin again. When he had first paroled, he would visit Franky and Elsa every other day and would take them out to breakfast every Sunday morning. But once he was back on the dope, he stopped coming around altogether.

Franky was crushed by the way things turned out. So when he came home from school one day and his mother sat him down to tell him the news of his father's death, she couldn't bring herself to do it. So Robert, being the asshole that he was, took the opportunity to make things worse and blurted out in a drunken slur, "For God's sake, woman, I'll do it. Your old man is dead, kid. He robbed a convenience store and things went bad and he ended up in a shootout with the cops." Franky was devastated, but he knew that Robert wanted nothing more than to see him break down and cry like a baby, so he didn't give the jerk the satisfaction. Instead, he sucked it up and didn't give the slightest hint of grief. He simply kissed his mother on the cheek and told her that he was going to the park to play football with some friends from school. He never spoke about his father's death with her again.

So Franky's decision to kill Robert after the latest family trauma came as no big surprise to Lil Joe. It was almost as if everything had been leading up to it.

"All right then, Franky," Lil Joe said, "your mom will still be in the hospital tonight. Right?"

Franky nodded. "Yeah."

"So after Elsa gets off work, she'll more than likely go visit her. Right?" Franky nodded again. "So then we can do it tonight. When Robert gets off of work, he'll go straight home for a couple of beers like he always does. Right?"

Franky grunted. "Yeah, we can count on that," he said. "Fuckin' lush."

"All right, look," Lil Joe said, "I still have twenty bucks that I got for my birthday stashed away in my bedroom. We can go get it, then head down to that liquor store on the corner of Seventh Street. You know the one the <u>chinos</u> [Chinese] own. They have those knives for sale under the counter, behind the glass. We can buy two of 'em, one for me and one for you." He paused for a moment to look Franky in the eye. "What do you think, Franky?"

"That sounds cool," Franky said, "but do you think the <u>chinos</u> will sell us the knives?"

"Man, of course they will, bro," Lil Joe said. "When have you ever known the chinos to pass up an opportunity to make a buck? Look man, don't worry about it. Everything will work out. Come on, bro, let's go to my house."

Lil Joe tried to loosen up the mood with a little small talk on the walk to his house. "So was it cold out here all night?"

"Hell, yeah!" Franky replied. "I froze my balls off!"

Lil Joe chuckled. "Well, it's a good thing you don't like girls cause they'd miss those."

They both shared a good laugh, which seemed to clear up the tension that lurked in the air. When they reached Lil Joe's house, Lil Joe's mother was at work and his younger brother at school, so the house was empty. Lil Joe made his way straight to his bedroom while Franky headed for the kitchen to find something more to eat. While Lil Joe was retrieving the twenty bucks from his stash box, he looked around his room as if to say goodbye, and his thoughts drifted to his mother. He felt a pang in his heart for what he was about to put her through. He knew that he and Franky were going to get locked up for what they were going to do. They didn't even have a very good plan, but he figured Fuck it! He was a loyal friend and Franky needed him. Besides, he thought, what's the worst that can happen. We're just kids.

Lil Joe shook off his thoughts, put the $20.00 in his pocket, and headed for the kitchen, where Franky was eating tortillas and butter. "Get enough to eat, homeboy?"

"Yeah," Franky replied, rubbing his stomach. But now I gotta take a dump.

"Aw, shit, Franky. Well hurry up, bro, cause we got some shopping to do. And hey, man, don't stink up my jefita's bathroom."

Franky grinned and said over his shoulder, "Don't worry, man, I'll leave a floater."

"Ugh, sick bastard," Lil Joe said with a chuckle.

On their way to the liquor store, they joked around and tried to lighten the mood. But the reality of the situation had already set in. When they got there, they went straight to the candy aisle. They both grabbed a couple of snacks and a soda and then made their way to the checkout counter. Behind the glass was an assortment of knives, marijuana pipes, lighters, and bongs. The Chinaman standing behind the counter saw that they were admiring the knives and said with a heavy accent, "Oh, you want to buy knife, eh?"

"Yeah, two of 'em," said Lil Joe.

"Okay. Which ones you want?"

Lil Joe looked at two buck knives lying next to each other on a red velvet cloth. He pointed to them and said, "Hey, Franky, how about those two right there?"

Franky looked at them and turned to Lil Joe, making eye contact. They stared at each other for a moment, both seeming to realize at the same time that they weren't just two kids buying knives; they were two kids buying weapons for the specific purpose of killing someone.

"I guess those will do the job," said Franky.

"All right, then," Lil Joe said looking at the clerk, "I'll take those two buck knives right there."

"Okie dokie," said the Chinaman. He opened the glass case and pulled out the knives.

"How much for all of this?" asked Lil Joe pointing at the knives and the snacks on the counter.

The clerk rang everything up on the register. "That's $17.17," he said.

"All right," said Lil Joe. Go ahead and throw in a pack of Camels.

The Chinaman frowned and gave him a funny look, but he quickly shrugged it off and put everything in a bag, including the cigarettes. Lil Joe handed the twenty dollars to the clerk and said, "Keep the change." Then he pulled the knives out of the bag and handed one to Franky. "Here you go, bro."

Lil Joe put his knife in his pocket and started toward the door. Just as he and Franky were about to step outside, the clerk yelled out, "Hey, boys, you don't buy those knives from me. Okay?"

Lil Joe snickered and looked back at the clerk. "Yeah, sure. Okay."

Lil Joe and Franky walked along the back streets and alleys on the way to the park. They ate their snacks, drank their soda, and smoked cigarettes on the way. At the park, there was some sort of family picnic taking place at their usual hangout spot, which was unusual for a

Friday afternoon. Usually big BBQ picnics didn't take place until the weekend. There were a lot of kids running around and an enormous amount of food on the picnic tables.

Lil Joe looked at his watch. It was already after three o'clock. The day had flown by. Just then an older, heavyset lady yelled out, "Come on, kids, it's time to eat." Then about twenty or so hungry kids started running towards the picnic tables. Lil Joe and Franky looked at each other, each knowing what the other was thinking. "Fuck it, man, let's eat," said Lil Joe and they grabbed paper plates and sat down at a table full of kids and helped themselves. No one seemed to notice that they were outsiders. There was a big assortment of food--BBQ meats like hamburgers, chicken, and hotdogs, and a variety of side dishes like potato salad, corn on the cob, and baked beans, along with several different desserts.

After stuffing themselves, Lil Joe and Franky slipped away from the picnic area and strolled around the park for a while. When they reached an unoccupied area on the far side of the park, they sat down on a park bench underneath a large acorn tree and pulled out their knives to get a feel for them.

"What time is it?" asked Franky.

Lil Joe looked at his watch. "Damn, it's already ten after six."

Franky nodded his head. "It'll be dark soon." The feeling of tension was back; it was getting real close to game time. "He'll be drunk off his ass by seven," Franky said. "Man, Lil Joe, I wish I would of visited my mom at the hospital, but man, I just hate to see her like that. You know?"

Lil Joe just sat back and listened, not really knowing what to say.

"Hey, Lil Joe, do you think our jefas will understand why we did this?"

Lil Joe shook his head in wonder. It was a good question. The truth was that he was thinking the same thing. "I don't know," he replied. "I mean, shit, it's to the point now where it's him or one of you."

"Yeah, I know," agreed Franky.

They sat quietly for a moment while they gathered their thoughts. Finally Lil Joe broke the silence. "It's about that time, Franky."

Franky looked up at him. "Yeah, let's go, bro."

CHAPTER FOUR

BY THE TIME THEY REACHED THE street Franky lived on, it was already dark and the street lights were on. The only car in the driveway to Franky's house was Robert's Chevy pickup truck. "Elsa's not home," said Franky. They stood at the corner of the short driveway staring at the house. Franky took a deep breath. "All right," he said, "look, we'll just go inside and check things out, but don't do anything until I make a move. All right?"

Lil Joe nodded. "Sure homeboy, you got it."

They made their way to the front porch and stopped short of the door for a moment to build up their nerve. The front door was open and they could hear the TV blaring through the screen door. They looked each other in the eye, communicating without the use of words. Lil Joe's stomach was in knots, and if the look on Franky's face was any indication, so was his. Lil Joe nodded to let Franky know he was ready to go. Franky nodded back and opened the screen door. They walked inside and immediately saw Robert slumped over in his recliner, loosely holding the neck of a bottle of beer.

"There you are, you little shit," he blurted out in a drunken slur as he noticed them standing there. "Your mother has been worried sick about you. She has me sitting here on house arrest waiting around for your dumb ass to show up." He looked over at Lil Joe. "What the fuck are you doing here anyway? Don't you have a home of your own to go to?" Lil Joe ignored him and Robert quickly turned his attention back to Franky. "Ignorant fucker!" he said, pausing to take a pull from his beer. "Don't you think I have better things to do than wait around on your sorry ass? I could have been at the hospital with your mom."

What an asshole, Lil Joe thought. All he ever does is sit on his ass at home and get drunk. It's his daily routine. If it wasn't for him, Franky's mom wouldn't of even been in the hospital. Lil Joe shook his head in disgust. He decided that he was going to enjoy killing the woman beater.

"Where the fuck have you been anyway?" Robert asked. "You were probably out being a hoodlum like your old man was." He grunted and paused to take another swig of his beer, but Franky had heard enough.

"Shut the fuck up, asshole," he yelled. "I'm tired of listening to your shit." Franky pulled the buck knife from his pocket and cocked out the blade and walked towards Robert. "At least my dad wasn't a piece of shit coward like you!" Franky spat. Lil Joe took that as his cue and pulled out his knife.

"What the fuck are you gonna do with that?" were Robert's last words. Franky and Lil Joe attacked him simultaneously, Franky sinking the first knife blow right into Robert's chest, making a loud thumping sound. Robert coughed up a short bloody breath and clutched his chest, then fell to the carpet with a horrified look on his face. Both Lil Joe and Franky then went into a stabbing frenzy. After a minute or so, their adrenalin wound down and they stopped their assault on Robert's mutilated body. Lil Joe stepped back and scanned the living room. It was a bloody mess. It looked like someone had slaughtered a cow. They knew Robert was dead and for a moment they just stood over his bloody corpse staring at what was left of it. Lil Joe broke the silence. "I think we're done, bro," he said, turning towards Franky just as he bent over and vomited all over the carpet where Robert's lifeless body was sprawled out.

"Are you all right?" he asked.

Franky straightened himself and wiped his forearm across his mouth. "Yeah, I'm all right, bro." Franky let out a little muffled grunt. "The son of a bitch is dead and he still makes me sick!"

Lil Joe swallowed hard and let out a snicker of his own. "I need a frajo, man." He wiped the palms of his bloody hands on the front of his gray khakis and pulled the pack of Camels and the lighter out of his pocket. After taking a couple of long drags from the cigarette to help calm his nerves, he passed it to Franky. "So what now?" he asked.

Franky looked as if he was in deep thought. "We should probably get outta here," he said. "We could go to your house."

Lil Joe shook his head. "No, bro, we can't. My mom is home from work by now. Why don't we just wash up here real quick and change our clothes. Then we can figure out what to do next."

"No, we can't stay here either," said Franky. "What if Elsa comes home while we're here? Or worse, what if she brings my mom home and they see us here like this." He pointed to their bloody clothes. "Nah, Lil Joe, we gotta split, bro."

"All right then. What about Jimmy's grandparents' house? We could go there. His tio, Lobo, will know what we should do."

Franky thought about it for a minute. "Okay, yeah, that sounds like a good idea. But what about the knives? What are we gonna do with them?"

"We'll figure it out on the way to Jimmy's. Come on, let's get outta here."

Outside under the streetlights, they noticed how much blood there was on them. Both of them were wearing plain white t-shirts and they were covered in blood. So were their hands and forearms. They even had blood spattered on their faces. "Damn, Franky, we look like something out of a horror flick, man. We gotta get cleaned up before someone notices us."

"Yeah, we should stick to the back streets and alleys on the way to Jimmy's. If we're cool, no one will notice us."

But they never made it to Jimmy's grandparents' house. Just a couple of blocks away from Franky's place, a San Bernardino P.D. cruiser patrolling the area drove past them. At first they thought maybe the cops hadn't noticed them, but that thought was short lived. The cop car pulled a quick U-turn and sped towards them in a hurry.

"We have to run, Franky! Come on. Look!" Lil Joe pointed to a schoolyard across the street. They ran for it and were on the fence and about to jump onto the school grounds when they heard a voice yell out, "Stop right there!"

"Shit! Guns!" said Lil Joe as he caught a glimpse of the two cops pointing their pistols at them. They slowly hopped off the fence, neither willing to risk getting shot. It was common knowledge on the Westside that the San Bernardino Police Department had a reputation for shooting suspects without hesitation, even kids.

One of the cops then yelled out, "Get face down on the ground and don't move!"

Lil Joe and Franky quickly complied with the instructions. As soon as they were lying on their stomachs, the same cop handcuffed them while his partner kept his gun on them. Once Lil Joe and Franky were cuffed up, the cops pulled them up and walked them towards the cruiser. One of the cops (the younger one) said, "You boys look a mess," and started searching through Franky's pockets. "Whoa!" he yelled when he discovered Franky's bloody buck knife. "What do we have here?"

His older partner quickly searched Lil Joe's pockets and found his knife. "Oh, we have another winner," he said as he pulled the knife out of Lil Joe's pocket.

"What have you boys been up to?" asked the older cop. Without waiting for a response, he asked, "Do either of you boys need medical attention? Are you hurt?"

Franky shook his head and Lil Joe quickly replied, "No."

"Okay then," the cop continued, "How about telling us your names." Neither Lil Joe nor Franky responded. "Well, have it your way, but if you don't cooperate with us, you'll regret it later."

Lil Joe had witnessed the S.B.P.D.'s unethical behavior on quite a few occasions so he already held them in contempt. So he decided to play hard ass with them. "We don't have to tell you shit," he said.

The cop frowned. "Is that so? Well, we'll just have to see about that, tough guy." He turned to his Hispanic partner and said, "Put them in the car. We'll take 'em to the station and see if they change their tune after we put them in the tank with Bubba." He smirked and slapped Lil Joe on the back with a heavy hand.

After his younger partner put Lil Joe and Franky into the back of the cruiser, he hopped into the passenger seat and they drove off. On the way to the police station, Lil Joe overheard the Hispanic cop inform Dispatch over the C.B. that they were bringing in two juveniles for questioning and to notify the gang unit sergeant. Lil Joe and Franky sat in silence looking out the windows wondering what would come next. About ten minutes later, they came to a stop in front of the Westside station house. "Well, here we are, boys," the older cop said. He and his partner helped Lil Joe and Franky out of the car and escorted them into the station and down a busy hallway past several interrogation cells.

Lil Joe and Franky were separated and the older cop took Lil Joe into a room, removed his handcuffs, and told him to sit tight. He then walked out and closed the door behind him. Lil Joe looked around the small room and the first thing he noticed was that there was no door handle on the inside, so trying to escape was out of the question. The only furnishings were a small wooden table and a couple of chairs. He decided to sit down and wait to see what would happen next.

After twenty minutes of silent anticipation, the door opened and a short, stocky, balding police officer walked in and introduced himself. "Hello, I'm Sergeant Moore. What's your name?" Lil Joe didn't answer. "All right, then, will you at least tell me why you and your friend down the hall were walking down the street drenched in blood and carrying bloody knives in your pockets?"

Lil Joe looked up at the sergeant. "So if I tell you my name and explain what happened, can we go?"

The sergeant shrugged. "Well, that depends on the situation. We'll have to investigate in order to verify your story and make sure you're being truthful with us. Because I gotta tell ya, kid, two young boys roaming the streets wearing bloody clothes and carrying bloody knives is serious business. Do you understand what I'm tellin' ya?"

Lil Joe nodded his head. "Yeah, I understand."

"Okay, good. First of all, what's your name and whose blood is that on your t-shirt?"

Lil Joe cut in. "It's not a person's blood. It's dog blood."

"Okay, okay," said the sergeant. "Why don't you tell me your name and then you can explain how you and your friend ended up with dog blood all over you."

"All right, my name is Joseph Hernandez."

The sergeant interrupted. "Where do you live, Mr. Hernandez?"

"What?" Lil Joe tensed up. "I don't see what that has to do with anything. This is just a big mixup."

"Okay, then, tell me about it," said the sergeant.

"All right. Look, man, me and my friend were walking down an alley on our way home from the Secumbe Park and . . . "

The sergeant interrupted again. "Do you recall what street the alley was on?"

"No, I don't," Lil Joe said with obvious frustration in his voice.

"Okay, so what happened in the alley, Joseph?"

Lil Joe sighed. "Well, like I was saying, we were walking down the alley when this big dog came out of nowhere and tried to attack us. But me and my friend pulled out our knives and stabbed it before it could bite us."

The sergeant frowned. "So a big dog attacked you, huh?" he said in an arrogant tone. "That's dog blood all over you and your friend?"

"Yeah, that's right," Lil Joe responded with an attitude of his own. "That's what I said."

The sergeant gave him a look of disbelief. "So why were you two carrying knives to begin with?"

Lil Joe shrugged. "Protection, I guess."

"Protection you say. Protection from what?" asked the sergeant.

Lil Joe could tell by the sergeant's attitude that he wasn't buying his story, so he gave him a cocky smile and said, "Protection from dogs."

"Uh huh, well, Joseph, I don't believe this little story of yours and I think you should be smart and start telling the truth. So I'm gonna give you time to think about it." The sergeant got up and walked out of the room, leaving Lil Joe to his thoughts. But he wasn't thinking about what Sgt. Moore had said. He was thinking about Franky and what story he would come up with.

After waiting for what seemed an eternity, the door to the interrogation room opened and in walked three men. Sgt. Moore came in first and then a tall, slim, elderly man wearing a suit and another pudgy police officer. "Well, Mr. Hernandez," said Sgt. Moore, "we've done some investigating and we believe you and your friend, Mr. Mu_oz, were involved in the murder of one Robert Ortiz, the stepfather of Mr. Mu_oz."

"What? Murder? Come on, man, you got the wrong kid," said Lil Joe.

Sgt. Moore cut in. "Look, Mr. Hernandez, you're in some pretty hot water here, so before we continue, we have to read you your

Miranda rights. Okay? And to make sure you understand your rights, we've brought in an attorney who has been appointed to you." He pointed at the elderly man in the suit.

"Hello, Mr. Hernandez. My name is John Williams and I'll be representing you as your legal counsel. Do you understand what that means?"

"Yeah, you're my lawyer," Lil Joe said with a bit of a wary attitude.

"Yes, good," the lawyer said. "This other gentleman is Officer Jacobs. He's here to witness the reading of your Miranda rights."

Lil Joe took a quick glance in the other cop's direction. "All right."

"Now, Mr. Joseph Hernandez, you have the right to remain silent. Anything you say, can and will be used against you in a court of law. You have the right to consult with an attorney, to be represented by an attorney, and to have an attorney present before and during questioning. If you cannot afford an attorney, one will be appointed by the court free of charge to represent you before and during questioning if you so desire. Mr. Hernandez, do you understand these rights?"

Lil Joe looked around the room at the men and then asked the attorney, "Can I talk with you in private?"

"Yes, you sure can."

Sgt. Moore and Officer Jacobs immediately left the interrogation room so Lil Joe and his lawyer could talk. As soon as they were gone, Lil Joe asked, "Are you Franky's lawyer too?"

"No, Mr. Mu_oz is represented by his own counsel, who, if I'm not mistaken, should be talking to him right now."

"All right, then," said Lil Joe, "how come the cops are charging us with murdering this Robert Ortiz guy?"

"Well, Mr. Hernandez, I won't know the exact circumstances by which the police came to their conclusions until tomorrow, but from what I've gathered so far, at approximately 8:40 P.M. tonight, Police Dispatch received a phone call from a young woman by the name of Elsa Mu_oz, the older sister of your alleged accomplice. Miss Mu_oz stated that she had just returned home from visiting her mother in the hospital and found her stepfather, Mr. Robert Ortiz, lying dead in a pool of blood on the living room floor. According to the dispatch officer, Miss Mu_oz expressed her concern for her younger brother, Frank Mu_oz, who, according to her, hadn't been seen by the family in almost twenty-four hours."

The lawyer sighed. "Uh, it appears that a detective who responded to the scene contacted Sgt. Moore to inform him of a possible connection to the case he was working, which happens to be your case, Mr. Hernandez. Now the police brought Miss Mu_oz for questioning, and I believe they are talking to her as we speak."

Just then there was a knock on the door and a couple of seconds later Sgt. Moore walked in and said, "Mr. Williams, may I have a word with you?"

"Sure. Uh, Mr. Hernandez, excuse me for a moment. I'll be back in just a minute," the lawyer said as he and the sergeant left the room.

Lil Joe was beginning to feel all the events of the day catching up with him. He was suddenly feeling very tired and just wanted to go to sleep. So he sat back in his chair and closed his eyes, hoping to catch a little rest, but about ten minutes later his attorney walked back in and announced, "I've got some more news for you, Mr. Hernandez. First of all, your mother is here."

"My mother?" Lil Joe said with surprise. He felt his heart sink into his stomach.

"Yes," said Mr. Williams. "Apparently someone called her and informed her that you were in custody. Now she is here demanding to see you. Sgt. Moore has promised her that she'll be able to visit with you in a short while."

Lil Joe didn't know what to think. He knew it had to be Elsa who called his mom. He did want to see her, but he just didn't want to see her right then. He didn't want to have to deal with the drama just yet.

The lawyer continued. "Sgt. Moore has just informed me of a statement that Mr. Mu_oz has given them in regard to the charges you two are facing."

Lil Joe was caught off guard. "What statement?" he asked with concern.

"Well, Mr. Hernandez, after the police questioned Miss Mu_oz about the death of Mr. Ortiz, they gathered some more information. According to Miss Mu_oz, after she learned of her brother's arrest, she made a statement to the effect that just recently Robert Ortiz , the deceased, beat their mother, causing her severe injuries and resulting in her being hospitalized. She further stated that if her brother Franky had anything to do with Robert's death, it would have had to be in self defense."

That's right, thought Lil Joe, at least she was trying to help out.

"So," the lawyer continued, "after the police finished questioning Miss Mu_oz ,they went back to question Mr. Mu_oz. Obviously the police used his sister's statement to get a confession out of him because he confessed to killing his stepfather in an act of revenge for the assault on his mother."

Fuck! Thought Lil Joe, what did he do that for?

"Also, Mr. Hernandez, you should know that Mr. Mu_oz has given a statement as to your involvement in the incident as well. He stated that you had nothing to do with it; that you just happened to show up while he was stabbing his stepfather, and that you tried to stop him. He said that you took one of the two knives he was holding and tried to restrain him, and that was why you had blood on your clothes and a bloody knife in your pocket."

Damn good story, thought Lil Joe.

"But, Mr. Hernandez, the police don't believe that story. There are some discrepancies in it. For example, if you were indeed trying to stop Mr. Mu_oz from further assaulting Mr. Ortiz, why didn't you call the police or run to a neighbor's house and have someone call the police? And why did you run from the police when they first saw you?"

Lil Joe didn't realize that his lawyer was expecting an explanation. "Well, Mr. Hernandez, anything?"

"I don't know," was all Lil Joe managed to say. He was tired and needed time to think, but according to his lawyer, he didn't have the luxury of time to do any thinking.

"As it stands right now, Mr. Hernandez, the police have a theory to go along with the evidence of your having been apprehended with bloody clothes and one of the murder weapons in your possession. They are going to try and prove that you were involved in the crime by having forensic experts analyze your clothes for the direction of the blood spatter. Right now the theory they have developed is that you knew what your close friend was going to do, and as a loyal fried you helped him murder his stepfather. Mr. Hernandez, I have to tell you that unless you can convince the police that you were somehow forced to participate in the crime and that the reason you didn't call the police or cooperate with them during questioning was because you feared for your own life, you're going to face murder charges."

Lil Joe knew that his lawyer was trying to get him to put the whole blame on Franky in order to save his own ass, but that wasn't going to happen. Lil Joe was only a youngster, but he still knew it wouldn't be right. No, he would ride this thing out with Franky. Besides, he had been aware of the consequences if they were caught. He had known what he was getting himself into, and he was prepared to face it like a man. Lil Joe looked his lawyer right in the eyes and said, "I'm no rat, and I won't sell out my homeboy."

His lawyer pleaded with him to reconsider. "You don't want to ruin your life with his, Joseph."

But Lil Joe wasn't having it. "No!" he yelled in anger. "I have nothing else to say."

"Very well, Mr. Hernandez," said the lawyer with a look of disappointment on his face. "I'll be back shortly with your mother to discuss what will happen next."

After the lawyer left the cell, Lil Joe sat quietly thinking about what he was going to say to his mother. He felt a little lightheaded. He was tired and stressed from the ordeal. He thought about what he and Franky had done to Robert, but he didn't feel any remorse. He didn't feel there was anything to be sorry about. The son of a bitch had had it coming! He thought. In fact, the only thing he was sorry for was the problems he was flinging upon his mother.

Just then the door opened and his attorney came in and held the door open for Lil Joe's mother. The look of pain and confusion on her face was enough to kill him ten times over. She looked like she had been crying, and her normally beautiful brown eyes were bloodshot and her face wrinkled with worry. Her long black hair was up in a sloppy ponytail and she was still wearing her work uniform. Lil Joe couldn't believe the look of hurt in her eyes. It was terrible. Then to make matters worse, he realized she was staring at the dry blood on his clothes. It was too much; he couldn't bare to look at her, so he put his head down and stared at the floor.

"Mijo, are you hurt?" She rushed over to examine him.

He quickly got to his feet. "No, Mam , I'm okay," he replied in a shamed whisper.

After examining him for herself, she grabbed him by the shoulders, tears streaming from her eyes. "Tell them you had nothing to do with it, mijo! Tell them so I can take you home." She pulled him into her embrace and squeezed him tightly.

Oh, God, thought Lil Joe, can this get any worse? He wished God would just strike him dead right there on the spot. "Por favor, Mam , don't cry."

"Oh, mijo," was all she could say in return.

"It's okay, Mom, it's okay." He tried to comfort her and after what was the longest hug of his life, she pushed him back and held him at arm's length.

Regaining her composure, she demanded, "What happened?"

"I don't know, Mam ," he said. "Don't believe anything these people tell you, okay? They don't know what they're talking about." He hated lying to her, but he had to protect her from the truth. There was no way she would understand it no matter how he explained.

She turned to his lawyer who was standing by the door of the small room trying to give them some kind of privacy. "What are they going to do with him?"

The lawyer gestured with his hand for them to take a seat. Once they did, he explained that Lil Joe and Franky would both be retained in custody and taken to Ward-B, a juvenile section of the county mental health unit. "It's county procedure for boys as young as Joseph and Franky to be evaluated for mental health problems when they've been charged with a crime such as murder. It's only a two week observation period, at the end of which the hospital's child psychologist will give his or her professional opinion and findings in a report to the Juvenile Superior Court. The child psychologist will either recommend mental health treatment in one of the state's mental health institutions or clear the boys for prosecution. If the boys are cleared for prosecution, we will start court proceedings soon after."

"Will I be able to visit him?" asked Lil Joe's mother.

"I would imagine so," the lawyer said. "I'll inquire about the visiting schedule at Ward-B and I'll contact you with the details no later than tomorrow evening."

Just then Sgt. Moore walked into the room. "Mrs. Hernandez, I'm sorry but we have to wrap this up. It's about 11:30 P.M. and we have to get the boys to Ward-B Intake."

"Okay," Lil Joe's mom said. She and Lil Joe stood up at the same time and she hugged him again. "You behave, mijo. Okay? I'll come visit you soon, I promise."

"Okay, Mom," said Lil Joe.

His mom let go of him and walked toward the door, turning back one last time to blow him a kiss before leaving. Lil Joe had to fight back his tears. He felt terrible for putting his mother through so much. She doesn't deserve this, he thought. She doesn't deserve this at all.

Just then Officer Jacobs walked into the room carrying a plastic bag and a blue sweatsuit. "Mr. Hernandez, we need you to change into these clothes and put your old ones in this bag. Okay?"

"All right," said Lil Joe.

CHAPTER FIVE

FOR THE FIRST TIME SINCE THEIR arrest, Lil Joe and Franky saw each other--when the arresting officers drove them to the county mental health unit. On the short drive there, Lil Joe and Franky talked in the back of the squad car. "It's been a long night, huh?" Lil Joe said.

Franky sighed. "Man, hell yeah. Hey, man, you know I tried to get you off of this shit."

Lil Joe nodded. "I know you did, Franky. My lawyer told me." He chuckled. "Shit, I thought it was a pretty good story myself, man. Too bad they didn't buy it."

Franky smiled.

"My mom showed up," Lil Joe said. "They let me visit with her, but I kind of wish they wouldn't have because I felt like shit seeing her all upset like that."

"Yeah, man. That's messed up, bro. They let me visit with Elsa, too, but they cut the visit short because she got all hysterical and shit." Franky shrugged. "I guess she kinda took it hard finding Robert like that, but I guess I can't blame her, you know?"

"Yeah. Hopefully she'll be okay."

Just then the older officer announced, "We're here, fellas," as he drove up into a parking lot and parked in front of a side entrance to a large concrete building.

The Hispanic officer opened the back door on Lil Joe's side and said, "Come on, boys, let's get you into Intake."

Lil Joe and Franky slid out of the car and the cops escorted them through the entrance and into a small cellie port that had a small glass bubble behind which a middle aged woman was stationed. As soon as they were all inside the cellie port, the older cop hollered into a tiny metal speaker box in the glass bubble. "We've got two intakes for Ward-B."

The woman behind the glass acknowledged him with a nod and pushed a button on the control panel in front of her. There was a loud buzzing sound and a door on the opposite side of the cellie port opened. "Come on through, boys," the younger cop said as he walked through and motioned for them to follow. Lil Joe and Franky walked through the door and into a small, occupied concrete waiting room with another glass bubble at the front.

As Lil Joe and Franky stood facing the glass staring at the elderly black man who was stationed behind it, the older cop pointed to an empty space on the concrete slab that stretched along the wall of the waiting room. "Go ahead and have a seat, boys," he said. Then the man behind the bubble slid two clipboards through a metal slot to the officers, who immediately began filling out the paperwork. While they were doing their custody transfer paperwork, Lil Joe and Franky sat next to each other and looked around at the other three people in the room. On the slab a couple of feet away from Lil Joe was an elderly, balding man with a long, straggly grey beard, and next to him was a middle aged, barefooted, blonde headed lady wearing a dirty white sock on one of her hands. The other was stuffed in her mouth.

Lil Joe chuckled at the sight of her, then nudged Franky with his elbow. "Hey, Franky, look." he said, nodding his head towards the "sock lady." "There goes your girlfriend."

They both laughed and then Franky nodded towards a filthy looking black man who was sitting in the corner across from them having a heated argument with himself. "Get a load of that guy bro."

Lil Joe wrinkled his brow in concern, noticing for the first time that he and Franky were the only people in the room wearing handcuffs. "Hey!" he yelled at the two officers. "What kind of place is this man, and how come we're the only ones with handcuffs on?"

The young Hispanic cop chuckled, obviously tickled by Lil Joe's question. "Don't worry, you guys won't be cuffed much longer," he assured him.

Then his partner grabbed his clipboard and slid both clipboards back through the metal slot and yelled to the man behind the bubble, "All done."

Just then the younger cop walked over to Lil Joe and Franky and said, "Okay, boys, go ahead and stand up so we can get those cuffs off you."

After the handcuffs were removed, his partner yelled to the man behind the bubble, "They're all yours," and both cops headed toward the door.

As they were being buzzed back into the cellie port, the Hispanic cop turned around and said, "Good luck, fellas." Then he and his partner left.

Lil Joe then turned to Franky and said, "Man, I'm dead tired, bro."

"Me, too," Franky said. "I gotta take a dump too."

Lil Joe shook his head and smiled. Good ol' Franky, he thought, always hungry and always having to shit.

About an hour later, a tall, skinny black man and a heavy set white woman dressed in the white outfits of orderlies were buzzed in through another door at the back of the waiting room and yelled out to the man behind the bubble, "We're here for the two goin' to Ward-B."

The man pointed to Lil Joe and Franky and the woman said "Come on, boys, let's get you to your ward."

Lil Joe and Franky followed her and her partner down several poorly lit hallways until they reached a door on which "Ward-B" was painted. "Here we are, boys," the lady announced. "The end of the road." She unlocked the door with a giant key and held it open for them and her co-worker. "Go on inside, boys, and have a seat over there." She pointed to a bench.

"I have to use the restroom," Franky said.

"Okay, honey it'll just be a few minutes. All right?"

After Lil Joe and Franky sat down, the lady joined her partner behind a staff desk across the room and began to write in a large green book labeled Unit Log on the outside cover. Lil Joe immediately began checking the place out. Directly behind where he and Franky were seated was a large dark room with big glass windows in the front. To the right of them was a glass door leading out to what he assumed was some kind of recreation yard, and to the right was a small television room with a TV sitting on top of a wooden hutch and a room full of soft cushioned chairs. To the right of the TV room was a hallway from which doors led to rooms which Lil Joe assumed were occupied by patients. The same kind of hallway was to the left of the unit.

"All right, boys, let's get you to your room," said the lady. "You two will be sharing a room over here. Follow me." She walked toward the left side of the unit. "This side is for the boys," she explained, "and the other side is for the girls."

Lil Joe and Franky's room was all the way at the end of the hallway. When they got there, the door was already open. "Everything you guys will need is in here," the lady explained. "Your linen and toiletries are there on your beds, and the bathroom's right there," she said, pointing to a closed door just to the left of the door to the room. "It has a sink, a toilet, and a shower. The daytime shift will be in at 6 A.M. They'll explain the daily routine, but for now it's sleep time."

She walked out and closed and locked the door behind her. Before walking away, she looked through the small, square window at the top of the door and said, "Goodnight, boys."

Lil Joe took a look around the room. "Well, Franky, here we are." The walls were yellow and the room was bare except for the two beds and a large dresser under a heavily screened window on the back wall with a nice view of the parking lot. "Well, I'm beat," said Lil Joe. He walked to the bed furthest from the bathroom and sat down.

Franky sat on the bed next to the bathroom door. "I gotta take a shit. You wanna go before I go in there?" he asked.

"Nah, go ahead, bro. I'm gonna crash. Buenas noches."

"Good night, Lil Joe. See you tomorrow," said Franky as he walked into the bathroom.

Lil Joe was too tired to even make his bed. He just lay down on it the way it was and instantly fell asleep.

The next morning, Lil Joe and Franky awoke to the sound of someone unlocking and opening their door. An elderly woman with a short crop of salt and pepper hair and smiling blue eyes poked her head around the door frame and greeted them with a cheery, "Good morning, boys. Breakfast will be here in about twenty minutes."

Franky jumped out of bed. "Good, cause I'm starving."

The lady smiled at Franky's spunkiness. "Good. Go ahead and wash up, then come join everyone for breakfast. Uh, by the way, my name is Edna. I'm the unit psychologist. If either of you boys need anything, just ask." They nodded in acknowledgment. "Okay, then, see you in a bit."

After Lil Joe and Franky washed up, they walked out into the unit, where Edna was waiting for them behind the staff desk. "Good. There you are, boys. Go ahead inside and have some breakfast." She pointed to the large room with the glass windows in the front. "The plates and eating utensils are on the table next to the food cart."

Now that the unit was bright with light, it was easier for Lil Joe to see everything. The big room that Edna had pointed to turned out to be some sort of dining area, and as soon as he and Franky walked in they noticed that there were four other kids, two boys and two girls, already inside eating breakfast. All of them stared at Lil Joe and Franky as they made their way to the food cart. There was a huge assortment of food to choose from--scrambled eggs, hash browns, pancakes with syrup, sausage patties, and little containers of milk and orange juice. After piling up their plates with food, they walked to a table across the room and away from the other kids and sat down. As soon as they sat down, Franky dug right in like a grizzly bear eating its first meal after hibernation. Lil Joe laughed at Franky's voraciousness.

"What?" Franky asked, looking up from his plate. "Shit, I'm as hungry as a stray dog." Lil Joe laughed and then dug into his own plate.

After breakfast, Lil Joe and Franky went back to their room for a shower. When they got there, there was a change of clothes for them on their beds. "Man, look at this shit!" said Franky, holding up a pair of Nutthugger underwear. "Hell, no, I'm not wearing these things. They remind me of my jefita's dust rags." Lil Joe laughed. It was true. Franky's mom never threw anything away. She found a use for everything, including old underwear, which she converted into dust rags. "Well, homeboy," said Franky, "you might wanna shower first cause I gotta feed the sharks."

"Shit!" Lil Joe said, "you don't have to warn me twice. I'll go first."

After they showered and changed clothes, they walked back out into the unit, where they were greeted by Edna again. "Oh, good, I see you boys found your change of clothes. We put fresh linen and clothes out for all our wards every morning except Sundays. The laundry service workers take Sundays off." She paused for a moment as if she were trying to remember something she wanted to say. "Well, that's about it for now. If you'd like, you can go out to the rec yard or watch television in the TV room with the others, whichever you prefer. Maybe you guys would like to get acquainted with the rest of the kids."

Lil Joe decided he liked Edna. She had a pleasant demeanor and was soft spoken, characteristics he liked women to have. There were two orderlies who worked the early day shift along with Edna, but as Lil Joe later learned, the rest of the day, including the night shift and most weekends, there were just two orderlies working the unit at one time. Basically they were just there to watch over the juvenile ward and make sure that nothing bad happened to any of the patients.

Lil Joe and Franky decided to go into the TV room. When they got there, the other four kids were all watching Saturday morning cartoons. Franky took a seat next to a pretty teenage brunette who was eyeballing him and greeted her with a smile. "Hey, what's up?" he said. She didn't respond. Instead, she got up and walked out of the room.

Lil Joe chuckled. "Hey, Franky, I think she likes you, man. It must be your face."

"Sarah doesn't talk," said a pretty redheaded girl sitting at the far end of the room. "My name's Kathy. This is Billy," she said, pointing to an Asian kid sitting next to her who was glued to the TV oblivious to what was going on around him. "And that's Travis," she said, tilting her head towards a spaced out looking blond kid who was sitting across from her.

"Nice to meet you, Kathy," said Lil Joe. "I'm Lil Joe Hernandez and this is my homeboy, Franky."

He pointed to Franky, who gave her a head nod and said, "What's up?"

Kathy appeared to be puzzled as she looked them both up and down. "I don't mean to be nosy or anything, but what are you guys doing in a place like this? I mean, you guys don't look like the kind of kids who would be in a place like this."

Lil Joe purposely avoided her question. He didn't know her well enough to tell her their business, so he pretended to be offended. "Hey, who are you calling kids?"

Kathy smiled deviously and in a sarcastically playful tone, said, "Oh, I'm sorry. With a name like Lil Joe I should of known not to refer to you as a kid."

Franky laughed at her sarcasm and Lil Joe shot him a playful scowl. "What are you laughing at, fucker?"

Kathy didn't notice that Lil Joe was only playing with Franky, so she took it the wrong way. "God, I was just giving you a hard time. There's no need to get all bent out of shape about it."

Before Lil Joe had a chance to respond, Travis, the spaced out looking kid, started yelling profanities out of nowhere. "Fuck! Bastard! Son of a bitch asshole! Dog shit cocksucker!"

Franky was caught off guard and immediately jumped out of his seat defensively. "Who the fuck are you talking to?" he shouted.

Travis responded by standing up and pulling off his pants, then running off onto the unit floor screaming curse words at the top of his lungs. Franky turned to Lil Joe with a twisted look of confusion on his face. "What the fuck was that, man?" Franky's reaction to Travis's outburst made Lil Joe laugh so hard he had to bend down and clutch his stomach in pain.

"Travis is a little off his rocker," Kathy explained while giggling over the situation. "He does stuff like that all the time."

Just then the unit orderlies caught up with Travis and physically restrained him. They took him into a room on the left side of the unit, strapped him down on a bed, and gave him a shot in his ass. Lil Joe and Franky were standing in the doorway of the TV room and witnessed the whole thing. "Did you see that shit, man?" Franky said with a disturbed look on his face. "Man, what kind of place is this, bro?"

Lil Joe tried to calm his nerves. "Hey, man, it's cool, Franky. Don't even trip on that shit. We're only gonna be here for a couple of weeks, man."

Franky shook his head. "Yeah, whatever, man. I'm cool as long as nobody tries to stick any needles in my ass!"

Lil Joe chuckled. "Don't worry, homeboy. I won't let nobody stick any needles in your ass." Franky smiled, then punched Lil Joe in the arm, and they shared a good laugh about the whole thing. They spent the remainder of the day talking to Kathy, who gave them the rundown on everything and everybody there in Ward-B, including herself.

Kathy was a sixteen-year-old Irish Catholic from Rialto, California, who had been admitted into Ward-B after taking half a bottle of her mother's sleeping pills in an attempt to commit suicide after her high school boyfriend broke up with her. According to Kathy, the other girl in Ward-B was Sarah Goldberg, a fifteen-year-old Jewish girl from Pomona, California, who never spoke a word to anyone. In fact, as Kathy put it, nobody there even knew if Sarah could talk. The only thing any of the kids knew about her was that she had been there longer than any of them.

The two boys were Travis Wheeler and Billy Schultz. They were both twelve year old and had serious problems. Billy was half Japanese and half German. He was from Cucamonga, California, and was a pyro-maniac. He had been admitted into Ward-B on several occasions for starting small fires around his neighborhood, but this time he'd been admitted for setting his grandmother's cat on fire, apparently as an act of vengeance because she wouldn't allow him to stay up late and watch TV.

Travis was Caucasian, was born and raised in San Bernardino, and came from a typical American background, but he suffered from just about every mental illness known to man. He also suffered from epilepsy and would often have seizures. Out of all the kids, Travis was by far the most memorable and was hands down the weirdest kid either Lil Joe or Franky had ever met.

Kathy also gave Lil Joe and Franky the basic rundown on Ward-B's daily routine. On Monday through Friday, there were mandatory group counseling sessions after breakfast with Edna. Kathy explained that Edna wasn't usually there on weekends, and that she was probably there that Saturday because they had shown up late the night before. According to Kathy, Edna always liked to be present when new arrivals came to Ward-B. Kathy said that visiting days were Monday through

Saturday from 5:30 P.M. to 8 P.M., and there was an 11 o'clock curfew during the week, with a midnight lockup curfew on weekends. So the only time any of the patients in Ward-B were locked in their rooms was after curfew until 6:30 A.M. unlock.

"Basically you just hang out all day and do whatever until they tell you you can leave," said Kathy.

After hearing that, Lil Joe was glad that he and Franky were only there for a quick evaluation period. The thought never even crossed his mind that he or Franky might end up having to stay.

A few times during the course of the day, Kathy would get up to change the TV from one soap opera to another, and when she did, Lil Joe and Franky would admire her nice, round, plump butt through her tight fitting sweatpants. A couple of times she noticed them staring at her in the reflection on the TV screen and blushed with embarrassment as she asked them what they were looking at. But they could tell that she liked the attention.

Later that first night, after dinner, Travis had another one of his spontaneous outbursts where he urinated on the staff desk while the orderlies were sitting behind it eating their dinners. They chased him down again and after strapping him down to the same bed as before, they gave him another tranquilizing shot in the ass. Lil Joe overheard one of the orderlies say they were going to leave Travis strapped to the bed all night and felt sorry for him. While the orderlies were manhandling Travis, Lil Joe thought about jumping in to help the poor kid out, but decided against it. He had enough problems of his own to worry about.

After dinner, Billy took his medication and went straight to his room to go to sleep, so Lil Joe, Franky, Kathy, and Sarah went into the TV room to talk and watch whatever came on until it was time for lockup, and that was pretty much the routine throughout the rest of the weekend. Come Monday morning, the routine began the same but after breakfast Lil Joe and Franky attended their first group counseling session. Edna held the session in the dining room, where she formed a circle with chairs and asked everyone to have a seat. The group sessions consisted of all the patients speaking about their specific problems that had landed them there and what steps they needed to take in the future to prevent themselves from making the wrong choices.

At the beginning of the first session, Edna explained to Lil Joe and Franky that the counseling sessions were completely confidential, but she didn't press them to talk about their case, so they didn't. Instead, they just sat quietly and listened to the other kids talk about their problems.

About an hour into that first session, Franky got upset with Sarah for staring at him and interrupted the session by yelling at her, "What the fuck. Why do you keep staring at me?"

Sarah didn't even blink and just kept staring, and Lil Joe could tell that Franky was getting worked up, so he cracked a joke to make light of the situation. "Hey, Franky, you know how I'm always saying that you got a face only a mother could love? Well, I take it back, man. Obviously I was wrong."

Edna smiled and started to say something, but her words were lost when Travis stood up and loudly announced that he had just shit himself. Then he fell to the floor and had a seizure, which naturally changed the mood in the room fairly quickly. Neither Lil Joe nor Franky had ever witnessed anyone having a seizure before and they found it kind of interesting how Travis flopped around on the floor like a fish out of water. The session ended then so that Edna and the orderlies could clear the room and attend to Travis.

Lil Joe, Franky, Kathy, Sarah, and Billy all made their way to the TV room to hang out and for some unknown reason Sarah decided to sit directly across from Franky and continue to stare at him, which caused him to blow his top. "What the fuck?" he yelled at her. "I'll give you something to stare at." He stood up and whipped out his dick and began shaking it around in Sarah's face. "Here, stare at this, bitch!" he said, laughing at her disgusted reaction.

Kathy stood up and yelled, "Leave her alone!" But it was too late. The damage was done and Sarah stormed out of the TV room crying. Although Franky's little outburst of perverted anger was somewhat cruel, it accomplished what he was shooting for. For the rest of their days in Ward-B, Sarah would never look at Franky again. In fact, she made it a point not to even be in the same room with him.

Later that night after dinner, Lil Joe received a visit from his mom and his attorney. He was happy to see his mom without tears pouring out of her eyes, but even though she wasn't crying, he could tell that she was still quite upset about the whole situation. She spent most of the visit checking out the unit and asking concerned questions about the place. She also brought word from Franky's sister, who asked her to relay a message to Franky. "Mijo, Elsa said to tell Franky that her and their mom will come to see him as soon as their mom is up to it, and she also said to tell him that they'll be moving soon."

"Elsa didn't say where to?"

"No, mijo, she didn't."

"It's okay, Mam_, I'll tell him. Thanks."

Lil Joe's attorney, Mr. Williams, brought him a copy of the police report of the incident. He highlighted the main facts of evidence in the report for Lil Joe because Lil Joe's mother had explained to him that Lil Joe didn't read very well. He knew enough to get by, but he still had trouble with words not known to the average thirteen year old.

At the end of their visit, Lil Joe's mom gave him $20 and a big hug. "I love you, mijo. You be good. Okay?"

"I will, Mom, don't worry."

After visiting hours ended, Lil Joe went to his room to read the police report. Most of the facts in the report were things he and Franky were already aware of. The only new information was that Robert had been stabbed thirteen times and died almost instantly from a stab wound to the heart. Lil Joe had had no idea that he and Franky had worked Robert over that bad. Just as he was finishing up with the report, Franky walked in. "Hey, bro, how was your visit?"

"Everything was cool. My mom says hello. She gave me twenty bucks so we can go to the commissary." Lil Joe held the police report out to Franky. "You wanna read this police report?"

"Nah, man, is there anything in there that we don't already know?"

"Not really, just how many times we stabbed him."

"Yeah, how many?"

"Thirteen times."

Franky whistled. "Damn! Must of hurt."

Lil Joe grunted at the twisted humor and put the report on his bed. "Oh, yeah, before I forget, your sister sent word with my mom. She said that her and your jefa will come to see you as soon as your mom is up to it and that they'll be moving soon."

Franky was surprised. "Moving? Where to?"

"I don't know, bro. Elsa didn't say." Lil Joe could tell Franky was disturbed by the news so he tried to change the subject. "So, hey, it's still early. What do you wanna do? We could go kick back with Kathy."

His attempt to change the subject didn't work. Franky's mind was still on his mom and sister. "Hey, bro, I'm kinda glad my mom hasn't come to see me yet. I'm not sure I can face her right now anyway. You know what I mean?"

"Yeah, I do man, but don't worry about it. Everything will work itself out."

Franky smiled. "Yeah, you're probably right. Come on, let's go see what's up with Kathy."

When they got to the TV room, Kathy was the only one there. She was getting ready to watch the 9 o'clock movie, some chick flick that she had already seen half a dozen times. Just before the movie started, the unit orderlies brought them some cookies for a snack. After they left, Franky jumped up and turned off the light just before Kathy got up to adjust the volume on the TV. As she did so, she bent over, placing her ass just inches from Lil Joe's face. The temptation was too strong; he just couldn't help himself. He leaned forward and gently bit her on the butt cheek, which caused her to jump forward and let out a yelp of surprise. She quickly turned around, flushed with embarrassment. "Oh, my God!" she said with utter disbelief. "Did you just bite me on the ass?"

Lil Joe half expected a slap across the face, but it never came. Instead Kathy smiled mischievously and playfully slapped him on the arm. Lil Joe knew he was in, so he went for it. He grabbed her by the waist and sat her on his lap. "Ooh," she purred, "I got the best seat in the house."

Franky laughed. "Yeah, yeah, get a room."

Hmm, that's not a bad idea, thought Lil Joe, but he settled for just making out with her throughout the movie until the orderlies came in at 11 o'clock to tell them it was time for lockup. "So I'll see you in the morning," said Lil Joe.

"Okay. Goodnight," said Kathy, and she kissed him and went to her room for the night.

Back in their room, Lil Joe and Franky talked a little before calling it a night. "So it looks like you're in with Kathy," said Franky.

Lil Joe smiled. "Yeah, man. Too bad it was already late, though."

"Shit, you'll pick up where you left off ma ana [tomorrow], bro."

"I hope so. Man, I'm beat, Franky. Buenas noches, bro."

Franky laughed. "Yeah, buenas noches. Try not to have a wet dream, Casanova," he joked.

Lil Joe laughed. "Ha! Sick bastard!" He went to sleep with Kathy on his mind. He knew that he and Franky were looking at a long stretch of time for what they had done, so he figured he should make the best of his time with Kathy while he had the chance. So next morning in the TV room after breakfast and group counseling, Lil Joe and Kathy picked up right where they had left off. Franky was the only other person in the TV room at the time, so he decided to give them their privacy and went out to the rec yard with Travis to play a game of H.O.R.S.E. on the basketball court.

Meanwhile Lil Joe took advantage of his one-on-one time with Kathy. They'd been fooling around for about ten minutes when Kathy stopped abruptly and asked, "What are we doing?"

Lil Joe thought that was a pretty dumb question, but he decided not to be a smart ass about it. Instead, he looked into her bright green eyes and said, "What's wrong, Kathy? Everything seems right to me."

Kathy had a concerned look on her face. "I know," she said, then gave a little sigh. "It's just, how old are you?"

"I'm fifteen." He lied, but figured, fuck it, what the hell did that matter anyway? He kissed her again and asked, "Are you cool?"

Kathy smiled. "Yes, I'm cool."

They began to make out again and Lil Joe wasted no time. He lifted her t-shirt up to her neck. She wasn't wearing a bra. Good girl! thought Lil Joe. He began to kiss and suck on her soft pink nipples, letting the heat of the moment take its course. Then after a few minutes of foreplay, Lil Joe was ready to go; he couldn't wait any longer. "Come on," he said, helping her off his lap. He walked over to the door to peek out and see what the orderlies were doing. They were all gathered around the staff desk playing cards, oblivious to their surroundings, so Lil Joe and Kathy snuck into her bedroom and sealed the deal. They went a couple of rounds before sneaking back out of her room about forty-five minutes later.

Lil Joe felt pretty damn good and he couldn't stop smiling. He was a man now, a man on top of the world. The thought made him stick his chest out.

The following few days were the same. Lil Joe took advantage of every opportunity to take Kathy to the side somewhere and wet his whistle. One time he pulled her into Travis's room while no one was looking and right in the middle of their screwing Travis walked in and went berserk. He stripped down naked and ran out of the room laughing like a crazy man while pissing all over himself and the floor. When the orderlies chased after him, it gave Lil Joe and Kathy an opportunity to sneak out of his room without being noticed.

Three days before the end of Franky's and Lil Joe's observation period, Franky still hadn't received a visit. Although he hid it well, Lil Joe could tell he was upset and wanted to do something to lift his spirits. And he knew exactly what would do the job. So on that day he decided to spring it on Kathy. They were alone in the TV room making out when he decided to try his luck.

"Hey, baby, you know me and Franky are looking at some time in C.Y.A., so I was wondering if you could do me a little favor and show Franky some love too."

Kathy looked as if she were giving it some consideration. Then after a moment she shrugged her shoulders and said, "Okay. Sure. Why not?"

Lil Joe kissed her. "All right. Cool." He smiled. He thought it was going to take a little more persuasion, but he was wrong; she was game. She seemed to really like all the attention. Thinking about it later, Lil Joe realized that before he and Franky got there, Kathy was a mess. She was depressed and wanted to kill herself, but the attention both he and Franky gave her seemed to help build back her self esteem. So in a small way they actually helped her get out of her depressed state of mind. Lil Joe was glad he'd been able to help.

So on their last three remaining days at Ward-B, he and Franky both spent their time screwing the devil out of Kathy every chance they got.

CHAPTER SIX

ON THE DAY OF THEIR HEARING, Lil Joe and Franky were escorted to Juvenile Hall where the juvenile court was located. The proceedings were held in a small building on the Juvenile Hall grounds. They were over quickly. Lil Joe barely had enough time to look over the courtroom before they rushed him and Franky out to get the next case in. But there wasn't much to look at anyway. The courtroom looked like a small church with its rows of varnished wooden benches and a wood podium up front with a large judge's bench. There was also a large stained wooden table directly in front of the judge's bench where Lil Joe and Franky, along with their attorneys, were seated. The assistant district attorney sat at a separate table which was somewhat smaller than theirs and on the other side of the courtroom.

Once everyone who was supposed to be there was in the courtroom, the proceedings started. The judge, an elderly man with a silver comb-over hairdo, began the proceedings by commenting on Edna's psychological report.

"All right, Mr. Hernandez and Mr. Mu_oz are both present. Have both parties received a copy of the Ward-B psychological report?" Both Lil Joe's and Franky's attorneys indicated they had. "And the assistant district attorney as well?"

"The district attorney's office has also received a copy, your honor."

"Well, okay then." The judge glanced at a stack of paper in front of him. "According to the report by Dr. Edna Towns of the Ward-B Mental Health Unit, neither of the defendants suffer from any apparent mental illness although Dr. Towns did recommend that both get professional counseling for anger management issues." He looked up from his notes and glanced at Lil Joe and Franky's table, then to the A.D.A.'s table. "Are there any objections to the report?"

"No, your honor, not on behalf of the people," the A.D.A. replied.

"Neither do we object, your honor," Mr. Williams answered, speaking for both Lil Joe and Franky.

"Okay, then." The judge sighed, then continued, "At this time I'll enter judgment and formally charge both defendants. Mr. Hernandez, Mr. Mu_oz, you are hereby charged with violating the California Penal Code 187, Murder in the Second Degree. How do you plead?"

"Not guilty," Lil Joe answered. His lawyer had coached him on how to reply before the proceedings began.

Franky also answered, "Not guilty, your honor."

Lil Joe held back a laugh, finding Franky's politeness humorous.

"All right," the judge said, "the court accepts the not guilty pleas from both defendants. I hereby order both defendants into Juvenile Hall custody, and I'm setting a preliminary hearing for two weeks from today. That's fourteen calendar days." He looked over to Lil Joe and Franky. "I'll see you two in two weeks. In the meantime, try to stay out of trouble."

After the arraignment, a bailiff took Lil Joe and Franky to a holding cell behind the courtroom, where they were met by their attorneys. Mr. Williams explained to Lil Joe what would happen next. "Mr. Hernandez, did you understand what the judge said in there?"

Lil Joe shrugged. "Some of it."

"Well, okay then, let me explain. After we're done here, you'll be processed into Juvenile Hall custody. Then in two weeks you'll be brought back here for your preliminary hearing. Now all that a preliminary hearing is, is a hearing of the state's evidence against you. The A.D.A. has to put up enough evidence against you to satisfy the court that there's reason to proceed to trial. Do you understand."

Lil Joe nodded. "I think so."

"Okay, well you do have any questions?"

Lil Joe thought about it. "Yeah, yeah I do. Can you tell my mom I'm here and let her know what's going on?"

Mr. Williams smiled. "Sure, I'll do that. Anything else?"

"If it's not too much trouble, can you tell her if she comes to visit me, to bring Franky's mom with her if she can so he can get a visit too?"

"Yes, Joseph, I'll run that by her." He looked at his watch. "I have to get going now. I'll see you in two weeks. Try to keep your nose clean. All right?"

Lil Joe nodded. "I'll try."

After their attorneys left, Lil Joe and Franky were taken into Juvenile Hall custody and put into a large holding cell that reminded them of a restroom at a fast food restaurant. After they showered, they changed into the clothes that had been set out for them--a pair of blue pocket less stretch pants and a plain white t-shirt, along with a pair of black "Wino" slip-on shoes. They were then taken to the violent crimes unit, walking past the unit's double door into the middle of a recreation dayroom where the song "Planet Rock" was blasting from a couple of speakers attached to corners of the dayroom's ceiling. The room was full of other teenage boys, mostly Mexicans and blacks. All of them stared hard at Lil Joe and Franky.

All right, Lil Joe thought, this is not Ward-B, and there's no Kathy here. The whole atmosphere was different, which made Lil Joe's attitude change. It was obvious to him that most of the kids were gang members, and right away he took notice of one of them in particular. He was a tall, skinny Mexican kid with slick black hair and a tattoo on his right forearm that read "E.S.V." in big block letters. Lil Joe grunted at the sight of it. The kid was an "Eastsider" and a sworn enemy to "Westsiders" like he and Franky. For as long as Lil Joe had been alive, each side had hated the other. According to a rumor, it was because of a dispute over a girl that took place years before and escalated into a neighborhood war. Although Lil Joe and Franky were only youngsters and weren't deeply involved in the neighborhood gang scene, their loyalties lay with the Westside. Yeah, Lil Joe thought, the whole scenario has changed.

As he looked around, Lil Joe observed that the unit actually pretty small. There were two wings of cells divided by the dayroom. To the back of the dayroom, just behind a row of shuttered windows, he noticed a small fenced-in recreation yard with a small basketball court.

One of the guards who brought Franky and him in, stayed with them by the unit's entrance while the other walked over to a small staff desk to speak with the two plain clothes unit staff members. While they stood there, Lil Joe continued to get familiar with his new surroundings. He noticed that the dayroom was split in two. The side where he and Franky were standing had several occupied plastic picnic tables and a ping-pong table just a few feet away from the door. Directly behind them was a separate room that appeared to be some sort of kitchen and dining hall, and across the dayroom, in front of the staff desk, was a TV area with several upholstered chairs and a wooden bench bolted to the wall. The television set was on top of a small panel that was also bolted up high in the corner.

As Lil Joe was finishing up his visual tour of the unit, the other escort guard, along with the two unit staff members, a middle-aged black man and a pretty, fair skinned, hazel-eyed brunette, approached Lil Joe and Franky. The two guards quickly left. "Hey, guys, my name's Mr. Jones," the black man introduced himself. "I'm one of the unit staff on the morning shift." He pointed to the pretty brunette who was standing beside him holding two mysterious looking red plastic bands. "This is Miss Birtch. She's also a unit staff member on the morning shift."

"Hi, boys," she said in a soft, feminine voice. She held up the two red bands. "Hey, guys, listen up. These are your name bands. They have your names and dates of birth on them. You'll need to keep them on your wrists at all times. Okay?" Lil Joe and Franky nodded their heads. "Okay, good. Now which one of you is Mu_oz and which one of you is Hernandez?"

Lil Joe spoke up first. "I'm Hernandez."

"All right. Give me your left hand."

After she put the wristbands on both of them, she said, "Okay, boys. There's still another hour or so left of dayroom, so go ahead and hang out. I'll show you to your cells after dayroom. Okay?"

"Okay, cool," said Lil Joe. He and Franky made their way over to the TV area and sat down on the bench while they scoped out their surroundings.

Shortly after they sat down, the tall kid with the Eastside tattoo strolled over wearing a mean mug look on his face and sat down directly across from Franky on one of the chairs. "Hey, fool, where you from ese?" he barked at Franky.

Lil Joe reacted immediately by jumping up and kicking the kid in the face, instantly knocking him to the floor. He and Franky continued to kick him until several staff members responded to the unit alarm and broke up the fight. As two of the staff pulled Lil Joe away from the kid, he spat on him and yelled, "Westside, puto. Don't forget it!"

As a result of the fight, Lil Joe and Franky were placed on program restriction for three days, which meant they were only allowed out of their cells once a day to shower. During those three days, every night after they were cell fed dinner, Lil Joe and Franky were let out to shower and they would take that time to talk with each other for a few minutes before being returned to their cells. On the last night, Franky said, "We'll be off this program restriction bullshit tomorrow."

"Yeah, I know man. About time."

Franky sighed. "Hell, yeah, I'm bored out of my mind in that cell. Hey, I heard they moved that other fucker to another unit. I found out a little about him. His name is Chuy. He's from the Meadow Brooks."

"Yeah, I know, bro. I saw his taca [tattoo]."

When Lil Joe went back to his cell, he did some thinking. The next day they would be getting off restriction. He felt that he and Franky had made a good first impression with the other kids. Everyone now knew where they were coming from and that they wouldn't accept any bullshit disrespect from anyone. He figured it would be smooth sailing from then on until, of course, they were new arrivals somewhere else.

For the rest of their stay in "Juvie" things did go pretty well for them. They were given jobs in the kitchen as food servers and clean-up crew, which worked out pretty good for them since they were able to eat all the leftovers. It was Franky's idea for them to start working out. He figured since they were eating good, it would be the perfect time to put on some muscle. "Besides," Franky said, "we're gonna end up in C.Y.A., and you know a lot of the guys in there are in pretty good shape. So we should yoke up a little and prepare ourselves for all the fights we'll be getting into."

Lil Joe thought about it. Franky was right. What he said made sense because the California Youth Authority was a gladiator school for teenagers. So every night after dinner and before showers, they would work out together in the yard. Usually they would find a vacant corner and do pushups and squats for an hour or so and then play some basketball if there was enough time before showers.

Their preliminary hearing came and passed quickly enough. Basically, al that took place at the hearing was testimony from state witnesses like Sgt. Moore and several others explaining the facts of the case to the judge. After hearing the state's case, the judge set a trial date two months later. Lil Joe and Franky were both being tried as juveniles for murder in the second degree, only because they weren't yet sixteen, a point that the judge stressed at the hearing.

The time before trial flew by quickly. Lil Joe received a couple of visits from his mom, but Franky had still not received any visits and it was starting to eat at him. During one of their visits, Lil Joe's mother told him that Franky's mother and Elsa had moved to a new place somewhere in the city of Colton, but she didn't know exactly where. Neither did Franky. His family never wrote to him either.

When Lil Joe first told Franky the news of his mother's move, he took it hard. "I can't even hear from her, man. She just cut me loose and forgot all about me. Man, my mom hates me."

"Nah, man, your jefita don't hate you."

Franky just lowered his head and muttered, "How can I tell?"

Damn! Lil Joe didn't know what to say. His best friend was going through a hard time, and there was nothing he could do about it.

The trial was held early in the morning. There was no jury in juvenile court, so everything was in the hands of the judge. After he heard the final testimony of the forensic investigators and that of Sgt. Moore and the arresting officers, it was a wrap. The judge found Lil Joe and Franky guilty of second degree murder and sentenced them to the California Youth Authority until their twenty-first birthdays.

The sentence took them both by surprise. Franky had just turned fourteen a few days prior to the trial and Lil Joe's fourteenth birthday was still a few months away. To boys their age, their twenty-first birthdays seemed like a lifetime away.

After the trial, there wasn't much for them to do except wait around to be transferred to the Youth Authority and as it turned out, they didn't have to wait very long. Early in 1986, Lil Joe and Franky caught the transfer chain together. One morning after breakfast they were taken to the Juvenile Hall holding area, where two transportation guards waited to take them to the Southern Reception Center of California (S.R.C.C.) in Norwalk. After waiting in a holding cell for about half an hour while the transportation team filled out custody paperwork, Lil Joe and Franky finally got on their way to the Youth Authority.

Along the drive, Lil Joe and Franky took in all the sights, figuring it would probably be a while before either of them saw the outside world again. They arrived at S.R.C.C. about an hour later and the younger of the guards pulled the van into a narrow driveway in front of a huge, solid metal gate and announced, "We're here, boys." Then he stuck his hand out the window and waved to a surveillance camera positioned at the top of the gate. Soon the big gate slowly slid open and exposed the spacious concrete box on the other side. After the driver pulled the van into the box, the big gate slowly slid shut behind them. Then the driver cut off the engine and announced in a loud, haughty manner, "Welcome to the end of the road, boys. The point of no return!"

Both Lil Joe and Franky ignored the man's comments and looked around the inside of the concrete box. The thought of escaping hadn't crossed Lil Joe's mind until that very moment, but after seeing the triple rows of razor wire that lined the top edge of the surrounding concrete wall, he wondered if it was even possible. From the look on Franky's face, Lil Joe figured that he was probably thinking the same thing. Lil Joe averted his attention to the right of the van, where there was a small steel staircase leading up to an open doorway on the side of the building.

After Lil Joe and Franky had stepped out of the van, the transportation guards escorted them into the building and removed their waist chains. "Have a seat," the older of the two guards instructed them, pointing to a small wooden bench bolted to the wall. Before sitting down, Lil Joe took a quick glance down a hallway leading to the back of the building, where he noticed two trustees folding laundry in the back room.

Just as Lil Joe and Franky sat down, a tall, corn fed, redheaded guard stepped out of one of the small windowless office rooms and looked them both up and down. "Welcome to C.Y.A., boys," he said in a deep, husky voice. "Good luck."

The younger of the transportation guards smirked at the comment and handed the redheaded guard two folders. "Here you go, Red," he said. "They're all yours." Then he and his partner left.

After glancing at the folders, the redheaded guard asked, "Which one of you is Hernandez?"

Lil Joe stood up. "I am."

"Okay, follow me."

Lil Joe followed him into the office he'd come out of earlier and sat in a chair directly in front of the guard's cluttered desk. The guard sat down behind his desk and put the two folders on top of a stack of folders, then grabbed a clipboard from his desk and pulled out a pen from the front pocket of his green jumpsuit. "Well, Mr. Hernandez, I just gotta take down some information on you and then we can get you over to the medical department for your physical." Lil Joe nodded.

"All right," the guard continued, "so what's your full name?"

"Joseph Miguel Hernandez."

"Okay, then what is your date of birth?"

"June 12, 1972."

"All right. Do you have any serious medical conditions at this time?"

"No."

"Okay then, last one. What street gang do you run with?"

Lil Joe knew better than to admit to being a gang member. "I don't run with any gang," he said.

But the guard didn't seem to believe him. He gave Lil Joe a funny looking frown and said, "Yeah, whatever. Look, I still need to take down some information on you, but it won't be until after I talk to the other guy. So go ahead back out there and have a seat and send in Mr. Mu_oz."

Lil Joe walked out of the office and told Franky, "Hey, you're up next, bro. He wants to talk to you."

A few minutes after Franky went in to Big Red's office, they both walked out. "All right, guys, we have a few more things to do, then we'll get you to medical. Come on, follow me."

They walked down the hall to the back room where Lil Joe had seen the two guys folding laundry. They were still there and now that he was closer to the two trustees, he got a better look at them. One was a chubby Asian kid who was wearing a big pair of round eyeglasses that made him look like a giant fly. The other was a peckerwood with a shaved head and a tattoo of a swastika on the side of his neck. The guard told the peckerwood, "Hey, Powers, I gotta go look for the scale. Why don't you get these guys set up with some clothes and I'll be back in a minute."

The peckerwood turned his attention to Lil Joe. "Hey, where are you guys coming from?"

"San Bernardino Juvenile Hall," replied Lil Joe.

The peckerwood smiled. "Is that right? Ol Berdoo, huh? Where are you guys from out there?"

"We're both from the Westside Verdugo [the Spanish name for the local Mexican street gang on the Westside of San Bernardino]. I'm Lil Joe and this is my homeboy, Franky."

"Nice to meet you guys. My name's Mike. I'm from outta San Bernardino County myself. Fontana to be exact."

"Hey, all right, Mike, it's good to meet you too," said Lil Joe.

"Hey, fellas, there are quite a few I.E. boys here. You guys will run into some of them a little later on."

Lil Joe knew that when Mike said there were a few I.E. boys there, he was referring to guys from the Inland Empire area of San Bernardino and Riverside Counties.

After Lil Joe and Franky gave Mike their clothing and shoe sizes, he brought their clothing rolls out from the back of the laundry room. "Here you go, fellas." He handed them their new wardrobes of blue jeans, a white t-shirt, a grey sweatshirt, and a pair of black Chuck Taylor Converse. "Brand new for the I.E. boys," Mike said with a wink.

Right away Lil Joe noticed that the t-shirts and sweatshirts had S.R.C.C. printed in black letters across the front. Well, that sucks, he thought, but Franky didn't seem to mind. After they dressed in their new duds, the guard returned carrying a scale and took down their weight and height for the Youth Authority records. At that time, Lil Joe stood five feet seven inches and weighed one hundred sixty pounds. Franky was a little shorter at five feet four inches and weighed in at one hundred forty-seven pounds.

After the weigh-in, the guard took them into another room and took their mug shots, then handed them each a piece of paper with a five digit number on it. "Memorize that number," he said. "You're now a ward of the state. That number is who you are. Your name is no longer of any significance. You're just a number now."

What an asshole, Lil Joe thought. The guy probably stands in front of a mirror in a John Wayne stance while he practices that speech. The image made him chuckle to himself.

"Hey, man, what's your number?" asked Franky.

Lil Joe looked at his piece of paper. "51188. What's yours?"

"51189. Just one digit different from yours."

"All right, boys," the guard interrupted, come on. Follow me. We're going over to Medical.

They followed him down a couple of dim hallways until they reached the medical clinic, where there was a waiting room for new arrivals. When they got there, there were already several wards in the waiting room waiting to see the doctors so they could go to their assigned units. The redheaded guard instructed them to have a seat and he hung their paperwork on a clip board in front of the examination room. He poked his head through the doorway and hollered, "There are two more intakes in the waiting room."

There were six other wards in the waiting room--two black teens who were at the far end of the waiting room caught up in conversation and four teenage Mexican boys who were grouped together in the seats across from Lil Joe and Franky. Right away one of them, a tall, slim kid with the Old English letters E.M.F. tattooed across his throat, hit them both up. "Where are you vatos from?"

Lil Joe answered, "We're both from Verdugo. I'm Lil Joe and this is my homeboy, Franky."

"Orale," the kid with the tattoo said. "I'm Cartoon de El Monte Flores."

Lil Joe nodded his head. "All right, Cartoon." He looked at the other Mexican kids. "Where are you guys from?"

"I'm Tortuga [turtle] de Florencia," said a short, pudgy kid who Lil Joe thought really did resemble a turtle.

"I'm Chino de San Fernando," said an Oriental looking kid who was sitting next to Tortuga.

The last one to introduce himself was a light complected kid with green eyes and a missing right arm. "My name's Lefty de Corona," he said.

Lil Joe and Franky bit their tongues so they wouldn't laugh at the irony of the guy's nickname. They spent the rest of the day in the waiting room getting acquainted with new arrivals as they came and went. Finally, after several hours, Lil Joe and Franky were called into the doctor's office by a gorgeous Chicana nurse with the face of an angel and the curves of a she devil. "Hernandez, Mu_oz, you guys are up next."

They followed her into the examining room. "Damn," Franky said under his breath, "look, bro." He nudged Lil Joe with his elbow and tilted his head in the direction of the Chicana nurse walking in front of them.

Lil Joe bit his lower lip as he noticed the way the nurse's pants hugged her shapely butt. "Son of a bitch," he muttered.

"Okay, boys, I have to take down some information before you guys can see the doctor, so you first," she said, pointing at Franky. "Come here." She patted the examining table with her hand. "Have a seat."

While the nurse examined Franky, Lil Joe took a seat across the room and admired the nurse's rear end. After a few minutes, she turned to him. "Okay, now, come on over here. It's your turn." He and Franky quickly switched seats and Franky immediately began enjoying the view. "Okay, Mr. Hernandez, what's your number?"

Lil Joe pulled the piece of paper from his pocket. "Uh, 51188."

"All right. Do you have any allergies to any medications or foods?"

"No, not that I'm aware of."

"Okay, then, I'm just gonna check your vitals real quick. All right?"

Lil Joe nodded his head. "Okay."

The nurse took his blood pressure and checked his pulse. Then she took a stethoscope and rubbed the receiver on her pant leg to get it warm, pulled up his t-shirt, and placed it on his chest. "Breathe in and out slowly, please."

As she moved the stethoscope over his back, he caught the sweet smelling scent of her perfume and was immediately charged with teenage sexual energy. To make matters worse, during the examination the nurse accidently brushed her breasts against his arm, causing him to panic. Oh, shit, he thought, please don't get a hueso [boner]. Please don't get a hueso! He was barely able to control his adolescent hormones and spare himself an embarrassing moment.

After the nurse finished examining his lungs, she set the stethoscope aside and asked, "Okay, Mr. Hernandez, just one more thing. Do you suffer from any medical conditions that the doctor should know about? Asthma, tuberculosis, anything like that?"

Lil Joe shook his head and said, "No, just a broken heart."

The nurse gave him a friendly grin and walked out of the room, saying over her shoulder, "The doctor will be with you boys shortly."

As soon as she was out of hearing, Franky grunted, "Damn, man, did you see all the junk in her trunk?"

Lil Joe sighed. "Hell, yeah, man! I'd eat a mile of her shit just to kiss her ass."

"Uh, you're a sick fucker. You know that?"

Just then a frail, white haired, elderly white man walked in and introduced himself. "Hello, boys, I'm Dr. Moorehead. I'll be with you two in a moment. Just let me look over your charts."

Franky smiled deviously. "Hey, Doc, what did you say your name was?"

"Dr. Moorehead," the doctor replied.

"Oh, okay, thanks." He and Lil Joe chuckled under their breath.

While the doctor was standing at the end of the examining table looking over their charts, Lil Joe looked him over as well. Damn! he thought, this guy has to be at least two hundred years old. The doctor was a hunchbacked old man with long white hairs protruding from his ears and nose, and he reeked of BenGay. Lil Joe chuckled to himself thinking, Who's going to examine this old fart? He looks like he's just a breath away from keeling over.

After looking over their charts, the doctor asked Lil Joe and Franky the same questions as the nurse had earlier. Then he gave them tetanus shots and a physical and sent them on their way.

When they walked out of the examining room, Lil Joe and Franky were met by the chicana nurse, who instructed them to sit in the waiting room until someone from their unit staff came to pick them up. They ended up sitting there for another couple of hours before an odd looking pair of guards, a tall black woman and a short Asian male, walked in. The woman pointed to Lil Joe and Franky. "Are you two Hernandez and Mu_oz?"

"Yeah, that's us," Franky replied.

Lil Joe couldn't help but stare at the Asian guard. He had a huge birthmark that covered half his face. But his attention was directed elsewhere when the female guard asked for their C.Y.A. numbers. To Lil Joe's surprise, Franky already had his memorized. "51189," he said.

Lil Joe fumbled through his pants pocket for the piece of paper with his number on it. He pulled the paper from his pocket and said, "51188".

The lady guard smiled. "All right, then, come on. Let's get you boys to your cottage." She opened the door leading into the main quad and waited for them to walk through. The quad looked like a small city and it was full of people on their way to and from somewhere, all of them teenage boys dressed in the same clothing as he and Franky. Just across the pavement from the clinic were numerous small trailers that the lady guard pointed out as the school area. To the far left were two huge buildings that the guard explained were the chow hall and gym. Directly behind the school area was a huge yellow and green grass field in the center of the quad with red brick cottages surrounding it. In front of each cottage was a square of blacktop with a basketball court on it. There were six cottages.

As they were walking up the pavement, Lil Joe overheard some of the kids in their cells talking with each other as they passed some windows. The lady guard explained that each cottage had forty double-bunk cells, each cottage housing eighty wards, except for the single-cell lockdown unit.

Later on, Lil Joe would learn that each cottage had a name and that each cottage was divided into two wings of twenty cells, with four showers to each wing. He would also learn that all the wards were housed with wards their own age.

Their first night in S.R.C.C., Lil Joe and Franky were taken to the orientation cottage, and as they were about to walk in, the female guard said, "You will only be here for tonight. In the morning, I'll be taking you over to my cottage." She pointed to a cottage across the quad. "That's Cabrillo Cottage," she said. "It's the fourteen year old and younger unit. My name is Rita. I'm the group supervisor for Cabrillo Cottage, and my quiet colleague here is Mr. Tsao," she said, pointing to the Asian guard. "He's the group supervisor for the orientation cottage."

Lil Joe and Franky nodded in acknowledgment as they followed her and the Asian guard to the orientation unit. Upon entering into the middle of the unoccupied dayroom, Lil Joe as always began familiarizing himself with his surroundings. The shiny waxed tile floors of the dayroom glistened like mirrors. He assumed the upkeep must have been done by inmate trustees just as they were in Juvenile Hall. To the back of the dayroom was a large plexiglass staff booth between the two separated wings of the unit.

"Well, okay, boys," Rita said, "I'll see you in the morning. Have a good night and stay out of trouble."

Lil Joe chuckled to himself, thinking that she sounded a lot like his mom encouraging him to behave or stay out of trouble.

After Rita left, the Asian guard pointed to the wing on the left side of the staff both. "You guys are both in Cell Number 10 on the left wing. Your fish kits and linen are on your bunks. Uh, it's already after program hours, so there won't be any more programs tonight. So go ahead and take it to your cell."

On their way to their cell, Lil Joe glanced at the clock on the wall of the dayroom. It was already past 6 o'clock. They had spent the whole day being processed through Intake. They walked down the left wing, checking the cell numbers on the doors, until they found Cell 10. They unlatched the metal sliding pins on the door and went in. Soon afterwards, the Asian guard came by to relock the door and make a quick head count.

The cell was cramped, with the metal bunk beds bolted to the right side taking up most of the space. Sitting on top of the bunks were two, thin, smelly, and dirty mattresses, along with their bedding, a fish kit, and a sack lunch. At the back of the cell was a window with a large metal screen welded over it. To the left was a porcelain toilet and a matching sink attached to the wall. There was no paint on the plain grey concrete walls, only graffiti that had accumulated over the years--"Tank, Big Hazard, 72, Chico, White Fence, 74, and many others.

"Well," Lil Joe said, "this place is a dump!"

"Yeah, it is," Franky agreed, "but speaking of a dump . . ." He smiled.

"Aw, shit, Franky, are you serious? Already?" Lil Joe said in disbelief. "We ain't even been here five minutes yet, man."

Franky shrugged. "Nature calls, bro. What can I say?"

Lil Joe shook his head. "Man, all right, wait up, let me cover up first." Lil Joe took off his t-shirt and tied it around his face from the nose down and walked to the back of the cell to stand in front of the window while Franky sat on the can and shit out what had to be the stinkiest turd in the history of the world. "Uh, that's foul, Franky."

Franky chuckled. "Sorry, bro, I've been holding it all day."

Lil Joe sighed. "Shit, it smells like you've been holding it the whole year."

After Franky finished and the air cleared, they ate their sack lunches, washed up, and called it a night.

In the morning, they awoke to the sound of a guard walking the tier banging on the cell doors and yelling, "Ten minutes till chow!"

They reluctantly got out of bed, washed up, and got dressed. Then they waited for the guards to open their cell door. Approximately ten minutes later, the unit guards returned and unlatched everyone's door for breakfast. Lil Joe and Franky stepped out and followed the other wards. They ended up at the dayroom where the rest of the cottage wards had formed two side-by-side lines in front of the exit. Three guards supervised the line from within the dayroom, and once every ward was there, the guard who stood in the doorway yelled out, "Okay, move it out!" and the two lines began walking toward the chow hall.

Lil Joe and Franky quickly jumped in the back of the line and followed along.

It was still dark and a little cold when they stepped outside, but the walk to the chow hall was a short one. Along the way, Lil Joe noticed that there was an apartment complex just to the right of the fence and he overheard a woman's voice from within the complex yell for someone named Brian to bring her her cigarettes.

The line stopped just outside the door to the chow hall for a few minutes while the wards that had just finished eating cleared out through the exit on the opposite side of the room. Once inside, Lil Joe scanned the large chow hall. The dining area in the front was lined with rows of circular steel, four-man tables. Behind the dining area was the main kitchen with a food service line at the front. Lil Joe took notice that most of the food servers were wards.

After Lil Joe and Franky picked up their trays and made their way through the serving line, they sat at a table with two black kids where there were two empty seats. While they were forcing themselves to eat their runny oatmeal and burnt French toast, a black kid sitting at the next table called out to one of the black kids at their table. "Say, C.K., what's up, blood?"

The chubby kid sitting to Lil Joe's right responded with a smile, "Hey, Coop, what's goin' on, blood? I didn't know you was here, brotha."

Lil Joe and Franky noticed that the other kid at their table had balled up his fists and adopted a twisted look of anger. "What's your name, cuzz?" he angrily blurted out to the chubby kid.

"Who you callin' cuzz, nigga? This is C.K. Crip Killa, everyday, Blood!"

Then they jumped out of their seats and began to fight. Almost immediately, the black kid at the other table jumped into the fight to back up his homeboy. It didn't take long for the guards to respond and several jumped right into the middle of the scuffle and began macing the three of them. Lil Joe and Franky tried to finish their breakfast, but it was ruined. Everything tasted like mace.

After the guards successfully contained the incident, they escorted the rest of the wards back to the cottage. When Lil Joe and Franky got back to their cell, they washed up and went back to sleep. They were awakened about an hour later by the lady guard, Rita, who knocked on their cell door. "Come on, boys, get your bedding and stuff together. You're moving over to my cottage." Lil Joe and Franky rolled out of bed and put all of their bedding and their fish kit belongings into sheet bundles. Rita opened the door and said, "Come on, follow me." They followed her outside and across the quad to her cottage. Once inside, Rita dropped a bombshell on them. "Hernandez, you're in Cell 24 on the right wing, and Mu_oz, you're in Cell 27 on the right wing."

Lil Joe was confused. "Hey, how come we're not in the same cell?"

"Well," Rita explained, "we didn't have any room until this morning when two wards were taken from her to another institution. But they weren't cellies and the guys left in Cells 24 and 27 didn't want to cell up together. Sorry, boys. But look, as soon as I get an empty cell, I'll move you two back in together. Okay?" She shrugged her shoulders. "Sorry, but that's all I can do."

"That's cool," said Franky, "we would appreciate it."

But on their way to their cells, Lil Joe protested, "Man, this is bullshit!"

"Yeah, I know," Franky said, "but at least we'll be in the same wing."

"Yeah, all right, man, but Rita better keep her word and cell us back up soon."

Franky ended up with a compatible cellie, a skinny, friendly kid from out of the Los Angeles area on Temple Street who went by the nickname of Bullet. Lil Joe, on the other hand, ended up in the cell with a weirdo named Martin from out of Chino. Martin was a mess. He was a fat, dirty, sloppy kid who slept all day and then stayed up all night making noise and keeping Lil Joe awake. To make matters worse, Martin was on Thorazine for mental problems. So after two days of living with Martin, Lil Joe had had enough. He decided that he would beat the shit out of Martin the next time he did something that he didn't like. So on their third day together as cellies, while Lil Joe was working out in the cell, Martin cut a loud fart and laughed about it. That was the straw that broke the camel's back. Lil Joe yanked Martin off the top bunk and fired on him with a round of punches. Martin managed to curl up in a ball on the floor next to the door while Lil Joe kicked him until he was winded. After he caught his breath, he told Martin, "When the juras run dayroom, you better tell them to move you to another cell cause you ain't comin' back in here."

After that, they both sat in silence until the guards unlatched everyone's door for dayroom program. Martin ran out of the cell screaming like a little girl. "Help! He's tryin' to kill me! Help! He's gonna kill me!"

Lil Joe remained calm as he stepped out of the cell. Franky was standing in the hall waiting for him when Martin threw his little fit, and when Lil Joe walked out of the cell, Franky stood beside the door with a confused look on his face. But Lil Joe didn't have time to explain because the guard who opened his door was on him. "What's going on, Hernandez?"

"Nothing, man," Lil Joe replied. "I don't know what he's tripping on."

By that time Martin was on the other side of the wing standing next to the staff booth hugging up to another guard's leg. Other wards stood in the hallway being nosey, but the guard at the staff booth told them to keep moving and clear the hall. "Well," said the guard standing in front of Lil Joe, "obviously something happened. Why else would your cellie run out screaming like that?"

"Nah, man, nothing happened. The dude's lost his marbles or somethin', man. Honestly I don't know what's goin' on with him."

The guard frowned. "Well, all right, you go ahead and take it to the dayroom. We'll sort this out and get back with you later."

"All right. Cool." Lil Joe hurried off to catch up with Franky at their usual spot in the dayroom.

The crew that Lil Joe and Franky had been hanging out with were at the table playing Spades when he got there. Besides Franky, there was Browny, a stocky, dark complected shy kid from the city of Compton. Next to him was Bullet, Franky's cellie. Then there was Snappy from out of San Diego, a fourteen year old Mexican kid with a quick temper. Hence the nickname. Last was Jorge, the joker of the group. He was originally from Vera Cruz, Mexico, but had been living in Orange County for about a year prior to his arrest. Jorge claimed to be fourteen years old, but he looked to be at least twenty.

As soon as Lil Joe reached the table, Jorge mimicked Martin in a thick accent. "Help me! He's trying to kill me!" Everyone at the table laughed.

"What happened anyway, bro?" asked Franky.

"Aah, man, that fuckin dummy's a weirdo, man. I just didn't want him in my cell anymore."

Franky grinned. "So what's next?"

"Well, I'm hoping to pull you over with me as soon as they move Martin."

"Yeah," Franky said, "maybe they'll move him tonight. Then tomorrow we can get Rita to move me over."

"Sounds like a plan, man," Lil Joe said, playfully shoving Franky by the shoulder. "Hey, you want your run back on some of those desserts you owe me?"

"Hell, yeah," said Franky, "rack 'em up."

Ever since they had moved to Cabrillo Cottage, Lil Joe and Franky spent most of their dayroom time playing pool for desserts. At that time, Franky was in the hole six desserts.

Most days, the dayroom program was run twice a day for about an hour and a half depending on the events of the day. Each weekday morning, every cottage would run school line, which was basically the guards from each cottage escorting wards who were approved to school to their classes. Only wards who were approved could go and the only way to get cleared for school was to take the T.A.B.E. test. The scores would determine what classroom wards went to. Once wards took the T.A.B.E. tests, they were placed on a school waiting list and would have to wait until other wards were transferred so as to make room for them. Lil Joe and Franky were on the waiting list.

Each day after school line, everyone left in the cottage would come out for morning dayroom. The dayroom wasn't much. There was a television, board games, cards, and a pool table, but mostly everyone just sat around and shot the shit with their friends. The second dayroom program usually took place before dinner while waiting for the call to go to the chow hall.

After dinner, everyone would go to the yard for a couple of hours before showers. Being outside was a big thing for most of the wards because of the feeling of freedom from being outdoors and out of a four-wall box, and being able to breathe in fresh air. But most of all, everyone liked the yard programs because they could be active and burn off some of their teenage energy. Some of them would play basketball and others would play football in the grass field in front of the cottage. That's what Lil Joe and Franky did during yard. They would scrounge up a handful of wards and play tackle football. The rules were that they were only supposed to play touch football under staff supervision, but in S.R.C.C. the rules were loosely enforced. Wards often got hurt playing tackle football with no protection, but everyone would pretty much suck it up and shake it off.

One night during a rough football game, Lil Joe dislocated a couple of his fingers, but he waited until the next morning to see the nurse so that he could say he hurt himself by falling off the top bunk and the unsupervised football games could continue without heat from the guards. But the main reason why he waited until morning was because the fine looking Chicana nurse worked the day shift and he wouldn't dare pass up an opportunity to see her strut around in her tight fitting white jeans.

After the incident with Martin, the guards moved Martin out of Lil Joe's cell. They knew that something had transpired between Lil Joe and Martin, but since they didn't actually see anything, they couldn't do anything about it and the very next day Rita moved Franky and Lil Joe back together.

Lil Joe was a fast learner and he quickly learned that S.R.C.C. was more than just a reception center for new arrivals to the Youth Authority. It was an initiation period into the incarcerated life of adolescent chaos. C.Y.A. was a breeding ground for future hard core criminals. If a kid wasn't the violent type when he walked into the Youth Authority, he would be when he walked out. Violence was the only way of life on the inside. It was what everybody depended on to make it through their sentence, and Lil Joe picked up on it right away. He knew that S.R.C.C. was just a taste of how life would be for the rest of his incarceration. He also knew that in order to make it through his sentence, he would have to be quick of mind and body, and willing to step up to any and every challenge. He could never let anyone get over on him or disrespect him in any way without paying the price. Although they were just kids, the Youth Authority was like any other prison when it came to the rules of conduct. For every action taken by one individual, there would be a harsher reaction by another. The best way to react to any type of challenge to one's pride or manhood was to deal with it in the most vicious and violent way imaginable.

Some guys weren't cut out for that sort of thing, and their reputation for being weak or a punk with no huevos would follow them around everywhere. They would be tormented, victimized, and taken for all their possessions their entire time in the Youth Authority. That was unacceptable to Lil Joe. He had too much self pride to ever allow himself to be treated that way.

Lil Joe received a couple of visits from his mother while he was at S.R.C.C.. She would always bring him money and whatever else he might need to get by. She was a true sweetheart who always made sure that he had what he needed. It was the same with his old man. Although he wasn't able to visit because of the distance, his dad always looked out for him. He was a good man and Lil Joe was extremely grateful for both of his parents.

Franky, on the other hand, was a completely different story. He had no one on the outside, so Lil Joe took care of him and made sure he had everything he needed. By that time it was pretty clear to Franky that his mother and sister had completely abandoned him; he still hadn't heard from either of them and they had basically left him to fend for himself in the cruel and harsh conditions of the California penal system.

But Franky and Lil Joe got by just fine. They had everything they needed--hygiene, food, even a radio Walkman each, which was really a necessity considering that they spent at least twenty hours a day in their cell. They would often pass the time listening to oldies on K.R.L.A., or sometimes they would listen to a local classic rock station that played a lot of their favorites--the Doors, C.C.R., Hendrix, Zeppelin, and many others.

Unfortunately, one night just before dinner, a crip who went by the nickname of Wacko from Pomona, snuck into their cell and stole their Walkmans and some food that they had bought from the canteen. Neither Lil Joe nor Franky were aware of it until Lil Joe went back inside to use the restroom in their cell in the middle of yard program. On the way there he was stopped by a friend who went by the nickname of Rascal from Inglewood. Rascal was on program restriction for a fistfight that he got into in the school area. He had seen Wacko sneak into Lil Joe and Franky's cell and sneak back out with their stuff and as Lil Joe was passing by his cell, he waved him over to his door. "Hey, Lil Joe, come here real quick."

"What's up, Rascal?"

Rascal shook his head and sighed. "Hey, man, that vato Wacko, the crip, went into your cell and took some of your shit. I saw him do it when you guys were at dayroom. He put everything in his cell."

The news made Lil Joe furious. "All right, Rascal, I'll take care of it. Good lookin' out." Lil Joe went straight to their cell to see what was missing. He noticed right away that Wacko had taken their Walkmans and some of their food. He figured there was at least half an hour before everyone came in for shower program, so he had plenty of time to do what he needed to. He knew what cell Wacko lived in. He also knew that Wacko was a bully who thought he could intimidate the other wards because he was a muscular black kid who had a reputation for being a good fighter. But Lil Joe didn't care about any of that. The way he saw it, the guy had fucked with the wrong people this time.

Lil Joe went straight for Wacko's cell and snuck inside to take his and Franky's stuff back, and to take any belongings of Wacko's that were of any worth. After he collected what he had gone there for, he decided to go a step further. He pulled out his dick and pissed all over the rest of Wacko's belongings while he muttered, "So you wanna steal from me, huh, you stupid mother fucker." When he finished vandalizing Wacko's cell, he walked back over to Rascal's cell and slid all the property he had stolen from Wacko under the door. "Here you go, homie, gracias for letting me know what was up."

Rascal stood at his cell door window wearing a big grin. "Gracias a ti, homie. Handle that shit, man!" He knew that Lil Joe wasn't going to leave it at that. Retaliation measures always had to be extreme; it was the way of life on the inside.

Lil Joe put his and Franky's belongings back in their cell and then went back out to the dayroom. When he got there, he heard one of the staff talking to someone on the left wing, so he took a quick look around to see if any of the staff were watching him. They weren't. He pulled two pairs of socks from his pocket and doubled each pair, making two separate doubled-up socks. Next he grabbed two pool balls off the table and put one in each sock. After he tied a knot in the socks to keep the balls in place, he put them in his front pant pockets and waited for yard recall. A few minutes later he heard one of the guards yell out, "All right, bring it in Cabrillo Cottage. Yard recall!"

Wacko was one of the first wards to come in off of the yard. Lil Joe eyeballed him as he sat down in one of the chairs in front of the TV. Franky was one of the last guys to come in and as he entered, Lil Joe walked over and handed him one of the sock packs. "Here, Franky, take this and follow my lead. All right?"

Franky looked concerned. "All right, bro. What's up?"

"That crip Wacko tried to jack us, man, but I'll explain everything later. Come on, let's do this shit."

"All right, let's go," Franky said. He didn't need to know any more; he trusted Lil Joe's judgment, as did Lil Joe his.

They walked over to where Wacko was seated and immediately began swinging their sock packs as hard as they could at his head. Lil Joe landed the first blow on top of Wacko's skull, making a loud cracking sound as the ball bounced off. Franky landed the second blow across Wacko's face, which immediately sent him to the dayroom floor dazed and bloodied. Both Lil Joe and Franky then stood over Wacko's feeble body and continued to strike him about the head and torso. He made several attempts to shield himself from the vicious blows with his forearms, but his attempts fell short. Lil Joe and Franky continued to strike him with hard blows for another twenty seconds or so before they were maced and restrained by the guards.

After they were handcuffed, Lil Joe and Franky were taken to the medical clinic to have the mace washed out of their eyes and to be examined for injuries. Wacko, on the other hand, was carted off on a stretcher to Medical, where an ambulance picked him up and drove him to a local hospital. Lil Joe later learned that Wacko never returned to Cabrillo Cottage, which was a little disappointing because he really wanted him to return to his cell to the smell of urine everywhere.

After they were examined by the night shift nurse, Lil Joe and Franky were taken to the disciplinary cottage (lockdown), where they would remain until they were transferred to another institution. They later learned that Wacko had sustained a fractured skull, a broken wrist, a smashed hand, and several other broken bones, including a couple of cracked ribs and a broken jaw. Lil Joe figured he probably looked like he'd been hit by a car, but he also figured that he got what he deserved.

Drake, the disciplinary cottage, was a lockdown program. The only time wards were allowed out of their cells was to shower. All of the cells were single ones and Lil Joe and Franky ended up three cells apart. After a few days, they figured out a way to talk to each other by yelling through the back windows of their cells.

Lil Joe knew that they wouldn't stay there very long. S.R.C.C. was temporary and they were only there for reception to be evaluated and classified in order to be sent to another juvenile institution. Everything depended on classification and age, schooling, and case factors played a big part in classification. After the evaluation period was over, Lil Joe and Franky would go to a Youth Authority board hearing, where the members of the board would determine what institution they would be sent to.

Lil Joe and Franky went to Board on the day of Lil Joe's fourteenth birthday, and it turned out to be a disastrous day altogether. The board decided to send Lil Joe to an institution in Paso Robles and Franky to one just around the corner from S.R.C.C. in Whittier. They were both pretty upset over the news.

"This is some bullshit!" said Franky. "Why are they splitting us up?"

"I don't know, bro," Lil Joe said with disappointment in his voice, "but it's fucked up, man."

"Maybe I can try to transfer to Paso Robles later on," said Franky.

"Yeah, that would be cool. You should try next Board."

Board hearings were held once a year for all wards, and during a hearing a guy could ask to be transferred to another institution. But unless there was a good reason for requesting a transfer, the board usually denied the request.

"Hey, Franky, I think Paso Robles is where Jimmy's at. I remember my mom saying that was where Jimmy's abuela said he was when she ran into her at the grocery store a while back."

"Man," Franky said, "it would be cool to see Jimmy again. Hey, if you do, tell him I said q-vo? [what's up]."

"Come on, bro, you know I will."

Later that day after they were finished talking, Lil Joe sat back on his bunk and did some thinking. He was looking forward to seeing Jimmy again, but he felt bad that Franky wouldn't be there with them.

Two weeks later, Franky caught the transfer chain to Whittier. He woke Lil Joe up early that morning hollering out to him through the window before breakfast. "Hey, Lil Joe!"

Lil Joe jumped out of bed to answer. "What's up, Franky?"

"I'm leaving, man! They"re taking me to Nelles in Whittier. They just told me to pack up right now.

The news woke Lil Joe up completely. "All right, Franky, make sure you write every now and then. All right?"

"You know I will, man," Franky replied. "Stay strong, homeboy."

"You too, Franky." Transportation came and took Franky about half an hour later.

After Franky left, his absence hit Lil Joe hard. It was the first time since their arrest that they had been separated from each other. Lil Joe found himself missing Franky right away, but more than anything, all he wanted to do now was move on to the next chapter of his life.

CHAPTER SEVEN

IT WAS THREE WEEKS EXACTLY AFTER Franky was transferred that transportation came to pick up Lil Joe and take him to Paso Robles. They showed up early in the morning, about an hour before Lil Joe usually ate breakfast. After he was shackled and escorted to the Institutional Program office, he was taken to a waiting blue Chevy van. There were several wards already inside and Lil Joe recognized Rascal from Inglewood, who greeted him with a smile. "Hey, what's up, Lil Joe?"

"Hey, all right, Rascal. How's it goin', man?"

"Cool, man. So it looks like we're headed to the same place, huh?"

"Yeah, man. Do you think it's a long ride."

"Probably. Say, where's Franky at?"

"He transferred to Whittier a few weeks ago," replied Lil Joe.

"That's cool. Hey, I heard you guys worked over that vato Wacko pretty good. I wish I could of seen it."

Lil Joe chuckled at the memory. "Yeah, fuck that fool!" He took a look around at everyone else and introduced himself to four of the other wards. There were two peckerwoods from Orange County who went by the nicknames of Skip and Crazy, and there were black twin brothers, both bloods, from out of the L.A. area who went by the nicknames of Fly and Shorty. There were also two dingbat crazies secluded in a cage in the back of the van, but Lil Joe didn't talk to them. He saw no point. Crazies were in their own world.

The ride to Paso Robles was long and boring. The transportation guard played nothing but country music on the radio the whole time and the only thing Lil Joe enjoyed was the scenery. The only place he had ever been outside of Southern California was the little town in Arizona where his father lived, so he took in all the sights of each town they passed through.

They arrived at Paso Robles late in the afternoon. The institution looked identical to S.R.C.C. except for a few differences. Paso Robles had several big shop class buildings for trade school and there was also a big academic school area consisting of numerous brick buildings. There was also a fire camp at the back of the institution and separate from the rest of the cottages. There was a gym with a swimming pool in front and a large grass track and field area behind it. But the main quad was structured the same as S.R.C.C..

It took about two and a half hours for everyone on the van to be processed through Intake, and when the processing was finished, all eight of the new arrivals were assigned to different cottages. Lil Joe went to a cottage called Nipomo and Rascal went to one named Cayucus. Lil Joe didn't know which cottages the rest of the wards were sent to since he left for his before they were assigned. The cottages were named after local cities and towns.

When Lil Joe walked into his cottage, there were a lot of wards in the dayroom and in the rec yard behind it. He could tell right away that the cottages were structured a lot different from those at S.R.C.C.. The smaller dayroom had several tables and rows of soft chairs, with a television set resting on top of a wooden panel that was bolted to a corner of the wall just above the rows of chairs. Across the dayroom was an open door that led to the recreational yard. Lil Joe stood in the doorway and took a quick look around, but there wasn't much to look at. The yard was just a small fenced-in square of blacktop crowded with wards. There were several wooden picnic tables spread around, as well as a tiny handball court, a pull-up bar, and a few weight benches with free weights. A quarter of the yard was shaded by a looming tin awning that was connected to the roof of the dayroom building. Lil Joe figured it was to act as a shield from rain during the winter and to provide a shaded area in the summer.

As he was taking in his surroundings, he was approached by one of the cottage youth counselors. "Hey, there, you must be Mr. Hernandez."

"Yeah, that's me."

The counselor cracked a creepy looking smile, which made Lil Joe see the guy's resemblance to The Joker from Batman. "Good, my name's Rick. I'm one of the Y.C.'s (youth counselors) here on the day shift, and that there is George." He pointed to another Y.C. who was walking towards them from the back of the yard.

He was a tall, elderly mulatto with a freckled face and a tiny white mustache. As he approached, he smiled and said, "So this must be our new booty."

Lil Joe hated the term "new booty." It was a degrading term that made him want to punch whoever used it.

"Yep, sure is," Rick replied. "This is Mr. Hernandez."

"Well, hello, Mr. Hernandez. I'm Y.C. George. Let's get you into the dorm so you can get situated. Come on, follow me," he said as he walked past Lil Joe and waved him towards the dorm area. Lil Joe followed him while the other Y.C. stayed behind to supervise the other wards in the yard.

The dorm was a large rectangular space that had single spring bunks and metal lockers lined on one side along a short brick wall and solid metal double bunks and lockers on the other side. All painted battleship grey. Rows of shuttered windows lined the double bunk wall, and on the opposite side of the dorm on the other side of the short brick wall was a wide hallway that held fourteen single man cells. The first two cells at the front of the dorm had solid metal doors, but the others had no doors at all. Lil Joe later learned that the two cells with doors were disciplinary cells used for solitary punishment and the others were for cottage workers and so-called honor wards, which basically meant wards who didn't get in as much trouble as everyone else. All the way at the end of the honor hall was a fire exit which ironically was locked shut with a chain and padlock.

George pointed to a single bunk along the short brick wall in the middle of the dorm. "There's your bunk right there, Hernandez." He handed Lil Joe a small piece of paper with a number written on it and pointed to a locker next to his bunk. "That's the combination on your locker there. Memorize that number and don't give it to anyone."

Lil Joe nodded and walked over to his locker to try out the number. There was a fish kit sitting on top of the locker and he put it in his locker and relocked it before making his way back to the front of the dorm. When he got there, George was sitting inside the small staff station doing paperwork, so while he waited for him to finish, Lil Joe took a look around at the rest of the dorm area. Behind the staff station was a small laundry room, and to the left of that was a large, green tiled shower area with eight showerheads lined up a couple of feet from each other. To the right of the laundry room was a restroom with two doors, giving access to it from the dorm and from the dayroom. The top half of the restroom wall was made of two large glass windows, which gave the staff visible access to the restroom from both the dorm and the dayroom. The restroom also had several small windows in the back towards the top of the high ceiling looking out over the outside area in front of the cottage. The restroom was split in two, with urinals and toilets on one side and sinks with mirrors above them on the other.

"You all set?" asked George.

"Yeah," replied Lil Joe.

"Well, then, go on out there with the rest of the people," George said, pointing towards the dayroom area.

Lil Joe walked out of the dorm and to the yard, where he was immediately approached by a pair of Mexican kids, one short and chubby and the other tall and skinny. "Hey, <u>ese</u>, where you from?" asked the chunky, dark complected one, who Lil Joe noticed had a lazy eye.

"My names Lil Joe de Verdugo. Where are you from?"

The chubby one spoke up again. "I'm Indio de Eighteenth Street. This is my homeboy Flaco," he said, pointing to the skinny kid standing next to him.

"<u>Mucho gusto</u> [nice to meet you], Lil Joe," said Flaco.

"<u>Igual mente</u> [likewise]," Lil Joe shot back. After shaking their hands, Lil Joe looked around. "So who's all here?"

"There are rides here from everywhere," Indio replied. "Los, I.E., San Diego, O.C., Chiquez--everywhere."

Lil Joe was already aware of the phrase "ride" or <u>ranfla</u>. A ride is a group of people who are from a specific area. And he knew that Los Angeles was often referred to as Los, that I.E. was his own hometown area of the Inland Empire, that O.C. was an abbreviation for Orange County, and that Chiques was the Spanish nickname for the Oxnard,

Ventura area. For the most part, everyone in the Youth Authority ran with people from their hometown areas and formed a ride.

"Hey, you got a few homies from the I.E. right over there," said Indio, pointing to a group of three across the yard who were lifting weights.

"Gracias," said Lil Joe and made his way towards the group. As he approached, they stopped what they were doing to see who he was. Lil Joe broke the ice. "What's up, fellas? I'm Lil Joe de Verdugo."

One at a time, each of the three boys walked up to him, shook his hand, and introduced himself. The first was a tall Chicano with slick black hair and a tattoo across his chest in big Old English letters that read "Black Angels. "I'm Cricket de Onterio," he said.

Next was a short, stocky Chicano kid with green eyes. "Hey, all right, Lil Joe. I'm Rebel de Indio."

The last was a gigantic Mexican who wore a pair of Murder One sunglasses and sported a handlebar mustache. "I'm Diablo de Redlands."

Lil Joe shook his hand. "All right now."

"Say, Lil Joe," Diablo said, "you know your homeboy Jimmy?"

"Yeah, where's he at? Is he in another cottage?"

"<u>Simon</u> [yeah]," said Diablo. "He's in the lockdown unit."

Lil Joe smiled at the news. "Is that right? What did he do?"

"He and another homie, Chato from Colton, packed some little rat who snitched on them for smoking weed in their shop class," Diablo said.

Lil Joe snickered. "Yeah, that sounds like Jimmy. So how long before he gets out of lockdown?"

"Shit," Diablo said, "he's been there for about six months already, so he has about six more months left. But he might not come back out here to this mainline."

Lil Joe wrinkled his brow. "Why not?"

"Well, he came from this cottage, so if they let him out here again, he'll come back here, but sometimes the disciplinary committee transfers people getting out of lockdown to another institution."

Lil Joe was disappointed hearing that he might not run into Jimmy again after all.

The remainder of the yard program, Lil Joe and his three new friends stood around shooting the breeze and taking turns doing bench press sets. During that time, his friends gave him the rundown on the daily program, covering every aspect of the routine in Paso, everything from dorm living, showers and school to visiting. After about an hour, the Y.C.'s called everybody off the yard and dayroom to take it to the dorm for showers. That was the daily routine. Every day before dinner, after all the wards returned from school and shop classes, it was shower program. From what the fellas explained to Lil Joe, he would only have seven minutes to shower, dry off, and shave before his shower time was up. Apparently it was that way because there were only eight showerheads and only a short period of time for all seventy-two wards to shower. During showers, the youth counselors made a shift change and two new Y.C.'s would come in for the afternoon/night shift.

Lil Joe absorbed everything that went on around him like he always did. During showers, one Y.C. would watch the dorm while the other supervised the shower area. The Y.C. supervising the showers would literally stand in front of the showers with a timer in his hand to make sure nobody went over their seven minute limit. As Lil Joe sat on his bunk waiting for his turn, he thought about something that Rebel had told him before returning to the dorm--that when he showered he should keep his back to the shower wall at all times. That way, no one could stare at his bare ass. Lil Joe didn't understand why a guy would want to stare at another guy's ass, but he knew there were weirdos in jail and decided to take Rebel's advice.

Just before it was Lil Joe's turn to shower, Diablo stopped by his bunk on the way back from his shower and gave Lil Joe a pillowcase full of hygiene items. "Here you go, homie. A few of us pitched in with a little something to hold you over until you can make the canteen."

Lil Joe smiled. "Hey, gracias, Diablo."

"No problem, man. You know how we do it."

Lil Joe made a mental note of the generosity. He was going to have to find out who all pitched in so he could thank them.

Lil Joe learned something that day. He learned that being part of a ride meant that you looked out for each other, and for the first time in his life he began to understand racial unity and appreciate it for what it was. In time he would also learn that there was power in unity and numbers and that on the inside, native respect and unity were vital necessities. Lil Joe preferred it that way. The way he saw it, it beat killing each other over petty conflicts like they did on the outside. In the short time he had been incarcerated, Lil Joe had picked up on a lot of things, but perhaps the most obvious was that the always violent and often cruel underworld of the California justice system forced the individual races of people on the inside to unite among their own in order to be strong and survive. It was somewhat ironic to Lil Joe because most of the young gang members on the inside were there for committing violence against their own people over street wars. However, he respected the change and his only regret was that it came after the fact.

As Lil Joe recalled, showers that day turned out to be quite eventful. The drain in the shower backed up and by the time he made it to showers, there was a foot of dirty water on the floor. So he showered from head to knees first, then dried off, put his boxer shorts on, and went back to one of the corner showers to stand on the outside while he washed the rest of his body. That would become his daily shower ritual.

After showers came dinner. All of the cottage wards lined up in front of the cottage and then walked to the chow hall just like they had done in S.R.C.C.. Chow time in Paso Robles turned out to be rush hour. In order for each cottage to get through the chow hall in a reasonable time, everyone had to eat as if it were an Olympic event. Lil Joe had no choice but to adapt. By the time he sat down to eat at the last table, the cottage staff was already clearing the first tables to line up to return to the cottage. So Lil Joe learned quickly that if he wanted to eat, he would have to wolf down his food as if there were no tomorrow. There were two hot meals, breakfast and dinner, served each day, which were eaten in the chow hall, and sack lunches were provided at the cottages during the midday break from school, or at noon on weekends.

The weekdays at Paso Robles consisted of the same program as S.R.C.C. and school was run the same way. Everyone assigned to school went after breakfast and returned in the afternoon. All of the wards who weren't assigned to school stayed at the cottages and hung out in the dayroom or the yard all day. On weekends there was no school, so everyone hung out at the cottages. Gambling and fighting were among the most common activities on weekends.

Lil Joe took an immediate liking to the gambling. He would spend the entire weekend fixing up wagers and keeping track of sporting pools. He even gambled on card games and dominos. Gambling was definitely one of his favorite pastimes. Fist fights were also a big pastime in Paso Robles on weekends. They usually took place in the dorms or the restroom, where the youth counselors couldn't see. Those places were referred to as blind spots, but most of the time the Y.C.'s were aware of what went on in the blind spots and would often wager money or canteen items on the outcome of the fights themselves. The weekend brawls were usually refereed by other wards who would call the fights and keep a lookout for the Y.C.'s, who would blow the whistle if they caught them in the act. Other wards besides the referees were often present and their job was to keep all of the matches one on one, because sometimes people felt compelled to jump in for a friend or homeboy who was coming out on the losing end of the fight. Most fights between wards were to settle little disputes over gambling debts or whatever, but some were over rival gang beefs and there was bad blood between the combatants. Nevertheless, for whatever reason there was behind the conflict, one thing was for certain--they were very profitable. Lil Joe won quite a few canteen payoffs from them and even made others a profit from his own fights.

Weekends were also visiting days for wards fortunate enough to receive visits. Weekends were also when most wards washed their clothes. The cottages changed whites on a daily basis during showers, but everything else had to be hand washed on the yard in little plastic buckets and then hung on the fence to dry. It never failed that every time Lil Joe hung up his clothes to dry, a bird would shit on them and he would have to wash them all over again.

Lil Joe adjusted to the Pasos program pretty quickly, and his time for the most part was flying by. He had heard from Franky a few times over the months. They would write to each other and exchange stories about their environments, along with some of the adventures they had both experienced while adjusting to their new world. Franky told Lil Joe in a letter that he had sent Lil Joe's mom a jewelry box that he made for her in a wood shop class for her birthday. Lil Joe thought that friendly gesture was pretty cool.

Lil Joe's mom came to visit him as often as she could. He always enjoyed seeing her and spending time with her catching up on things. For Lil Joe, the visits were a pleasant break from the chaos that went on behind the walls, and for a short time visiting with his mother brought him back to a reality he once knew. Usually after a visit with his mother, Lil Joe was humbled and would be in an overall good mood for a couple of days.

However, it wasn't always the case. On one visit, Lil Joe's mother broke the news to him of his grandmother's passing. He returned to his cottage in a foul mood, and it was just his luck that when he went to shower and get ready for dinner, something happened to bring his anger to the surface. When he stopped by the laundry room to pick up a fresh linen roll, the cottage laundry worker, Tia, a homosexual Asian kid, put an extra small pair of boxer shorts in his shower roll. When he realized it and return to the laundry room to exchange them for a bigger pair, Tia caught an attitude with him and told him if he asked nicely, he would think about it. That was all it took for Lil Joe to blow his lid. He didn't like homosexuals as it was. He felt that they were disgusting, and he didn't even like being anywhere around them. So there was no way in hell he was going to let the little cocksucker get away with talking to him that way.

Visiting hours always ran past the regular cottage shower time, so at that time the others had already showered and were out on the yard or in the dayroom waiting for the call to go to chow. Lil Joe took a quick look around and saw that none of the staff were in the dorm area; they were all out in the dayroom or yard supervising the rest of the wards. He pushed Tia into the back of the laundry room and beat the attitude out of the little queer. When he finished with Tia, Lil Joe grabbed a bigger pair of boxers from the shelf and turned to the bloody sissy lying on the floor and stuffed the extra small pair into his mouth.

"Listen, you little bitch, you're lucky I don't finish your weak ass off right now, but you're not worth a shit to me, so it's like this. From now on you're gonna make sure that everyone in my ride gets good linen rolls or I'll catch your punk ass in here again. You got it?" Tia whimpered some kind of an acknowledgment and Lil Joe showered and went on his way.

After dinner, Lil Joe and Diablo were doing sets of pull-ups on the yard when a tall, skinny Puerto Rican kid with a goatee named Gary from out of Hayward approached them and asked Lil Joe if he could talk to him. "Sure," said Lil Joe, and took Gary to the side so they could talk in private. "What's up, Gary? What's on your mind?"

Gary avoided making eye contact with Lil Joe. "Aah, man, nothin' much."

Lil Joe could tell by Gary's body language that he was nervous. "Speak your mind, Gary. What's up?"

Gary nodded his head. "Yeah, all right. It's just that you beat up my "boy" Tia without even getting at me first, and that ain't right, man. I feel disrespected."

Lil Joe's blood began to boil. His first impulse was to smash the guy right there on the spot, but he kept his cool. He knew that wasn't the way things were done in Paso. Personal problems between wards were supposed to be handled in a blind spot at the earliest opportunity so there would be no interference from staff and the combatants would have enough time to come from the shoulders and work out their problems.

Lil Joe had heard enough; he didn't want to drag out the conversation and have to listen to the idiot any longer than he had to. So he cut Gary short. "Look, man, I don't know what you're getting at, but I don't have to ask nobody's motherfuckin permission to do shit. So what do you wanna do?"

Gary looked frightened and swallowed hard before he replied. "Well, I think an apology oughta cover it."

Lil Joe laughed in his face. He couldn't help himself. He thought, Who the fuck is this asshole with his apology shit? "Fuck no!" he sscoffed, "I ain't apologizing to no fuckin ass licker! Sabes que, I'll set it up--me and you this weekend--the first blind spot available."

Gary nodded his head. "Okay, then, if that's the way you . . . "

Lil Joe didn't hang around long enough for the dummy to finish what he was saying. He went back to the pull-up bar and told Diablo what had happened, and they both had a good laugh about it.

Later on in the week, just before the weekend, Gary pulled Lil Joe to the side and apologized to him for what he had said and explained that he wanted to squash the problem between them. Lil Joe couldn't believe the joker. First he wanted an apology for beating up his queer boy, and now he was apologizing and asking to squash everything. Lil Joe quickly assessed the situation. He was a pundit when it came to his surroundings, and he could tell that Gary was weak. So he took advantage of the whole ordeal. "Okay, look, man, you came to me with some disrespectful bullshit, and it won't just go away with an apology. You owe me."

Gary appeared eager to please. "Okay, what can I do to make it right?"

Lil Joe and Cricket were the only two in their ride who made it to the commissary on a regular basis, so Lil Joe figured he would milk Gary for money. "You and your boy make it to the commissary, right?"

"Yeah, right."

Lil Joe caught a hint of protest in Gary's voice so he decided to put more fear into his heart to seal the deal. "Check this out, motherfucker!" Lil Joe said in a harsh, intimidating voice. "I want half of yours and your boy's commissary every time you go. It's either that or I'll stab your fuckin ass! So what's it gonna be?"

Gary didn't hesitate. "Okay, okay, man, it's cool." He agreed to Lil Joe's terms and that was that.

Later that night, Lil Joe lay on his bunk thinking about how he was adjusting to his new world. A year had gone by since his arrival into the Youth Authority and what he had learned so far was that the rules to the animal kingdom were the only rules in effect. There were predators and there were prey. He knew which one he wouldn't be, which only left him one other choice. Lil Joe was witnessing himself go through changes, and he knew it was only the beginning. It was like he was in the driver's seat of a car going a hundred miles an hour but his hands weren't the ones on the wheel and his foot wasn't on the gas. All he could do was sit back and enjoy the ride, and he wondered what kind of a person he would be at the end of the trip.

CHAPTER EIGHT

ABOUT SIX MONTHS AFTER LIL JOE arrival at Paso Robles, his old friend Jimmy Vasquez got out of the lockdown unit and returned to Nipomo Cottage. Lil Joe was sitting at one of the tables in the dayroom ironing his pants when Jimmy walked in. He looked up to see who it was and couldn't figure out who the familiar face belonged to until he heard him talk.

"What's up, dawg?" Jimmy greeted him with a big smile and gave him a bear hug. "Man, I heard you were here. I see you've been hitting the weights," he said while he squeezed Lil Joe's arm.

"Man, bro, it's good to see you again. I didn't recognize you at first. You stretched out some."

Jimmy laughed. "Yeah, man, every time I wake up, I'm a little taller."

"So hey, man, how did you know I was here?" Lil Joe asked.

Jimmy smiled. "It's a small world, bro. I know a lot of things--like what you and Franky did to Robert and how you two put it down on some crip in Norwalk."

Lil Joe was surprised. "How did you find out about all that?"

"Aw, shit, man, what you and Franky did to Robert was big news. Mi abuela wrote to me after it happened and told me everything. As far as your little trip in Norwalk, shit, I heard that story from a peckerwood named Mike from Fontana. He was in lockdown with me. He said he met you and Franky in S.R.C.C.."

Lil Joe nodded. "Yeah, I remember him. He was a trustee in the reception building when me and Franky first drove up. But hey, how did you know I was here?"

Jimmy smiled. "Come on, bro, why you sweatin' me?" He playfully punched Lil Joe on the arm. "I'm just jokin', man. Franky wrote to me a couple of months back. He told me you were here."

Lil Joe raised a brow. "Damn, it is a small world. Well, come on, let's go out to the yard with the fellas."

When they walked outside, the whole crew stopped lifting weights and walked over to greet Jimmy. "Hey, Jimmy, man, what's up?" Diablo said with a smile and a handshake.

"It's good to see you again, Jimmy," said Cricket, patting Jimmy on the shoulder.

"Hey, Jimmy, where's Chato?" Rebel asked.

Jimmy pretended to be hurt. "What's up, man? You ain't happy to see me?" Rebel turned red with embarrassment. "Oh, nah, man, I'm glad to see you. I just thought you guys would of come out together.

Jimmy grabbed Rebel in a headlock and gave him a coscoron [knuckle rub] across the top of his head. "Come on, homie, I'm just fuckin with you. Chato transferred out to Y.T.S. in Chino a few weeks ago."

"Is that right?" Diablo said. "Lucky fucker!"

After the fellas welcomed Jimmy back to the cottage, they spent the rest of the day catching up on lost time.

That weekend, Lil Joe and Jimmy washed their clothes together on the yard and took advantage of their one-on-one time to talk to each other as two old friends. "So, I hear you've been making your mark here," said Jimmy.

Lil Joe shook his head, half smiling. "Nah, man, not really, bro. I just deal with whatever falls in my lap."

Jimmy nodded. "Yeah, I hear you, man. Hey, I hear you're in Cindy's art class at school."

"Yeah, I've been in there for a couple of months now."

Jimmy stared at him. "You know what time it is with her, right?"

Lil Joe smiled. "I've heard the rumors."

"They're not just rumors, bro. I was in her class before I was sent to lockdown. All I could think about in there was getting back out here and back into her class."

Lil Joe was surprised. "So it's true that she messes around with us?"

"That's what I'm telling you, man," Jimmy said with a smile. "I have first hand knowledge, bro. But she won't just mess around with any ol' hard on; she has to like you."

Lil Joe was definitely interested. Ever since he had been in Cindy's class, he had heard many rumors about her having sexual encounters with other wards. "So how do you know if she likes you?" he asked.

"She'll give you hints, man," Jimmy explained. "Like if you're working on an art project and she stops at your desk pretending to be interested. She'll get real close to you and rest her tits on your arm or something."

Lil Joe cut in, "Man! She's done that to me before, but I thought it was just an accident or something."

Jimmy laughed. "Nah, it's no accident, bro. If she's been doing that, you're in. Look, next time she does that, just rub your finger across her nipple a couple of times to let her know you're all good to go."

"Come on, bro, are you serious?" asked Lil Joe.

Jimmy laughed. "Of course I'm serious. Trust me, homeboy, I wouldn't bullshit you about something like that. But you have to be discreet about it. Don't front her off and make it obvious in front of other people. If you do, she'll flip out and make a scene." Jimmy chuckled. "She did that to a guy when I first got here. He just reached out and rubbed her ass in front of the whole class. Man, she screamed and slapped the hell out of him. Then she walked out of the classroom and told the guard on post that the dude groped her. About ten guards came to her rescue and snatched the guy out of the class and beat the dog shit out of him."

Lil Joe laughed at the story. "That's fucked up, man."

"Trust me, bro, just be discreet."

Later that night, while lying on his bed trying to sleep, Lil Joe thought about what Jimmy had said. He had school the next day, but he hadn't made up his mind about whether or not to make a move on Cindy. It was a risky business, but he was a horny teenager. He decided to sleep on it.

Cindy was a very attractive brunette in her early forties who obviously took good care of herself. She had a rock hard, athletic body with a beautiful, shapely ass and an amazing set of bright green eyes. Lil Joe had always had a thing for brunettes with green eyes. Cindy was a very desirable woman, especially to a sex crazed teenager who was incarcerated.

Lil Joe had heard all the rumors about her. Supposedly she was this nymphomaniac who could hardly control herself when it came to teenage boys, but so far Lil Joe hadn't seen anything that suggested the rumors were true. Guys in the Youth Authority had a tendency to exaggerate things and make them appear to be more than they really were. However, now that he'd heard it from his homeboy Jimmy, Lil Joe began to think about it a little harder. He recalled several occasions when Cindy asked someone to stay after class to help her clean up the classroom during the twenty minute break between third and fourth periods. At the time, that seemed perfectly logical, but now Lil Joe couldn't help but think there was more going on than cleaning the classroom.

By morning, Lil Joe had decided to make a move on Cindy the next time she gave him a good enough sign to act upon. It didn't happen right away, but about two months later, just before Christmas, Lil Joe was between art projects and wasn't really doing anything when Cindy approached him and asked, "Will you help me hang up Christmas decorations around the room?"

"Sure. What do you want me to do?" he asked.

"Here." She handed him a long Christmas tree pattern made out of green paper. "Could you tape this along the border of the classroom ceiling?"

"Sure, no problem."

After he finished with that, Cindy called him over to help her at the front of the room. "Can you hold the chair for me while I hang up these Christmas lights?"

"Yeah, okay." Lil Joe thought the precaution was a little excessive since the chair only stood two feet off the floor. Nevertheless, he complied with her request, which turned out to be a good thing for him. He held the chair in place by the spine as she stepped up onto the seat.

As Cindy leaned forward to hook the wire onto the hook, the front of her t-shirt lifted up above the waistband of her jeans and exposed the soft skin below her navel. Lil Joe couldn't help but notice the light shadow of peach fuzz running from her navel to her pubic area. He stood there gawking and when she leaned forward even further, that area was pressed into his face. Lil Joe was overwhelmed with teenage lust and acted before he thought. He pressed his lips to the exposed area of soft skin and kissed it. Lucky for him, she didn't make a scene. She only paused for a moment to smile down at him and give him a shocked look. Then she continued to hang up the Christmas lights. When she finished, she announced to the class, "Okay, class, five minutes until next period. Time to clean up." Then she turned to Lil Joe and asked, "Whose class do you have next?"

"Mr. Miller's math class."

"Well, I have my lunch break next period," Cindy said. "I was going to finish up with the decorations. Would you like to stay and help?"

Lil Joe tried not to smile. "Sure," he said, trying to sound casual. But actually his heart was racing with excitement.

"Good," she said. "I'll call Mr. Miller real quick and ask if I can borrow you next period since you're so helpful."

Lil Joe couldn't believe what he was hearing. It was just like Jimmy had said. He was in. He heard Cindy on the phone. "Hello, Dave, this is Cindy. Fine, thanks, and you? That's great. Listen, I'm calling to ask for a favor. I have Mr. Joseph Hernandez here with me. He's been helping me with a class project and I was wondering if I could borrow him next period." After a pause, she continued, "Yes, he has your class next period. Okay, thanks, you're an angel. Bye-bye now."

After she hung up, she announced to the class, "That's all for today, class. I'll see you tomorrow. Have a nice day."

After everyone had left, Cindy locked the door and walked into the supply room at the back of the room. She didn't say anything to Lil Joe, so he just stood there like a big dummy until finally Cindy called out to him, "Are you going to join me or what?"

What a dipshit! Lil Joe cursed himself. What were you waiting for, a written invitation.

When he entered the supply room, Cindy snatched him by the t-shirt and pinned him against the wall. "You made me so horny kissing me like that!" she said with a crazed look in her eyes. Then she kissed him aggressively on the mouth and wasted no time getting down to business. She undid his belt buckle, unbuttoned his pants, and pulled them, along with his boxers, down to his ankles. By then, Lil Joe was hard as a rock. He couldn't believe what was happening.

Then Cindy lifted her shirt and bra up to her neck, releasing her beautiful breasts. She had the largest nipples that Lil Joe had ever seen. He reached out and cupped her breasts in his hands and leaned forward and took one of her erect nipples into his mouth. Cindy moaned with pleasure while Lil Joe eagerly sucked on her nipple like a hungry infant. Suddenly she pulled her breast from his mouth and dropped to her knees to return the favor. The feeling was so intense that Lil Joe could barely stand up. He had never received a blow job before.

Cindy stopped just short of him blowing his load and looked up at him, waving her finger at him. "No, no, not so fast," she said. She stood up and peeled off her jeans and panties, exposing the rest of her firm body. Then she walked to the back of the supply room and hopped onto a small table and curled her knees up to her chest. "Kiss me there again," she demanded. She didn't have to ask him twice. Lil Joe dove right in. Although he had never performed oral sex before, his memory of the pornos he had seen as a kid came into play, and obviously he did it right because Cindy moaned in ecstasy as he hungrily ran his tongue over her womanhood.

Suddenly Cindy lifted his head from between her thighs and with lust in her eyes, said, "Fuck me! Fuck me hard!" Lil Joe happily obliged and did just that until he spent himself inside her. Afterwards, they sat there on the small table in silence while they regained their composure. Then Cindy looked at Lil Joe and said, "We should talk."

"Okay," Lil Joe said, feeling a lot more relaxed about the whole situation.

"You can't speak of this to anyone."

"I won't," Lil Joe assured her. "I'm not like that."

Cindy smiled, then grabbed him and pulled him close to her. "You can't act out in front of everyone like you did today, either. Okay? Because someone might see you."

Lil Joe grinned. "Okay, I won't."

"Okay, good." Cindy pressed her body against his and purred. "We still have at least twenty minutes to kill before my next class."

Lil Joe smiled. "Say no more."

Later on back at the cottage, Lil Joe met up with Jimmy at the pull-up bar on the yard. "Hey, Jimmy, ask me how my day went, bro."

Jimmy had been hounding him for weeks about making his move on Cindy, so Lil Joe was eager to break the news to him. "Come on, what the fuck, man?" Jimmy replied. "What? Do I look like asking you how your day went?"

Lil Joe chuckled. "Come on, fucker!" he growled. "Just ask me."

"All right, honey," Jimmy said sarcastically, "how was your day?"

Lil Joe grinned. "I don't know. Why don't you ask Cindy."

Jimmy smiled. "About fuckin time, man. I was just about ready to give up on you. That's right, homebody. Hey, man you gotta get me back in her class. I miss that big ol' hairy muffin of hers. You don't mind sharing with your homeboy, do you?"

Lil Joe frowned. "Hell, nah, bro. Just as long as I can go first."

They both broke out in laughter. Then Jimmy got Lil Joe in a headlock and gave him a coscoron.

The next couple of years flew by for Lil Joe. His time had been going by pretty smooth. He was just about to turn seventeen and was developing into a strong, solid, muscular young man, in part due to inherited genes and also from all the weight training he'd been doing. He weighed about 190 pounds and stood about 5 foot 11 at the time. He was growing a lot physically and mentally. He was still receiving visits periodically from his mom and his little brother Marco. Marco was growing up too. He was now twelve and pretty tall for his age. Lil Joe's mom always expressed her happiness with how good Marco was doing in school, and he was glad to hear it. At least one of them gave her something to be proud of.

Lil Joe had even received a couple of visits from his father, which was great for him because he could talk with his old man about things he couldn't talk to anyone else about. His dad was doing well and enjoying his life, which made Lil Joe happy for him because he hadn't exactly had an easy life.

In 1988, Paso Robles began having Catholicism study classes on Saturday nights. People from the local Catholic church would come in to teach and support young Catholic wards in the institution. When Lil Joe first became aware of it, he signed up himself and his whole ride. He figured there might be some young women from the church who would show up, and he was right.

On the first Saturday in October, Lil Joe and his crew went to their first class, which was held in the visiting room. About thirty other wards (all Mexican) showed up. Altogether sixteen volunteers from the local church were there, three men and thirteen women. Six of the women were older, but seven were the teenage daughters and granddaughters of the older women. On that first meeting, everyone just got acquainted with one another. The volunteers brought in some pan dulce (Mexican sweet bread) for the wards, which turned out to be a good ice breaker.

Lil Joe made an immediate connection with one of the teenage volunteers. Her name was Valerie Acosta. She was a very beautiful young chicana from Pismo Beach with long brown hair and the softest pair of smiling brown eyes Lil Joe had ever seen. After talking with her the entire two hours of that first class, Lil Joe took a real liking to her. Aside from being beautiful, she turned out to be a real sweetheart who was one hundred percent dedicated to her faith and her religious quest to help others. She was totally naive as to the kind of life Lil Joe had lived, but it made him like her all the more.

At the end of that first class, Lil Joe decided to make the class his Saturday night routine, and he attended every class for almost nine months. During that time he and Valerie developed a strong friendship, and they even began writing letters to each other during the week. Although Lil Joe was attracted to Valerie, he always kept things respectful. He never hit on her or did anything to jeopardize their friendship. Even if she had suggested that she wanted more, he wouldn't have been able to act. They were under constant supervision by the guards. So he just kept things simple. Valerie was his friend and he was content with that.

However, Lil Joe's Saturday night routine came to an abrupt end when yet another problem unexpectedly dropped into his life, taking him for another cruise down chaos avenue. One afternoon when he returned to the cottage from school, he found Jimmy arguing with a couple of youth counselors. They were accusing him of beating someone up in the restroom. One of the Y.C.'s attempted to handcuff Jimmy, Jimmy resisted, and the two Y.C.'s tried to wrestle him to the ground. Lil Joe didn't hesitate to jump in. There was no way he was going to let them put their hands on his homeboy. He knocked one of the Y.C.'s out cold with a hard right hook to his temple. As soon as the other Y.C. realized what was happening, he pushed his panic button and the electrical alarm went off, alerting other guards to respond to the cottage.

But before the other guards and Y.C.'s could respond, Lil Joe and Jimmy dropped the other Y.C. to the floor and proceeded to kick him senseless. When the other staff members showed up, they maced them both until they stopped their assault. They then handcuffed Jimmy and Lil Joe and escorted them to the lockdown unit, where they took their revenge. Once they were out of view of other wards, the guards maced Lil Joe and Jimmy again, slammed them to the floor, and took turns kicking them for the rest of the afternoon. Lil Joe and Jimmy were handcuffed the entire time, but Lil Joe managed to spit out a couple of insults between blows from the guards' boots.

It wasn't until the following morning that Lil Joe was able to wash the mace from his eyes because when the guards had finally put him and Jimmy into their cells the night before, they purposely turned off the running water. To make matters worse, sometime during the night Lil Joe was bitten by something in his sleep. When he woke up, his right knee was swollen to the size of a cantaloup. So when a nurse walked the tier early that morning for sick call, Lil Joe called her over. When the nurse approached his cell window, she said, "What's wrong, baby?"

Lil Joe backed away from the door so she could see his knee. "Something bit my leg."

The nurse wrinkled her face in disgust. "Ooh, honey" she said with a grimace, "that's ugly. We'll have to get you to the clinic so the doctor can take a look at that."

Lil Joe nodded his head. "Okay."

"All right now, honey, you just hold tight while I go find someone to help me escort you to the clinic. Okay?" As she walked away, she yelled over her shoulder, "I'll be back soon. In the meantime, try to stay off that leg."

After the nurse left, Lil Joe attempted to clean up his cell. The night before he and Jimmy weren't put into their cells until it was late and too dark to see anything. Not that it mattered much. The mace in his eyes had impaired his vision something terrible. He couldn't see a thing and was dead tired from all the physical abuse. As soon as he'd been put in his cell, he lay down on his bunk and went straight to sleep. The next thing he knew it was morning and his knee was sore and looked like hell.

The nurse came back for him about an hour later with a wheelchair and a couple of escort guards. "Mr. Hernandez, we're here to take you to the infirmary. Are you ready?"

Lil Joe yelled out, "Yeah, I'm ready!"

One of the guards looked through his cell window. "Hey, Hernandez, we're gonna open up your door now so we can cuff you. You're not gonna do anything crazy now are you?"

Lil Joe could tell by the look on the guard's face that he was genuinely frightened. He smiled. "No, I ain't gonna beat you up, man. I just wanna go get my knee checked out."

The guard frowned and then slowly opened the door while he and his partner cautiously kept their eyes on Lil Joe. After they handcuffed him, Lil Joe hobbled out and sat down in the wheelchair. As the nurse wheeled him down the tier, he saw that Jimmy was standing at his cell door window. As Lil Joe was rolled past, Jimmy smiled and yelled, "I like your new Cadillac! What happened, did the juras break your leg?"

"Nah, bro, I think somethin' bit me."

The nurse stopped the wheelchair short of the exit. "We gotta hold up a minute baby. Count ain't cleared yet, but it should be clear anytime now, honey," she explained while glancing at her wristwatch.

While Lil Joe waited for count to clear, he took a look around the lockdown unit. There were two separate wings of twenty cells, with a shower area at the end of each wing. Between the two wings were two small dayrooms, a staff station, and a small kitchen. Across the hall from the entrance was an open door leading out to a fenced in recreational yard. Not a very big unit, he thought. Just then he heard a female voice announce over the loud speaker that count was clear. "That's our cue," said the nurse. One of the escort guards unlocked and opened the door and the nurse pushed Lil Joe outside and across the quad to the infirmary.

At the infirmary, Lil Joe was examined by the on-duty doctor, an elderly Asian man who informed him that he had been bitten by a poisonous spider. "It looks like the work of a brown recluse spider," he explained. "We'll have to get you to the local hospital for treatment."

Lil Joe was then taken by van to the local hospital's emergency room, where he was seen by another elderly doctor who agreed with the diagnosis and treated Lil Joe with an anti-venom shot and some antibiotics. When he was returned to the institution that afternoon, he was admitted into the infirmary overnight so the doctor could check up on him the first thing in the morning. Lil Joe liked the infirmary because he was able to watch cable TV in the dayroom and eat all of the leftovers from lunch and dinner.

Later that night after being locked in his room, Lil Joe heard an alarm go off. About ten minutes later, he watched through the window as the medical staff carted someone in on a gurney. The next day while Lil Joe was waiting to be escorted back to the lockdown unit, he found out from the nurse on duty that the ward they had wheeled in the night before had died. She explained that he and another ward were playing a game called Chest where they took turns punching each other in the chest until one of them (the loser) called it quits. Unfortunately in that particular game, the loser died. His breastbone shattered and one of the bone fragments punctured his heart, causing him a painful death. Lil Joe thought it was sure a terrible way to die.

Earlier that morning, the doctor checked up on Lil Joe and prescribed him some pain medication for his swollen knee. Lil Joe had never been bitten by a spider before, and he found it fascinating that a creature so tiny could cause so much damage to the human body.

Back on the lockdown unit, Lil Joe and Jimmy had to spend ten days on CTQ (confined to quarters) before they were able to attend their daily dayroom program for one and a half hours. CTQ was a punishment that all lockdown unit wards had to go through when they first arrived, but it didn't really matter much as far as the lockdown program was concerned. Lockdown was already a slow, solitary program of twenty-two and a half hours a day in the cell and only one and a half hours out of the cell to shower and spend time in the dayroom or sometimes the yard.

This was Lil Joe's second time in solitary confinement in the four years he had been incarcerated. He knew that this new stint would last at least a year, so to keep the cell time from driving him crazy, he adjusted by staying occupied throughout the day. That way the time would go by faster.

The daily routine never changed. Except on Sunday, after breakfast were showers and then dayroom or yard programs. On Sunday mornings, bare knuckle fights were held on the wing tiers. After the staff picked up the breakfast trays, someone would yell out, "If you want to fight with someone, stand at your window." Then, two at a time, they would let out the wards who wanted to fight and give them three minutes on the tier to settle their differences. When the three minutes were up, they would be locked back into their cells and two more fighters would be let out. That would go on for an hour or so depending on how many wards had problems to settle. Then the staff would mop the blood off the tier and run regular programs of showers and dayroom.

The lockdown staff held the Sunday morning brawls for a couple of reasons. One was to try and control one-on-one incidents from escalating into small riots, especially when the combatants were of different ethnic backgrounds. The other reason for the controlled fights was so the unit staff didn't have to write up time consuming incident reports for good old fashioned fistfights. Not to mention, it was entertaining for them to host the underground pit fights while they gambled on the outcomes. But neither Lil Joe nor any of the other ward seemed to mind. They were used to it; their lives revolved around violence and chaos.

But what Lil Joe personally liked most about the Sunday morning brawls was that the unit staff was not exempt from the action. If a ward called one of them out, they would have to fight too unless they wanted to be viewed by their colleagues as punks or cowards. And that was where both Lil Joe and Jimmy got their get back for that first night. There were only a few rules to the Sunday morning pit fights. There was no kicking while someone was down and after three minutes the fight was over, no matter what. If the fight resulted in a knockout, it was over regardless of whether or not the three minutes were up. And the number one rule was that if a person got hurt during a fight, there was no complaining to the nurse unless the injury could be blamed on something other than the fight.

After dayroom and yard programs were shut down for the day, it was all about cell time. Lil Joe learned that the best way to deal with extensive cell time was to stay busy. It was a lesson he was grateful to have learned at a young age because later in life he would spend the majority of his time in solitary confinement somewhere. After morning dayroom, Lil Joe would usually read or do school work for a couple of hours. There was a teacher assigned to the lockdown unit Monday through Friday. He would slide a variety of school books and lesson sheets on different subjects under everyone's door and collect them as the lessons were completed. Everyone was allowed to work at their own pace. After they completed a lesson, they received credit towards a high school diploma. But there were a lot of wards who didn't participate in the school studies because if they didn't understand something in a lesson there was nobody around to help them. So the only wards able to take advantage of the program on lockdown unit were wards who were good at self learning.

After his reading and studying period was over, Lil Joe and Jimmy would work out together for about an hour and a half, taking turns calling out exercises through their doors. By the time they were finished working out and bird bathing, it would be about diner time. After dinner, Lil Joe usually wrote letters so he could send them out at mail pick-up at around 9 P.M.

At first, he had kept in contact with Valerie. They would write to each other at least once a week until suddenly after about three months, he stopped receiving letters from her. After almost three months of not hearing from her, Lil Joe figured she had probably just moved on with her life and forgotten all about him. That was until the day he received the news of why Valerie had stopped writing.

One day in December 1990, Jimmy went to a board hearing in the main quad. His eighteenth birthday was right around the corner and his time on lockdown was coming to an end, so he had to go in front of the board for a status review, at which time they would decide what to do with him. While he was outside the boardroom waiting to be called in, Jimmy ran into Indio from Eighteenth Street, who was also attending board that day. While they waited, they caught up on the chismes (gossip).

"So what's new on the mainline?" asked Jimmy.

"Nothing much. Same old shit."

Jimmy nodded. "I hear ya. Hey, Indio, when you get back to the cottage, extend mine and Lil Joe's saludos [regards] to the fellas."

"Sure. No problem. Say, Jimmy, is my homeboy Rocky still there on the lockdown unit?"

"Simon [yeah}, he's still there."

"That's firmé [cool]," said Indio. "Give him my regards tambien [also]. Okay?"

"I will," said Jimmy.

They stood quietly for a moment, then Indio broke the silence. "Say, Jimmy, did you vatos hear about what that dingbat J.R. did at the Catholic studies class?"

"No, what happened?" Jimmy asked, curious to hear the story.

"Aw, shit, man," Indio said, shaking his head as he remembered. "That vato J.R. tried to get all touchy feely with that ruca [broad] your homeboy likes. Como se llama [what's her name]?" He snapped his fingers while trying to remember.

Jimmy asked, "you talkin' about Valerie?"

"Simon [yeah], that's it. That's the one--Valerie." Indio frowned. "Yeah, man, J.R. was grabbing on her and shit, so she turned around and slapped his ass." Indio paused for a moment and laughed as if the whole scene was playing out in his mind. "Yeah, she slapped his ass hard too. Pero [but] J.R. got mad and beat her down, man."

Jimmy shook his head, disgusted with the news. "That's fucked up, man. Lil Joe's gonna flip when he hears this. So where's J.R. now?"

Indio sighed. "I think they put him in the caja [box], but he probably won't be there very long."

Jimmy smirked. "Yeah, you're probably right." Jimmy knew that crazies like J.R. were never housed in the lockdown unit. Wards who were documented as mental health care wards could pretty much do anything they pleased and never get punished. The medical staff would just up the dosage on their medication and that was it. Not that Jimmy cared, but at least if J.R. were sent to the lockdown unit, he and Lil Joe would eventually be able to get hold of the little coward and get him back for what he did to Valerie.

Just then a female guard walked out of the boardroom and announced, "We're ready for Vasquez now."

Jimmy turned to Indio. "Hey, that's me, homie."

"All right then, Jimmy, take it easy, huh."

"Yeah, you too."

The lockdown escort guard walked Jimmy into the boardroom. He was in and out within five minutes. The board had decided to put him on the transfer list to the Youth Training School in Chino, California. It was good news for Jimmy because he was being transferred close to home, but he felt bad that he would be leaving Lil Joe behind.

When Jimmy got back to the lockdown unit, he told Lil Joe the news of his up and coming transfer, but he didn't mention the news about Valerie because he didn't want to yell it over the tier. He waited until the following morning at dayroom, but Lil Joe kicked off the conversation with talk about Jimmy's transfer. "Damn, Jimmy, that's cool that you're going to Y.T.S. At least you'll be close to home and can get some visits from your abuela."

"Yeah, I know man. It'll be nice. Hey, maybe you can try to get transferred to Y.T.S. when you go to board."

Lil Joe smiled. "Shit, you thought I wasn't? Wouldn't it be cool if me, you, and Franky ended up there together."

"Hell, yeah!" Jimmy said. "It's been a long time since I saw Franky. It would be cool to kick it with him again."

"I know. What do you think he's doin' right now?"

Jimmy grunted. "Probably takin' a dump."

He and Lil Joe laughed at the joke, but then Jimmy got serious. "Hey, bro, I gotta tell you some bad news, man."

Lil Joe wrinkled his brow. "What's up, man?"

Jimmy shook his head and told Lil Joe everything that Indio had told him about what had happened between Valerie and J.R. The news disgusted Lil Joe. He felt terrible for Valerie as he pictured the scene in his mind. Later that day while he was alone in his cell, he lay on his bunk thinking about the situation. He knew who J.R. was. He remembered him from a shop class they were in together about two years before. J.R. was a scrawny, shaggy haired chicano kid from Fresno who was on several different medications for mental health problems. But as far as Lil Joe was concerned, J.R.'s mental problems were no excuse for what he did to Valerie.

Lil Joe knew that the institution's disciplinary committee was lenient when it came to punishing wards with mental problems. He knew that was why J.R. wasn't on the lockdown unit for his actions. However, Lil Joe wasn't going to worry about it. He knew that the Youth Authority, just like any other prison or jail, was a small world. He knew that he would run into J.R. sooner or later, and when he did, he would hold J.R. accountable for his actions.

For the next few days, Lil Joe pondered whether or not to write a letter to Valerie. He decided to go ahead and do it.

Dear Valerie,

My best wishes and utmost respects to you. I was recently informed of the terrible experience you went through while attending the Catholic study class here in the institution. I'm very sorry for what happened and I deeply regret not being there for you when it happened because I know the outcome would of been very different. I will completely understand if you choose not to write back in response to this letter. However, if our friendship ever meant anything to you at all, then you will take into consideration what I'm about to say in this letter. Valerie, you have one of the most beautiful spirits that I've ever been blessed to know, and I beg you, please don't

> allow one unfortunate incident in your life to change who you are as a person because it would be a great loss to the world we live in if you didn't allow your true self to shine like a light for those of us who are in the dark. It may not mean much coming from someone like me, but it's the truth, and it's the way that I feel. So with that being said, I'll end this letter with all my respect and best wishes.
>
> Always your friend, Lil Joe

He mailed the letter out that night, but Lil Joe would never hear from Valerie again.

A few weeks later, Jimmy was transferred to Y.T.S. Lil Joe was glad to see his friend get out of lockdown, but at the same time he was sad to see him leave. It made him reminisce about the times when he, Franky, and Jimmy were on the outside together, and to think about how much things had changed over the past five years.

After Jimmy was transferred, Lil Joe pretty much kept to himself. He wrote to his mother and father on a weekly basis and on occasion he even wrote to Marco, but for the most part he lost himself in books. He read just about anything he could get his hands on, but he enjoyed history books the most, especially books on war and warlords around the world. War was a subject he never grew tired of and he read just about every book about war history that the library had. He felt there was a lot to learn about humanity from war because not only did it bring out the worst in people, it also shed light on the human spirit and its nature.

Lil Joe was a great admirer of warlords and military strategists who fought against tyranny as underdogs and won. Although he respected all military geniuses like Genghis Khan, Attila the Hun, Julius Caesar, and many others for their intellect on the battlefield, he admired most the greats who fought for the little guy and crushed their oppressors. One of his idols was Emiliano Zapata, the Mexican revolutionist who fought for the indigenous people of Mexico against a corrupt Mexican government. Lil Joe figured you had to respect any man or woman who fought and died honorably to free his or her people from the suffocating grip of oppressors.

As Lil Joe read, he took the knowledge learned from history books and began applying it to his own life, which helped him develop his character and principles as a young man.

In addition to history books, Lil Joe enjoyed folk tales of ancient times. The Aztecs of Mexico and the Celtics of Ireland were among his favorites. He also liked stories of the Japanese Samurai. He felt that the character of the people of those times was impeccable. He related to their way of life and often felt as though he belonged in the past himself and as if the universe had somehow made a mistake and put him in the wrong place and time. Lil Joe knew that he was a warrior at heart, and it was because of that that he was considered an outcast and locked inside a cage. He felt as though the modern world didn't understand his kind, but there was nothing he could do about it. He figured life was what it was, and all he could do was be his true self and hope for the best.

CHAPTER NINE

A COUPLE OF WEEKS AFTER LIL Joe's eighteenth birthday, he received a letter from Franky, who had recently been transferred to Y.T.S. and had landed in the same unit as Jimmy. According to the letter, he and Jimmy were having a ball and the only thing missing was him. Franky told him to try real hard to get transferred to Y.T.S. so the three of them could be together again. However, it was too late. Lil Joe had already been to Board, and although he asked to be transferred to Y.T.S., they had something else in mind. They put him up for transfer to a new institution located just outside of Stockton, California, called Chaderjian School for Boys--Chad for short. The board informed Lil Joe that he would be transferred to Chad within a month.

After he went before the board, Lil Joe wrote to his family, as well as to Franky, to inform them of his transfer news. But it was obvious to him that Franky hadn't yet received his letter when he sent his own.

Although Lil Joe was looking forward to getting out of the lockdown unit, he wasn't thrilled with the idea of being sent all the way up to Stockton. It was too far away from his family for him to expect any visits. But there was nothing he could do about it. While he waited to be transferred, he mentally prepared himself for the change, and about two weeks after Franky's letter, he was taken to the new institution.

The transportation team picked him up early in the morning and put him in the van along with seven other wards on their way to Chad. To Lil Joe's surprise, J.R. was among the seven. Besides J.R., there were three other Mexican wards. The chunky, hairy guy sitting next to him introduced himself as Grizzly from Norwalk, but Lil Joe thought the guy looked more like the old wrestler, George, the Animal, Steel. In the seat directly behind Grizzly was a baby-faced kid who went by the nickname of Gizmo. He was from the Compton Barrio Tortilla flats, and although he was eighteen like Lil Joe, he looked barely fourteen at the most. Next to Gizmo was Huero (Whitie), a twenty-year-old blue-eyed, dirty blond-haired Mexican from the Riverside County area. After Lil Joe talked with him for a few minutes, he learned the he was only forty-five days away from being paroled. There were also two black wards and one peckerwood on the van.

The two blacks, Reggie and Snow, were both from the Hoover Street crips in Los Angeles. The peckerwood was a pudgy nineteen year old who went by the nickname of Porky, which Lil Joe thought fit him well. He was actually from Stockton, so he was practically on his way home.

The drive to Stockton from Paso Robles was pretty long, and all Lil Joe could think about the entire ride was getting his hands on J.R. However, he hid his emotions well the few times that J.R. attempted to spark a conversation with him. Lil Joe didn't yet know exactly what he was going to do to J.R., but he had patience; he would figure it out soon enough. For the time being, he decided he would treat J.R. as if everything was cool between them. He didn't see any point in putting J.R. on his toes by making him aware he had ill intentions. After all, Lil Joe knew that J.R. was a little bit on the looney side and unpredictable, so he figured it would be smart to keep J.R. oblivious to what was coming.

Lil Joe had a window seat on the van, but there wasn't much to look at. There were a lot of grassy fields filled with grazing livestock (mostly cows) and there were also some orchards and a few fields of crops, but nothing spectacular.

They arrived at Chaderjian sometime in the afternoon, and the first thing Lil Joe thought upon entering the grounds was that the place was a lot different from anywhere he had been before. At first glance, it looked like a prison instead of a Youth Authority school. There were quite a few huge, white cinder block buildings that Lil Joe assumed were housing units. There were also several large buildings that Lil Joe figured were classrooms and trade school rooms. The quad was really spacious, with a few smaller buildings opposite the housing units. In between was a large grass field that resembled a football field. The only thing missing was bleachers. Just beyond the entrance gates there was another white cinder block building somewhat smaller than the others which had an engraved wooden sign hanging above the door that read "Receiving and Release."

The van came to a stop in front of that door and the wards were escorted into the building by the transportation guards. Once inside, Lil Joe and the rest of the wards were directed towards a long wooden bench that sat against the wall on the left side of the room. The room was empty except for the bench and a small desk at the back that had stacks of case folders on top of it. As soon as everyone was inside and seated on the bench, a guard took a quick roll call of all the new arrivals. Then the transportation guards removed their restraints and gave them new clothes to change into.

After they were all dressed in their new clothes--blue pocket less stretch pants and white t-shirts, several guards showed up to escort them to their housing units. On the walk across the quad, Lil Joe overheard one of the guards tell the peckerwood, Porky, that most of the units were on lockdown status due to racial and gang melees. The news didn't come as a surprise to Lil Joe. He figured that jail was jail no matter where it was.

When they arrived at the other side of the quad, the guards split the group in two. Lil Joe, Porky, and J.R. were taken to one unit and the other five wards were taken to the unit right next door to theirs. Once inside, Lil Joe checked out his new surroundings. The first thing that caught his eye was the glass bubble control tower that protruded from the middle of the wall to the right of the door. The wall divided the unit from the unit on the other side, but Lil Joe noticed that there was a closed door on the far end of the tower wall that gave access to the other unit.

Before going inside, Lil Joe had taken a look around and counted four identical housing buildings. He assumed they were all the same. To the left of the housing unit were the cells. There were two tiers, one on the dayroom floor and one on the second floor. There were two wide steel staircases on opposite sides of the dayroom that connected the tiers. Each tier had two two-man showers, one located in the middle and one at the end, all four in plain view of the tower guard.

The dayroom had a few octagon shaped metal tables with four metal seats around them. Just left of the control tower was a television set on top of a small wooden panel that was bolted to the wall about six feet above the floor. Facing the TV were six rows of blue plastic chairs. To the right of the TV area and directly underneath the tower was a small wooden podium used as a Youth Authority station for the staff, and to the right of that were two pay phones and a large baby blue painted door leading to a small chow hall. Next to the chow hall was a microwave set on a small wooden stand and beside it was a water fountain and another door leading to an unknown room. In the back of the unit just behind the plastic chairs was another door that Lil Joe later learned led to the yard.

There were no other wards on the unit floor, but Lil Joe could see a few looking out of their cell windows to catch a glimpse of the new guys. One of the unit guards told the escort guards, "We need to get the new arrivals to their cells because it's almost time to cell feed." Apparently the wards didn't eat in the chow hall, but instead, as Lil Joe later found out, the guards cell fed all of them because it was more convenient for the guards.

About five minutes later, Lil Joe, J.R., and Porky were all assigned to cells. Lil Joe's was on the top tier--cell number 27. J.R. and Porky both ended up on the bottom tier. Before making his way up the stairs to his cell, Lil Joe took a quick count of the unit cells. He counted twenty on the bottom and twenty on the top. As he walked up the stairs, he heard a loud popping sound and his cell door opened up. He knew it was his because the cell numbers were painted in big black letters on the outside of the door. When he first heard the noise and saw his door open, he looked around in confusion for a moment, but then it dawned on him that it had to be the control tower's doing. He turned to look at the tower and saw that the guard was standing behind some sort of electrical control panel. Lil Joe laughed to himself, thinking, Wow! Pretty high tech stuff for a Youth Authority facility.

As Lil Joe opened his cell door the rest of the way and walked inside, he saw out of the corner of his eye that the control tower guard was waving his hand around trying to get his attention. When Lil Joe nodded his head toward the guard in acknowledgment, the guard motioned with his hands for him to close his cell door. "Oh," muttered

Lil Joe, "you can open it, but you can't close it, huh?" He grunted and let out a little chuckle at the irony, then closed the door behind him.

As he looked around his cell, Lil Joe overheard other wards talking to each other through the ventilation ducts. He remembered one of the escort guards telling Porky on the walk to the housing unit that hardly any of the wards had cellies because they wanted to fill up all the cells before they double celled anyone. So Lil Joe thought it was pretty cool that the wards had figured out a way to talk with each other.

The cell was similar to those at S.R.C.C. with just a few differences. The new cell had a stool and a metal desk, bolted to the back wall, in front of a long narrow window with a view of the yard. To the left were two metal lockers bolted to the wall about four feet off the ground. To the right of the door was a stainless steel sink and toilet, and a couple of feet from them was a metal bunk bed frame with a thin, plastic mattress on the bottom bunk. Lying on top of the mattress was fresh linen and blankets, along with a clean clothing roll and a fish kit.

Lil Joe grabbed a towel and a bar of soap from the fish kit and cleaned the cell. After he'd made it more livable, he filled the sink with water and took a quick bird bath. Shortly after he had dried off and dressed, the guards passed out dinner and to Lil Joe's surprise, the food wasn't that bad. He had tacos with rice, side dishes of beans and corn, and an ice cream sandwich for dessert. A few minutes after Lil Joe finished his dinner, the guard came by to pick up the trash.

Then Lil Joe took a look through his fish kit to see if there were any writing utensils and stationery so he could write to his family. There was, but as soon as he sat down at the desk, the control tower guard popped open everyone's cell door for voluntary dayroom program. When Lil Joe stepped out of his cell and closed the door behind him, he was met by a heavyset black male guard who searched him with a quick pat down. Lil Joe looked around while he was being searched and saw that the guards were patting down everyone who came out of their cells, so he took it to be a common practice.

After the pat down, Lil Joe made his way down the stairs to the dayroom and walked over to the back row of chairs and sat down with his back facing the wall. He picked that exact spot because it gave him a good view of the entire dayroom floor. So he just sat there by himself watching all the other wards interact with one another. As he looked over the dayroom, he saw that most of the wards were hanging out in small groups of four or five talking with each other. There was no sign of J.R. anywhere in the dayroom and Lil Joe remembered hearing J.R. ask one of the guards along the walk to the unit if he would be issued his medication. The guard explained that he would have to see the psych first and that it might not be for another day or two.

Lil Joe knew that people on psychiatric medications sometimes went through bad withdrawals when they missed a few doses. He had witnessed it happen before when he was in S.R.C.C., so he figured that J.R. was probably going through withdrawal and wouldn't come out of his cell for a couple of days. That's cool, he thought, that'll give me time to decide what to do with the little punk.

Lil Joe shook away his thoughts when he noticed a group of five Mexican wards walking towards him and quickly hopped to his feet. The tallest of the group spoke first. "Hey, loco, where you from?"

"My name's Lil Joe de Verdugo. Where you from?" he shot back.

"I'm Shotgun de Eastside Longo [Long Beach]," the tall kid replied. "Mucho gusto."

"Igualmente [likewise]," said Lil Joe.

Shotgun then pointed to the short, small framed kid with a shaved head standing next to him. "This is Tiny de Compton 70s."

"All right now," Lil Joe said in return.

The other three guys then stepped forward and introduced themselves. "I'm Oso [bear] de Shelltown San Diego," said the medium height, bulky kid who looked a little bit too old to be in the Youth Authority.

The other two introduced themselves as Sporty and BamBam from the Cochella Valley in Riverside County. They were brothers, although Lil Joe would never have guessed it by looking at them. They were exact opposites of each other. Sporty was dark complected with a tall, slender build and BamBam was short and chubby with fair skin.

"Hey, Lil Joe, where did you come from?" asked Oso.

"I came from Paso Robles. How long have you guys been here?"

"We all came on the same van from Preston about a week ago," said Oso. Lil Joe knew that Preston was another Youth Authority facility further north in California.

"Hey, Lil Joe, check it out!" said Shotgun. "We already got all of our property that we came down with, so we'll all put together a little care package for you to get you by until you get your stuff."

"All right. Cool. Gracias." Lil Joe didn't pack very much property with him when he left Paso. Instead, he left most of his belongings in the lockdown unit with a few friends who didn't have much.

For the remainder of that dayroom, all five of Lil Joe's new found friends ran him down with the daily routine in order to help him adjust to the new program. He learned that all meals were eaten in the cells and that dayroom programs were run twice a day, once after breakfast and again after dinner--for about an hour each time. He also learned that every day following the afternoon count, the unit guards ran a two-hour yard program. Then afterwards was shower program. Shotgun explained to Lil Joe that there were school and trade shop classes on weekdays, but they had been suspended for a couple of weeks because of a race riot that took place in the school area a few days earlier.

After dayroom, Lil Joe went back to his cell and wrote letters to his parents. After the guards passed by to do mail pickup, he called it a night.

On Lil Joe's second day, during the afternoon yard program he walked laps around the small, fenced-in yard, enjoying the fresh air and the afternoon sun, while the majority of the wards played basketball or handball on the small square of blacktop. Lil Joe explored every square inch of the yard as he paced around it from corner to corner. As he did so, one particular corner where the housing unit connected with the fence caught his eye. Right in plain sight just beyond the fence were three six-inch nails lying in a crevice between the building and the yard. He figured that the construction workers who built the place accidentally left them behind.

The nails looked to be within reaching distance if he could just squeeze his hand far enough through the crack between the fence and the building. So he squatted down on his heels with his back against the wall of the building in the corner and took a look around the yard to see if anyone was paying any attention to him. No one was, so he quickly reached through the crack and snatched up all three of the nails. Once he had them firmly in his possession, he pulled his hand back through the crack in the fence and slowly worked the nails into his shoes, one in his right shoe and the other two in his left. After they were securely in place, he stood up and made his way to the other side of the yard and leaned against the wall pretending to be interested in a basketball game that was taking place. He stood there for the remainder of the yard program.

Once he was back in his cell, he pulled the nails out of his shoes to examine them. All three were identical, so he put two to the side while he sharpened the other by scraping the point back and forth across the rough concrete of his cell floor until it was sharpened to a fine point. When he came out for his shower a little while later, he put all three nails in his clothing roll and took them with him.

Lil Joe ended up sharing one of the upstairs showers with Shotgun. After they finished showering and drying off, Lil Joe made sure that the tower guard wasn't watching him and handed one of the nails to Shotgun. "Here you go, that's for you," he said.

Shotgun was surprised. "Oh, hell, yeah, Lil Joe. Where did you get it?"

"I found a few of them on the yard today."

"Man, get on, Lil Joe, this will work." Shotgun admired the nail for a few seconds before wrapping it up in his towel. "Muchas gracis, Lil Joe."

"No problem, homie."

On his way back to his cell from showers, Lil Joe stopped by Sporty and BamBam's cell and slid the other extra nail under their door. "Hey, that's for you guys. Don't hurt yourselves now." They both smiled and thanked him as they took turns inspecting it.

On the way back to his cell, Lil Joe thought about Sporty and BamBam being cellies. They were the only wards on the unit who were double celled at the time and that was only because they were brothers. At first Lil Joe thought it would probably be pretty cool having your own brother for a cellie, but then he thought about his younger brother Marco and decided it wouldn't be very cool at all rotting away in the same jail cell with your brother. It made him sad to even think about it, and he wondered if Sporty and BamBam felt the same way.

When he got back to his cell, he ripped several thin strips of cloth from his sheet and used them to make a small handle for his little homemade shank. After tying the cloth tightly around the bottom of the nail, there was still at least three and a half inches of the nail point protruding.

Lil Joe had already made up his mind earlier in the day when he first found the nail that the first chance he got, he was going to punish J.R. for what he did to Valerie. He would teach him a lesson he would never forget. So after dinner he washed up and got ready for dayroom, slipping his little shank into the side of his shoe. He then stood by his cell door waiting for the tower guard to pop it open. When the door finally opened, he quickly stepped outside and closed the door behind him. A black female guard was patting down his neighbor and she gestured with her hand for Lil Joe to wait by his door. A few seconds later she approached him and said, "Assume the position."

Lil Joe stood with his feet spread wide apart and his arms out to his sides while she quickly patted him down. He was a little nervous about being caught with the shank before he was able to use it. He had given it a lot of thought while he was in his cell all afternoon. He was still angry about what J.R. had done to Valerie, but he wasn't enraged about it like he was when he first heard the news of the incident. No, he was going to punish J.R. based on principle more than anything else. Not only did J.R. beat up a woman, he beat up a young woman Lil Joe cared for, and although Lil Joe knew that Valerie wouldn't approve of what he was about to do, there was no way he could let J.R.'s actions go unanswered.

In the world Lil Joe had grown accustomed to, things were dealt with in a certain way, and he had come to accept it in his life as the only way. J.R. would have to suffer the consequences of his actions.

The thought did cross Lil Joe's mind that the last person he stabbed had died and it was possible that he would end up killing J.R. as well. However, the little voice of reason in his head had long ago been strangled to death by the corruption of growing up inside the California Penal System. Throughout the course of his life, those warning signs within him that should have put up a red light for him to stop and think about the consequences had long ago faded away into the darkness of a predominately violent world. As a young boy, violence was his way of expressing his anger, but now as a young man, his surrounding world had molded violence into his religion.

When the guard finished patting him down, Lil Joe made his way downstairs and onto the dayroom floor. He took a seat in his usual corner in the back row of the plastic chairs, where the fellas soon joined him.

J.R. had come out earlier that day for the morning dayroom program, but he didn't go to the afternoon yard program. Lil Joe was hoping he would come out for that nighttime dayroom. He did. J.R. was one of the last wards to be let out of his cell and after one of the guards patted him down, he sat down at an empty table by himself in the middle of the dayroom. He looked as if he had just woke up from a nap. His long curly hair was messy and he looked a bit disoriented. Lil Joe almost felt sorry for him.

After all five of the fellas sat down next to him, Lil Joe broke the news. "Hey, fellas, check it out. I have some business to deal with that followed me up here from Paso, so don't trip on it when you see me doing my thing. I just wanted to let you guys know ahead of time so it wouldn't catch you by surprise."

Sporty looked at Lil Joe with a concerned expression. "What's up, homie?"

His brother BamBam chimed in, "Yeah, Lil Joe, shit, we'll go with you, homie. Who is it?"

Lil Joe couldn't help but grin at their reaction. "No, hey, I'm flattered by your loyalty, fellas, really. But this is personal business that I gotta handle solo." The two brothers nodded their heads in understanding and Lil Joe then turned his attention to Shotgun. "Hey, Shotgun, did you bring out your plastic cup?"

Shotgun leaned back in his chair and picked his cup up off the floor. "Yeah, I got it right here."

"Can I use it to heat up some water?" asked Lil Joe.

Shotgun knew what he was up to. "Sure, go ahead, man, it's yours."

He handed the cup to Lil Joe. "Gracias, Shotgun." Lil Joe took the cup and walked over to the water fountain and filled it up with water. He then put it in the microwave and set the timer for twenty minutes. Afterwards, he walked back over to the chairs and held somewhat of a mediocre conversation with the fellas while he waited for the water to heat. He didn't intend to sound distant when the fellas attempted to talk with him, but he couldn't really hold a conversation at that time. His adrenalin was pumping and he was completely focused on his mission. He was pretty sure they understood.

When Lil Joe heard the microwave timer bell go off he quickly pulled the shank from his shoe and placed it under the front of his waistband, covering the protruding handle with his t-shirt. He then stood up and shook the hands of his five comrades. "You guys take care and keep those other nails handy." He looked around the unit. "Something about this place tells me you'll be needing them."

Lil Joe took a deep breath and slowly exhaled. It was game time. As he walked across the dayroom, he took a quick glance in J.R.'s direction to make sure he was still sitting at the table alone. He was. Good, thought Lil Joe, everything should go as planned. When he reached the microwave, he grabbed a towel that was lying on top of it and used it to pick up the cup of hot water. He then closed the microwave door with his free hand and very calmly strolled over to where J.R. was sitting. As he approached, J.R. looked up to greet him. "Hey, Lil Joe, how's . . . "

J.R. never finished his sentence. Lil Joe cut him off. "Shut up, bitch!" he said as he threw the scalding hot water in J.R.'s face.

"Ahhhh!" J.R. screamed and clutched his face with his hands.

Lil Joe wasted no time. He set the cup on the table and pulled the shank out. "This is for Valerie, you fuckin' punk!" Then he stabbed the shit out of the little dingbat.

Whenever Lil Joe committed a violent act, he was relentless. He would fly off the handle into a fury and there would be no stopping him until he was finished doing what he had set out to do. Unfortunately for one of the unit guards, he learned that the hard way. During his assault on J.R., one of the guards attempted to restrain Lil Joe and stop him from attacking J.R. But the guard's interference only enraged Lil Joe more and he began stabbing the guard as well. He took turns stabbing them both until finally two more guards responded to the incident and tackled him from behind, managing to restrain and handcuff him.

Once the guards had Lil Joe securely restrained and lying face down on the floor they maced him and began their vengeful assault by hitting and kicking him repeatedly. It was nothing new. Lil Joe was used to it and had come to expect the cowardly act as a given.

After a good five minutes of physically abusing him, the guards decided to pull Lil Joe off the dayroom floor and carry him outside, where they assaulted him some more before throwing him head first into the back of an escort van. Soon after, they drove him to the clinic, but it wasn't until hours later that he was placed in one of the clinic holding cells waiting to be examined by a nurse.

The nurse on duty was a young Asian woman who walked up to the door of the holding cell and introduced herself. She put her face in the small square window in the door and said, with a slight accent, "Hello, I'm Nurse Santos. Are you in need of medical attention?"

Lil Joe looked towards the door and squinted in an attempt to see her, but the mace blurred his vision. "No, I'm all right," he said.

The nurse could see for herself that Lil Joe was beaten up. "Are you sure? Because you look like you've been injured. I should take a look at you."

Lil Joe knew that the guards had worked him over pretty good. He could feel the soreness setting in already, but he wasn't about to give them the satisfaction of complaining about it. As it turned out, he didn't have to. Two of the guards who had brought him in were standing right outside of the cell and they cut right in. "Don't worry about him. He don't deserve medical attention," Lil Joe heard them say.

The nurse attempted to argue with the guard, insisting on treating Lil Joe's injuries, but the guards laid the intimidation down pretty thick and discouraged her from attempting to do her job. "Fuck him," one of the guards said, "it's because of this asshole that one of ours has twenty holes in his back," he exaggerated.

"Yeah," the other guard piped in, "fuck him! He don't have shit coming, so go about your business, lady."

They managed to scare her off with their verbal attack, so it turned out to be a long, painful night for Lil Joe. He spent the whole night in the clinic holding cell and even though it was cold, he managed to sleep some of the night on the dirty concrete floor. When he couldn't sleep, he just lay there thinking about how bad things had turned out and wondering what would happen next. He hadn't planned on stabbing a guard, but it happened. There was nothing he could do about it now.

Early the next morning, a sheriff's transportation van came to pick him up. Two deputies walked inside the clinic. Lil Joe was standing at the window of the cell door when they came to get him. "Hey, Mr. Hernandez," the taller of the two said, "we're here to transport you to the local prison reception at D.V.I."

Damn! Lil Joe thought. D.V.I.? He knew that the Dual Vocational Institution, also known as Tracy, was an adult prison. Things had happened so fast and now, bam! just like that he was on his way to the penitentiary. Well, he thought, what did you expect?

The tall deputy's shorter partner was holding waist chains and leg irons. "Mr. Hernandez," the tall deputy said, "we're gonna need you to turn around and kneel down on the floor, cross your ankles, and put your hands on top of your head."

"All right," said Lil Joe. He complied with the deputies' instructions. Once he was in position on the floor, one of the C.Y.A. guards unlocked and opened the door. Then the two deputies came inside and placed the restraints on him. They then helped him to his feet and escorted him to the sheriff's van parked in front of the clinic building.

When they reached the van, the taller deputy attempted to make small talk with Lil Joe while his partner opened the side door of the van. "You sure did spook these Youth Authority guys," he said. "They were in a hurry to get you outta here."

"Yeah," his partner chimed in, "usually when one of you Youth Authority boys gets rowdy, they just put you in the lockdown unit or stick you in the local county jail. But not you. They think you're too dangerous for that. Now you're goin' in with the big boys."

Lil Joe didn't respond to either of them. Instead, he just nodded and stepped into the van. During the short drive to Tracy, Lil Joe thought about what the two deputies had said. There he was on his way to the state penitentiary and he didn't even know whether or not he had killed J.R. or the guard. Man! he thought, here opens another chapter in my life.

CHAPTER TEN

THEY ARRIVED AT D.V.I. ABOUT HALF an hour later. When the tall deputy pulled the van off the highway and onto the prison grounds, Lil Joe's mood turned real serious, real quick. He didn't know exactly what to expect, so he mentally prepared himself for the worst. When they were past the gates, the van pulled up into an area of blacktop and parked in front of the doorway to a building that had the letters "R & R" (Receiving and Release) painted above the door. Almost immediately, a group of angry looking guards stepped out to greet Lil Joe. "Greeeaat!" Lil Joe muttered, "here we go again."

After his warm welcome consisting of another ass kicking while he was restrained with chains, Lil Joe was escorted to K-Wing, the prison's administrative segregation unit, also known as The Hole. He was taken to a cell on the first tier that the guards kept referring to as The Dungeon. They threw him into the cold dark dungeon wearing nothing but a pair of boxer shorts.

Once his eyes adjusted to the dark, Lil Joe understood why they called the cell a dungeon. It was a dark, morbid cell inside a larger cell. It looked like it had been carved out of rock, and the first thing he noticed was the stench. The cell stank of death, which appeared to be coming from the disgusting, thin cotton mattress which was lying on top of a short concrete slab towards the back of the cell. To the left of the slab was a stainless steel sink and toilet. Neither of them looked like they had been cleaned in a decade. The rest of the cell was empty with the exception of a pile of trash on the floor through which several mice were rummaging.

Lil Joe laughed to himself and said to the mice, "So how long have you guys been here?" He decided not to mess with them. He was too exhausted from the past two days. Besides, he figured they had gotten there first. However, he did attempt to move some of the trash out of the cell by pushing it through the bars into the larger cell with his foot. Midway through his half assed cleaning job, three guards walked into the outer cage of the dungeon. "Hernandez!" said a porky black male guard approaching the bars of the cell. "The lieutenant is here to see you. Back up to the bars and cuff up. We're gonna take you out to talk to him."

Lil Joe sighed and thought, What now! Does the lieutenant want to get a few kicks in too? He cautiously complied and let the guard handcuff him. Then the guards escorted him out of the dungeon and down to the front of the tier to a holding cell, where an elderly, grey haired man with a matching moustache, wearing a pair of green slacks and a beige dress shirt was waiting for him. After the guards locked Lil Joe in the holding cage, the lieutenant stepped to the front of the cage holding a piece of paper in his hand.

"Mr. Hernandez, I'm Lieutenant Smith. I'm here to notify you of the reasons for your placement in segregated housing and to give you a copy of your lock-up order." He held the piece of paper up for Lil Joe to see. "Since you're handcuffed, I'll just read it to you. How's that?"

"Sure," Lil Joe said, "knock yourself out."

The lieutenant smirked at Lil Joe's response and then read the lock-up order out loud:

> Joseph Hernandez, you were received by the institution D.V.I. on 7-16-1990 from the California Youth Authority as a result of your attempt to murder a C.Y.A. officer and a C.Y.A. ward on the date of 7-15-1990. Because of the above stated reasons, you will be retained in administrative segregation pending the outcome of a court ruling on your behalf.

After the lieutenant finished reading the order, he said, "Mr. Hernandez, do you understand what I've just read to you?"

"No," Lil Joe replied, "not really, but all of this stuff is new to me."

The lieutenant sighed. "Okay, look, basically you're gonna have to stay in the hole until you're done with court because the Youth Authority is pressing charges on you. As a matter of fact, someone from the Youth Authority will be here tomorrow to read you your rights and state the charges against you."

Lil Joe nodded. "Okay, so what happens in the meantime?"

The lieutenant appeared confused by the question. "What do you mean?"

Lil Joe sighed. "Well, for starters, when will I be able to clean that dungeon you guys put me in, and how about getting me some clothes and bedding, and maybe a fish kit or something."

The lieutenant seemed a little surprised. "You don't have any of those things in your cell?"

By that time, Lil Joe was tired and quite irritated by the whole mess, so he didn't see any reason to be polite. Instead, he was blunt and to the point. "Look, man, I don't have shit, and your guards have been doggin' me since I got here."

The lieutenant didn't seem to mind his bluntness. In fact, he reacted by calling one of the guards and giving him instructions to let Lil Joe clean his cell and to make sure he got everything they were required to give him. Then he turned his attention back to Lil Joe. "They'll take care of everything," he said.

Lil Joe nodded in acknowledgment. "So how long am I gonna be in that dungeon?"

The lieutenant grinned and let out a low grunt. "It sucks, huh? Well, you should see the disciplinary committee within the next ten days or so and at that time they'll approve you for a yard. After that, they'll probably move you up to the second or third tier with the rest of the inmates. Okay?" Lil Joe nodded.

After the lieutenant left, the guards escorted Lil Joe back to the dungeon and a couple of hours later they brought him some cleaning tools along with fresh linen, a fish kit, and a clean mattress. Shortly after he finished cleaning the cell, a rugged looking female guard came to retrieve the cleaning materials and decided to be snooty with him.

"There, is that better?" she asked in a sarcastic tone. "Because you know we're here to please you."

Lil Joe didn't let her attitude get to him. Instead he played it cool. He looked around the dungeon and smiled. "Yes, thank you, it's pure utopia."

She must not have liked his response because she fixed an ignorant look upon her face, shook her head, and stormed off down the tier. Lil Joe couldn't help but laugh out loud at her frustration. He muttered to himself, "What a nice lady."

For the next ten days, Lil Joe's daily routine consisted of working out, bird bathing, and sleeping, but his sleep patterns were somewhat disturbed by the constant screaming all through the night by an obviously mentally disturbed person in a dungeon next to his. Sometimes throughout the day Lil Joe would hear people talking on the tier, but he could never make out the words. For the most part he was pretty much bored out of his mind the entire time. He had nothing to keep himself busy with--no reading materials and nobody to talk to. To make things worse, he couldn't even brush his teeth because the toothbrush that came in his fish kit looked as though it had been used already, so he didn't dare use it.

But after ten days, things began to look up. He was finally able to see the disciplinary committee on the morning of his eleventh day in the dungeon. About an hour after the guards passed out breakfast, they came to his cell to take him to the committee. He was happy just to be getting out of the cell for a while, even if it was only down the tier to a small room in the front of the unit. In the ten days he had been in the hole, he had only been out three times--once to talk to the lieutenant the first day, once for a shower, and once on his second day when a lieutenant from the Youth Authority came to read him his rights and serve him with a piece of paper formally charging him with two counts of attempted murder. So he was grateful to be able to stretch his legs for a while.

When the guards escorted him into the small committee room, they had him sit on a chair in front of a large table where six committee members were seated scowling at him. All six let their disgust for him be known by verbal assassination and then cleared him for a yard group and told him he would remain in administrative segregation until he was transferred to another prison. Afterwards, one of the guards informed him that he would be moving up to another tier a little later in the day, which meant he was going to get out of the dungeon. That news alone made his day. However, about an hour later he was surprised when two guards came to his cell and informed him that transportation was there to take him to court.

Lil Joe was caught a little off guard by the news. No one had told him that he had a court date scheduled, so he hurried and washed up, used the toilet, and let the guards handcuff him so he could get on his way. He was escorted outside down a long concrete corridor that was crowded with general population prisoners on their way to or from somewhere. A few acknowledged Lil Joe with a head nod or a "What's up?" as they passed, but most just walked by without even looking in his direction.

The guards walked him to the same receiving and release building he had come in through when he first got there. A bit wary, Lil Joe's stomach tightened a little as he walked through the door. He half expected to be greeted by the same welcoming committee for another friendly round of kick the guy in the handcuffs. But to his relief, there were just a couple of transportation guards waiting to take him to court. After he was shackled with waist chains and leg irons, Lil Joe hopped into the back of the van and was driven to the local courthouse in Stockton. The ride only took about twenty minutes, but Lil Joe enjoyed every minute even though there wasn't much to look at along the way. As far as he was concerned, it beat staring at the corroded walls of the dungeon.

After pulling off the highway and making a couple of left turns, they were on the courthouse property. The driver pulled the van into a large, dark garage area that was connected to the courthouse and parked in front of an open doorway which led into the building. The transportation guards then escorted Lil Joe into the courthouse. Just beyond the doorway was a short, narrow hall with four small holding cells on the left. The guards put Lil Joe in one of them and he stayed there for about an hour until a couple of courthouse sheriff's deputies came for him and escorted him into one of the courtrooms for his arraignment hearing.

The courtroom looked identical to the one he had been in five years earlier in San Bernardino County. One of the court bailiffs, a short, pudgy faced man who walked with a limp, hobbled his way over to Lil Joe and instructed him to stand in front of the wooden railing across from the judge's bench. Then he announced to the courtroom, "In the matter of the State of California versus Joseph Hernandez, case number SC-05-9139SCR, penal code violation 664/187."

When the bailiff had finished reading Lil Joe's charges, the judge, an elderly, curly haired woman who Lil Joe thought bore a strong resemblance to Mrs. Roeper from the television show "Three's Company," looked at him and asked, "Mr. Hernandez, do you understand the charges against you?"

"Yes, I do," he replied.

The judge nodded and said, "Okay, Mr. Hernandez, I'm going to enter a plea of not guilty on your behalf and assign an attorney to represent you." She paused for a moment to shuffle through some papers and then continued. "I'm going to schedule a preliminary hearing on this matter for two weeks from today." Then she looked at Lil Joe and said, "That's it for now, Mr. Hernandez. You'll be coming back in two weeks."

Lil Joe was then taken into a small conference room where he was met by his assigned lawyer, Luis Flores, a tall, sharply dressed, middle aged Puerto Rican who introduced himself as a private attorney. During their brief meeting, Lil Joe and the attorney went over some of the facts of his case. Then his attorney cut the meeting short, explaining that he had to leave and attend court on another matter. But before he left, he promised to visit Lil Joe at the prison a little later in the week after he'd had time to familiarize himself with the case.

Lil Joe was then taken back to the prison and a couple of unit guards escorted him to a different cell, one on the second tier on the east side of the wing. It was the last cell, being in the corner at the back of the tier, which suited him just fine since he had developed somewhat of a reclusive personality over the past five years.

Along the walk to his new cell, Lil Joe passed by at least twenty or so other cells, all occupied. Most of the occupants stood at the bars of their cell door to see who the guards were taking into the empty cell.

When he finally reached it, Lil Joe noticed that the guard had already moved his bedding and toiletries into the new cell.

After the guards put him into his cell and removed his handcuffs, he took a look around. The cell was pretty much the same as the dungeon except for a couple of differences. The bunk area was metal instead of concrete and it was located to the right instead of being at the back. In addition, it wasn't inside another cell as the dungeon had been.

As soon as the guards who had brought him in left the tier, Lil Joe heard another prisoner yell out, "Second tier is clear!" which sparked his curiosity. He later learned that whoever was in the first cell on the tier took the responsibility of warning the rest of the prisoners on the tier when the guards were walking the tier and letting them know when they had left. The reason for the warning was obvious. After all, it was a prison, and the last thing any prisoner wanted was guards sneaking up on them while they were doing something which wasn't allowed. Lil Joe knew how things on the inside were, so he figured the warnings were a good idea.

After looking over his small cell, Lil Joe walked to the front and stood at the bars looking around the tier. He saw that the tier was divided the long way by a steel cage. He would later learn that the narrow space behind the cage was known as a catwalk, and its purpose was to give the guards safe access to the tier when there was a conflict. There was a third tier and another catwalk right above his tier. Behind the catwalk was a long brick wall with rows of windows stretching the entire length of the tier. The window directly in front of Lil Joe's cell gave him a good view of two small fenced-in recreation yards which were divided by a huge concrete handball wall and a gun tower.

While Lil Joe was standing at the front of his cell looking outside, he heard his neighbor knock on his cell wall and call out to him in a coarse voice, "Hey, neighbor!"

"Yeah," Lil Joe answered.

"Hey, what's your name?"

"My name's Lil Joe de Verdugo. Who am I speaking to?"

"This is your neighbor, Rojo de San Jose."

"All right now, Rojo, do I have any camaradas [comrades] right here?"

"Yeah, you have a few homies from your way right here."

Lil Joe knew the deal. Prison was the same as the Youth Authority in the sense that everyone ran with their own people or race from their hometown areas.

Lil Joe heard Rojo knock on his other neighbor's wall. "Hey, what's up, Rojo?" his neighbor asked.

"Say, Crow, you have another camarada who drove up next door to me in Cell 224. Se llama Lil Joe [his name is Lil Joe]."

"All right, gracias, Rojo."

"No problem. Hey, Lil Joe, there goes your camarada Crow."

"Okay, gracias," said Lil Joe.

Just then he heard Rojo's neighbor call out to him. "Hey, Lil Joe, this is Crow de Pacoima right here. I'm in Cell 222 on the other side of Rojo. Say, Lil Joe where are you from?"

"I'm from Verdugo Westside."

"All right now, Lil Joe. Mucho gusto."

"Likewise."

"Hey, Lil Joe, where did you come from?"

"I came from the dungeon on the first tier. But before that, I came from C.Y.A."

Lil Joe heard Crow chuckle. "Orale, a Youth Authority reject, eh? Hey, let me put something together for you and I'll get back at you in a few minutes. All right?"

"Sure," said Lil Joe.

While he waited to hear back from Crow, Lil Joe decided to clean up his cell. About ten minutes into his cleaning, Crow hollered over to him again. "Hey, Lil Joe!"

"Yeah," he answered.

"Hey, I'm gonna send my line down to you. Let me know when you see it."

"Okay." A few seconds later a condiment packet of syrup tied to thin, twisted nylon fishline slid in front of his cell. "I see it!" Lil Joe yelled out.

"All right, Lil Joe, go ahead and pull it into your house."

"All right." Lil Joe reached out underneath the bars and snatched up the line and quickly pulled the end into his cell. He untied the folded piece of paper tied to the end of it and called out to Crow, "I got it."

"All right, go ahead and check that out and get back at me when you're done."

Lil Joe unfolded the little piece of paper and read what was written on it:

> Lil Joe, it's just me, Crow, getting at you to extend my regards and welcome you into our company as a camarada. Por favor don't take this the wrong way, like if I'm being nosey or anything, but it would be appreciated if you could tell me about how you came to the hoyo. Again, it's not my intentions to come off as being nosey, but it's necessary to check out new arrivals to make sure they're trustworthy. I'm sure you understand where I'm coming from anyway, gracias for your time and cooperation.
>
> Con respeto [with respect], Crow.

Lil Joe put the kite to the side and thought about what Crow had written. He understood where he was coming from so he wasn't offended by the question of how he ended up in the hole. After all, it was prison. Lil Joe figured it was pretty good practice to know what kind of people were in your surroundings. He searched through his belongings for the lock-up order that the lieutenant had given him on his first day and decided to send it to Crow so he could see for himself. He slid the fishline back towards Crow's cell. "Hey, Crow, do you see that?"

"Yeah, I got it."

Lil Joe folded his lock-up order and tied it to the end of the line and yelled out, "Go ahead and pull it!"

A few minutes after Crow had pulled the line back into his cell, Lil Joe heard him call out to a few different people on the tier and let them know that there was another camarada who drove up by the name of Lil Joe de Verdugo. Lil Joe wondered if there was anyone there he knew. He figured there probably was because during the five years he'd been in the Youth Authority, he'd heard of a lot of people who had paroled from C.Y.A. and ended up in the California Department of Corrections.

About half an hour later, Crow sent back his fishline. "Hey, Lil Joe, do you see that?"

Lil Joe walked back to his cell door and pulled the weight of the line into his cell. "I got it."

"Okay, homie, go ahead and pull it."

When Lil Joe pulled in the other end of the line, he saw that there was a big brown paper bag tied to it. It was folded perfectly to fit under the bars of his cell door. When he had everything inside his cell, he called out to Crow, "I got it, homie. Gracias."

"All right now, Lil Joe, it's just some necessities for you. I'll get my line back later."

"Okay, Crow. Muchas gracias."

After he untied the line, Lil Joe sat on his bunk and opened the bag. Inside was a tube of toothpaste, a stick of deodorant, two bars of Irish Spring soap, and a pair of rubber shower shoes, along with a bag of instant coffee and a mysterious bundle of cellophane. Crow had also returned his paperwork and sent his own for Lil Joe to read. There was another kite attached to the front of Crow's paperwork and Lil Joe read it right then:

> All right now, Lil Joe, it's just me again getting at you with some necessities and returning your paperwork. It looks like you got off on that vato and that guard pretty good, youngster. I know a lot of us around here can sure appreciate a move like that. Anyhow, I'm sending you my paperwork to check out for yourself as well. It's only right. I got busy on a punk ass child molester out here on the general population yard. I peeled his fuckin' cap on the weight pile with a dumbbell. Anyway, you might of noticed the small bundle of cellophane that was in the bag. When you're finished reading this, go ahead and unwrap it. It's

> for you. But you got to keep it on you at all times, especially when you go to yard because that's when you'll need it the most. Everyone on this tier goes to one of two group yards, either our yard, which is us camaradas and a handful of gavachos [white boys] or the others and blacks yard. We have yard tomorrow morning, so I'll run you down the whole program then. In the meantime, you have a good day down there and I'll try to scrounge up some reading books for you.
>
> Con mucho respeto, Crow.
>
> P.S. If you have any questions regarding anything just ask. I'm here for you.

Lil Joe was curious to see what was in the bundle of cellophane. When he unwrapped it, he found a small knife made of plexiglass and a little plastic baggy full of hair grease, with another note wrapped around it. "Damn!" he muttered. "Welcome to prison." He took the note from around the little baggy of grease and read it:

> Lil Joe, I wanted to write this separate because it's important for you to know this. In the morning after the guards pick up breakfast trays, you'll have about a half an hour to get ready for yard so you'll have to hoop the piece before yard because the juras strip search us before letting us out to the yard. We all do it, mostly as a precaution just in case someone lands on our yard that don't belong there. A while back committee cleared two vatos for our yard that had come back here to the hole for stabbing up one of our camaradas on the G.P. yard. These guards are some crooked

> motherfuckers who like to play games and set people up on the yards for their own amusement. I don't mean to add any stress to your life, but since you're back here for stabbing a guard, they might try to set you up. So be careful and be cautious.

Lil Joe sat there for a moment taking in what he had just read. He figured there might be more repercussions for what he did to that guard. He was well aware of how the guards made examples out of guys who assaulted other guards. They would often take vengeance on another guard's behalf as an intimidation tactic to discourage other prisoners from doing the same thing, but at that very moment Lil Joe wasn't really thinking about what kind of reprisals the guards had planned for him in the future. Instead, he was caught up in the immediate issue at hand, and what a dilemma it was.

He sat there for a moment staring at the little knife and the baggy of grease. "Son of a bitch!" he muttered to himself. He had known as soon as he laid eyes on them that it was bad news; he had felt it in his gut. Lil Joe had heard the rumors before, but he never really imagined having to do it himself. He knew what the slang word hoop meant and he dreaded just the thought of it; he was going to have to sneak the knife to yard by shoving it up his ass. As much as he hated the idea of having to do such a thing, he realized that he was now in an all around ugly environment where he didn't know what to expect. He figured Crow wouldn't have brought it all up if it wasn't necessary, and the last thing Lil Joe wanted was to find himself in a situation he wasn't prepared for. No, he thought, I'd rather be safe than sorry any day.

For the remainder of the day, Lil Joe sat back and listened to what was going on around him. Throughout most of the day, people had short conversations on the tier while others played games of chess with one another. The chess players had a unique way of playing the game over the tier which Lil Joe thought was pretty cool. Since everyone in the hole was single celled, the chess players had developed a number system that allowed them to exchange moves by calling out numbers. He later learned that they hand made their own chess boards and pieces out of paper and then numbered each square the same in order to play the game.

In Lil Joe's five years of incarceration, he had seen people making things out of nothing, and he was often amazed at how crafty people on the inside could get. But he figured, hey, give a guy enough dead time to do, especially in solitary confinement, and he'll find a way to keep himself occupied. Either that or he'll go crazy, which was a regular occurrence in any solitary confinement unit.

One thing that Lil Joe quickly picked up on during his first day on the second tier was the level of respect with which the prisoners treated one another. If there were a couple of guys talking with each other or playing chess, nobody would talk over them or even flush their toilet without excusing themselves first. Lil Joe knew that there was a reason for that kind of respect among convicts. He was well aware that respect was a universal law in any jail or prison; it was the number one rule to survival on the inside. Disrespectful behavior among prisoners was never tolerated, and it always resulted in violent consequences. If the Youth Authority had taught him anything, it was that any self respecting man who was thrown into the treacherous world of the California Penal System valued his pride more than anything. The inside was a cruel world that would eat a man alive if he didn't.

Lil Joe knew that a man's pride was the only thing the system couldn't strip him of, and it was the only thing that a man had left when he stepped into a prison. So behind the walls, disrespect was always viewed as a personal challenge to a man's self pride, and most men on the inside would rather die than be stripped of the only part of their manhood they had left.

Fortunately for Lil Joe, he was a quick learner and was blessed with a keen sense of awareness. He always absorbed what went on around him and learned from it. So he took what he was learning from his new surroundings and quickly adapted to the change. He knew that he was looking at a long sentence for what he did to J.R. and the guard, so he figured that adopting the prison's code of conduct would be a good idea. He also knew that he had to take on a more serious attitude. He had heard all the stories about prison. He knew it was a whole other ballade compared to the Youth Authority, especially when it came to conflicts among convicts. In the Youth Authority, most conflicts among wards resulted in fistfights but conflicts among convicts in the penitentiary usually resulted in death. The reality of his situation made Lil Joe realize that it wasn't just about doing time anymore. It was now about survival, and behind the walls survival and respect went hand in hand.

Lil Joe had learned through experience that on the inside respect was earned not only by conducting yourself respectfully, but by demanding respect. And he was ready to do what he had to in order to get the respect he demanded, even if it meant making sacrifices that could keep him in prison longer. After all, he was a man before anything and he wouldn't compromise his manhood for anything in the world.

Lil Joe was well aware that on the inside respect was often obtained through fear. When people feared you, the respect was automatic, and he was prepared to be one vicious motherfucker if necessary in order to earn respect. He had learned long ago that inside was no place for a nice guy.

The next morning, Crow gave Lil Joe an early morning wake-up call, which gave him enough time to wash up, brush his teeth, and clean up his cell before breakfast. Right after he finished his breakfast, he drank a strong shot of instant coffee and sat down on the toilet to take a dump. He had been dreading his next move all night, but it had to be done. It was time for him to "put away" the knife, and what an event it turned out to be. He had never done anything as disgusting in his whole life, and it hurt like a son of a bitch. But after a few tries, he was able to do it. What a fuckin' mess, thought Lil Joe. This shit is definitely going to take some getting used to.

As he waited for the guards to start running the yard program, it suddenly dawned on him that if a situation occurred on the yard that called for the use of his knife, he would have to shit the thing out in time to use it. Ugh! That's some gross shit. Literally! he thought. He laughed at himself and thought, Well, I've adjusted to everything else that the system has thrown my way; I can adjust to this too.

The guards began to run yard program about five minutes later. They pulled everyone out of their cells and escorted them to small holding cages in the front of the unit to be strip searched and released to the yard. During Lil Joe's search, he was a little nervous even though he had no reason to be. It wasn't like the guards had x-ray vision, but still he half expected to hear one of them yell out, "Hey, this guy has a knife up his ass!" But of course nothing of the sort actually happened. The strip search was uneventful and he made it to the yard all right.

The yard wasn't much. Aside from the handball court, there was a pull-up bar cemented into the concrete and a drinking fountain next to it. There was also a three-head shower area next to the fountain with a grungy looking porcelain toilet on the other side. The rest of the yard was blacktop and concrete. At the top of the yard gate just above the large handball wall that divided the two small yards was a compact gun tower occupied by a guard holding a mini 14 assault rifle. As Lil Joe approached the gate, he noticed that there were quite a few people standing at the back of the yard looking at him. Once he entered the yard, the guards who escorted him closed the gate and had him back up and stick his hands through a square slot in the gate so they could unhandcuff him. Then one of the guards yelled out to the gunner, "He's the last one."

"Okay, thanks," said the gunner. Then he yelled down to everyone, "Resume yard."

As soon as the gunner said that, everyone standing on the opposite side of the yard quickly spread out in different directions. Lil Joe later learned that everyone had to stand on the opposite side of the yard from the gate until the guards were finished putting everyone in the yard.

As Lil Joe made his way across the yard, he was greeted first by Crow, who walked up to him wearing a big smile. "What's up, youngster? It's me, Crow," he said, extending his hand for a handshake.

Lil Joe shook his hand firmly. "Hey, all right, Crow. How's it goin'?" The image he had created of Crow in his mind was completely different from what he really looked like. Lil Joe had expected him to be some big, mean looking Mexican covered in tattoos like convicts were portrayed in the movies, but he was actually quite the opposite. He was a medium built, dark complected, middle-aged man with slick black hair and a thick salt and pepper mustache. Lil Joe could tell by his hardened facial features that the guy had been through a rough life.

The next guy to introduce himself totally took Lil Joe by surprise. It was Raul, the older brother of his childhood crush, Melissa. Lil Joe hardly recognized him. He had gained about thirty pounds and appeared to have aged twenty years. Obviously his time in prison had been taking a lot out of him, and it made Lil Joe sorry for him, but there was nothing he could do about it. When Raul shook Lil Joe's hand and introduced himself, Lil Joe said, "I know who you are, man. I used to go to the ditching parties you used to throw in the old neighborhood when I was just a young pup."

Raul seemed surprised. "Orale, well, hey it's good to have someone around from the old neighborhood. Say, Lil Joe, do you play handball?"

Lil Joe did, but his thoughts instantly went to the knife in his ass. "Uhh, no, not really, man."

"All right then." Raul shrugged it off. "Well, hey, I'm gonna go hit the court, get some exercise. We can partner up if you change your mind."

Lil Joe nodded. "All right, man. Gracias."

As Raul walked off, Lil Joe thought of Melissa. He was curious to find out how she was, but there was no way he would ask Raul about her. It just wouldn't be right.

After Raul made his way to the handball court, the other five cons on the yard introduced themselves and went on their way to play handball or work out. There were two old timer peckerwoods from Orange County who went by the nicknames of Crazy and Woody. There were also three other Mexicans, a short chubby youngster nicknamed Sapo (frog) from San Gabriel Valley, another old timer from the Los Angeles Harbor area who went by the name of Smiley, and Pete, another youngster in his late teens from out of the Bakersfield area who had recently drove up to Tracy from the Wasco reception center. Pete was a scrawny youngster with a shaved head and a crazed look in his eyes which for some reason reminded Lil Joe of Franky.

After everyone went about their business, Crow and Pete stayed behind with Lil Joe. "So how's prison life treating you so far?" asked Crow.

Lil Joe smiled. "I'm still adjusting."

"I hear you, man. So hey, you sure did manage to catch yourself a hot case. How's it lookin'?"

Lil Joe shrugged. "I don't know yet, man. I barely went to my arraignment yesterday, so it's still too soon to tell. How about you. How long have you been here?"

"Where? Here in prison or in Tracy?"

"Both," said Lil Joe.

Crow let out a long sigh. "Well, I've been in prison since 1978, but I've only been here in Tracy for a little over a year. I'm just waiting to transfer out to Corcoran S.H.U. right now, so I should be catching the chain anytime."

At that time Lil Joe had no idea what a S.H.U. was, but he decided to ask about it later. "Say, Lil Joe, I'm gonna head off to the handball court, man. Why don't you and Pete hang out and he can run you down with the program."

"Sure," said Lil Joe. Then he wrinkled his brow and added, "I don't know how you guys can play handball like this," he said referring to the keystered shanks. "Shit, I can barely walk."

Crow and Pete chuckled. "Don't trip, Lil Joe," Crow said. "You'll get used to it after a while." He looked to the handball court. "All right, youngster, I'm gonna go school these vatos on the court. I'll catch you later." As he made his way to the court, he yelled out, "I got Tallie!"

Lil Joe thought about what he had said. He couldn't imagine getting used to having a shank up his ass. For the rest of that first yard, Lil Joe and Pete talked in their secluded corner of the yard. They took a liking to each other right off and after Pete ran Lil Joe down with the daily routine there in the hole, they got to know each other by sharing their stories about how they ended up in Tracy's hole together.

Lil Joe learned that Pete was only a year older than he was and had recently begun his eight year stretch for a first offense drug beef. According to Pete, a dope fiend trying to get off on a residential burglary case, snitched on him in exchange for leniency, claiming that Pete was a big time speed dealer. After the local sheriff's department raided Pete's house and seized only half a kilo of crystal meth, they quickly realized that he wasn't the big fish they were after, but the assistant district attorney tried to pressure Pete into giving up his supplier in exchange for a one-year probation deal. However, Pete wanted no part of it and instead kept his dignity by refusing to become a stool pigeon for the

D.A.'s office. After Pete told the A.D.A. to suck his supplier's name out of his cock, they prosecuted him and made sure he received the maximum sentence allowed by law.

Pete told Lil Joe he landed in the hole just a week after he arrived in Tracy because he kicked the shit out of a homosexual who tried to proposition him on the main yard. Lil Joe thought that was pretty funny, thinking he would have done the same thing. All in all, he liked Pete's style and figured they would become good friends.

As the yard time came to an end, the unit guards came and escorted everyone off the yard one at a time, returning them to their cells. Lil Joe was the last one to be taken off the yard and while he stood there waiting for the guards to come get him, the gunner, an angry looking red faced man, called him over towards the tower. "Hey, Hernandez, come over here for a minute." When Lil Joe was standing under the tower, the gunner continued, "So, I bet you're real proud of yourself for what you did to that guard, huh?" Lil Joe didn't respond. "Well," the gunner said, "it's all right. You'll regret it soon enough, and just so you know, that guard you stabbed up is the husband of my wife's best friend." He stuck his mini 14 rifle out of the tower window and pointed it at Lil Joe's head. "I got my eye on you, so you better hope you don't fuck up on my watch." Then he smirked and let out a muffled grunt, obviously satisfied with getting his threatening message across to Lil Joe.

Lil Joe didn't say anything. He knew it wouldn't help matters any. At least now he knew exactly what to expect. If given the opportunity, the guards would kill him. He quickly put the thought out of his mind, figuring that whatever was going to happen, would happen, so there was no point in stressing over it. He wasn't about to let them get into his head and drive him crazy with worry. Lil Joe smiled at his serene outlook and shrugged it off. Fuck them, he thought, I'm not letting these cowards put fear in my heart.

When the guards finally came to take him off the yard, they informed him that he had a lawyer visit. The news surprised him; he hadn't expected to see his lawyer again so soon. Great timing, he thought. The entire time on the yard, all he could think about was getting back to his cell and getting that damn knife out of his ass, but now he would have to wait until after the visit. The guards escorted him out of the unit and down the long busy corridor to a special visiting area on the second floor of the G.P. program office. Once inside, the guards took him up a flight of stairs and into a small conference room furnished with a fold-out table and a few plastic chairs. Lil Joe took a seat and a few seconds later Mr. Flores, his lawyer, walked into the room accompanied by a gorgeous, tall, blonde woman wearing a blue skirt and dress shirt and carrying a black leather briefcase.

After they took seats, the two guards left and closed the door behind them. "Hello, Mr. Hernandez, how are you this morning?" Mr. Flores asked.

"Fine, and you?" asked Lil Joe while he eyeballed the pretty blonde.

"Fine, thanks. This is my investigator, Miss Sheldon."

"Good morning, Mr. Hernandez," she said in a soft gentle voice.

"Good morning," Lil Joe said, shooting her one of his most charming smiles.

His lawyer cut in. "Well, Mr. Hernandez, we're in quite a pickle. It looks like the district attorney's office is going to try to make an example out of you. I brought you copies of all the crime reports and a memorandum from the D.A.'s office."

The investigator opened her briefcase and pulled out a stack of papers and handed them to Lil Joe's attorney. "Okay, here they are. Well, Mr. Hernandez, what you're looking at if convicted for both counts of attempted murder is twenty-five years to life." Mr. Flores paused for a moment to give Lil Joe time to absorb the news. "That's a long time, Mr. Hernandez."

No shit, thought Lil Joe.

"The thing is, if it weren't for one of your victims being a guard, you and I both know that the district attorney's office isn't particularly interested in what young gang members in the Youth Authority do to each other. But since a guard was victimized, they're obligated to prosecute to the fullest extent. However, there might just be some light at the end of the tunnel."

He paused again long enough for Lil Joe to ask, "What is it?"

"Well, there was a complaint filed by a nurse at the Youth Authority regarding this matter. Her name is Mrs. Santos. You may remember her."

Lil Joe nodded to acknowledge that he did remember her.

"Well, good," Mr. Flores said. "In her complaint she states that the guards who brought you into the clinic after the alleged incident wouldn't allow her to treat you. She states that you had sustained several visible injuries and that when she attempted to treat them, she was physically intimidated by several guards who wouldn't allow her to do her job. She further states that she overheard the same guards bragging about how they got their "get back" on you for what you did, and that she believes your injuries were the result of an assault by the guards as an act of reprisal."

"Okay, so what does that all mean?"

The pretty blonde investigator answered. "This information could work as leverage for you to strike a deal."

"How so?"

"Well, Mr. Hernandez," she continued, "you're still under the state's care as a juvenile since you were, and still are, serving a sentence administered by a juvenile court. What that means is that while you were in the custody of the state under a juvenile conviction, you were physically assaulted by state employees and denied medical treatment, which brings forth both civil and criminal charges against the state and its employees. Since there is a state employee witness to these claims, your chances of striking a deal are very good."

Mr. Flores cut in. "Do you understand what that means?"

"Sort of, but why don't you explain it to me anyway."

"Okay, basically the plan is to go interview Mrs. Santos and find out if she would be willing to testify to the contents of her complaint in court. If she is, we can possibly use that as leverage for a deal with the D.A. The deal, of course, would be a plea bargain for a sentence shorter than a life term, and in return you would agree not to press criminal charges and civil charges against the state and the guards who assaulted you. Now, Mr. Hernandez, nothing will be official until we can talk to Mrs. Santos and the A.D.A. However, I'm pretty sure we'll be able to make a deal for less than fifteen years. That is, of course, if you're willing to do so."

Lil Joe was giving it some thought when Miss Sheldon re-crossed her long legs and threw his whole train of thought. Damn! he thought, what kind of deal can I make for a piece of that? Lil Joe came close to telling his lawyer that they could execute him right there on the spot if they would guarantee that he would be reincarnated as a pair of Miss Sheldon's panties. Ha! Sick fucker, he silently scolded himself.

Mr. Flores interrupted his x-rated thoughts of Miss Sheldon. "Well, Mr. Hernandez, what do you think?"

Lil Joe knew that at this point anything other than a life tops was a good deal. "Sure, if you can work it out like you said, then I'm on board with it."

"Okay, good. I have court this afternoon, so Miss Sheldon will head over to the Youth Authority and talk with Mrs. Santos. If that goes well, I'll approach the A.D.A. this afternoon with the deal. You do understand, though, that if the deal goes through, you'll be formally waiving your right to sue the state for compensation?"

"Yeah, I understand, but shit, if you can make the deal happen, I'm not worried about suing."

Mr. Flores smiled. "You're actually pretty lucky that your case landed on me as one of my pro bono cases for the year because I seriously doubt any public defender would have bothered to raise the issue of the nurse's complaint."

Lil Joe nodded. "So you're pretty confident that the A.D.A. will accept those terms of a plea bargain?"

"Well, it will be kind of hard for the Youth Authority administration to swallow, but the actions of their guards leave them and the district attorney's office no choice. They can't afford to chance the public outcry and negative publicity that would come with that kind of case. They'll do almost anything to keep that kind of thing quiet."

"All right, everything sounds good."

His attorney and Miss Sheldon stood up. "Okay, then, Mr. Hernandez, I'll see you at the prelim. Until then stay out of trouble, and if anything new comes up, I'll contact you either by mail or visit. All right?"

Lil Joe nodded. "All right, then. Thanks."

Lil Joe was then escorted back to his cell, where he immediately shit out the little shank and took a bird bath. While he was finishing up, Crow hollered over to him. "Hey, Lil Joe, you all right down there?"

"Yeah, I'm cool. Why, what's up, homie?"

"Shit, after you didn't come back from the yard, we all kinda thought maybe the placas got to you and buried you out in the yard somewhere."

Lil Joe heard a few chuckles on the tier and even smiled himself. Shit, he thought, if the gunner had it his way, that's exactly what would have happened. "Nah, homie, I went out to a lawyer visit."

"Any good news?"

"Maybe. I'll find out at my preliminary hearing."

"All right then, Lil Joe, I'll let you get back to what you were doin'. I just wanted to check on you and make sure you were cool."

"Hey, all right, Crow. Gracias."

Lil Joe then sat on his bunk and read his copy of the incident report his lawyer had given him. The way it was written made him out to be some kind of psychopath, and he noticed that the author of the report somehow managed to leave out all the physical abuse he endured after the incident. Go figure! he thought. He found a couple of new facts he hadn't already known. According to the report and the D.A.'s memorandum on the incident, J.R. had suffered second degree burns to his face and neck and nine puncture wounds to his upper torso. One of his lungs had completely collapsed and the other partly. The D.A.'s memorandum stated that J.R. was in stable condition and expected to make a full recovery.

Lil Joe also learned from the report and the memorandum that the Youth Authority guard had suffered four puncture wounds to his upper torso, with one of them resulting in a collapsed lung. The D.A.'s memorandum stated that the guard was stable and had been discharged from the hospital three days after the incident.

After reading the reports, Lil Joe sat back and thought about the whole thing. What if I do end up with a life sentence? he thought. Does it even matter any more? "Aw, fuck it!" he muttered. He shook off his thoughts, deciding to let fate take its course without worrying about it.

The next couple of weeks flew by, and before he knew it, he was back at the courthouse sitting in a different holding area waiting to be called into court for his preliminary hearing. The holding cell area had cells and tanks on both sides of the hallway, and all of the cells had big plexiglass windows in front. Right across from Lil Joe's single cell was a tank full of women from the local county jail. Most of them looked like rugged truck drivers or crackheads, but a few were eager to flash him their titties and bare ass cheeks so he wasn't complaining.

When his court number was called, Lil Joe was taken to another conference room for a quick meeting with his attorney, Mr. Flores, before going into the courtroom. "Well, Mr. Hernandez, I've got pretty good news considering the circumstances. The D.A. has agreed to a plea bargain."

"What is it?"

"It's what we talked about during our last visit. In exchange for you agreeing to waive your right to press charges and sue, they'll accept a guilty plea with a recommended sentence of thirteen years."

"Whoa, wait a minute," Lil Joe said, "what do you mean 'recommended sentence'?"

"Oh, that's nothing to worry about. The judge always goes along with what the D.A. recommends. In any event, if for some strange reason the judge doesn't go along, you can always withdraw your plea. But don't worry about it; I assure you it'll be fine."

"All right, then, let's do it."

"Okay, good. So here's what will happen next. You'll go into the courtroom and the judge will read off the charges. Then the A.D.A. will formally announce that there is a plea bargain agreement and that both parties wish to waive the preliminary hearing. At that time you'll plead guilty to the charges and we'll ask to waive the probation hearing and request immediate sentencing. After that, the A.D.A. will recommend to the judge that you be sentenced to thirteen years as a part of the plea agreement. That's pretty much it. Do you have any questions?"

Lil Joe thought about it for a moment, then replied, "No, I'm good."

"Okay, then," said the attorney. He pulled a pen and several pieces of paper from his briefcase and put them on the desk in front of Lil Joe. "Read over that plea bargain agreement, then sign and date it when you ready."

Lil Joe read the agreement. It was legit as far as he could tell. It basically stated everything that his lawyer had already explained to him. So he signed and dated it and give it back to Mr. Flores. "All right, Mr. Hernandez, you'll receive a copy of this before the end of the day. Now let's get you into the courtroom."

The court proceedings went by quickly. Lil Joe was in and out all within half an hour. He pled guilty and was sentenced to thirteen years in state prison just like Mr. Flores had assured him. After sentencing, the judge, an elderly, grey haired man with a deep tenor voice, took a few minutes to lecture Lil Joe on how he would have plenty of time to think about his course of life and, hopefully, make a change for the better. The statement made Lil Joe wonder if the old man really believed he had a chance of rehabilitation after serving that kind of a stretch in the California penal system. He was often amazed by how naive people on the other end of the system could be when it came to the reality of it all. The system simply didn't work. The California prison system was a cutthroat world that turned troubled young men into vicious killers, and that was only if they could survive their time. The ironic thing was that the only people who seemed to realize that or acknowledge it were the people doing hard time. Even though Lil Joe was still young and hadn't been around as long as some of the old-time convicts, he was well aware of what a stretch of time in the system could do to a man since he had grown up on the inside. To Lil Joe there was nothing worse than a man witnessing himself changing into some creature other than a human being and not being able to do anything to help himself.

A week after court, Lil Joe went in front of the disciplinary committee for the second time. They informed him that they had received an abstract of the judgment from the court and that within the next few months he would be classified and transferred to a maximum security prison. The committee also decided to retain him in the hole, stating that because of his violent history, he posed a threat to the safety and security of the institution.

Lil Joe thought that was a load of crap, but what could he do? The only thing he could hope for was to be transferred soon. However, he knew that at any time, anything could happen to put a hold on his transfer. Prison was just unpredictable that way.

CHAPTER ELEVEN

A COUPLE OF MONTHS LATER, TROUBLE once again found its way into Lil Joe's life. He was lying on his bed reading an old western novel when Crow called out to him, "Hey, Lil Joe!"

"Yeah, what's up, homie?"

"I got a kite down here for you from Pete. I'm on my way down."

"All right. Come on down."

After he fished in the kite from Pete, Lil Joe sat back and read it:

> Qvo, Lil Joe? How you doing down there? It's just me, your ol' buddy from Bakers getting at you to extend my regards and ask you a big favor. I was just informed that some vato from my hometown named Spanky was recently cleared for our yard by the committee. But they still got him on the first tier because there's no empty cells on our tier. Anyway, I remember that vato from the county jail. He had got stabbed in my unit the first day I got there. The fuckin' punk was convicted for raping his twelve-year-old stepdaughter. Word of his case was circulating the unit and I read it myself. Anyway, look, homie, since I'm the only one here who knows about him, I'm

> obligated to take care of it. So tomorrow at yard I'm going to whack the motherfucker. The thing is, he's a big ol' boy so I was wondering if you would spot me just in case something goes wrong? I know I'm asking a lot from you considering all the time you just caught in court, so I'll understand if you can't do it. Anyway, por favor, get at me a.s.a.p. with a response. Gracias for your time.
>
> Con mucho respeto, su camarada P.

Lil Joe didn't even have to think about it. Of course he would be there for Pete. But he wasn't just going to spot him; he was going to help him take care of it. Pete was a little guy who barely stood five foot four, if that, and probably only weighed a buck thirty-five soaking wet. So there was no way Lil Joe could let Pete go at the big "Rapo" by himself. Besides, Lil Joe believed in what Pete was doing. He despised rapists and would take great pleasure in sticking it to the guy.

Right away he sat down and wrote a quick note to Pete letting him know that he was in for the whole deal and would see him tomorrow on the yard. Then he had Crow do him a favor and fish the response down to Pete. Five minutes later, Pete hollered out to him, "Hey, Lil Joe!"

"Yeah."

"I got that, homie. Gracias. I'll see you tomorrow."

"All right, Pete, see you tomorrow."

That night Lil Joe decided to write a letter to his mom. He didn't have the heart to tell her that he had caught more time because she would have asked him why, and it would have been impossible for him to explain. So he avoided the whole thing altogether by telling her that he had been transferred into prison custody because he was now eighteen and the Youth Authority was no longer housing adults. He hated lying to her, but he couldn't tell her the truth; it would break her heart. Besides, he decided to stop telling his family when he was supposed to get out. There were no guarantees that he would get out, so he figured there was no point in getting anyone's hopes up, especially his own.

After the guards passed by for the evening count and mail pick up, Lil Joe decided to call it a night; he wanted to be well rested for the next day. He slept soundly through the night and morning came fast. He got up a little earlier than usual in order to prepare himself for what lay ahead. To his surprise, he had butterflies in his stomach, but he knew they weren't from the anticipation of violence. He had gotten over those kinds of butterflies long ago in the Youth Authority. No, the butterflies he felt that day were from wondering if he would come out alive. The threat from the yard gunner had resurfaced in his mind and was causing him to think about dying. He wasn't able to eat breakfast and instead bagged it up and put it to the side. Then he cleaned up and got ready for yard.

By the time the guards began picking up breakfast trays, his stomach was in knots. He knew that the gunner wasn't going to pass up an opportunity to carry out his threat. "Fuck it," he muttered. He psyched himself up to get rid of his nervousness. "That son of a bitch rapo motherfucker has it coming."

Lil Joe decided to say a little prayer before yard, figuring it wouldn't hurt. He said, "Dear God, I know you probably don't approve of what I'm about to do, and for that I'm sorry, but if you could just pull me through today, I would really appreciate it. Thanks."

He was the first one to make it out to yard that day, and he was hoping that by some kind of miracle the sadistic gunner who had threatened him wouldn't have shown up for work, but he had. Fuck it, he thought, we all got to die sometime. Lil Joe knew that if he had told Pete about the gunner's threat the night before when he wrote him the note, Pete would never have let him go on the hit with him. But that wasn't Lil Joe's style. He wouldn't have been able to live with himself if he allowed fear to control his life and make him set aside his principles. After all, aside from his friendship with Pete, his principles played a major part in his decision to go along for the ride. The hatred that he harbored towards sexual predators made the decision easy for him. When he thought about how easily it could have been one of his family members or a loved one who had been victimized by the rapist, it deeply enraged him.

Pete and Spanky, the rapist, were the last two people to be brought out to yard. Once everyone said their hellos and shook hands, Lil Joe pulled Pete to the side to talk. "So how do you wanna do this?"

"Why don't we get our shit out of the hoop and then call him over here away from everyone and take it from there."

"Okay, sounds good," said Lil Joe.

One at a time they squatted down to retrieve their pieces while the other kept a lookout to make sure the gunner wasn't paying attention. "What you workin' with, Pete?"

"Oh, a box cutter."

"Ouch. Does anyone know what we're gonna do?"

"Just Crow," Pete replied. "I told him last night so he could let the homies know afterwards why we did it."

Lil Joe nodded. "Makes sense. You ready to go?"

"Ready when you are, man."

"All right, give me a second." Lil Joe pulled the cellophane off the point of his shank and put it in the waistband of his boxer shorts and covered it with his t-shirt. "Okay, call him over."

"Hey, Spanky," Pete waved him over. "Come here, man."

As Spanky approached from across the yard, Lil Joe whispered under his breath, "He's a fat motherfucker, ain't he."

Pete chuckled. "Yeah, he is."

At the beginning of yard, Lil Joe had purposely avoided introducing himself to Spanky so if by chance he and Pete got away with whacking him and he lived, he wouldn't be able to name Lil Joe as one of his assailants. However, now that Lil Joe knew how they were going to do it, he knew that his precautions didn't matter. In fact, as Spanky walked up to them, the first thing Pete did was introduce him to Lil Joe. "This is my good friend Lil Joe from Verdugo."

Spanky extended his hand. "Mucho gusto, Lil Joe."

"Likewise," Lil Joe said in return, hiding his contempt.

"Say, Pete," Spanky asked, "how long have you been here?"

"A few months. I'm waiting on a transfer to another joint right now."

Spanky nodded. "Cool, man, I'll probably hit this reception yard soon. The committee only has me in the hole because I was in the hole in the county jail." He gave Pete a suspicious look. "Were we in the county together."

Pete played it cool, shrugging his shoulders. "We probably were, but we were probably in different units."

Just then Crow yelled out, "Who wants to be my handball partner?" from the other side of the yard. It diverted Spanky's attention for a moment, which couldn't have happened at a better time. Lil Joe was growing anxious to stab the fat jerk.

As soon as Spanky looked towards the handball court, Lil Joe knew that was their chance to make their move. He glanced at Pete for a second, giving him a nod, and then pulled his piece out and slammed it hard into the rapo's gut. Almost simultaneously, Pete grabbed Spanky by the forehead, pulled is head back, and slit his throat from ear to ear. The rapist instantly lost his footing and fell to the ground, taking Lil Joe with him. Lil Joe quickly jumped on top of the rapo and continued to bury the piece into his gut while cursing him.

The tower gunner yelled, "Get down!" several times, but Lil Joe couldn't hear; he was completely focused on the task at hand and had shut out everything that was going on around him. He didn't even hear the gunshot from the mini 14 ring out from the tower, but he felt it. It crashed into his left shoulder blade with so much force that it spun him around and knocked him flat on his back. He lay there for a moment blurry eyed and a little confused. Everything around him fell completely silent and for a second he wondered if he was dead.

Then a familiar voice broke the silence. "Lil Joe, are you all right, homeboy?" asked Pete.

Lil Joe looked over at Pete, who was lying on his stomach a few feet away from where they first started their assault on Spanky. "I think so," he replied.

"I can't believe that punk shot you, man. Fuckin' bitch ass puto!"

Right then the gunner yelled out, "Shut the fuck up! No talking!"

A few seconds later, the small yard was packed with guards and medical staff. Lil Joe lay there in pain while he watched the medical staff attend to the rapist first. They picked up his half limp body and placed him on a gurney and wheeled him off the yard in a hurry. Lil Joe looked over at where the rapo had been sprawled out and saw a huge puddle of the fat bastard's blood, which made him smile, content with the feeling that he and Pete had done a good job.

The medical staff returned a few minutes later accompanied by several guards. A cute, young, red headed nurse pushed a wheelchair towards Lil Joe. He sat up as she approached and asked him, "Excuse me, sir. Can you get yourself up and into the wheelchair?"

Without responding, Lil Joe very slowly pulled himself to his feet. He was a little dizzy and lightheaded from the loss of blood and was barely able to stand long enough to stumble towards the wheelchair and plop down in it. One of the escort guards who responded to the incident stepped towards him brandishing a pair of handcuffs. He frowned. "Sorry, we gotta cuff you, man," he cuffed Lil Joe's wrists in front and the nurse wheeled him off the yard. The rest of the convicts on the yard were lying flat on their stomachs. All of them rewarded him with a smile and a wink as he rolled past.

Lil Joe was taken to the infirmary to wait for paramedics to pick him up and take him to the local hospital. By the time he got there, the loss of blood and adrenaline comedown had taken its toll. He felt weak and tired, but he figured since he hadn't died yet, he was probably going to be all right.

In the Emergency Room, the doctor, a tall Middle Eastern man with a heavy accent, explained the situation to Lil Joe. "Mr. Hernandez, we have to get you to x-ray so we can determine the extent of the damage caused by the bullet."

Lil Joe nodded. "Sure, Doc, whatever you gotta do."

When he returned from being x-rayed, Lil Joe waited about ten minutes before the doctor returned to talk with him. "Well, Mr. Hernandez, after looking over your x-rays, I found that the bullet didn't do any major damage. In fact, it appears that it only tore through some of your muscle tissue and then lodged itself in the bone of your left shoulder blade. I would say that you were pretty lucky not to have suffered any serious damage."

One of the prison guards who was assigned to guard Lil Joe at the hospital was sitting in a chair in the corner of the examining room. "Yeah," he said and chuckled.

Lil Joe turned his attention to the pudgy, red faced man. "What's so funny?" he asked.

"Oh, uh, I'm not laughing at you. Seriously, man, I'm just saying you were real lucky considering the kind of round you were shot with."

"Is that right? How's that?"

The guard's eyes widened. "Man, you were shot at close range with a high power rifle round. That alone makes you lucky not to be dead, but what really makes you lucky is how the bullet lodged in bone. You were shot with a round that we call a traveler," he explained. "Its whole purpose is to tumble around inside of you until it loses its velocity."

Lil Joe smirked. "So the point is a guaranteed kill!"

The pudgy guard shrugged. "Well, the point is to make sure that the bullet stays inside of the intended target, and in this case the intended target was you."

Lil Joe absorbed the news silently. He decided that he was indeed very lucky not to have died from the wound. However, the day wasn't over. He looked up at the doctor. "So what's next?"

"Well, Mr. Hernandez," the doctor started, then paused to scratch his head. "I think it's best that we leave the bullet where it is."

"What!" Lil Joe protested. "Wait a minute. You mean to tell me that you plan on leaving this bullet in my back?"

The doctor could tell that Lil Joe was getting upset. "Please, let me explain, Mr. Hernandez. As it stands right now, if left alone, the bullet won't pose a significant threat to your health, whereas with surgery there's always a substantial risk of permanent nerve damage or worse."

Lil Joe got the feeling that the doctor was blowing smoke, but he was too exhausted to put up the energy for an argument. Instead, he decided to let it go. "Yeah, whatever, man. You're the doctor."

"All right then, Mr. Hernandez, I'll have a nurse clean you up and then stitch and dress your wound. Then you can be released back into the prison's custody."

A few minutes later while a nurse was stitching up Lil Joe's wound, another chubby, middle aged guard walked into the room. "Hey, Gil, how's it going?" he asked Lil Joe's escort guard.

"Hey, what's goin' on, Sammy?" Lil Joe's guard replied.

"Aw, not much. I was assigned to the victim, but he's in surgery right now so I thought I'd come and hang out." He pointed to Lil Joe. "Is this the one who got shot?"

Lil Joe's guard looked toward Lil Joe. "Yeah, that's him."

Spanky's guard looked at Lil Joe and said, "You guys really stuck it to the other guy. He's in surgery right now, but it doesn't look good for him; he might not make it."

Lil Joe grunted under his breath, thinking, Shit, that was the whole point.

Shortly after he was stitched up, Lil Joe was discharged and taken back to the prison, where he spent the night in the infirmary. The following morning, one of the doctors there gave him enough pain medication to last him two weeks and then cleared him to return to his unit. When he got to his cell, Lil Joe found all of his property spread out all over the floor. The guards had tossed it pretty good, leaving him quite the mess to clean up, but he was up to the task.

After a good twelve-hour sleep and a couple of hearty meals in the infirmary, he had a miraculous comeback in physical energy. Other than being a little sore, he felt pretty good, which in part was more than likely attributable to the powerful dose of pain medication running through his veins.

After the guards who brought him back had left the tier, Crow hollered over to him. "Hey, Lil Joe!"

"Yeah, what's up, Crow?"

"Not much. What's goin' on with you, killer? How are you doin'?"

Lil Joe laughed at the handle "killer." "I'm all right, man, gracias. Hey, where's Pete? I noticed his cell was empty when I walked by."

"The placas moved him to the dungeon last night," Crow said.

"Aw, man, that's fucked up."

"Yeah, I know. Say, Lil Joe, I have some things down here that Pete left behind for you when they moved him."

"All right. Cool. Just let me clean up and bird bath and I'll give you a holler. Okay?"

"Sure, homie, just let me know when you're ready and I'll come down."

"Okay, Crow. Gracias."

Lil Joe took his time cleaning his cell. Even though he felt all right, he didn't want to chance injuring himself. He didn't finish up until later in the afternoon, and by that time he was a little drowsy, so he decided to take a nap until the guards passed out dinner. But about ten minutes before dinner, he was awakened by a female nurse who was making her rounds passing out medications. "Hernandez!" she called out.

Lil Joe answered in a groggy voice, "Yeah, what's up?" He got out of bed and walked to the cell bars.

"I have fresh dressing for your wound. Can you put it on yourself or should I . . . "

Lil Joe cut her short. "I can do it. Thanks."

"Okay, then." She passed him the gauze and medical tape through the tray slot and said, "I'll be by to bring you fresh dressing once a day until you're all healed up. Okay?"

Lil Joe nodded. "Okay. Thanks."

After the nurse left, Lil Joe cleaned his wound with soap and water and redressed it before dinner. He had a hard time reaching the area of the wound, but he preferred to do it himself. He was a little wary about trusting prison medical staff to do their jobs properly. After dinner he took a couple of his pain killers and waited for the guards to pick up the trays so he could call down to Crow and get whatever it was that Pete left for him, but as it turned out, Crow beat him to the punch. As soon as the guards left the tier, he slid his line down to Lil Joe's cell. "Hey, Lil Joe, you see that?"

Lil Joe reached out and grabbed the line. "I got it."

"Go ahead and pull it."

Lil Joe pulled in the heavy brown paper bag tied to the end of the line and hollered out, "I got it, Crow. Gracias." He sat back on his bunk and opened the bag. Pete had left him some hygiene, instant coffee, and a stack of smut magazines. Lil Joe smiled at the names of the magazines. "Ass Parade," he muttered and chuckled to himself. Inside one of the magazines was a kite from Pete. Lil Joe quickly unfolded it to read it and discovered a little folded piece of cellophane with a black sticky substance inside. He knew it was heroin. Pete had offered it to him before, but he had always rejected it, having heard nasty rumors about getting hooked on it and figuring it wasn't worth the hassle. He removed it from the kite and set it to the side so he could read what Pete had written.

> Qvole, Lil Joe? I hope that you're doing all right, man. Homie, that was some fucked up shit, that jura shooting you like that! If I would of known that was going to happen, I never would of involved you. Sorry, homie! Serio [seriously], man, fuck that faggot ass gunner! Anyway, look, homie, I kinda figured these placas would put me in the dungeon so I put together these few things for you to have when you got back. Take care of my girls and don't hurt yourself. Ha! Ha! As for that other stuff I sent to you, I know that you don't fuck around, but considering everything you've been through, I thought maybe you might want a little something to help calm your nerves and take the edge off. Besides, I figured you might be in some pain with the bullet hole in your back and all, and this shit works wonders for dulling pain. So anyway, it's up to you. Take it easy, Lil Joe, and gracias for having my back out there. I owe you.
>
> Con mucho respeto, su camarada, P.
>
> P.S. If you do decide to put what I sent you to use, you should half it because there's enough there for two good shots. Just mix half of it in a hot shot of coffee and once it melts, down it.

After reading the kite from Pete, Lil Joe sat there and stared at the little chunk of heroin for a few minutes contemplating whether or not to try it. "Fuck it," he finally muttered, "might as well." He filled up a ziplock bag with water and set it on the light bulb in the back of his cell. While he waited for the water to heat up, he unwrapped the cellophane and split the chunk of heroin in two with his plastic spoon, putting half of it into his coffee cup. Once the water was hot, he poured it into his cup. He added a spoonful of instant coffee and quickly stirred the water to dissolve both of the contents, then lifted the cup to his nose to smell it. All he could smell was the water. "Well, here goes nothin'" he muttered and downed the coffee in three quick gulps. Almost immediately, he tasted the foul, bitter flavor of the tar heroin. "Ugh, yuck!" He wiped his chin with the back of his hand and quickly refilled his cup to chase "the fix" down with cold water.

Almost immediately, Lil Joe began to feel the effects of the heroin. For the first ten minutes or so, he sat back and enjoyed the head change and body numbing feeling that crept up on him, but then he suddenly felt nauseous and his stomach began to turn. The rest of the night was rough and consisted of him running back and forth from his bunk to the toilet until he eventually puked himself to sleep. When he woke up the following morning still feeling the aftereffects of the night before, he flushed the other half of the heroin down the toilet and vowed never to touch the stuff again. He decided that trying it at all was probably one of the most regretful decisions of his life. However, he was also grateful for the experience because it made him realize how low prison could take a person. From that day forward, Lil Joe decided to fight with all his might not to allow the corruption of prison life to destroy his soul.

A few days later Lil Joe went in front of the disciplinary committee again, where they acted to put him on "Walk Alone" status, which meant he would only be allowed to go to yard by himself and wouldn't be allowed to come into contact with any other prisoners. The committee also informed him that he would remain on Walk Alone until he was transferred to a security housing unit at another prison, but he wouldn't be transferred until the outcome of his D.A. referral for attempted murder of an inmate was known. The committee informed him that the district attorney's office would let the institution know within thirty days whether or not they intended to prosecute.

Later on that week, one of the unit prison guards informed Lil Joe that more than likely the D.A. wouldn't pick up his case because the incident wasn't caught on video tape. The guard insisted that the district attorney only accepted prison violence cases that were caught on camera. Lil Joe wasn't sure that what the guard said was true, but it did give him some hope. Crow even expressed his doubt that the D.A. would pick up the case. According to him, since he had been there in Tracy, the only cases that had been prosecuted by the D.A.'s office were murders and violence caught on video tape. Lil Joe wanted to believe that things would work out well for him, but he knew his luck wasn't all that great and he would just have to wait it out.

During that period of thirty days, Crow was transferred out to Corcoran State Prison's S.H.U. and Pete was brought back from the dungeon and moved into Crow's old cell. Lil Joe and Pete spent the duration of that time talking with each other on a daily basis. They talked about all sorts of things except their pending case. They knew it was never a good idea to discuss an ongoing case over the tier because there could be a jail house snitch listening in, and the last thing either of them needed was a snitch knowing their business.

Lil Joe was actually surprised that Spanky had lived, especially after reading the prison incident report and finding out how much damage he and Pete had done to the fat rapist. Well, he thought, I suppose some people are just lucky that way.

At the end of the thirty day wait, the disciplinary committee brought Lil Joe in front of them once again to inform him that the district attorney's office had rejected his case, and that they were putting him up for transfer to the S.H.U. at Pelican Bay State Prison. Although the news of his case being rejected took a huge weight off his shoulders, it was somewhat of a bittersweet moment for Lil Joe because now a new burden replaced the old. He had heard some pretty disturbing rumors about Pelican Bay and even though the prison hadn't been open for two whole years, already it was considered to be the worst prison in the entire nation. Not only was it the most high tech maximum security institution to date, it was notorious for violence and administrative corruption. One of the rumors circulating about the place that interested Lil Joe in particular was that the guards were setting up tier fights between known enemies and then shooting them as part of their no tolerance policy. Well, he thought, it looks like I'm in for a bumpy ride.

Two weeks later, right after the New Year, Lil Joe caught the bus to Pelican Bay. The prison was located on the outskirts of one of the towns near the Oregon state border. The drive there turned out to be the longest, most boring and uncomfortable ride of his life. It took over fourteen hours and by the time they got there, it was too dark for Lil Joe to catch a good look before the bus drove down into the S.H.U. pit. Other than a few huge concrete buildings and several perimeter gun towers, there didn't appear to be much to look at anyway.

On the drive up, Lil Joe had overheard one of the transportation guards tell one of his co-workers that the prison was built in an old forest swamp area and that it rained nine months out of the year. After hearing that bit of information, Lil Joe thought of how great that kind of weather would go along with the bullet in his back.

When the bus pulled into the S.H.U. pit, all the prisoners were processed off the bus and crammed into S.H.U. holding cells. A few minutes later a couple of female nurses came by and gave everyone a quick health check, then a group of S.H.U. escort guards showed up and began taking them to their housing units. Two corn fed male escort guards wearing green jump suits came to take Lil Joe to his assigned housing unit on the C-Facility of the S.H.U.

Along the walk down the long, dim corridor to his cell block, Lil Joe visually absorbed his surroundings. The place reminded him of an underground military facility like the ones in the movies. When they arrived at an open door at the beginning of another corridor, one of the guards instructed Lil Joe to face the wall next to the door and then yelled into the block, "One Block, we got an escort coming in!" Then he motioned for Lil Joe to walk into the unit, saying, "Okay, come on."

Once inside, the first thing that Lil Joe noticed was the circular gun tower just a couple of feet above his head. He also noticed the gunner inside standing behind an electrical control panel gripping his mini 14 assault rifle. "He's goin' into E-Pod, Cell 219," said the gunner. He pushed a button on the panel and Lil Joe saw a steel gate open up a few feet away.

"Come on," one of the escort guards said, "let's get you into your cell."

Lil Joe walked past the open steel gate and into the small cell pod. He immediately noticed several other prisoners standing on their steel mesh cell grills to get a look at the newcomer. The two escort guards walked Lil Joe up the steel staircase onto the second tier towards an open cell door with 219 painted in big white numerals right above the door. "There's your new condo," one of the escort guards said, pointing at the cell. Lil Joe grunted at the comment and walked into the empty cell. The door slammed shut behind him. One of the guards opened the metal tray slot in the door so he could remove Lil Joe's handcuffs. "Come on, back up to the tray slot," he instructed. Lil Joe stuck his hands through the slot and the guard removed his cuffs and left the pod.

Someone then yelled out to Lil Joe by calling out his cell number. "Hey, Cell 219!"

"Yeah."

"Hey, this is Cell 119. I'm right below you. What's your name?"

"My name is Lil Joe."

"All right, now, my name is Manny. Say, where are you from, Lil Joe?"

Same old song and dance, thought Lil Joe. "I'm from Verdugo. Where are you from?"

"I'm from Santa Nita, Orange County," Manny said. "Hey, Lil Joe, where did you come from?"

"Oh, I came from D.V.I, Tracy."

"Orale, all right then, Lil Joe, I'll go ahead and let you get situated. I'll stop by your cell first thing in the morning to run some things by you. Okay?"

"All right then, Manny. Hasta ma ana [until tomorrow]."

After talking with Manny, Lil Joe cleaned his cell, bird bathed, and went straight to sleep. He was exhausted from the long bus ride and slept like a rock all through the night.

The next morning, Lil Joe woke up when he heard Manny call out his name. "Hey, Lil Joe, buenos dias."

"Hey, all right now, Manny, buenos dias."

"Say, Lil Joe, do you drink coffee?"

"Uh, yeah, I do."

"Okay, I'll bring some out to you when I come out for yard. I have some cosmetics for you down here too."

"Hey, all right, Manny. Muchas gracias."

After his brief early morning conversation with Manny, Lil Joe wiped the crust from his eyes and got out of bed. Shortly after his morning wash up and cell cleaning ritual, the guards passed out breakfast trays and then returned about half an hour later to pick them up. After his food settled, Lil Joe contemplated working out. He hadn't attempted exercise since he was shot but he figured he had given his body enough time to recover and decided he would ease his way back into a good workout routine.

A couple of hours later after Lil Joe had worked out and bird bathed, Manny came out for his yard time and stopped by his cell. "Here you go, Lil Joe," said the tall, slim, clean shaven man as he slid a bag of hygiene and a couple of books and a baggy of coffee under Lil Joe's door. "There's some writing paper and a few envelopes for you in the big bag. I wrote the prison's address on one of the pieces of paper along with a quick rundown about this place."

Just then the tower gunner yelled out, "let's go, Marquez, take it to yard!"

"All right, Lil Joe, I gotta go, man."

"All right then, Manny. Gracias," Lil Joe hollered out as Manny hurried down the stairs on his way to the yard. Then he sat down on his bunk and read the kite that Manny had put together for him.

> All right now, Lil Joe, buenos dias y mucho gusto [good morning and nice to meet you]. I'm just writing a few things down to give you a quick rundown on what's going on right here. We're the only two camaradas in this pod. There are a few other sure os in this block, but they're all in different pods. This block right here is the violence control unit. So you probably won't be here very long. Mostly everyone here are dings, but some of us are here for taking care of business. I myself have been here for almost two months. A few of us camaradas cell extracted in another block because the placas were tripping. Anyway, everyone else in our pod are locos, so just

be on your toes and stay on the lookout, because these guards like to rack the doors open on us to see if we'll fight with each other. Other than that, there ain't shit happening around here. We're allowed to go to the yard by ourselves for an hour and a half a day, but it's nothing to get excited about. The yard is just another concrete box a little bigger than our cells, and there ain't shit on that motherfucker either. We get showers three times a week. They rotate the shower days between tiers except on Thursdays. There are no showers on Thursday. Today is the top tier's shower day. The placas usually run the showers at around 2 o'clock right after shift change. I'll give you a warning call to let you know when it's almost that time so you can be ready. The showers are at the front of each tier, one on the bottom next to Cell 117 and the other on the top tier next to Cell 217. Well, that's about it. If you need anything, just let me know.

Con respeto, M.

After reading the kite, Lil Joe ripped it into little pieces and flushed it down the toilet. Then he sat back and thought about some of the things Manny had run him down with in the kite. He couldn't help but wonder if it was by coincidence that he landed in the violence control unit or if it had been planned that way. Well, he thought, I'll find out soon enough when I go to my committee review. Lil Joe also thought about how Manny had ended up in the violence control unit and wondered if cell extractions were a common thing in the S.H.U. He figured they probably were.

Cell extractions were something Lil Joe hadn't yet experienced but he had heard some of the older convicts talk about them. He knew that in order to get the guards to cell extract you, you had to purposely do something to disturb the institutional program. He also knew that cell extractions were a last resort when there was a problem between convicts and guards because a physical altercation like that held serious consequences. People got hurt during cell extractions and depending on the circumstances, some convicts could even lose their chance of parole. So it was common knowledge among convicts that cell extractions were to be avoided unless they were absolutely necessary, especially since most physical conflicts in prison involved large groups of people. Convicts always backed up their own kind and war was war, whether it was a race war or a conflict between convicts and guards.

Lil Joe recalled a story that Crow had told him about a time years before at Folsom State Prison when Crow was just a youngster and experienced his first cell extraction. Apparently the warden had suspended visiting privileges of all the cons in the hole for an undisclosed reason. So every convict in the hole decided to cell extract over it. All of them held on to their food trays, refusing to turn them in. They wouldn't even allow the guards to walk the tier to conduct counts or do any other parts of their job. Every time the guards even attempted to walk the tier, prison made spears would come flying out of every cell, sending them running for safety. Eventually, they returned, strong in numbers, geared up and protected by plexiglass shields, tear gassing and ultimately cell extracting every convict in the hole. But after three days of that kind of dangerous and exhausting activity, the warden was forced to re-evaluate his asinine decision to take away visiting privileges and he eventually lifted the ridiculous ban. The only explanation he ever gave for taking away the visiting privileges in the first place was a vague statement about institutional security precautions.

Lil Joe knew that it was only a matter of time before he would experience his first cell extraction. Prison was just one giant revolving door of madness, and he knew that there was no escaping any part of the chaos that went on behind the walls. He decided to sit down and write some letters. He wrote to both of his parents first, then scratched out quick letters to Franky and Jimmy. By the time he finished, it was his turn to go to the yard.

As he made his way to the yard, he noticed that none of the other prisoners in the pod had cellies, but a few of them had a radio or a television for entertainment. When he stepped out onto the tiny concrete yard, he laughed out of utter disbelief. But in truth there was nothing funny about it. "What the fuck kind of bullshit is this?" he muttered. The yard was a completely bare, compact concrete box just a little bigger than his cell. The gloomy grey walls bore distorted looking images of screaming souls embedded in the concrete. The roof was so high that the sunlight barely reached halfway down the wall. The roof was completely covered with a steel screen and there was a thick plastic cover on one half. There was a security camera surrounded by razor wire on the other side. Lil Joe shook his head in disbelief. Boy, isn't this special, he thought. After getting over the initial shock, he ended up pacing the length of it until the tower guard popped open the yard door for him to come back inside.

Shortly after Lil Joe returned to his cell, the guards exchanged shifts and ran shower program. Manny gave Lil Joe a warning to get ready for showers just like he said he would and a few minutes later the tower guard popped Lil Joe out for his shower. They gave him ten minutes to shower and shave and then he returned to his cell and began reading one of the books that Manny had lent him. It was entitled "The Art of War" by Tsung Tsu.

About an hour into his reading, an incident occurred there in his pod that would turn out to be one of the most disgusting and disturbing things he would ever witness. After finishing up with the shower program, the tower guard popped out Lil Joe's neighbor for his yard program. When the young black man stepped out onto the tier, the stench hit Lil Joe like a sledge hammer. He stood on his cell door to see where the stink was coming from and saw that his neighbor had come out of his cell stark naked with feces smeared all over his body. Lil Joe quickly pulled his t-shirt off and tied it around the lower half of his face in an attempt to keep from breathing in the stench.

As soon as his neighbor stepped onto the bottom tier floor, the tower guard popped open the bottom tier shower door and yelled out, "Hayes, step into the shower!" But the ding ignored the gunner's instructions. Instead, he squatted down right in the middle of the tier and defecated on the floor. Lil Joe was flabbergasted by the whole thing. He stood at his cell grill looking downward and whispered to himself, "How does a man get to that point?"

The gunner repeated his earlier instructions. "Hayes, step into the shower now!" However, the ding ignored him again. Instead, he scooped up a handful of feces from the tier and flung it through the bars of the control tower, splattering feces all over the tier.

"Ugh, nasty," Lil Joe muttered.

The stench nearly made him puke, but his nausea soon passed when he heard a gunshot from the gunner's rifle echo through the pod. The ding's body hit the floor in a twisted position and Lil Joe heard another prisoner yell out, "Damn, they shot his ass!"

Lil Joe looked down to see if the ding was dead, but he was still alive at that moment, squirming around in a puddle of his own blood and excrement. Damn! thought Lil Joe, the whole scene seemed unreal. He heard a loud alarm ringing in the S.H.U. corridor, along with the sound of heavy footsteps and the rattling keys of the responding guards. A moment later, the pod door slid open and a small army of guards suited in riot gear ran into the pod yelling, "Roll over on your stomach!" After they had handcuffed the wounded man's hands behind his back, the guards allowed the responding medical staff to enter the pod and attend to him. As the medical staff wheeled in the gurney and lifted the wounded man onto it, Lil Joe saw the gaping hole in the man's chest and wondered if he would make it.

About an hour after the medical staff carted the ding off, two unit guards entered the pod carrying mops and a large bottle of liquid bleach. As they began mopping up the blood and feces, Lil Joe stood at his cell door and watched. A few seconds into their cleaning, one of the guards, a heavy set redneck, turned to his skinny colleague wearing a disgusted look on his face and said, "Nasty fuckin' animal! We should of made him clean this shit up before we let medical take him."

"Yeah," his partner chimed in, "we can always leave it here for him to clean up when he gets back."

"Yeah," the heavyset guard grunted. "If he comes back." They both broke out into fits of laughter as if the ding's life was some sort of hilarious joke. It wasn't until that very moment that Lil Joe became aware of how much he had grown to hate prison guards. He knew that over the years he had developed a certain amount of disdain and animosity towards them, but it wasn't until that day that he realized just how much of a burning hatred he really had for them.

CHAPTER TWELVE

TWO WEEKS AFTER LIL JOE ARRIVED at Pelican Bay, he went in front of the prison's disciplinary committee and was informed that he would be retained in the S.H.U. until he completed his disciplinary S.H.U. term for attempting to murder another prisoner. Although the district attorney's office in San Joaquin County didn't prosecute him for stabbing Spanky, he was still punished administratively for the act. However, Lil Joe considered himself lucky; he figured he had lucked out on the whole ordeal by not receiving more time from the courts.

The day after Committee, Lil Joe was moved from the violence control unit to another cell block on the "D" facility of the S.H.U., where he was double celled with one of his fellow camaradas, a short, bearish looking Mexican who went by the fitting nickname of Shorty. Shorty was a thirty-seven year old lifer, originally from the northeast Los Angeles area, who had begun serving his life sentence for two counts of vehicular manslaughter shortly after his nineteenth birthday. He was also on one of the first bus loads of convicts to be sent to the Pelican Bay S.H.U. when it opened in 1989.

By the time Shorty and Lil Joe were celled up together, Shorty was already well adjusted to the solitary confinement of the S.H.U.. However, neither he or Lil Joe had had a cellie in quite a while, so it took a while for them to adjust to double cell living. In the time that Lil Joe was celled up with Shorty, he learned a lot from the old con--not only was Shorty smart in the ways of prison survival, he was also an extremely skilled jailhouse lawyer who spent the majority of his time helping fellow convicts with their appeals and other legal matters.

Since Lil Joe was a fast learner, he picked up on the legal trade fairly quickly, which would later come in handy.

It didn't take Lil Joe long to get adjusted to the S.H.U. program. He understood right away that the S.H.U. was more than just another solitary lockdown unit; he knew it was purposely designed to break the human spirit, but he took the psychological warfare as a personal challenge. There was no way he would allow the system to break his spirit. The idea was to get into a daily routine and stay busy with activities like exercising, reading, and writing, even taking up hobbies such as drawing or creative writing--anything to stimulate the mind.

Lil Joe knew what too much solitary confinement could do to a man's mental state, and he refused to fall victim to the slow tortuous process. He figured just because his body was locked in a cage it didn't mean that his mind had to be as well. Unfortunately, not everyone within the S.H.U. possessed his vigor, and he would witness many prisoners fall victim to the extremely inhumane conditions. Some would even go so far as to commit suicide to escape the psycho punishment.

The thing about the S.H.U. that Lil Joe could never understand was that it was a permanent housing for only some of its occupants. Most of the convicts housed there were serving indeterminate terms and would never get out of the place alive while others would serve determinate S.H.U. terms and be released back to the general population yards around the state. The Department of Corrections administration somehow justified the unequal treatment by categorizing the convicts serving indeterminate S.H.U. terms as security risks to the safety and security of the general population, which Lil Joe personally thought was a bunch of horse shit. After all, it was prison, not a daycare center.

Most of the convicts Lil Joe met in the S.H.U. were real stand-up guys who stood up for what they believed in and stuck to their principles and beliefs no matter what. But for some strange reason, that kind of character was considered a security risk by the prison administrators.

Fortunately for Lil Joe, he still had a chance to see a G.P. yard; the prison disciplinary committee hadn't welded him in yet.

While he was in Pelican Bay, Lil Joe continued to stay in contact with both of his parents, as well as his two pals Franky and Jimmy. He was too far from either of his parents to get visits, but he wrote letters to them as often as he could. In the summer of 1992, he received a letter from Franky reminding him that he and Jimmy were less than a year away from being released back into society, and that neither of them would forget about him on the outside. The letter made Lil Joe realize how many years had gone by and that he, too, would have been getting out if it weren't for a couple of unfortunate occurrences that took place.

The years had gone by so fast it was hard to believe he was just months away from turning twenty-one. It felt like a whole lifetime had gone by since he was first incarcerated, but not in the sense of time because after the first couple of years he had stopped paying attention to the time. It was more along the lines of maturity. He had grown so much mentally over the years that he felt much older than he really was. He attributed the growth to all the obstacles he had already overcome. Even though most of them were surreal in nature, he didn't regret any of them. Instead he viewed them as important learning experiences that would eventually mold him into the man that he was meant to be.

Sometime towards the end of 1992, Lil Joe's younger brother began writing to him on a weekly basis. Lil Joe was real proud of Marco. Somehow he had managed to stay out of trouble in the old neighborhood and was even getting ready to graduate from high school. When Marco wrote to Lil Joe, he would share his goals and dreams of one day opening his own restaurant. Lil Joe would always respond with supporting words of encouragement and would send Marco drawings that other convicts did for him as often as he could, which Marco always appreciated.

One thing that Lil Joe learned about prison was that the time brought out the artistic nature in a lot of the convicts. Some would draw, some would write, and others were crafty in other ways. But Lil Joe admired most the drawings that convicts brought to life. He was often amazed at what some of them could do with just a pen and a piece of paper. Lil Joe wasn't very talented when it came to drawing, but he did adopt quite a talent for writing. He especially liked to write poetry, and it was one of his favorite pastimes. Writing helped him overcome the solitude of his environment, and it often served as a way for him to vent some of his anger and frustrations. Throughout the years he had even entered several poetry contests and ended up getting some of his work published.

At the end of 1992, Lil Joe's old friend Pete from Bakersfield drove up to the Pelican Bay S.H.U. from the S.H.U. in Corcoran State

Prison. He was transferred to Pelican Bay after being convicted on a bogus murder beef that he picked up in Corcoran. Shortly after Lil Joe got word that Pete had driven up, they celled up together and Pete explained how he had ended up catching a prison murder beef. The story didn't surprise Lil Joe. He had long ago grown accustomed to the horrors of prison realities.

According to Pete, the guards at Corcoran S.H.U. had been setting up dog fights among convicts who were known enemies by putting them together on a integrated S.H.U. yard, knowing that they would fight with each other. Pete explained that the dog fights had been going on for a couple of years and that they were still taking place when he left. In Pete's case, the guards had set him up by putting him on the same yard with a known child molester, knowing that Pete wouldn't pass up the opportunity to assault the pedophile. So when Pete assaulted the molester, the tower gunner took the opportunity to shoot and kill the guy, ultimately placing the responsibility for his death on Pete. The prison referred the case to the local district attorney's office and they eventually picked it up and prosecuted Pete for murder, sentencing him to twenty-five years to life.

This was typical of California prison officials and their corrupt antics. There was no doubt in Lil Joe's mind that the guards at Corcoran had planned to execute the child molester all along, and Lil Joe didn't have any problems with that. He figured that the guy had it coming. What he did have a problem with was the guards using Pete as a scapegoat and taking away his life in the process.

So Lil Joe took the legal knowledge that he had learned from his ex-cellie, Shorty, and scratched up a writ of habeas corpus for Pete, challenging his conviction. After a year and a half of handwritten arguments, an appeals court finally granted Pete a re-sentencing hearing under the lesser charge of involuntary manslaughter, which held a sentence of only six years. It wasn't exactly what they'd been shooting for, but at least Pete no longer had a life sentence. In California, anything was better than a life sentence. Every convict in the California Penal System knew that the state parole board never granted parole to a lifer. It was an unwritten policy. Lil Joe had run into convicts who had been incarcerated since the late 60's on a five years to life sentence who were still awaiting parole in 1992. It didn't make much sense to Lil Joe, but it was the way the state played it.

In mid 1993, Lil Joe's mother sent him pictures of Marco's high school graduation. Like always, Lil Joe was proud of Marco, but he was especially happy for his mom. Although Lil Joe knew how much his mother loved him, he could never shake the feeling of being a disappointment to her, so his brother's accomplishments brought him the great satisfaction of knowing that at least she had something to be proud of.

For Lil Joe's twenty-first birthday, he received a birthday card, some pictures, and $300 from Franky and Jimmy, who by then were both free men living in the old neighborhood. Neither of them were on parole because they had both maxed out their sentences. State law prohibited the California Youth Authority from placing wards on parole if they completed their entire sentence in custody. So Lil Joe was happy for Franky and Jimmy because he was aware of how hard it was to successfully complete parole in the state of California. The system was structured to keep parolees caught up in the revolving door as long as possible. Since Franky and Jimmy weren't on parole, Lil Joe figured they had a pretty decent chance of making it on the outside, and he wished them all the luck in the world.

Over the next few years, both Franky and Jimmy stayed in contact with Lil Joe by writing to him periodically. But Franky was the one who would always elaborate in his letters about their daily lives on the outside. Lil Joe always enjoyed their letters and stories and lived vicariously through them to the point where he often felt as if he were on the outside with them.

But their letters weren't always about how great things were in the free world. At times Franky would express his frustration over how hard it was for an ex-con with a murder on his jacket to get a decent job. Basically, for their first four years as free men, they struggled with crummy jobs and dishonest employers until one day they were approached by a mutual acquaintance who offered them an opportunity to make a substantial amount of money on the streets. Of course the work involved criminal activities, but Franky and Jimmy were at the end of their ropes and the temptation was too great for them to ignore. So after four hard years of attempting to make things work legitimately, Franky and Jimmy accepted another course of life, one that they were already too familiar with.

CHAPTER THIRTEEN

IN THE SUMMER OF 1997, LIL Joe received a letter from Franky enclosing a check for $2000. The surprise caught him considerably off guard, and although he definitely appreciated the gesture, he wondered how Franky was able to afford such generosity. Franky's letter was vague. He only wrote that he and Jimmy were doing a lot better financially and that he would be receiving a lot more such letters in the future. Although he was extremely grateful for the gift, he couldn't help but worry that Franky and Jimmy had gotten themselves into something that would eventually lead them back to jail or worse.

Later that night, he sat down and wrote a thank you letter to both of them and expressed his concern. He tried to remind them of how much life on the inside sucked, but when they wrote back, they just sent another grand and told him not to worry about them, that everything was all right. But Lil Joe couldn't help himself; he knew that whatever it was that Franky and Jimmy were involved in, it was bad news.

Nevertheless, he put the money they sent to good use. For a few years Lil Joe had been paying a lot of attention to the stock market news on television. So after several months of receiving thousands of dollars from Franky and Jimmy, he decided it would be a good idea for him to invest his money in the steadily growing bull market of technology. Before he did, he did his homework and ordered all sorts of reading material on stock market trading, including a subscription to the Investors Business daily newspaper. He spent the better half of the year learning as much as he could before he felt confident enough to open up an account.

Finally, late in 1998, with the help of his dad, he opened an account with an internet brokerage firm and invested in technology stocks. He did pretty well on his first portfolio for a new investor and made a decent profit that first year. However, his stock market success was short lived. One morning about halfway through his second year of trading, while he and Pete were in the S.H.U. rec yard, a couple of guards tossed their cell and confiscated all of Lil Joe's investment materials, claiming that prisoners weren't allowed to participate in the stock market.

Lil Joe was furious and he and Pete talked about what actions they would take for what the guards had done. "Fuck these sorry motherfuckers, man!" Lil Joe spat. "They can't just take all my shit like that. What the fuck kind of explanation was that anyway." He mimicked the guard who had told him why they had confiscated his investment materials. "'Prisoners aren't allowed to participate in the stock market.' Fuck that shit! Is that even a real regulation? I've never heard of no bullshit like that before!"

Because Lil Joe was extremely pissed over what had happened, Pete decided to go along with whatever he wanted to do. "Yeah, fuck them, man. They're full of shit. Look, Lil Joe, I'm down with whatever you wanna do, man. I mean, we can't let these bitches get away with that kind of bullshit!"

Lil Joe smiled. He knew what time it was. "Are you sure?"

Pete grinned wickedly. "Hell, yeah, fuck them!"

Lil Joe nodded. "All right, then, let's do this shit."

He and Pete began barricading their cell grill with sheets and blankets in order to prepare for a cell extraction. At that time, they were the only two camaradas in their pod, so neither of them were concerned about getting anyone else involved. Neither were they concerned about any administrative consequences since a few years earlier the prison disciplinary committee had acted to retain both of them in the S.H.U. on indeterminate status, claiming that they were security threats to the safety and security of the general prison population. That meant that neither of them would ever see a prison G.P. yard again, so they figured they had nothing to lose from cell extracting.

Later that afternoon, one of the guards walked the tier to make a count and wasn't able to see inside their cell because of the barricade.

He attempted to talk Lil Joe and Pete into uncovering their cell grill. "Come on, guys, you don't wanna do this shit!"

"Fuck you!" yelled Pete. "That's not what your mama said."

"Is that right?" the guard said, "well, then, have it your way. I'll go get the sergeant."

Pete grunted and yelled back, "Fuck the sergeant! Shit, if we're gonna have our way, then go get your mama, punk!" He and Lil Joe belted out in laughter as the angry guard stomped off muttering an assortment of four letter words.

Lil Joe and Pete had been around long enough to know what would happen next, so as they waited for the sergeant to arrive, they prepared themselves for the expected. They began tossing cups of toilet water on the barricade to soak the linen so it would absorb the pepper spray fumes. Then they wet their t-shirts and tied them around their faces from the nose down to keep from inhaling any fumes that might make it past the barricade.

Right around that time the sergeant showed up and instructed them to take down the barricade. "Hernandez, Porras! Remove the barricade now!"

"Fuck off, asshole," Pete hollered back.

The sergeant responded by opening the door's tray slot and spraying two large canisters of pepper spray into their cell. Then he repeated his earlier instructions. "Take down the barricade and cuff it up."

Lil Joe chuckled and yelled out, "Take down these boxers and cuff up this dick, motherfucker! As a matter of fact, why don't you just run up in here so I can kick another hole in your ass, punk!" Pete laughed out loud at Lil Joe's vulgar remarks, but then Lil Joe overheard the sergeant instruct one of the guards to retrieve the block gun. "Shit!" Lil Joe said, "Quick, Pete, grab your mattress. Here comes the bertha!" They hurried and pulled their mattresses from the bunks and then stood side by side, holding their mattresses in front of themselves as shields against the wooden projectiles of the block gun.

A few seconds later, they heard the sergeant's voice again. "Last warning. Take down the barricade and cuff up."

Neither Lil Joe nor Pete responded. Instead, they braced themselves for the block gun's impact. The first shot echoed with a loud boom, then a couple of wooden projectiles made their way past the barricade and ricocheted off the walls of the cell. The second and third shots quickly followed and then suddenly everything fell silent. Lil Joe listened intently until finally he heard the extraction team assembling outside the pod. "I think they're gettin' ready to come in." He hurried and dumped a container of shampoo on the floor in front of the door and lathered the area up with his hand to make it as slippery as possible. "There, Pete, that oughta take some of their advantage away. Make 'em lose their footing."

Pete raised his brow in astonishment. "Hell, yeah, man, that'll work." Just then they heard the sound of foot traffic and boots scuffling the floor in front of the door. "Here goes nothin'" said Pete seconds before their cell door slid open and six guards suited in riot gear rushed in yelling, "Get down!"

Lil Joe and Pete snatched up the first guard to make it past the barricade and slammed him to the floor, where they were able to kick him several times before the cell was full of baton swinging guards. Lil Joe and Pete fought hard, punching and kicking the uncoordinated guards for a couple of minutes before they were restrained, beaten, and taken to the S.H.U. clinic for a medical evaluation. But Lil Joe was satisfied. At least he got his get back for them taking away his investment materials without answering for it. His actions may not have amounted to much, but at least they were more than nothing. His dignity wouldn't allow him to just do nothing.

After the cell extraction, the guards split up him and Pete. They figured that the two of them together were too much trouble. Pete was moved to the violence control unit and Lil Joe was returned to the same cell that he and Pete had been living in. When Lil Joe returned to the cell, the first thing he noticed was that all of his personal belongings were scattered all over the place. The guards had tossed his cell and totally disrespected his property. Half of his things had ended up in the toilet bowl, including his family photos and address book. "Fuckin rat ass motherfuckers!" he muttered.

Although the guards' actions angered him, he wasn't surprised. He was very familiar with the retaliation tactics of the prison guards. After cleaning up the mess, Lil Joe sat back and thought about the events of the day. He knew that if he had had a chance of ever seeing a general population yard, it was gone now. Fuck it, he thought, there's nothing going on out there except extensive lockdowns anyway. He was just going to have to sit back and watch the solitary time soak up more of his soul.

A few months later, Lil Joe was able to roll over his money from his stock market account into two separate growth funds where he had a better chance of managing his money from within the confines of the prison. After he squared away his money affairs, once again he wanted to apply himself to something productive and decided to commit himself to getting a better education. He took advantage of a new G.E.D. course that the institution provided and earned a G.E.D. certificate. Shortly afterwards, he decided to take a paralegal course by mail. He paid for the course by using some of the money that Franky and Jimmy had been sending him. Within a year, he became a certified paralegal and earned a paralegal diploma.

Throughout his incarceration, and especially during his time in solitary confinement, Lil Joe maintained the attitude that just because his body was locked up, it didn't mean his mind had to be as well.

CHAPTER FOURTEEN

FOR A LITTLE OVER THREE YEARS, Franky and Jimmy had been working as legmen for a local speed and ecstacy dealer by the name of Ernie Ortiz. They met Ernie through a mutual acquaintance, an ex-con named Freddy Lerma. Freddy was a small time pusher for Ernie Ortiz and he approached Franky and Jimmy with a proposition to earn some cash acting as muscle for him.

The opportunity came at a trying time for both Franky and Jimmy. When they first got out of the Youth Authority, their intentions were to join the work force and do what they had to in order to make it and stay away from the kind of life that would lead them back into the system. However, after being laid off, let go, and even cheated out of money by a number of different employers, they became discouraged.

Freddy Lerma was aware of that and since he knew Franky and Jimmy were both young, vigilant, and trustworthy guys, he offered them a chance to make a lot of money. According to Freddy, Ernie Ortiz was a local high roller who had a good setup and treated his crew generously. At the time Freddy approached them with the proposition, Franky and Jimmy were unemployed, so they agreed to meet with Ernie Ortiz. Soon afterwards, they began taking on jobs doing various illegal activities for him.

At first Franky and Jimmy were content with what Ernie paid them for their work. However, as time progressed and their jobs began to get more risky, they felt that Ernie wasn't putting up enough cash for their troubles. Since they had been working for him for quite a while and had developed a trusting friendship with him, they decided to sit down with Ernie Ortiz and attempt to negotiate better positions for themselves within his crew. Unfortunately, that's when things got ugly. Ernie agreed to meet with them one afternoon at a local strip club where he frequently hung out. The club was owned by one of Ernie's top pushers and it was one of the few places where he actually felt comfortable. Paranoia was a big issue for Ernie. He had a lot of enemies and rival dealers who were looking to put him out of commission, so he had a hard time trusting anyone.

As time passed, Franky and Jimmy began noticing that Ernie's paranoia was worsening. They even suspected that he was addicted to his own product. Nevertheless, they kept their noses out of his personal business and did what he paid them to do.

When Jimmy and Franky arrived at the strip club that afternoon, they noticed that with the exception of a few alcoholic stragglers, the place was pretty much empty. As soon as they walked inside, they were met by a couple of bouncers who escorted them to a secluded booth in the back of the place where they had complete privacy. As they approached, Ernie stood up to greet them. "Hey, fellas, come have a seat and join me in polishing off this bottle of tequila," he said, extending his arms. He sat down and pointed to a half empty fifth on the table. He looked exhausted and stressed, his usual slick, neatly groomed black mane messed up and out of place. His brown, sleep deprived eyes were deeply set in wrinkled sockets, and his usually healthy frame appeared to be deteriorating. They noticed how loosely his neatly pressed Italian suit hung on his sickly looking body. He looked like he had lost at least twenty pounds since they had last seen him--two weeks earlier at a birthday party Ernie had thrown for one of his top dealers.

"Damn, Ernie, you look like you haven't eaten in a while. You doin' all right?" Franky asked as he slid into the booth next to Jimmy.

Ernie poured three glasses of tequila while he responded. "Who needs food when you got good tequila in your belly?" He lifted his glass. "Salud," he said and downed his drink.

"Salud," Franky and Jimmy said in unison as they downed theirs.

"So," Ernie said as he refilled all the glasses. "What can I do for you guys?"

Franky looked to Jimmy. They had decided to let him do the talking. "Well, Ernie, we don't wanna take up too much of your time," Jimmy said, getting straight to the point. Ernie nodded in acknowledgment. "It's just that lately, lately we've been taking on some risky jobs, like the warehouse hijacking job." Jimmy was referring to a job he and Franky had done for Ernie two months before when they robbed a warehouse full of ecstacy belonging to one of Ernie's main rivals. "As you know, things got a little hairy, and I got shot twice."

Ernie nodded again. "Yes, I recall. You guys did one hell of a job. It takes balls to do what the two of you do."

Jimmy cut in. "That's our whole point. We've been putting ourselves on the line to keep your business on top, and we feel that we've earned your trust and also more profitable positions within your crew."

Ernie immediately took offense. "So this is about money then? You fuckin' vatos think I owe you something?"

Franky and Jimmy were caught off guard. "Whatcha trippin' on, Ernie?" Jimmy said. "You act like we're tryin' to rob you or somethin'. We ain't tryin' to shake you down, man. You know us better than that."

Ernie smirked. "Let me tell you somethin'. I don't owe you thugs shit! Everything you have is because of me. I pulled you vatos outta the gutter. If it wasn't for me, where would you be now? Shit, I built my own setup from the ground up, and I took you two vatos in at a time when you didn't have nada! Now this is how you repay me, by trying to twist my fuckin' arm for more money? Fuck that!"

Franky and Jimmy hadn't expected Ernie to overreact like that, but they both knew nothing good would come from dragging the conversation on any further, so Franky cut in, "You know, Ernie, we apologize. We didn't mean to come off sounding ungrateful. Maybe we can just put this whole conversation behind us and move on. Obviously you have other matters to attend to so we won't waste anymore of your time."

Ernie sat back and stared at them in silence for a moment. Finally he smiled. "Okay," he said in a humbled tone, "it's forgotten. But you're right, I do have other business to attend to so I'll get back with you later."

Franky nodded. "All right, then, mas alrato [later on]." He and Jimmy slid out of the booth and made their way out to the parking lot.

Jimmy spoke first. "What the fuck was all that about?"

Franky shook his head in disbelief as he hopped in Jimmy's dark metallic green Hummer. He waited until Jimmy started the motor and pulled off the parking lot before he answered, "Something's up with that motherfucker! Where does he get off talking to us like we're some dumb dicks that don't know what's up?"

"Yeah, fuck that shit, man," Jimmy spat. "I got somethin' for that fuckin' tweaker son of a bitch!"

Franky shook his head. He knew what was running through Jimmy's mind. "Nah, Jimmy, we can't handle it like that, bro. Not this time."

Jimmy hissed, "Well, what the fuck, Franky, are we supposed to just let that fuckin' punk get away with that bullshit? We could take him out easy. Him and his two primo [cousin] bodyguards. Fuck them!"

Franky knew how Jimmy always lost his cool when he was worked up about something, but he could always find a way to get him to listen to reason and think logically. "Look, bro, I'm pissed off about this shit too. But killin' ain't the answer this time, man."

Jimmy took his eyes off the road for a moment to look at Franky. "So what then? We just act like that didn't just happen? We keep workin' for that motherfucker until we end up dead?"

"Nah, Jimmy, listen, man!" Franky sighed heavily and then continued. "Remember when we were in that auto body trade shop in the Youth Authority?"

"Of course I remember."

"Okay, then, so then you remember what we wanted to do when we got out. How we wanted to save up enough money to open up our own body shop and fix up old cars. Do you remember that?"

Jimmy smiled. "Yeah, man, I remember."

"Good. Then why don't we do it? Maybe this shit that happened today was a wake up call. You know? I mean, shit, we got ourselves into this because we didn't have anything else. But now, now we're doin' all right. There's no need for us to be greedy. We can't do this kind of shit forever."

Jimmy was silent for a moment while he pondered what Franky had said. "Look, Franky, I hear what you're saying, bro, but what that asshole had to say . . . " Jimmy's face twisted in anger. "I can't let that go."

"Come on, Jimmy, think about it. What did Ernie's sorry ass say that was so disrespectful that you can't get over it. Really, bro, he was obviously drunk and stressed out when he was wolfing that shit, but he didn't threaten us. He's no threat to us. Look at him. We both saw him today. The game's sucking the life out of him. He's on his way down anyway."

Jimmy shook his head. "Aw, man, I don't know, Franky. I think we made an enemy out of him today, and it's bad for our health to have an enemy like him. Somethin' tells me it would be a mistake to let this shit go. You know the law, bro--move first or die first."

"I know, Jimmy, but if we just hold off and do our thing, I think things will work out all right, and it's not like we don't know what to watch for. If we get a bad vibe comin' from his direction, then we'll down his fuckin' ass."

Jimmy thought about it for a moment. "Okay, suppose we do things like you suggest. I know we got some money stashed, but I doubt we have enough to open our own body shop just yet."

"Well, you're probably right. I was thinking about that myself. The way I see it, we can keep a better eye on Ernie from the inside." He shrugged. "Shit, we can take a couple more jobs just to get our money right, and if he doesn't make a move by then, more than likely he never will."

Jimmy snickered and looked over at Franky. "All right, man, you've sold me. But if I feel anything--anything, Franky, we take him out."

Franky nodded. "You got it, bro."

As it turned out, Franky and Jimmy did make an enemy out of Ernie that day, and his paranoia wouldn't allow him to overlook what had transpired. The fact of the matter was that Ernie feared Franky and Jimmy. He knew what they were capable of, and he wasn't about to chance becoming the next victim of their wrath. He also knew that it would be too risky for him to attempt to have Franky and Jimmy killed. Too many things could go wrong. Ernie knew that in order to get them out of the picture he was going to have to think of something foolproof, something that would get them out of his way and at the same time cover his own tracks.

CHAPTER FIFTEEN

A COUPLE OF WEEKS AFTER FRANKY and Jimmy's meet with Ernie had gone south, Ernie contacted them and asked to meet with them at the same place and time as before. Franky and Jimmy agreed to the meet, and later that afternoon they showed up at the club ready to talk things out. The club was as empty as it had been on their previous meet. However, Ernie was cleaned up and of sound mind. As soon as they approached his secluded booth in the back, he greeted them with open arms. "Hey, fellas, you're lookin' good! Please have a seat."

Once they were all seated in the booth, Ernie gestured for them to pour themselves a drink from the full bottle of tequila on the table. Both Franky and Jimmy politely declined with a hand gesture. "All right, then," Ernie said, "straight to business." He leaned forward with his elbows on the table and fixed his eyes on them. "Look, things got a little carried away the last time we met. I wasn't quite myself that day, and for that I humbly apologize. You two have contributed a great deal to my business, and I would like to show my appreciation and gratitude for your loyalty and hard work. So please accept my apologies. I am in debt to both of you."

Both Franky and Jimmy were a little bit wary of Ernie's sudden change of attitude. Nevertheless, they led Ernie to believe they weren't suspicious of him at all. "Ah, nah, Ernie," Franky said. "There's no need to apologize."

"Yeah," Jimmy chimed in, "it was all forgotten the moment we walked outta here."

Ernie leaned back in his chair, appearing to be more relaxed. Franky studied him for a moment, thinking, Either this guy is a great actor or he's genuinely apologetic. Ernie interrupted his thoughts. "Well, fellas, I'm humbled by your willingness to forgive so easily. Anyway," he took a deep breath and continued, "the other reason I called you was for business purposes. I gave a lot of thought to what you had to say the last time we talked." He paused for a moment to pour himself a glass of tequila. After filling his glass, he tilted the bottle towards Franky and Jimmy as an offering gesture, but they again politely declined.

"No, gracias. So what's the job?" Jimmy asked.

Ernie quickly swallowed his glass of tequila with a grimace and put the empty glass on the table. "Yes, the job. Well, as I was saying, I got to thinking about what you guys said, and the truth is, you vatos are good at what you do. I can't even imagine anyone else taking care of business like the two of you. But," he said and shrugged, "I understand your position, and I think I have a solution that will accommodate all three of us. As you guys know, lately I've been having problems with some of my shipments coming from down south being hijacked." He frowned. "Now obviously that's a problem I have to do something about."

Franky and Jimmy were aware that a few of Ernie's shipments had recently been hijacked by his rivals. They nodded in agreement and Ernie continued. "Anyway, moving shipments is a good paying job, a lot more than what you have been making. So here's what I propose. You two start moving bi-weekly shipments for me coming from down south and I'll pay you ten grand a piece for each delivered shipment. That way, you make more cash and I can rest easy knowing that my shipments are being protected by the best. You guys can even take on an escort if you want, and I'll pay him a quarter of what I'll be paying you." He leaned back and clasped his hands together. "So, fellas, do we have a business deal?"

Franky looked to Jimmy, who nodded in agreement. "Yeah, Ernie, we got a deal."

Ernie smiled. "Bueno, I'll contact you guys in two days with the necessary information about a shipment that will need to be picked up Thursday night."

"All right then," Jimmy said, "we'll talk to you then."

Franky and Jimmy were satisfied with the way the meet with Ernie had gone, and although they thought that Ernie's compromise and change of attitude worked out well for them, it didn't change their plans to go legit and open up their own auto body shop. In fact, since they had agreed to do it, they had been looking into making it happen as soon as possible.

Franky had already looked into what it would cost to lease a shop and buy the necessary equipment, and Jimmy was in the process of finding out what kind of licenses were needed and what kind of paperwork would have to be furnished. They were well on their way to putting their criminal lifestyles behind them and make their adolescent dreams come true. All they had to do was take on a couple more jobs for Ernie and they would have enough money to put their plans into effect.

For the next two days following their meet with Ernie, Franky and Jimmy prepared themselves for their next job. Jimmy prepared his Hummer for the trip and he and Franky decided not to take on an escort. Instead, they decided to drive to the pick up spot together in Jimmy's Hummer and Jimmy would then drive the shipment back solo while Franky escorted him in the Hummer. They figured that bringing someone else in was unnecessary. They worked good together and they knew and trusted one another's judgment and reactions in difficult situations. So they felt more comfortable keeping their team a duo.

Ernie called them with the pick up and drop off information Wednesday afternoon. They were to head out deep into the state's southern desert to the city of Blythe Thursday morning and contact a man by the name of Jerry by phone when they got there. He would then give them directions to the pick up spot. Once they picked up the shipment, they were supposed to drive it up and drop it off at an old storage warehouse in Rialto.

Franky and Jimmy prepared themselves for the possibility of trouble during the trip and loaded a secret compartment in Jimmy's Hummer with extra fire power and ammunition. Usually, they each only carried a couple of semi-automatic handguns, but with the threat of being hijacked, they decided to take a couple of heavy duty spray guns as well, so they added an Uzzi and a twelve-gauge street sweeper to their arsenal. Once they were fully prepared for the trip and had gone over their defensive plans in case of trouble, Franky and Jimmy split up for the night to tend to personal affairs. Jimmy headed off to a girlfriend's and Franky jumped into his cherried black 1984 El Camino and did the same.

Franky had been secretly seeing Ernie's youngest sister, Teresa, for about four months, and Jimmy was the only other person who knew about it. Franky didn't care too much for keeping his relationship with Teresa a secret, but it was her idea. She was afraid that if Ernie found out, he would react badly, which Franky figured was probably true. He knew how Ernie preferred to keep his personal life and his business life separate. As far as Franky knew, none of the people who worked for him even knew where he lived except for his two bodyguards, who also happened to be his twin cousins. Neither of the two humongous twins were ever more than a few feet away from Ernie at any given time.

But now Franky found himself in quite a dilemma. He was beginning to have real feelings for Teresa, and he had no idea how he was going to tell Ernie about their relationship, especially now that he was going to have to deliver the double whammy of their relationship and the news that he and Jimmy were retiring from their life of crime. He chuckled at the thought of how it would sound. Say, Ernie, Jimmy and I are retiring from the business, so you're going to have to find some other guys to take our places. By the way, I've been screwing your baby sister for the last four months. "Ha!" he laughed, thinking that maybe Jimmy was right and they would be better off if they just killed Ernie. "Yeah, Franky boy," he muttered, "you sure have gotten yourself in a bind this time."

Jimmy had warned him that getting involved with Teresa was a bad idea, and he knew it was true, but he couldn't help himself. He had been spellbound from the moment he first laid eyes on her. He still remembered everything about that night. It was Ernie's thirty-eighth birthday and his two cousins had put together a surprise party for him at one of his favorite hangouts, a downtown club owned by a good friend. Franky and Jimmy weren't even invited; they just accidentally crashed the party while they were out looking to have a good time. The club bouncers recognized them and let them into the private party, figuring they had been invited.

Apparently Ernie thought the same thing, because as soon as he realized they were there, he greeted them and thanked them for showing up to celebrate his birthday. Upon realizing that they had crashed the party, Franky and Jimmy decided to leave, but just as they were about to do so, Ernie asked them to stay to talk business after the party. So they stuck around and mingled among Ernie's family and close friends. Sometime during the course of the night while Jimmy talked with a young cocktail waitress, Franky made his way to the open bar at the other end of the club, and that was when he laid eyes on Teresa for the first time. She was standing in front of the bar holding a martini and looking off into the crowd of people on the dance floor as if she were searching for someone in particular.

At the time, Franky had no idea who Teresa was. All he knew was that he wanted to find out. He was absolutely stunned by her beauty, the way her knee-length red cocktail dress hugged the curves of her voluptuous, petite figure tightly, and how her wavy brown, shoulder-length hair complimented the honey-brown color of her eyes. Franky hadn't even realized that he was standing just a few feet in front of her gawking like a moron until her cute angelic face lit up with a smile and she asked, "Are you gonna come talk to me or are you gonna stand there like that all night?" That wasn't exactly the kind of first impression he liked to make with a woman, but he managed to make up for it with several hours of good conversation with her. He found out that Teresa was Ernie's younger sister, but he agreed to see her again when she suggested it. So, four months later, they were still seeing each other.

Franky shook off his reminiscences as he pulled up and parked along the curb in front of Teresa's house. As he approached the front door, Teresa opened it and stood in the doorway wearing a purple negligee and a tempting smile. "Hey, baby, it looks like I'm just in time," he said and scooped her up in his arms, walked inside, and kicked the door shut behind them.

CHAPTER SIXTEEN

EARLY THE NEXT MORNING, FRANKY LEFT Teresa asleep while he showered, dressed and left for Jimmy's place. When he arrived, Jimmy was ready to go, so they wasted no time getting on their way. By 10:30 that morning, right after rush hour was over, they were on the freeway heading south towards the Cochella Valley. They arrived in Blythe later that afternoon and after making a quick stop at a local gas station to clean up and gas up the Hummer, Jimmy made the phone call to their contact, Jerry. While he was on the phone, Franky bought a few snacks and made a quick visit to the restroom. When he came out, Jimmy was parked right outside waiting for him. "Did you get it all out?" he joked.

"Yep." Franky patted his stomach. "All clear."

Jimmy laughed and said, "Come on, let's go."

When Franky opened the door, he noticed that Jimmy had taken the street sweeper and Uzzi out of hiding and placed them on the back seat. "So we're all set, huh?"

"Yeah. The pick up spot is just a few miles from here."

"All right, let's do it," Franky said as he hopped into the back seat and began loading the guns.

When they arrived at the pick up spot a few minutes later, a tall, barrel-chested Indian with a head full of long grey hair stood in front of a fenced-in driveway smoking a cigarette. Jimmy parked the Hummer along the curb on the opposite side of the street and stepped onto the pavement. The big Indian swaggered over to greet them. "Hey, there, you must be Jimmy," he said with a friendly grin.

"Yeah, that's me. And this is my partner, Franky," he said as Franky walked around the back of the Hummer carrying both the street sweeper and the Uzzi.

The Indian's eyes widened. "Well, hot damn, you fellas sure did come prepared! Must of heard about the recent hijackings, huh?" Before they had a chance to respond, he continued, "Well, I'm Jerry. Nice to meet you fellas."

"Likewise," Jimmy said.

"All right then," Jerry said, "let's get you guys squared away." He gestured for them to follow him up the driveway towards a white cargo truck parked in front of a small warehouse garage. He directed them to the back of the truck and the open cabin. "There goes your ride." He pointed to the truck.

Franky and Jimmy peeked into the cabin to find it full of furniture and cardboard boxes. "What's all that shit?" asked Franky.

Jerry chuckled. "That's just a diversion in case the cops pull you over. You can tell them you're moving out of the county." He patted the bed of the cabin with his hand. "Now that's where the good stuff is at. You see, if you look carefully, you can see that the bed is about four inches thick." Jerry knocked on the bed. "It's hollow in between. I welded another bed on top of the original, leaving a good gap in between to store the goods." He grinned with pride as he explained. "I structured four trucks just like this one." He pointed to the thick metal railing welded across the end of the bed to cover the gap between the two separate beds. "All you have to do is remove this railing here to retrieve the goods."

Franky and Jimmy were impressed. "Damn," Franky said, "I would of never guessed it on my own."

Jerry smiled. "Yeah," he said, scratching his head, "but I don't get the reason for splitting the shipment in half. There was plenty of room in one truck for the whole load."

Jimmy looked at Franky with a suspicious frown. "Oh, yeah, Jerry," he said, "where did the other truck go?"

"Same place this one's goin'. A couple of guys came and picked it up around this time yesterday."

"Hmm." Jimmy smiled and patted Jerry on the back. "Well, thanks man. You've been real helpful. We'll take it from here."

"Well okay, fellas." Jerry handed the keys to the truck to Jimmy. "Here you go. You two have a safe trip back. Oh, and if you don't mind, could you lock the gate before you head out? The lock's loose on the gate there." He pointed to the fence.

"Sure," Franky said, "we'll take care of it."

"All right then. See you fellas." Jerry walked down the driveway and across the street to a dusty blue 1985 Cadillac and drove off.

As soon as he was gone, Jimmy turned to Franky and said, "So what do you think about this two shipments bullshit? It smells a little fishy to me, bro."

Franky nodded. "Yeah, I know what you're thinking, man. But before we jump to any conclusions, let's just think about it for a minute. We know that Ernie's been getting robbed lately along this route." Franky shrugged. "Maybe he split the shipments as a precaution. It's a logical explanation."

Jimmy clamped his jaw shut and exhaled a long, powerful breath through his nostrils. "I don't know, Franky. I mean, what you said makes sense, but my gut tells me something's not right, man."

Franky nodded. "All right, then, what do you wanna do?"

Jimmy stood silent for a moment collecting his thoughts. Finally he sighed, shaking his head. "What can we do? I mean, shit, all we can do is play this thing out and see what happens. Our only other choice is to make a move against Ernie on my hunch, and you're right, we can't just jump to conclusions and act."

"Okay, then we'll go along as planned and just stay on our toes." He paused for a moment giving Jimmy the chance to think it over. "Are you ready, bro?"

"Yeah." Jimmy sighed. "Yeah, I'm ready. We'll stop at that rest stop outside of Grand Terrace just like we planned. Just keep your eyes open, okay, Franky?"

"You got it, bro." Then he handed Jimmy the street sweeper and walked down the driveway towards Jimmy's Hummer with the Uzzi in hand cocked and ready to spray.

CHAPTER SEVENTEEN

THE DRIVE UP TO THE DROP off point was uneventful. Franky and Jimmy had stopped at a rest stop to rest and kill a couple of hours before they drove the last thirty minutes. They were both familiar with the drop off spot. On several occasions they had taken hijacked shipments to the old storage warehouse. When they finally reached the drop off point a little after 6 o'clock that Friday morning, the warehouse was already occupied by people awaiting their arrival. The doors at both ends of the warehouse were open and Franky and Jimmy could see people moving about as they approached.

Franky left the engine running as he parked the Hummer across the street from the back gate to the warehouse property where he had a good view of the entire area. Jimmy passed him and drove the cargo truck around to the front gates. Their plan was to drop off the truck and be on their way as soon as possible. Neither of them had a good feeling about the whole thing. Something about what the big Indian, Jerry, had said didn't sit right with either of them.

As soon as Jimmy parked the cargo truck inside the warehouse and stepped down onto the pavement, all hell broke loose. It was a raid. A dozen San Bernardino County sheriff's deputies swarmed the warehouse entrance with their guns drawn, yelling out orders that Franky couldn't make out from where he was. Before he even had time to think of a reaction, a gun battle broke out from within the warehouse. He heard several volleys of gunshots within seconds, and then he saw Jimmy make a break for it out the back entrance. Jimmy ran out firing shots over his shoulder with his Barretta while making his way towards Franky.

As soon as Franky saw Jimmy running in his direction, he gunned the Hummer, running in right through the chainlink fence to meet him halfway. He hit the brakes and brought the Hummer to a screeching halt several yards in front of Jimmy. Then he opened the passenger side door, yelling out, "Vamanos, Jimmy, come on!" But Jimmy didn't make it. Two of the deputies opened fire and shot him down just a few feet away from the Hummer. Franky saw his head explode as one of the deputy's bullets hammered into the back of his skull, blowing fragments of bone and brain matter into the air. "No! Fuck!" Franky yelled. He knew Jimmy was dead.

As soon as Jimmy's body hit the ground, Franky returned fire with the Uzzi, emptying the entire fifty-round clip in the direction of Jimmy's killers before punching the gas and driving the Hummer back into the street. Once he was a few blocks away, he dumped the Hummer in an alley and made his way towards the nearest main street. He knew that a police department helicopter would be looking for the Hummer soon, so he had to get as far away from it as possible.

Franky tossed the Uzzi in a dumpster behind a doughnut shop just before he spotted a city transportation bus coming towards him. He hurried off towards the bus stop in front of the shop to catch the bus and get away from the area. He took a seat next to the back door and his mind began racing. He couldn't believe that Jimmy was dead. "Fuck! Son of a bitch!" he yelled while he punched the empty seat in front of him. An elderly black woman sitting across from him gave him a frightened, wide-eyed look, which made him get hold of himself and plan his next move. He had already figured out what had happened and how it had happened. Ernie was a rat. He had set them up to get popped with the shipment. He knew that for a fact. Franky had worked for Ernie long enough to know that he had cops on his payroll, both the local P.D.'s and the county sheriff's department. So there was no way he wouldn't have known ahead of time that one of his warehouses was going to be raided. Ernie had planned the whole thing. He had planned to get rid of Franky and Jimmy by having them arrested for possession and transport of enough illegal narcotics to guarantee them at least a twenty-year sentence.

Except his plan didn't work out. Jimmy ended up dead and Franky was on the loose. Franky knew he had to move quick; it was only a matter of time before Ernie got word that his plan failed.

Franky got off the bus a couple of blocks from Teresa's house and walked the rest of the way there. He checked his watch when he got to Teresa's. It was ten minutes after seven. He knew she would still be asleep since she never got out of bed until at least noon. He also knew that she kept a spare key to her front door buried in a flower pot on the front porch. After he found it and let himself in, he made his way straight to her bedroom. When he walked inside, he stood at the foot of her bed for a moment staring at her while she slept. He felt bad that he was going to have to involve her in what he was about to do, but there was no other way. She was his key to getting to her brother.

"Teresa, wake up!" he yelled. "Come on, get up!" he said as he shook her leg.

She stretched her arms and yawned before propping herself up on her elbows. "What's going on?" she asked.

"Come on, we're goin' for a ride."

Teresa rubbed both of her eyes and yawned again. "A ride? What time is it?"

Franky lost his patience. "Come on, Teresa. Fuck! Snap out of it. Let's go!"

"Franky, why are you yelling at me? What's wrong?"

Franky sighed. "Look, Teresa, I don't have time to explain everything, but I need you to listen carefully. You have to get up and get dressed quickly, and then I need you to take me to your brother's house."

Teresa's eyes widened. "Why I can't take you there, Franky, you know that."

"Bullshit!" Franky yelled in frustration. "Just get the fuck outta bed and take me to your brother. Now!"

"Franky, stop yelling at me. Please just tell me what's wrong."

Franky knew that he was going to have to manipulate her in order to get her to drive him to her brother's house. "Okay, look, something went wrong with a job me and Jimmy took care of. Your brother's in danger. I have to get to him now."

Her eyes widened again. "Oh, God, should I call him first?"

"No! The cops could be listening."

"Okay, I understand. I'll hurry."

After Teresa got dressed, she drove Franky to a suburb on the north end of San Bernardino known as the Shannon Hills area. Franky instructed Teresa to park a couple of houses down so he could check the area for cops before he got out of the car. He had thrown in that extra part hoping it would keep her from asking him anymore suspicious questions.

When they came to Ernie's street, Teresa pulled her silver BMW along the curb two houses down from a large Spanish villa on the corner. Franky recognized Ernie's black Lexus SUV in the driveway before Teresa pointed to the house and said, "That's it."

"Good. Who else should I expect inside besides your brother and your cousins?"

Teresa shrugged. "Maybe Marlene, Ernie's girlfriend. Why?"

"I just need to know what I'm dealin' with." Franky pulled his twin .45 semi-automatic pistols from out of his waistband and cocked back both of their slides.

Teresa panicked at the sight of the guns. "Franky, you're scaring me! What's going on."

He saw the worry in her eyes and it hit a soft spot in his heart. He figured that he at least owed her an explanation for what he was about to do. He took a deep breath, then exhaled and looked her in her eyes. "Jimmy's dead, Teresa. Ernie set us up and Jimmy was killed."

Teresa's eyes widened at the realization of what was going on. "Oh, my God! No . . . " she shook her head. "No, Ernie wouldn't do that. It's a mistake."

That brought Franky's anger to the surface. "What the fuck are you talkin' about? You don't know shit about nothin'. Come on, get your ass outta the car. Let's go!"

Teresa began to act hysterical. "No, Franky, don't! You can't do this!"

Franky put his guns back into the waistband of his pants. "Fuck this shit!" He got out of the car and walked around to the driver's side and opened the door. "Get the fuck out!" he said, grabbing Teresa by the arm and yanking her out of the car.

"Franky, stop it, you're hurting me. Please," she pleaded, "stop this! Let me talk to Ernie. I know this is just a misunderstanding. Please, Franky!"

She glared at him with pleading brown eyes. Franky sighed. He knew the only way he would be able to pull off his plan was to be tough with her. Otherwise, he would be the one to end up dead. "Shut the fuck up, Teresa!" he said through clenched teeth. He grabbed her firmly by the elbow. "Let's go. Walk."

She tried to struggle loose from his grip. "No, Franky, let go of me!"

Franky yanked her arm hard, pulling her body into his. "Listen, Teresa," he whispered into her ear, "you need to calm your ass down. This is gonna happen regardless of how much you try to stop it. Jimmy is dead. You hear me, dead! So I don't give a fuck about how you feel right now." He spun her around to face him so she could see how serious he was. "Look at me, Teresa! Either you come with me quietly or I leave you dead right here on the fuckin' street"

Teresa understood just how serious Franky was, so she submitted without any further protests. Franky walked her all the way up Ernie's driveway and onto his front porch. "Okay, look, Teresa, just ring the doorbell when I tell you to, and don't act stupid. I don't want to have to shoot you." She fixed her hurtful gaze on him then nodded. "Okay, good," said Franky. He pulled both of his .45's out and stood to the left of the door out of view of the peephole. He had taken notice of the large window to the right of the door and figured that the living room was more than likely behind it. "All right, Teresa, now!"

Teresa hesitated for a moment, staring down at her feet as if she was lost in thought, but just as Franky was about to tell her again, she reached out and pushed the doorbell twice. A few seconds later, the door opened and one of her cousins greeted her cheerily. "Teresa!"

Franky didn't give Teresa time to say anything. He immediately stepped between her and her cousin and shot him in the forehead. He heard Teresa's scream and out of the corner of his eye saw her run off, but he wasn't worried about her. Before her cousin's body had collapsed to the hard wooden floor, Franky had moved past him and entered the living room where Ernie and his other cousin were seated on a large brown leather sofa. Before either of them had time to react,

Franky fired two shots into the face of Ernie's remaining cousin, killing him instantly.

Ernie stared at Franky in shock as he wiped his cousin's blood from his face. "Get up, you lousy cocksucker!" Franky spat.

Ernie slowly stood up with his hands to his face. "Look, Franky, you don't understand. I . . . "

"Shut up, you fuckin' rat piece of shit!" Franky yelled. "What makes you think I'll listen to anything you have to say?" Franky backed up toward the front door, stepping over the body of Ernie's cousin, and kicked it shut. He chuckled at Ernie's frightened demeanor. "It looks like your guard dogs were asleep on the job."

Ernie tried to speak again. "Come on, Franky, it doesn't have to be this way, man."

"That's where you're wrong, Ernie. It does have to be this way. It's because of you that my brother is dead, you fuckin' rat coward!"

"Please, Franky, don't shoot me," Ernie pleaded. "We can work this out."

Franky laughed. "Where's all that tough talk now, Ernie? Come on, die like a man <u>con ganas</u> [with balls)." Franky scoffed. "But don't worry, Ernie, I'm not gonna shoot you. No, I have something special planned for you." Franky took a quick glance around the house. "Where's your kitchen?"

Ernie's eyes were wild with confusion. "What? My kitchen?"

"Yeah, Ernie, your kitchen." Ernie hesitantly pointed to a doorway behind Franky. Franky smiled. "Good. Tell me, Ernie, have you ever heard of death by a thousand cuts?"

CHAPTER EIGHTEEN

As Franky was finishing up with Ernie's mutilated corpse, he heard a man's voice yell out over a bullhorn. "Mr. Mu_oz, this is the San Bernardino Police Department. We have the house complete surrounded. Surrender yourself now! Come out of the house peacefully and unarmed."

Franky grunted. "So that's what Teresa ran off to do," he muttered. "Like brother, like sister, huh?" He stood up and put the big kitchen knife on the counter next to his two .45's, then wiped his bloody hands on the front of his pants. "All right, my work is done here," he said as he took one last look at what was once Ernie. Then he made his way to the front door. He opened the door slowly and stepped out onto the front porch. He raised his hands in the air as he saw the small army of San Bernardino cops at the end of the driveway with their guns pointed in his direction.

Once they realized he was unarmed, two male uniformed officers approached him and instructed him to lie face down on the ground. As he complied, one of the cops handcuffed him. Then two other uniformed officers, one black male and one Caucasian female, passed by him with their guns drawn and entered the house. Just as the two cops who had handcuffed him had lifted him off the ground to escort him to one of the cruisers at the end of the driveway, the female officer ran out and vomited on the front porch.

Just then a heavyset plain clothes detective with a brown curly shag hairdo approached from the end of the driveway carrying a camera. "Well, it looks like you left a nasty mess in there, Mr. Mu_oz." When he got within a couple of feet, he said, "Now stand still," and began taking snapshots of Franky. "Okay, I'm finished," he said. "You guys can take him to the house."

As the two cops escorted him down the driveway to their police car, Franky saw Teresa standing a ways off talking with a detective. He made eye contact with her and held her gaze for a moment before he was put into the back of the cruiser and driven off to the police station.

CHAPTER NINETEEN

A FEW WEEKS LATER, LIL JOE received a letter from his mother breaking the bad news of Jimmy's death and Franky's arrest.

August 18, 2001

Dear Joseph

Hello, mijo. I hope that all is well for you and you are under God's loving care. Unfortunately, I'm writing you this letter to tell you some really bad news. Last night I received a phone call from Franky. He's in the San Bernardino County Jail. Anyway, he asked me to relay a message to you. He said to tell you that Jimmy was killed a couple of weeks ago in a shootout with the police, and later on that same day he was arrested. He said to tell you to be expecting to hear from him soon. Mijo, I'm so very sorry about Jimmy. It's such terrible news. I hope you are okay. I'm going to visit with Franky at the jail later on this week, and then I'm going to drive out to see you next weekend. I'll find out what I can about Jimmy from Franky and I'll let you know

> everything at our visit. I love you, mijo. Be good and I'll see you soon.
>
> Love always, Mom.

The letter came as a shock to Lil Joe and it took a moment for the news to really sink in. He saw that his mom's letter was dated a week earlier, so that meant she would be up to see him that weekend. He was anxious to find out how Jimmy ended up in a shootout with the cops and how Franky ended up in jail. He read the letter three times before finally setting it aside. For the next few days, all he could think about was Jimmy being dead. He could hardly wrap his mind around it. Although he didn't know the exact circumstances of what had occurred, he knew it had something to do with the kind of work that Franky and Jimmy had gotten themselves mixed up in.

The following Saturday morning, Lil Joe was called out for a visit. When he got to the visiting area, his mother was waiting behind the glass of their assigned visiting cell. Although he was happy to see her, the grief-stricken look on her face overshadowed his joy, reminding him of the purpose of her visit. After the guards removed the handcuffs through the door slot, Lil Joe sat down on the tiny wooden stool and picked up the telephone. "Hello, Mam_, you look well."

She gave him a halfhearted smile. "Oh, mijo, I'm so sorry about Jimmy!"

Lil Joe nodded. "I know, Mom. What do you know about what happened?" He didn't really expect her to know much, but he figured she would know enough to give him a good idea of what went down.

"Mijo, it's just so sad. I don't understand it." She had such a hurtful expression on her face that Lil Joe wanted to reach out and hug her, but he couldn't. The glass that separated them wouldn't allow it. "I know they both had it hard," she said, referring to Franky and Jimmy, "but they seemed to be doing so well. They always came by the house to see me and make sure I was okay. They're such nice boys."

She began to cry, and it killed Lil Joe to see her upset like that. It reminded him of a time he would rather forget. "It's okay, Mam_, please don't cry."

He sat in silence for a moment to give her time to regain her composure. "I'm sorry, mijo, I just can't help it. I think of you boys as you were as kids, having fun together and enjoying your youth. And now . . ." She searched the visiting booth with her eyes. "And now all of this. It's just so tragic."

Lil Joe knew it wasn't her intention to hurt him with her words, but nonetheless they were like daggers piercing his heart. "Do you know what happened, Mom?"

She nodded. "Yes, mijo, but not the whole story. I went to see Franky in the jail. He said to tell you that he has hired a private attorney and he will be pulling you down for court soon." The news didn't surprise Lil Joe. He expected as much. Franky would probably pull him down for trial as a character witness so they could talk and Franky could run him down with what happened.

Lil Joe's mom cut through his thoughts as she continued. "He said that he would explain everything to you then." She paused again. "Mijo, all that I know about what happened is that Jimmy was involved in a shootout with the police during some sort of a raid, and that was how he was killed. When I visited Franky, he told me it was probably better for me that I didn't know the whole story." She paused again for a moment and then with a worried look in her eyes, said, "Mijo, you're not involved in any of this, are you?"

"No, Mom, I don't know what happened," he assured her. "I'm just as surprised by the news as you."

His words seemed to comfort her and she looked somewhat relieved by his response. Throughout the remainder of the visit, she caught him up on all the family news. "Your brother just got engaged."

He smiled at the news. "Really? That's cool. Who is she?"

His mother bit her bottom lip. "I probably shouldn't of said anything because I know Marco was planning on writing to you and telling you the news in a letter, but it's exciting news and I can't help it." Lil Joe smiled at her happiness. He was glad to see her sadness replaced with joy. "Mijo, please don't tell him I ruined the surprise."

Lil Joe laughed. "I won't, Mom. I promise." He repeated his earlier question. "So who is she?"

"Oh, mijo, I'm sorry. Her name is Tina. She's a wonderful young woman and I think she's perfect for your brother."

Just then a guard passed behind his mother and announced, "Visiting hours are over in five minutes. Wrap it up."

"Well, mijo, it looks like it's time to go." She frowned. "Oh, before I forget, as you know Franky and Jimmy stopped by the house quite often to make sure I was okay." Lil Joe nodded. "Well, mijo, the last time, Jimmy gave your brother an envelope full of money and told him to give it to me on my birthday." She paused with her eyes wide. "Mijo, there was $7000 in it! I didn't spend any of it. I was planning on giving it back the next time they came by, but now . . . "

Lil Joe cut in. "Don't worry about it, Mom. Keep it; that's why they gave it to you."

"But mijo," she protested, "it's a lot of money."

Lil Joe smiled at her. "Mom, listen to me, okay?. With Marco getting married, the money will be useful to you. Besides, he'll probably make you a grandma soon, so keep it, okay?"

Evidently she liked his prediction that she'd soon become a grandmother because her face lit up with a smile and she dropped the subject. "Oh, mijo, I love you! Be good, okay? I want you to come home again and have a normal life."

He smiled. "Okay, Mam_, I'll be good. I love you too. Bye."

They put their phones down and she blew him a kiss and waved goodbye as she walked away.

When Lil Joe returned to his cell, he sat back and thought about what he'd learned from his mom regarding Jimmy's death. He couldn't quite figure out how Franky had been arrested, and the absence of information was eating at him. But there was nothing he could do about it. He was just going to have to wait until Franky pulled him down for court to find out what happened. He didn't have to wait very long. A few weeks later he received a consent form and a letter from Franky's attorney asking him to sign the form giving him permission to have him transferred to the county jail for Franky's trial. Lil Joe signed the consent form and mailed it back to Franky's lawyer.

Within two weeks, a tri-county transportation van picked him up and took him to the San Bernardino county jail. He left on a Tuesday morning and didn't arrive at the jail until Wednesday night. Once he was processed through Intake, he was taken to the high power lockdown module. After he arrived in the unit and got himself situated, Lil Joe asked around to see if anyone there knew Franky and where he was, but none of the prisoners knew anything about him. Lil Joe assumed that Franky was on one of the general population units and that he wouldn't be able to see him until court, or possibly an attorney visit, which turned out to be the case.

That Friday, Franky's lawyer pulled Lil Joe and Franky out at the same time for a lawyer visit. As soon as Lil Joe walked into the attorney visiting area, he recognized Franky. He was standing on the grill of his visiting cell door wearing a huge grin; he hadn't changed one bit. He looked exactly as he had the last time Lil Joe saw him except that he had grown a few inches and gained about thirty pounds.

The two deputies who had escorted Lil Joe to the visiting area put him in the cell directly across from Franky. Once they removed his handcuffs and left, Franky happily greeted Lil Joe. "Damn, bro, you sure blew up and stretched out! Look at you, man, you're like the fuckin' jolly green giant!"

Lil Joe couldn't help himself; he grinned like a boy virgin in a whorehouse. It had been so long since he and Franky had seen each other, but they seemed to have picked up right where they had left off like no time had passed at all. "It's good to see you, too, short shit!" Lil Joe said with a smile. But he quickly changed his expression. "Too bad it's under these circumstances."

Franky frowned. "Yeah, I know, man," he said, lowering his head in shame.

Lil Joe noticed a man in a suit sitting behind the glass on the other side of Franky's visiting booth reading from a stack of papers. He pointed to him. "What's up with the suit? Is that your lawyer?"

Franky took a quick glance behind him. "Oh, yeah, that's my lawyer, but don't trip on him, bro. He's just gonna sit there and do some legal research on my case while we talk."

Lil Joe nodded. "So what happened, man?"

Franky clenched his jaw and shook his head. "Fuck, man, it's still hard to swallow, you know?"

"Yeah, I know."

Franky sighed. "You know I'm facing a possible death penalty case, man. I killed all of those motherfuckers, bro. For Jimmy, I killed 'em all for Jimmy.

Lil Joe could see that Franky was deeply disturbed about what had taken place. "Talk to me, Franky. What happened, man?"

Franky sighed again. "It's a long story, bro." He shrugged. "But that's why I had you pulled down here. I knew you would wanna know everything." Franky ran Lil Joe down with the whole story, starting from the time he and Jimmy got out of the Youth Authority until the time of Jimmy's demise and his arrest.

When he finished, Lil Joe just stood there in silence for a moment while his brain processed all of it. "Damn, Franky, that whole trip is crazy, man."

Franky sighed and ran his fingers through his hair. "I know, man, but I got those motherfuckers, Lil Joe, I got 'em back."

"Yeah, homeboy, you got 'em back, bro."

"You know, Lil Joe, it's my fault that he's dead. Jimmy knew that Ernie was up to somethin' and I talked him outta dealing with Ernie when he wanted to."

Franky's words hit Lil Joe hard. "No, Franky, you can't take the blame for what happened. These kinds of things are bigger than you and me, bro. You did what you had to to make things right as a man, and you held the right people responsible for their actions. But you can't blame yourself for Jimmy's death. We're not that powerful, Franky. We don't decide life and death, man. We're all just puppets on a string--no more and no less."

Franky stared at Lil Joe for a moment, nodding his head while he took in what Lil Joe said. "Thanks, bro, I'll take your words to heart."

Lil Joe figured it would be a good idea to change the subject. "So how long before I have to go back to the Bay?"

"Aw, shit, I'm not sure, man. My lawyer's talking about putting off the trial for a while. He thinks if we let the case collect a little dust, I might be able to work a deal that don't involve the death penalty." Franky shrugged. "I suppose it's all about money. If I pay this suit long enough to drag this case out and waste the state's money, the D.A. will be more willing to put up a plea bargain just to be done with it."

Lil Joe grunted. "Yeah, that sounds about right. So I'll probably head on out real soon then. Well, shit, we might as well catch up on things before I'm sent back. Hey, man, I appreciate how you and Jimmy looked after my jefita while you were out there. I appreciate you guys looking out for me too."

Franky waved it off. "Nah, man, that was nothin', bro. We're family, man."

Lil Joe smiled. "That's right, Franky. Speaking of family, were you able to find your mom and Elsa out there?"

Franky frowned. "Yeah, I spent two months tracking them down when I first got out. But once I found 'em, it hit me. They didn't want anything to do with me, bro. They made that clear long ago, so I just left things as they were, you know? Why disrupt their lives after all that time?"

Lil Joe understood Franky's logic even though it was somewhat of a tragic story. But he knew that it was true that some things were better left alone.

Lil Joe and Franky's visiting in was short lived. Franky's attorney was able to postpone his trial like he had planned, and since it was postponed indefinitely, Lil Joe wasn't allowed to stay in the county jail. However, he and Franky were able to see each other twice more at lawyer's visits before transportation came to pick him up. During their last visit, Franky promised Lil Joe that he would bring him back down if his case made it to trial.

Altogether, Lil Joe spent ten days in the San Bernardino County Jail before the tri-county transportation van came to pick him up and take him back to Pelican Bay. Since his mind wasn't preoccupied with stressful thoughts of Franky and Jimmy, he was able to enjoy the ride back, especially when the van stopped at the Ventura County jail to make a pick up. As the young driver pulled the van into the Intake and Release area, his partner, a young black man, turned towards the plexiglass divider and hollered into the back of the van, "Hey, Hernandez, we're gonna pick up some company for you! She'll be riding with you all the way up to Humboldt County."

Lil Joe was glad to hear he would have someone to talk to along the long drive up and was especially ecstatic to hear that it was a female. It had been a long time since he had talked with a woman. He pretty much expected her to look like the ones he had seen while attending court in the San Joaquin Courthouse, but that wasn't the case. When one of the guards opened the side door of the van, Lil Joe was caught by surprise when he saw how pretty the young woman was. As she struggled to step into the van while restrained with leg and waist chains,

Lil Joe admired her beauty. The first thing he noticed was her long, straight black hair and the golden brown tone of her face. As she got into the van, she smiled at Lil Joe, revealing beautifully shaped full lips and gleaming white teeth.

She sat down right next to Lil Joe and met his gaze with friendly brown eyes. "Hi, my name's Patience," she said in a soft, feminine tone. "I like your face. What's your name?"

Lil Joe couldn't help but smile at her delightful directness. "My name's Lil Joe. Nice to meet you, Patience."

She smiled again and shyly looked away towards the side door of the van as the black transportation guard yelled inside, "You two be good back there, okay?" before closing and locking the door.

Lil Joe waited until they were on the road before he sparked up a conversation with Patience. "So, Patience, huh? That's a unique name."

"Yeah, I know." She smiled. "I hear that a lot."

"Is there a story behind it?"

"Actually, there is. I was born a week and a half late, so my dad figured the name would suit me."

Lil Joe smiled at her again. He was really enjoying being in her company. He wasn't sure whether it was just because he hadn't been in the presence of a woman in so long or if it was her style, but he found himself drawn to her.

"So," she asked, "where are you headed, Lil Joe?" She wrinkled her brow. "And why do you go by the name of Lil Joe? There doesn't seem to be anything little about you." She looked him over with curious eyes.

He grunted a muffled laugh at her flirtatious manner. "You're just a little firecracker, aren't you."

"When I wanna be," she teased.

Lil Joe nodded. "My dad is Joe Senior, so instead of calling me Junior, my family always called me Lil Joe."

"Oh," Patience said, "I get it. So where are you on your way to?"

Lil Joe sighed. "I'm on my way back to prison from being out to court."

"What prison?"

"Pelican Bay."

She raised a brow. "Oh, I've heard of the place." She looked him up and down. "You don't look like some big mean killer to me."

Lil Joe smiled at her bluntness. "Well thanks, that's good to hear."

He and Patience spent hours talking and getting to know each other during the day and a half ride. Lil Joe shared his story with her, explaining how he had ended up doing so much time but not including all the unnecessary details. In return Patience ran Lil Joe down with her story and how she ended up in trouble with the law. She was a twenty-four year old Mexican/Yaqui Indian who was born in San Diego but raised in the small northern California town of Watsonville, where her family moved when she was just six. According to Patience, she began getting into trouble with the law when she was a teenager. She started using drugs and hanging out with the wrong crowds, which eventually landed her in jail on numerous drug possession charges. By the time she was nineteen, she had already been in jail four times, twice as a juvenile and twice as an adult.

She claimed to have been clean for three years prior to her most recent arrest, but she relapsed when she got involved in a relationship with a small time speed dealer who recently hung her out to dry. According to Patience, they were living together in Humboldt County when the local police raided their house and found a substantial amount of bathtub crank and the materials to make it in their basement. Both of them made their bail at their arraignment using money from their illegal sales. However, three days after she made bail, Patience was informed by her attorney that the district attorney's office had approached her boyfriend with a deal. The deal was for him to finger her as the dealer and put all the blame on her in exchange for first offense probation instead of jail time. Since Patience had a record of narcotics possessions and her boyfriend had never been arrested before, the district attorney knew that Patience would receive more time if convicted by herself as opposed to being prosecuted as a co-defendant.

Patience's attorney was aware of that fact as well and informed her that if her boyfriend accepted the deal, she would be looking at a lengthy sentence in a women's correctional facility. He suggested that she beat her boyfriend to the punch and agree to testify against him. However, that wasn't her style. She couldn't bring herself to stoop to that level. Instead, out of fear that her boyfriend would accept the district attorney's deal, Patience skipped out on her bail and fled to Ventura County to stay with her older sister and brother-in-law, where eventually she was arrested on an outstanding warrant.

Patience explained to Lil Joe that just two days earlier her attorney from Humboldt County had come to visit her at the Ventura County Jail to let her know that her boyfriend did accept the D.A.'s deal, and that she would be returning to Humboldt County to face the charges as a single defendant.

Lil Joe wasn't surprised by the story. He had heard plenty of others just like it, but he couldn't help but think of how much of a coward Patience's boyfriend was for doing what he did.

After several hours of conversation, Patience had talked herself tired. "I'm gonna take a nap. Put your back against the van so I can use you as a pillow."

Lil Joe readjusted his position and leaned his back against the wall of the van. Then Patience nuzzled herself against his chest and went to sleep. Lil Joe was a little drowsy himself, but he wasn't able to fall asleep. He hadn't had a woman that close to him in a long time, and he had never had that kind of non-sexual intimacy with a woman, not even in a prison transportation van. The feeling was something new to him, and he didn't want to miss it by falling asleep. Instead, he sat there and watched Patience nap comfortably with her body pressed against his, and for a short time, Lil Joe was able to escape the reality of his life and enjoy another part of life that was unknown to him.

Before nightfall, the guards made a stop in a small town in central California to gas up and get something for all of them to eat and to make a quick restroom call. They pulled into a small mini-mart/gas station and parked right next to the restroom. While the black guard escorted Patience to the restroom and waited outside the door for her, his partner stood just outside the van's open side door and attempted to make small talk. "So, Hernandez, you two sure looked cozy back there." He smiled at his own remark. Lil Joe didn't say anything in return, so the guard quickly avoided an awkward silence. "Hey, we don't give a shit about that, man. Neither me or my partner are hard asses. We're just two guys collecting our minimum wage, man."

Lil Joe could tell the guy was sincere, but he wasn't accustomed to talking about such things with guards so he just smiled and nodded, hoping it would be an acceptable response. At that moment, Patience hobbled out of the restroom and made her way toward the van, greeting him with a smile as she approached. "It's all yours," she said as she stepped into the van and sat down in another seat so he could get out easily.

After Lil Joe finished using the restroom and got back in the van, the guards pulled the van around to the front of the mini-mart to gas up. While one of the guards filled up the tank, his partner hollered through the plexiglass divider, "Well, down the street we got a McDonald's, a Burger King, and a Carl's J.R. Which one do you guys want for dinner?"

Lil Joe looked to Patience. "I like Burger King," she said.

Lil Joe nodded. "Did you hear that?" he hollered to the guard.

"Yep. Burger King it is."

After gassing up and making a quick run through the Burger King drive through, they were back on the road. While Lil Joe and Patience ate their double cheeseburgers and French fries, the white guard yelled out, "Hey, you guys, in about three hours we're gonna make a stop in Sacramento and you guys will be switching vans. Two other drivers will take you the rest of the way."

Lil Joe had figured as much. They had done the same thing on his way down from Pelican Bay. "Hey," he yelled back, "how about letting us get some music back here?"

The black guard yelled back, "We got oldies and rock and roll. Which do you wanna listen to?"

"What oldies do you have?" asked Patience.

"I got the Dells," the black guard replied.

"I love the Dells," Patience said.

Lil Joe hollered out, "Put the Dells on."

The black guard gave him a thumbs up and a few seconds later music from the Dells blasted through the speakers in the back of the van. Patience's face lit up with happiness. "Oh, I love this song," she said as she sang along, "The love we had stays on my mind." She looked at Lil Joe with smiling eyes and Lil Joe thought, Wow, this girl's so full of life even though she knows that many struggles lie ahead of her. He appreciated her spirit and it made him realize how the events of his life had cast such a dark shadow upon his. As he sat and watched her sing and smile, Lil Joe silently pledged to himself that he would use her as a reminder not to allow his spirit to fall into a dark pit.

As nightfall came and it darkened within the van, Patience snuggled up to Lil Joe once again. "I can't believe how patient you've been with me," she said, smiling up at him.

Lil Joe wrinkled his brow. "How do you mean?"

She laughed. "Come on, what are you, some kind of boy scout?" she teased. "You gotta have more will power than any man I've ever known."

Lil Joe knew what she was talking about. "Is that so?"

"Yeah, that's so. I would of expected a man who's been locked up as long as you to of been all over me by now."

"Yeah, well, just because I've been down a long time doesn't mean that I've lost my manners."

Patience smiled up at him. "You wouldn't know that I was flirting with you if it was tattooed on my forehead. Kiss me, Lil Joe."

Then she raised her lips to his and they kissed heavily for at least ten minutes before Patience pulled back and said, "I have an idea." She reached down and unbuttoned the bottom of Lil Joe's jump suit and pulled out his manhood. Lil Joe was hard as a rock. Patience gave him a wink and then positioned herself in the spooning position alongside him and managed to wiggle herself free from the bottoms of her two piece jump suit. Once she pulled the bottoms and panties down past her waist chains, she curled her legs up into the seat and Lil Joe positioned himself behind her.

Lil Joe was so caught up in the moment that he didn't even bother to look and see if the guards were paying any attention to them. He cuddled up next to Patience and entered her from behind. Her warmth and the caress of her buttocks against his pelvis was enough to send him into climax, but he held back as long as he could. Then he spent himself inside her twice before they straightened themselves out and fell asleep nestled close together. They were awakened soon after by the black guard hollering out, "Wake up back there, it's time to change vans."

His partner pulled the van into a large garage and parked next to an identical van with a blonde female guard standing next to it smoking a cigarette. As soon as the guards transporting Lil Joe and Patience stepped out of their van, the blonde's Hispanic partner made his presence known. He walked around from the other side of the van carrying a clipboard with paperwork attached and handed it to the black guard. His partner opened the side door and walked over and opened the door of their van. "Come on out, guys. Your new ride awaits," she said, gesturing toward her van.

Lil Joe and Patience slowly stepped out of the first van and into the other. The new van was empty, which Lil Joe was grateful for. That meant that more than likely he and Patience would be alone together the entire trip up to Humboldt. After the black guard and his partner signed Lil Joe and Patience over into the custody of the new transportation team, the white guard saluted Lil Joe and gave him a wink through the window of the van before leaving. Lil Joe chuckled to himself, figuring that the guard must have seen him and Patience doing their thing in the back of the van.

As soon as their old transportation guards drove off, their new ones followed suit. They drove the remainder of the night, not stopping until early the next morning when the blonde guard pulled into a gas station for gas and to allow Lil Joe and Patience to use the restroom. Afterwards, they went through a Burger King drive through for breakfast for Lil Joe and Patience and got right back on the road.

A couple of hours later, the blonde guard hollered out into the back of the van, "We'll be arriving at Humboldt County in about an hour!"

Instantly Lil Joe's and Patience's moods changed to a sad reality as their time together was quickly coming to an end. Patience snuggled herself close to Lil Joe and rested her head on his chest while they sat in silence. A few minutes later, Patience broke the silence, saying in her gentle, little girl voice, "You know, as funny as this might sound, I think these past two days were the two best days I've ever spent with a man considering the circumstances."

Lil Joe chuckled.

"You're right, that's pretty funny." Patience smacked her lips and pulled her head away from his chest. "But don't laugh, it's true," she said in a hurt tone and with a painful look in her eyes.

That look hit him like a punch in the gut. "I'm sorry, I didn't mean to hurt your feelings."

Her hurt expression quickly changed to a smile. "Admit it, Lil Joe, I got under your skin."

Lil Joe held her gaze for a moment and then nodded. "Yeah, Patience, you did," he sincerely agreed.

Satisfied with his response she leaned back against him and kissed him. Lil Joe looked towards the front to see if either of the guards were paying any attention to them. They weren't. He kissed Patience back passionately, holding nothing back. For all he knew, she could be the last woman he would ever kiss. They kissed each other as if they were trying to make sure that neither of them would forget about the other. Then suddenly Patience pulled back, wearing a naughty looking grin. "You're never gonna forget about me, Lil Joe," she said. Then she slouched down in her seat so that she could reach his crotch. As soon as she had freed his manhood from his jump suit, she crouched down and took him into her mouth.

"Aah, son of a bitch," Lil Joe muttered as he sat back in bliss while Patience gave him a marathon blow job. She finished him off just minutes before they arrived at the Humboldt County Jail.

The guard pulled the van into a large garage and parked in front of a door. As soon as she cut off the van's engine, her partner got out and opened the side door. "Come on, Sosa, we're here. Let's go," he said, waving for Patience to step out of the van.

Patience gave Lil Joe a sad look and slowly slid out of her seat and stepped out of the van. Before walking away, she turned back and said, "Maybe if life is good to us, we'll meet again, Lil Joe."

Lil Joe gave her a halfhearted smile. "Yeah." He nodded. "You take good care of yourself, Patience."

CHAPTER TWENTY

IT WAS BACK TO REALITY FOR Lil Joe as the van parked inside the prison's checkpoint. While the duty guards inspected the van, Lil Joe stared out the window at the grey, gloomy day that surrounded him. The past two weeks already seemed like a distant memory as his eyes searched over the gun towers and razor wired electrical fences hung with signs that read "No Warning Shots! Lil Joe grunted and thought, Yeah, thanks for the warning.

After the gate duty guards finished inspecting the van, they waved it through past the second gate and onto the prison compound. Lil Joe sighed as the blonde driver pulled the van down into the S.H.U. pit and parked in front of the back door. "You're home!" she yelled out cheerfully as if it were something to be excited about.

"Yeah, lucky me," Lil Joe said with sarcasm. Once past the S.H.U. intake booth, Lil Joe was placed in a holding cage in the S.H.U. committee area, where he waited for a few hours until the guards could find him a cell. Finally he was taken to a cell block on the "D" facility of the S.H.U. and celled up with a con with the nickname of Speedy.

Speedy was a thirty-two year old Salvadorian who had been in the S.H.U. only three months. However, he had been incarcerated for a little over six years before being placed in the S.H.U. indeterminately for being labeled a prison gang associate.

Lil Joe was familiar with the departmental process. He had helped several convicts file appeals on the administrative policy which allowed the administration to house prisoners in the S.H.U. indefinitely based on bogus prison gang affiliation labels. As far as Lil Joe was concerned, the policy was unjust. Convicts who were labeled as prison gang affiliates by the Department of Corrections were deemed a threat to the safety and security of the general population and were forced to live in solitary confinement until they died or were paroled or debriefed. Which meant that once a prisoner was labeled a prison gang affiliate, whether it was based on unreliable information or not, the only way out of the S.H.U. other than parole or dying was to snitch on other convicts and their illegal activities associated with a prison gang.

Although there were many problems with the policy, perhaps the most disturbing was that the majority of the convicts who were housed in the S.H.U. were victims of the corrupt policy, and even more shocking, the majority of them had been labeled prison gang affiliates by confidential statements given by other prisoners. It was an insane policy that many convicts were challenging in both the state and federal courts. However, the policy had already been in effect for almost twenty years and showed no promise of change any time in the near future.

Lil Joe had helped Speedy put together a state writ of habeas corpus challenging his indeterminate placement in the S.H.U., but when it was denied all the way through the California Supreme Court, Speedy became discouraged and gave up even though Lil Joe offered to help him get a federal writ into the federal courts.

After several months had gone by following the denial of his writ, Speedy began showing signs of mental deterioration. He began to sleep away most of the day and all night, and he often became irritable for no apparent reason. Lil Joe had been around long enough to recognize what was happening to Speedy, so he attempted to help him overcome his depression by finding ways for him to occupy his time and get his mind off the solitude. He did so in the hope that Speedy would be able to pull through and maintain his sanity. However, Speedy chose another way to escape the grips of the S.H.U..

One afternoon while Speedy was on the pod's recreation yard, Lil Joe was in their cell catching up on some letter writing when one of the unit floor officers came onto the tier to pass out the incoming mail. As he passed Lil Joe's cell, he looked inside and then slid a magazine and a piece of paper under the door. Lil Joe got up from his bottom bunk area where he had been writing a letter to his dad and strolled over to the cell door to retrieve the mail. As he picked up the magazine, he saw that the piece of paper on top was a committee chrono for his cellie. But just as he was about to place it on top of Speedy's bunk, something typed on it caught his eye. The word "drop out" was printed next to Speedy's gang status.

Lil Joe was well aware of the meaning of the phrase. There was only one way for a convict labeled a prison gang affiliate to be determined a gang drop out, and that was by debriefing. Lil Joe shook his head in disgust as he read the whole chrono word by word. After he finished, he crumbled it up and flushed it down the toilet. It had confirmed what he was already thinking--that Speedy was a rat. He had debriefed earlier in the month when he attended a disciplinary committee. "Fuckin' punk!" Lil Joe muttered. He checked the clock on his TV to see how much time he had before Speedy would come back from the yard. It was 3:45 P.M. He had only half an hour to decide how he was going to handle the situation.

There was no way he was going to allow Speedy to stay in the cell with him, and there was no way he could just let him walk out of the cell either. It really wasn't much of a dilemma; he knew what he had to do. Even though he wasn't affiliated with any prison gang, he still had an obligation as a stand-up convict to deal with his cellie. The convict laws were universal. All snitches, child molesters, and rapists were dealt with in the same way. But it was no skin off Lil Joe's back. Killing Speedy wasn't going to be a problem for him. He despised snitches, especially jail house snitches. He had no compassion for anyone who chose to live their life as a criminal and then turned around and snitched on others to avoid punishment. He had absolutely no respect for people like that, and when it came to jail house snitches, the way Lil Joe saw it was that life in prison was hard enough as it was without having some rat humping the man's leg and making things worse for everyone.

Lil Joe scrambled to come up with an idea on how to deal with Speedy. At the time he didn't have a knife or a razor blade, and he knew he couldn't waste any time trying to acquire one. So he looked to the shoestrings in his shoes. Well, he thought, they'll have to work. He quickly pulled his shoes off and unlaced them. Then he put his shoes under his bed in the back of his locker. Next he checked the clock again. Speedy would be returning from the yard in ten minutes.

Lil Joe twisted both of the shoe strings together to strengthen the homemade garrote. Then he lifted his t-shirt and loosely tied it around his waist. Lil Joe had never used a garrote on anyone, and although he stood half a foot taller than Speedy and outweighed him by at least fifty pounds, he still didn't underestimate the guy. He was well aware of the kind of physical strength a man could summon when fighting for his life. He was definitely going to need the advantage of surprise to pull it off.

When Speedy came back from the yard, Lil Joe sat on his bunk and pretended to be interested in something on television. "Wow, it's cold out there," Speedy said as he rinsed his hands off in the sink.

"Is that right?"

"Yeah, man. Say, Lil Joe, you wanna get a game of chess in when you're finished with your letters?"

Lil Joe looked to the half written letter on his bunk. "Uh, yeah, sure."

"All right. Despensa, I gotta piss." Speedy turned his back to Lil Joe to stand over the toilet. Lil Joe knew that was as good an opportunity as he was going to get so he quickly lifted his t-shirt and untied the garrote from around his waist. He then quickly wrapped the ends around his palms for grip. Just as Speedy was finishing up, Lil Joe crept up behind him and tossed the garrote around his neck and jerked his arms back hard, tightening the reins.

Speedy immediately began to panic and dig his fingers into the flesh of his neck in an attempt to free himself fro the garrote. He began making loud retching, gargling sounds so Lil Joe tried to pull him away from the cell grill to keep the guards from hearing him. But Speedy put up a hard fight and when he realized that Lil Joe was too strong for him, he began kicking the cell door in attempt to get the guard's attention. In response, Lil Joe yanked back on the reins as hard as he could to pull Speedy away from the door, but the garrote snapped in half near his right hand. "Shit!" Lil Joe cursed as he tossed the broken garrote to the floor and began kicking Speedy repeatedly while he lay balled up on the cell floor gasping for air.

The unit guards heard all the ruckus and immediately responded. A few seconds later, half a dozen guards ran into the pod and straight to Lil Joe's cell. "Get down! Get down!" Several guards repeated the order several times, but Lil Joe was too worked up with adrenalin to stop. He ignored their orders and continued to assault Speedy until the guards finally soaked him with a gallon of pepper spray through the tray slot.

After Lil Joe discontinued his assault and allowed the guards to handcuff him, he and Speedy were taken to the S.H.U. clinic for medical treatment. Soon after a nurse washed the pepper spray from Lil Joe's eyes, he was discharged and returned to his cell. When he got there, he found that the guards had already removed all of Speedy's property from the cell and had searched through all of his belongings.

After cleaning up the mess the guards had left, Lil Joe took a bird bath and washed the rest of the pepper spray off his body.

While he was being evaluated at the clinic, Lil Joe had missed out on dinner, so after his bird bath he got into his canteen stash and ate a bag of crackers. Then he sat back and finished the letter to his dad before the guards came by to pick up the outgoing mail.

CHAPTER TWENTY-ONE

ALMOST A YEAR AFTER THE INCIDENT with his cellie, Speedy, Lil Joe received a letter from Franky in which he explained that he had recently taken a plea bargain deal that didn't include the death penalty. According to Franky, after a long investigation and a little help from his ex-girlfriend, Teresa, the district attorney was able to link him to the warehouse shootout with the county sheriff's department. However, the D.A. didn't have quite a strong enough case to prosecute him for that. So the district attorney's office offered to exclude the death penalty if Franky admitted his involvement in the warehouse shootout and agreed to plead guilty to all the charges against him.

So at the end of the day, everyone got what they wanted. Franky managed to avoid the death penalty and instead received a sentence of two hundred years to life, and the D.A. was able to close two high-profile cases and add another notch to his belt. Personally, Lil Joe thought that the sentence was a bit excessive and a waste of the state's money since it meant that Franky would be eligible for parole when he was two hundred thirty years old.

Lil Joe laughed at the idea. Yeah, he thought, I'm sure he's looking forward to that. Then he frowned, wondering if Franky would still think taking the deal was better than the death penalty after he had twenty years of hard time behind him.

A month later, Lil Joe had a little luck with his own legal matters when he received a notice from the Del Norte County district attorney's office rejecting his referral for prosecution for attempting to murder Speedy. The reason cited on the notice was that there was no material evidence available to support the charges. Apparently whoever it was that searched Lil Joe's cell after the incident absentmindedly disposed of the shoestring garrote, mistaking it for trash. So once again Lil Joe managed to dodge another bullet.

Later that same year, Lil Joe received a letter from Marco enclosing some pictures of his newborn baby girl. The news that he was an uncle made Lil Joe's entire year. After reading the letter, he just sat on his bunk and stared at the pictures for hours, admiring his beautiful baby niece, Rebecca. He was amazed at how much love he felt for her from just looking at the photos. He could hardly wait to meet her in person and that thought made him realize how close to parole he was.

He was thirty years old and just around the corner from being released back into society. He began to give everything a lot of thought. The idea of being a free man seemed strange. He had been just a thirteen-year-old boy when he first began his journey through the treacherous California penal system and now, almost eighteen years later, he was just about ready to step back into the free society. And he had no idea what to expect from the outside world.

Throughout Lil Joe's time in prison, he had done many things to prepare himself for life on the outside. He was self educated and mentally strong. However, something deep down inside made him feel uneasy about it all. Although he had never admitted it to himself, the truth was he had never really expected to make it out. But now that the reality of freedom was so close, it made him realize just how unprepared for the outside world he really was. After all, he had grown up on the inside and was accustomed to life on the inside. Prison had molded him into a man and he knew how to live and survive in prison. As much as he despised the place, it was his home, or at least the only home he was used to. He knew nothing of the world beyond the prison walls, and it bothered him deeply knowing he feared a positive change in his life.

After the incident with Speedy, Lil Joe had been placed on single cell status by the disciplinary committee, so when he felt like socializing with somebody, he would usually call his neighbor, Luie, over the tier for a bit of conversation. Luie was an old Mexican convict originally from the City of Santa Paula in Ventura County. He was also one of

Lil Joe's favorite old timers. He had character and Lil Joe learned a lot from him.

Luie had been in prison since 1967 when he caught his first offense for a robbery at the age of nineteen. His original sentence was a twelve-year stretch, but just like many other convicts, Luie caught more time when one of prison's uncontrollable situations occurred. Near the end of his original sentence, he got into a knife fight with another convict and managed to salvage his own life while taking another. In the end it didn't matter much because he was prosecuted for murder and sentenced to life in prison.

Lil Joe knew how that much time in prison could destroy a man, and he also knew how bitter and angry at the world a man could get after being locked in a cage for so long. However, that wasn't the case with Luie. In fact, Luie was one of the smartest and most level headed individuals Lil Joe had ever met, and he also possessed an excellent sense of humor.

Lil Joe shared his concerns about paroling with Luie, and in return Luie shared his thoughts. "Youngster," he said, "you have a lot of things going for you, man. You're still a young man and you're bright and have a sense of direction. I can tell from our conversations that you want something more out of life than this. Am I right?"

"Yeah, Luie, you're right, man."

"Well, then," Luie continued, "all you have to do is stay focused, man. You have an opportunity to leave all this behind you. That's more than most of us in here will ever have. Plus, you still have a family out there who loves and supports you and has stuck with you throughout all this. That's rare, man."

"Yeah," Lil Joe agreed.

"Look, youngster, your family will help you adjust and get on track. Plus, like I said, you're bright. You'll figure out what to do once you get used to being out there. Most motherfuckers paroling from outta here act like they got a fuckin' hard on for this place. Like they can't wait to come back here. Shit, I don't know why because there ain't nothin' in here but this fuckin' tomb we live in. Hey, man, just don't get discouraged. Things might not be too easy at first, but hey, they could be a lot worse. At least you're not some dope fiend that's gonna get out chasing some fuckin' needle. You know what I'm saying?"

Lil Joe smiled at the old man's words. "Yeah, Luie, I do. That's why I like talkin' to you."

Satisfied that he had gotten through to Lil Joe, Luie lightened up the conversation with a little bit of his raw humor. "Shit, youngster, do you know what I would do if they let me out right now?"

"Nah, Luie, what would you do?"

"I'd take my old crusty ass out there and find a good young woman to love, and I'd hump her like crazy until the day I died."

Lil Joe burst out in laughter, as did the rest of the cons in the pod. Luie had a way of drawing other people's attention whenever he talked to someone. It was just his character; he was a likeable guy.

Later that night while Lil Joe lay on his bunk listening to the radio, he thought about all the things Luie had said to him., and everything made sense. Luie had put everything in perspective for him and had helped him get rid of most of his worries. For the most part, Lil Joe figured he was about as ready for the outside as he would ever be. The only thing that sat heavy on his mind was the never ending threat of those uncontrollable situations that can occur and bring a man to the darkest point of his nature.

Just two months before Lil Joe was due to parole, his friend and neighbor, Luie, passed away. He had been battling with liver disease for quite some time and one night it got the best of him. Shortly after eating his dinner, Luie began vomiting blood. When the unit guards came by a few minutes later to pick up his dinner tray, Luie informed them of his problem and they escorted him to the clinic. The nurse admitted Luie into the infirmary and he died during the night.

Early the following morning, one of the guards came into the pod to collect Luie's personal belongings, and while the guard was placing it onto a roller cart, Lil Joe asked, "Hey, where's Medina going?"

The guard sighed and ran his fingers through his hair. "Uh, Hernandez, uh, Medina passed away last night in the infirmary."

"Damn!" Lil Joe hung his head while he digested the news. It didn't catch him too much by surprise; he had pretty much figured it out when he saw the guard clearing out Luie's cell. He had just hoped that maybe he was wrong. Lil Joe spent the majority of that day just sitting on his bunk thinking about his friend and the many conversations they'd had. Although he was saddened that Luie was dead and gone, he was also glad for Luie. At least he was finally a free man.

Lil Joe smiled at the memory of something Luie had told him several months earlier when he'd returned from the infirmary after suffering a similar episode. They were talking about death and the afterlife when Luie mentioned that he had never seen the Aztec ruins in Mexico and that if there was an afterlife, he would take his spirit home and spend eternity among his ancestors. Luie was big on the ancient culture and religion of the Aztecs. He often expressed his disappointment at how things were for the modern day Mexican society and how what was once a noble and proud race of people had ended up struggling to survive in the gutters of the free world. Luie was especially heartbroken about how his people were killing each other on the streets over drugs and turf wars, and he longed for the day to come when his people would unite and become strong as one.

Luie was old school, and he had a good heart. Lil Joe remembered how Luie would go out to the tiny concrete S.H.U. yard everyday in hopes of catching a glimpse of the sun, or maybe even feel the warmth of its rays. As he reminisced over his deceased friend, Lil Joe was inspired to write a poem to honor his memory. He entitled it "One Last Time" because it was Luie's wish to see the sun one last time before he died.

ONE LAST TIME

I know it's out there, yet it's something I never see.
Just to feel its warmth means so much to me.
The caress of its rays and the life it gives,
The way it lights up the heavens in which it lives,
For I am of the people of the sun, I yearn to be free.
The blood in my veins shines a light through me.
Yet I am condemned in this dark hole where I am
forced to dwell,
A world without sunshine is a world of hell.
As time passes and darkness takes it toll,
The underworld grips my battered soul.
After holding on with all of my might,
My only wish is to die under the sunlight.

CHAPTER TWENTY-TWO

LIL JOE RECEIVED A LETTER FROM Franky just a few days before he was due to parole. Franky explained that he had recently been transferred from the Tehachapi State Prison reception center to the new Folsom State Prison in Sacramento. He wrote to wish Lil Joe good luck on the outside and to let him know he'd be hearing from him again in a few weeks after he'd had time to settle in at home. Franky said that in his next letter he would send Lil Joe a phone number of a friend to contact on the outside who would be able to help him get on his feet.

Lil Joe spent his last few days in prison sorting out his personal property. He put aside the things he had to pack up to take home and passed out the rest to other convicts in his pod. The night before the big day, he hardly got a wink of sleep. He was too anxious with anticipation of his release. The morning of his parole, one of the night shift guards came to give him a half hour warning just before the morning shift change.

"Hey, Hernandez," the guard said knocking on his door with his flashlight.

"Yeah."

"Hey, Hernandez, we're gonna get you over to R&R in about fifteen minutes."

"All right. Thanks." Lil Joe got out of bed and cleaned up. Then he put all his bedding in a sheet bundle and tossed it next to the cell door. The rest of his property was waiting for him at the receiving and release building, where his unit guards had taken it the day before. Next, Lil Joe drank a strong shot of instant coffee and sat down to use the toilet. He figured it was a good idea to empty out his bowels and take a quick bird bath before the long bus ride home. After he finished, he washed his hands and stood at his cell door searching the cell over with his eyes. It was as if he were saying goodbye to the place that had taken up so much of his life.

Two night shift guards showed up a few minutes later to take him to the receiving and release building just outside of the S.H.U. compound. Two male hillbilly transportation guards were waiting to drive him to the local bus station when he got there. After they had all of his parole paperwork in order, one of the guards removed his handcuffs so Lil Joe could dress in his parole clothes. It was the first time in thirteen years that he was free from restraints while outside his cell. He took a moment to adjust to the unfamiliar feeling before he put on his white t-shirt and brand new pair of beige khakis. After he was dressed, one of the transportation guards handed him a pen and a property receipt and pointed to his 12x12 cardboard box of property which was sitting on the plywood counter in front of him.

"Go ahead and look through your stuff and make sure everything is there. Then sign that property receipt."

Lil Joe nodded and began rummaging through the small box to make sure it was all there. It was, so he signed the receipt and handed it back to the guard. "All right then, Mr. Hernandez, you're the only one we got paroling today, so let's get you to the bus station." He motioned for Lil Joe to follow him and his partner outside to the van.

Lil Joe felt distant from himself as he sat in the back of the van staring out the window as they passed countless redwood trees along the drive to the local bus station. Everything about the day felt surreal. He kept thinking that at any moment, he would awaken from this dream he was having and would once again be surrounded by the four walls of confinement. But it wasn't a dream and the reality of the situation slowly sunk into his brain.

They reached the bus depot just ten minutes after they'd left the prison grounds, and as the driver pulled into the parking lot and parked in front of the entrance, Lil Joe snapped out of his enchanted trance and instantly became aware of his surroundings. The tall, husky guard who had been sitting on the passenger side stepped out and opened the side door. "Come on, Hernandez, let's go get you a ticket so we can get you on your way." Lil Joe stepped out of the van carrying his little box of property while he looked around the empty parking lot, taking in his first real moment as a free man. The guard chuckled and spit a wad of chewing tobacco out on the blacktop. "It's been a while, huh?"

Lil Joe nodded. "Yeah, it's been a while." He followed the two guards inside the bus depot, where an elderly black woman was stationed behind a ticket counter. Lil Joe noticed the bus schedule hanging just above the counter and looked to see when the bus heading down to Southern California was due. According to the schedule, it was due at 6 A.M. Lil Joe looked at the clock hanging on the wall behind the ticket counter. It was 5:45 A.M. He would be on his way soon.

The husky guard bought Lil Joe's ticket from the lady behind the counter and handed it to Lil Joe. "Here you go. Your bus should show up here in a few minutes. Here, let's just have a seat until it shows up." He pointed to a row of linked plastic chairs positioned in the middle of the floor. "We have to stay with you until you get on the bus." He shrugged. "It's policy." Lil Joe nodded and he and the two guards sat down. While the guards talked to each other about fishing, Lil Joe took a look around the small depot. With the exception of a couple of vending machines, the place was pretty much empty, so there wasn't much to look at.

Lil Joe had been growing anxious to be on his way and get as far away from Pelican Bay as possible and thankfully the bus showed up on time. As it came to a stop at the side entrance, the guards walked Lil Joe out onto the loading dock. After an elderly couple stepped off the bus and retrieved their luggage, the husky guard handed Lil Joe five twenty-dollar bills and said, "This is what's left of your gate money. We deducted a hundred bucks for your clothes and the bus ticket."

Lil Joe smirked, then took the money and put it in his pocket. "All right, then," he said and picked up his box and boarded the bus. After greeting the driver with a head nod, Lil Joe showed her his ticket and made his way to the back. On his way, he saw that there were only half a dozen other people on the bus, which he found comforting since he wasn't used to being in the presence of a lot of people. Shortly after he settled into a window seat at the rear of the bus, the driver pulled off the parking lot and onto the road.

Once they were cruising along the northern California highway, Lil Joe sat back in his seat and stared out the window while he thought about how much his life was about to change. He thought it somewhat ironic that he was feeling the same uncertainty and nervous anticipation that he had felt on the drive to the police station so many years before when he and Franky were first arrested. On the ride south, the bus made several stops to drop off or pick up passengers. When it stopped in San Joaquin County, a female parolee boarded the bus and sat directly across from Lil Joe. After exchanging formal greetings, she and Lil Joe talked until she got off in her home town of Salinas. Her name was Mindy and she was a cute, energetic blonde who had just completed an eighteen-month stretch in a women's correctional facility in Stockton for a second offense drug possession. But according to her, she had learned her lesson and had vowed to stay drug free and out of jail. Lil Joe commended her for wanting to make a change in her life for the better and wished her all the luck in the world.

As the bus got closer to home, Lil Joe began thinking about what he had to do when he got there. He was supposed to contact his parole officer within twenty-four hours of release so that they could schedule meetings at the parole office and go over his parole conditions. The only thing he knew about his parole officer was that she was a female. He had her name and phone number on his parole papers that a prison counselor had given him a week earlier. He decided that if it wasn't too late when he arrived at the bus station, he would call her.

The bus arrived at San Bernardino a little after 6 o'clock. As the driver pulled onto the off ramp, Lil Joe read some graffiti that had been spray painted on the side of a bridge overpass just above the exit. "Welcome to Verdugo. Bandit, Seventh Street Locos." Lil Joe smiled as he was reminded of childhood times in the old neighborhood. Then he took a deep breath. "I'm home," he muttered. "About fuckin' time."

It had already begun to get dark when they arrived at the downtown bus depot, but Lil Joe was still able to catch a glimpse of some of the traffic and buildings. Everything had changed in the eighteen years he'd been gone. Everything looked so different from how he remembered it, but it still felt like home. When the bus came to a stop in front of the loading dock, Lil Joe stood up and stretched his legs for a moment then grabbed his little 12x12 box of property and walked to the door. As he stepped off the bus and onto the pavement, he was instantly hit with an assortment of smells coming from the night air of the business street, mostly smells from fast food restaurants and the fuel exhaust from passing cars. However, the smells brought back fond memories of a life he had once known and was happy to return to.

Lil Joe made his way from the busy dock and into the crowded bus station where there were pay phones he could use. All the phones were in use, so he made his way past a mixed crowd of people toward the restrooms at the back of the building. After relieving himself, Lil Joe strolled over to the opposite side of the building to the change machine to get some quarters for the pay phone. However, the machine only accepted five and one dollar bills. He looked at the ticket counter and saw that it was unoccupied, so he walked over to the counter hoping to change one of his twenties. As he approached the young, fair skinned brunette standing behind the counter greeted him. "Hi, how can I help you?"

"Uhh," Lil Joe held up a twenty dollar bill that he'd pulled from his pocket. "Can I change this for some fives?"

"Sure," she said in a cheerful tone.

Lil Joe slid the twenty through the metal slot in the plexiglass window and the cute brunette took it and put it in the register, withdrew four five-dollar bills, and slid them through to him. She smiled and said, "You have a good evening, sir."

Lil Joe smiled at her use of the word <u>sir</u>. "You, too," he said and made his way over to the change machine. After putting the five dollars in quarters in his pocket, he walked across the floor to the pay phones and waited for one of them to be free. While he waited, he looked around at all the faces. He half expected to see his mother's, but he had told her in a letter a week earlier that he would just call her when he got there. That way she wouldn't have to wait around in the depot for him to show up. Downtown wasn't exactly a nice place for a woman to hang out, especially at night.

While he was still on the bus, Lil Joe had retrieved his parole papers from his box and put them in his pocket. When one of the pay phones freed up, he put his box on the floor in front of his feet, retrieved his papers from his pocket, along with a handful of quarters, and put them down on the pay phone shelf next to a thick phone book. After picking up the receiver and wiping it off on his t-shirt, Lil Joe put two quarters into the slot and slowly dialed his parole officer's number. Two rings later, a coarse female voice answered. "Hello, you've reached Georgia at the San Bernardino Parole Office. How may I help you."

"Uh, yeah, this is Joseph Hernandez. I'm calling to check in with my parole officer, Mrs. Cummings."

There was a short pause and what sounded like paper shuffling on the other end of the line. Then the lady spoke again. "Yes, Mr. Hernandez, I'm your parole officer, Georgia Cummings. Did you just get home?"

"Yeah, I just got off the bus," Lil Joe replied. "I'm at the bus depot."

"Okay, good. Uh, I've recently spoken with your mother. Actually, I went by her house the day before yesterday to meet her and go over some things regarding your parole conditions. She's going to drive you over to see me here at the parole office in the morning so we can go over some things. Okay?"

"Yeah, okay."

"Listen, Mr. Hernandez, I'm glad that you were able to get through. I'm usually clocked out at 5 o'clock, but today I was just swamped with paperwork. You're the last of six new additions to my parole caseload. Anyway, you have a good night and I'll see you around 10 A.M. tomorrow."

"Okay then."

Lil Joe then put another quarter into the slot and dialed his mom's number. He was a bit surprised that she had kept the same phone number all those years, and he was even more surprised that he still had it memorized. The phone rang several times before he heard his mother's voice. "Hello, mijo, is that you?"

He smiled at the realization that she had been waiting for him to call. "Yeah, Mam_, it's me."

"Oh, mijo, I'm so happy. We're coming to get you right now."

"Okay, Ma, I'll see you soon."

"Okay, mijo, bye bye."

After he hung up and retrieved his change, Lil Joe headed across the floor to the vending machines. He hadn't eaten all day and was practically starving. He bought a couple of snacks and a Dr. Pepper soda and then walked outside and stood along the building facing the parking lot while he ate his snacks and waited for his mother. As he stood there, he watched the evening commuters pass by in cars and on foot. It had been a real long time since he had been outdoors at night, and he was enjoying that little bit of freedom.

Just then two nearly naked hookers walked past him on their way to a car parked in the parking lot. Lil Joe chuckled and mumbled to himself, "Some things never change." Then he saw something he had never seen before. Two raunchy looking transvestite hookers emerged from behind the depot and propositioned a young black man standing just a few feet away from him. "Uh, yuck," he muttered with a disgusted look on his face. "Maybe some things do change."

His attention was then diverted to a tan Buick Regal that pulled into the parking lot and came to a stop just a few yards in front of him. "Mijo!" he heard the familiar voice of his mother yell out as she stepped out of the car to greet him. He tossed his snack wrappers and empty soda can into a nearby trash container and picked his box up and walked towards his mother.

"Mom!" he happily greeted her. Then he set his box down next to the Regal and wrapped his arms around her, giving her a gentle bear hug. "Hi, Mam_," he said as he kissed her on the cheek.

She smiled at him with tears in her eyes as she cupped his face in her hands and stared at him lovingly. "Oh, mijo, I'm so happy you're home. I love you so much!"

Lil Joe hugged her again and whispered in her ear, "Te quiero mucho [I love you very much], Mam_."

Out of the corner of his eye, he then saw Marco step out of the car wearing a huge grin. "Hey, big brother, how's it goin'?"

Lil Joe smiled. "Damn, bro, look at you!" He walked around to the front of the car to greet his young brother and was surprised to see how grown up and distinguished looking he was. He stood just a couple of inches shorter than Lil Joe's six foot two and was very athletically built, with thick, wavy black hair and strong, dark facial features. Lil Joe embraced his brother. "It's good to see you again, Marco."

"You too, Joe."

Their mother cut in. "Well, come on, boys, let's go home," she said as she placed Lil Joe's box on the back seat of the car.

Marco smiled. "She cooked a big meal for you, man. I think she's in a hurry to get you home and feed you."

Lil Joe rubbed his stomach. "Ah, man, that sounds good to me. Let's go!" He jumped into the back seat next to his box and Marco drove them home.

During the short ride home, Lil Joe's mother turned sideways in the seat and began to catch him up on family news. "Tina and the baby, Rebecca, are waiting to meet you at home. Tina's pregnant again, six months already, so your brother has been working twelve hour days at the restaurant trying to save up a little extra money. Since he's gone a lot, we all thought it would be best for Tina and the baby to be at home with me. Since I'm retired, I'm at home all day and I'm able to help Tina with the baby."

"More like spoil the baby," Marco cut in. "You should see the way she spoils Rebecca, bro. It's crazy. If Grandma would of spoiled us like Mom does Rebecca, Mom would of had a fit."

Lil Joe saw his mom's face light up with a smile. "It's true," she confessed, "but I can't help it. She's so precious."

Lil Joe laughed. "Hey, Marco, so you've been working a lot, huh? Did you get that management position you mentioned in your last letter?"

"Yep, I've had it now for almost a month. The pay's great, but I work most of the day so we've been living with Mom for a couple of weeks now. She takes care of Tina, and spoils her granddaughter rotten, while I'm at work. It's only temporary, though. After Tina has the baby, we'll find a new place."

Their mom cut in. "You guys are welcome to stay as long as you like."

Marco laughed. "She only says that because of the baby."

"That's not true, Marco," she scolded him.

Marco chuckled. "I know, Mom, I'm only teasing."

Lil Joe was having a hard time believing that he was actually there in the presence of his family interacting with them the way he was. Feelings that he thought were lost began to resurface.

"Hey, mijo," his mother said, "I'm throwing you a welcome home party this weekend. Everyone will be there. All of your cousins and other family members you haven't seen in so long."

Lil Joe wasn't very excited about the news of the party. The only other people he wanted to see were his dad and of course Tina and his baby niece, but he didn't have the heart to tell his mother. She had obviously already planned the whole thing, so he figured it wouldn't hurt for him to at least pretend to be excited. "That's great, Mom. It sounds really nice. Oh, before I forget, I called my parole officer when I got off the bus. She said you were gonna drive me over to the office to meet her tomorrow morning."

"Yeah, mijo, she came by the house and let me know about your parole conditions."

Marco cut in. "She told us to keep you away from all the knives in the house."

Lil Joe laughed. "What? She said that?"

"Nooo," his mom said, "she didn't say it like that. She said you're not allowed to have any weapons in your possession or in your bedroom--not even kitchen knives."

Lil Joe grunted and changed the subject. "So is this your car, Marco?"

"No, it's Mom's. I got a Ford Explorer at the house, but Mom doesn't like to ride in it. She's still spooked over the tire thing that happened years ago."

Lil Joe noticed that his mom hadn't stopped smiling since they left the bus depot. It warmed his heart to see her in such good spirits.

"Well, we're here," Marco announced as he pulled the Regal onto the street where they had grown up as children. "Look familiar, Joe?"

Lil Joe nodded as he stared at the big flaxen stucco house with the concrete porch and small front yard. His brain was immediately flooded with childhood memories.

Marco pulled the Regal into the narrow driveway and parked it right behind his black Ford Explorer. "We're home, mijo," his mom proclaimed. She looked at him curiously while he stared unbelievingly at his childhood home. He smiled at her.

"Yeah, Mam , we're home."

She and Marco got out of the car and his mom pushed the front seat forward so he could get out. He grabbed his box and stepped out. He pointed to Marco's Explorer. "That's pretty nice," he said.

"Thanks, bro, I like it."

Their mom stood on the front porch waiting impatiently. "Come on, mijo, let's go inside so you can meet Tina and the baby. You'll have plenty of time to talk about cars with your brother later."

"She would of made a good prison warden, huh?" Marco joked.

Lil Joe chuckled. "Okay, Ma, we're coming."

He and Marco walked up the steps as their mother opened the door. "Tina, we're home," she announced. Lil Joe followed Marco in and set his box down on the floor. Then he walked up to his mom and hugged her as he looked around the house. Surprisingly, not much had changed since he left. He noticed a few new pieces of furniture and a large, stained-wood entertainment center that hadn't been there before, but his mother's living room walls were still decorated with her beloved painting of the last supper and a large crucifix right next to several family photos.

Lil Joe shook his thoughts away when a very pretty, and very pregnant, petite brunette walked into the living room carrying a baby girl he immediately recognized as his niece, Rebecca. "Hi, Joe, I'm your sister-in-law, Tina, and this is your niece, Rebecca." She looked at Rebecca, who was staring wide eyed at Lil Joe. "That's your tio, mija."

Lil Joe walked over to Tina and kissed her on the cheek. "It's great to finally get to meet you."

Tina smiled at him. "It's great to finally be able to meet you too, although I feel like I've known you for a long time. Your mother and brother talk about you all of the time."

Lil Joe smiled. He took a liking to Tina instantly. She had a mild mannered pleasantness and he could definitely see what Marco saw in her.

Marco noticed that Lil Joe was admiring Rebecca, so he asked, "Would you like to hold your niece, bro?" Before he had a chance to respond, Tina was already placing Rebecca in his arms. As soon as she was firmly in his grip, she looked up at him with her big brown eyes and rewarded him with a big loving smile. Lil Joe fell in love with her instantly. He smiled back at her and then she put her hand in his mouth and made a cheerful noise.

"Ah," his mother said, "she loves her uncle. Well, mijo, I'm sure you're hungry so I'm going to go fix you a hot plate of food. Why don't you guys go relax and catch up. Your food will be ready in a few minutes."

"Okay, Ma, thanks."

Lil Joe sat down on the couch with Rebecca on is lap, and Marco and Tina shared the leather love seat across from him. "So, how's it feel to be home, bro?" Marco asked.

Lil Joe looked down at Rebecca, who was admiring one of the tattoos on his forearm. "It feels great, man. More like a dream than reality though, you know?"

Marco nodded. "Yeah, but hey, it's great to have you home again, brother."

"Thanks, brother."

Rebecca began to giggle and laugh out loud, which made Lil Joe laugh along with her. "Does she talk yet?"

"No, not yet," Tina said with a hint of disappointment in her voice, "but she's been trying. She just hasn't said anything comprehensible yet."

Lil Joe smiled down at his niece. "So, do you guys know what the new baby's gonna be?"

"She doesn't want to know," Marco said. "She wants it to be a surprise." He shrugged. "We'll find out sooner or later. Mom says it's gonna be a boy. She says she can tell by Tina's appetite for certain foods."

"Hmm." Lil Joe raised his brow. "Speaking of food, have you guys eaten already?"

"Oh, yeah, we had just finished when you called."

Lil Joe tickled Rebecca's tummy. "What about you? Have you eaten yet?" She smiled at him again.

"Boy, she's just full of smiles for you," Tina said. "She really likes you."

Lil Joe stared into his niece's eyes while he held her in his arms. She's so small and fragile, he thought, yet she generates such loving energy. As he sat there witnessing her beautiful smile, he thought,

Wow! This tiny little angel holds enough power in her smile to heal eighteen years of internal wounds.

His thoughts were interrupted when his mom came into the living room carrying a huge plate stacked with his favorite meal of tostadas, beans and rice, corn, block cheese slices and plenty of spicy, homemade chilé. "Here, mijo, why don't we trade?" she said, referring to Rebecca.

"All right, but only for a little while." He looked down at Rebecca. "Sorry, sweetheart, but I can't eat you."

Rebecca giggled as if she understood what he'd said. Lil Joe's mom handed him his plate of food and scooped up Rebecca from his lap. While Lil Joe enjoyed his first home cooked meal in almost two decades, he and his family talked and watched the evening news on television. One of the segments on the news caught Lil Joe's attention. It was about the newly elected governor of California, Arnold Schwarzenegger, and his proposal to help get the state out of debt. Usually Lil Joe didn't follow politics since a convicted felon wasn't able to vote anyway, but he got a kick out of the new governor/actor, mostly because of the controversy that surrounded the guy. He smiled as he recalled some of the nicknames that some of the cons in the S.H.U. had come up with for the governor: Governor Groper, The Governator, and Lil Joe's personal favorite, Conan the Governor.

After eating and talking with his family for a couple of hours, Lil Joe's mother showed him to his old bedroom. Evidently she had been using it as a storage room because the entire room was cluttered with boxes full of miscellaneous household junk. In the middle of all the clutter was a bed with his box of property on it as well as a few other boxes of what appeared to be items from his childhood. The sight of some of his old stuff took him back in time for a moment. "Sorry about the mess, mijo," his mother apologized. "I haven't found the time to go through all of this stuff and decide what to keep and what to give to the shelter."

"Don't worry about it, Mom, I'll help you with that later. And don't worry about the mess; I've lived in way worse."

"Oh, mijo." She clasped his face in her hands and kissed him on the forehead. "I'm so glad you're home."

Lil Joe smiled. "Me too, Ma."

He stood there for a moment familiarizing himself again with his mother's face. She had aged well over the years, and although there were a few visible laugh lines and her long black hair was streaked with strands of grey, she was still a very beautiful woman. "Hey, Mom, is it all right if I call Pop in the morning? I haven't been able to talk with him in a long time."

"Sure, mijo. Why don't you invite him to come up in June for your birthday and stay the week so you guys can catch up."

Lil Joe liked the idea even though his birthday was still a few months away. But he knew his dad would need at least that much time to get ready to take time off work. "Sure, Mom, that sounds great. I'll do that."

"Well, okay, mijo, I'm tired so I'm going to take a bath and go to bed. I'll see you in the morning, and don't forget we have that appointment with your parole officer tomorrow morning at 10 o'clock."

"Okay, Mam_. Goodnight." He kissed her on the cheek. "Oh, before I forget, Mom, about a month ago I cashed in one of my mutual funds and opened a bank account with the Wells Fargo Bank. Anyway, I was wondering if tomorrow after stopping by the parole office, maybe you could take me to the bank to make a withdrawal and then take me somewhere to buy some new clothes."

She yawned and nodded. "Yeah, mijo, sure. Tomorrow we'll spend the whole day together, just you and me."

Lil Joe smiled. "That sounds good, Ma. Thanks."

She yawned again. "Oh, also mijo," she said pointing to his small box of belongings, "I put a toothbrush and some other stuff in your box so you'd have your things to wash up with in the morning."

Lil Joe took a quick glance at his box. "Oh, okay, Mam_. Thank you. I appreciate that."

She smiled. "Goodnight, mijo."

A few minutes later, Marco stopped by with Rebecca to say goodnight. "Hey, Joe, I just thought I'd bring her by to say goodnight."

Lil Joe smiled at the sight of his niece. "Thanks, Marco." He kissed his niece on the top of the head. "Goodnight, angel face." Rebecca giggled and reached out to touch his chin.

"She's just all laughs with you, bro."

Lil Joe smiled. "Yeah, well, she's probably never seen this much ugly before."

Marco laughed. "Well all right, Joe, I'm gonna head off to bed. Goodnight, man."

"Goodnight, little brother." Then as Marco was about to leave the room, Lil Joe said, "Hey, Marco!"

Marco turned around. "Yeah?"

"I'm proud of you, man. You got a good thing goin' for you, bro."

Marco nodded. "Thanks, Joe. I'll see you tomorrow."

After Lil Joe heard his mother come out of the bathroom, he stepped in to take a quick shower and then called it a night himself. However, at some time during the night he was suddenly awakened by his bubbling stomach and had to make a run for the bathroom. Apparently his stomach couldn't handle his mother's rich, home cooked food just yet and he paid for it dearly with a bad case of the midnight runs. Unfortunately for him, his stomach's disagreement with the food he had eaten wasn't the worst of his problems. He had forgotten what hot chilé could do to a person who hadn't eaten it in a long time, and his mom, God bless her, made some of the hottest chilé he had ever tasted. So while Lil Joe sat on the toilet cursing the chilé during his late night crisis, he muttered to himself, Damn, my ass feels like a blowtorch. If that lady wasn't my mother, I'd sue her! After about half an hour of burning torture, Lil Joe finally made it back to bed, grateful to be finished with it all, and happy to finally be home.

CHAPTER TWENTY-THREE

THE NEXT MORNING, LIL JOE AWOKE to the aromas of hot brewing coffee and chorizo con huevos. After stretching and retrieving his hygiene items from his box, he made his way to the bathroom for his morning wash-up ritual, then headed to the living room to call his dad. After having a good conversation with him, he was in good spirits and joined his mom, Marco, and Tina in the kitchen for a hot cup of coffee.

"Good morning, mijo," his mother greeted him. "Did you sleep well?"

"Good morning, mom. Yeah, I slept pretty good." He decided to keep his midnight escapade with the toilet to himself.

"Did you call your father, mijo?"

"Yeah, I just got off the phone with him."

"How is he?"

"He says he's doing good, Ma. He said to tell everybody hi."

"Did he say if he would make it out for your birthday?"

"Yeah, Ma, he said he would make it."

His mother started to get up. "Would you like some breakfast, mijo?"

"No, Ma, please sit down. Coffee's fine, thanks." He decided to take it easy on the rich foods until his stomach was able to handle it.

After an hour or so of breakfast table chitchat, Lil Joe and his mom left to meet with his parole officer. They arrived at the office half an hour early, so they sat in the waiting room talking until at about 10 o'clock an elderly black receptionist escorted Lil Joe into the office of his parole officer. "You go ahead and have a seat," she said. "Mrs. Cummings will be with you shortly."

"Okay, thanks." Lil Joe took a seat in front of the desk and a few minutes later his parole officer entered the room.

"Hello, Mr. Hernandez, I'm Georgia." She extended her hand. "Or Mrs. Cummings, whichever you prefer."

"Okay," Lil Joe said and stood up to shake her hand. "Nice to meet you." He was a bit taken aback by her appearance. With her short, dirty blonde "butch" hairdo and her tanned, wrinkled face, he thought she bore a strong resemblance to the old-school rock star Rod Stewart.

"Okay, Mr. Hernandez, please take a seat. I'll try not to take up too much of your time." She walked around her cluttered desk and sat down. "Well, Mr. Hernandez," she said while looking around on her desk, "I know your file is around here . . . Ah, here it is." She retrieved a thick folder from a stack near her computer and opened it. After she shuffled through the contents for a few seconds, she removed a piece of paper and set the file to the side. "Okay, well," she said, frowning, "you've been gone an awfully long time." Lil Joe nodded in agreement. "I imagine it will take you a while to adjust to the outside world, huh?" She looked up at him. "Have you considered getting some counseling to help you with the adjustment?"

Lil Joe held up his hands in protest. "No, I'm okay with that. My family will help me adjust. Thanks."

She sighed. "Well, okay then, I just have a few questions for you and then I wanna go over your parole conditions. But first just let me say this: you'll find that I'm a fair parole officer. I'm not a hard ass, and I'm not one of those parole officers looking to send you back to prison just to lighten my caseload. As long as you keep your nose clean and stick to your parole conditions, I'll stay out of your business and let you live your life. Do you understand?"

"Yeah. Sounds cool to me."

She smiled. "Good. Now what do you plan on doing for income?"

"Well, right now I wasn't planning on doing anything until I get used to the change of being out here."

Mrs. Cummings cut in, "But you're gonna need money to live on."

Lil Joe nodded. "Sure, but I'm doing okay with that right now. I have a substantial amount of money in my bank account to lean on for a while. But to ease your concern, after I've adjusted to this new life, I plan on attempting to find work with a small private practice attorney as a paralegal. I'm certified so I shouldn't have much trouble landing a job."

"Well, okay, it looks like you have a plan. So that's good. I just have to make sure you're not gonna be out there selling drugs or robbing people. You know?" she said with a halfhearted smile.

"Yeah, I hear ya."

"Okay, good, but just in case your plans don't work out, you can come see me and I'll get you set up with work somewhere. All right?"

Lil Joe nodded. "Okay."

"All right then, Mr. Hernandez, now to your parole conditions." She began reading from the paper that she had retrieved from his folder. "You're not allowed to have any weapons in your possession at any time. This includes your living quarters at your mother's house. Uh, you know what constitutes a weapon, right? Guns, knives (even kitchen knives), loose razor blades, explosives, clubs, brass knuckles, etc."

Lil Joe nodded. "Yeah, I get it."

"Okay, so you're not allowed to have any controlled substances in your possession, nor are you allowed to be under the influence of any type of controlled substance."

Lil Joe interrupted. "What about alcohol?"

"You can drink alcohol if you choose, but I would take it easy. Okay?"

"Okay."

"Okay, where was I. Oh, right, you're only allowed to be in the possession of drugs that are prescribed to you personally by a licensed physician. Uh, you're not at any time allowed to leave the county or state without permission from this office. You're not allowed to be in the company of any other parolees or people on probation supervision. This includes lady friends. Last, but not least, you're to check in, that is make a physical appearance, here at the parole office with me once a week. At any time you may be subject to random drug testing, and I may even show up periodically at your mother's house to check on you. Do you understand everything I've just explained to you?"

"Yeah."

"Do you have any questions?"

"Just one. What day of the week am I supposed to come check in with you?"

"Uh, good question. Let's see." She began searching through an appointment book on her desk. "How about you check in on Tuesdays any time before 5 P.M.. When you get a job, if we need to change the day to work around your work schedule, we'll do that."

"All right," Lil Joe said. "Is that all for now?"

"Yep, that pretty much covers it. You take it easy and I'll see you next week."

"All right."

Just as Lil Joe was about to leave, Mrs. Cummings said, "Oh, just one more thing, Mr. Hernandez. Keep your cool out there. Okay? When somebody pisses you off, and someone will, it's inevitable, just try not to kill anybody. All right?"

Lil Joe almost smiled at her candor, but instead he just nodded and left.

The remainder of the day, Lil Joe and his mom drove all around town while he shopped for his new wardrobe, and by the end of the day he had everything he needed and then some. The last stop they made was at a grocery store, where Lil Joe bought enough groceries to stock his mother's house for a month. When they finally got home late in the afternoon, Marco had already left for work and Tina and the baby were home alone.

After a long day of non-stop shopping, the last thing Lil Joe wanted to see was his mother cooking everyone's dinner, so he talked her and Tina into letting him treat them to dinner and a movie. A couple of hours later they were on their way. Tina had dressed Rebecca in a little pink dress that Lil Joe had bought for her while he was shopping. When Tina thanked him for thinking of Rebecca, she also warned him not to spoil his niece too much or he would create a monster, but Lil Joe wasn't worried about it. In fact, he had already planned to spoil his baby niece rotten.

After surprising his brother by showing up to eat at the restaurant he managed, Lil Joe, his mom, Tina, and the baby went and saw a movie. By the time they got home, it was already nearly 11 o'clock, so after his mom and Tina were done using the bathroom and had gone to bed, Lil Joe showered and called it a night himself. While he lay there in bed trying to fall asleep, he thought about all those nights in prison when he would lie in his bunk and think about what he would be doing if he were a free man. Even though he hadn't pictured things exactly as they were at that moment, he had no complaints. He was enjoying being surrounded by his family.

The next couple of days flew by and before he knew it, it was Saturday morning and his little welcome home family get together was scheduled to kick off that night. While his mom prepared the house for the party, Lil Joe went with Tina to the neighborhood supermarket to buy some last minute party items. While they stood waiting in the checkout line, Tina said, "Please don't be upset with me, but I sort of invited one of my girlfriends to the party tonight. Her name is Vanessa. Me and her have been friends for a really long time. Your brother knows her too. Anyway, we kinda thought that you two would hit it off if we introduced you guys to each other. She's really down to earth and really pretty too. I really think you'll like her."

Lil Joe smiled at her persistence. "I'm not upset. Hell, no. I think that's pretty cool of you to wanna introduce me to one of your friends. I could use some female companionship."

Tina smiled. "Whew, I'm relieved. I don't know why, but the more I thought about it, I kept thinking that I screwed up and that you were gonna be upset with me."

"No," Lil Joe assured her. "I've been in prison for eighteen years. Why would I be upset with you for fixing me up with a woman?"

Tina laughed. "I don't know. I guess I was just being silly."

When they got back home, there were still a couple of hours to kill before the party so Lil Joe helped his mom with a few chores and then took a quick shower and got ready. Ever since Tina told him about her friend who was coming to the party, he had been a little more excited about the whole thing. To his amazement, he even had butterflies in his stomach. Sissy, he teased himself. What? Are you scared of a girl? He laughed at himself for being nervous.

People began showing up for the party around 6 o'clock. At first everyone greeted Lil Joe and welcomed him home, but as the crowd grew larger, every new arrival just grabbed a beer and blended in with everyone else, but Lil Joe didn't mind. He hardly recognized any of them anyway. For the first couple of hours, Lil Joe shyly mingled among some of his cousins hoping to get reacquainted. Instead, they managed to make him feel alienated with their never ending questions about prison. Lil Joe didn't get it. He didn't understand what they found so fascinating about prison life. None of them seemed interested at all in getting to know him personally; they just wanted to know what it was like in prison. What Lil Joe wanted to tell them was to go out and get a gun and shoot each other and find out. But he kept his cool; he didn't want to do anything that would ruin the party his mother had worked so hard to put together.

Finally, he just grabbed a couple of beers from the refrigerator and slipped away and found himself a secluded corner seat in the living room right next to one of the stereo speakers. He sat there for a few minutes sipping on one of the beers and listening to the mixed party disc that was playing until suddenly Tina walked in accompanied by a gorgeous, long haired brunette. Wow! he thought as he looked the brunette over from head to toe. She was just an inch or two taller than Tina and had a flawless, olive brown skin tone to go along with her athletic curves. She wore a knee length denim skirt and a short white top that exposed her flat, firm stomach. Right away Tina spotted Lil Joe and brought her friend over to meet him. "Hi, Joe, this is my friend Vanessa I was telling you about."

Lil Joe stood up and extended his hand to her. "It's nice to meet you, Vanessa. I'm Joe."

She smiled and took his hand. "It's nice to meet you too."

Lil Joe stood there for a moment staring into her big, brown, almond shaped eyes, absolutely captivated by her beauty. He suddenly realized that he had been staring at her and tried to appear less dumbfounded by offering her the extra beer in the chair next to his. "Would you like a beer?"

"Sure. Thanks."

"Well," Tina said, "I'll let you two get acquainted. I have to go pee." She shrugged. "Sorry. You know how pregnant women get."

After Tina made her subtle exit and hurried off, Lil Joe pointed to the chair next to his. "Would you like to sit down?"

"Sure."

As she took a seat, Lil Joe sat back down and took a long pull from his beer. Vanessa looked around the crowded house at all the people standing around drinking and talking and said, "So this is your welcome home party, huh?"

Lil Joe took a quick glance around the living room. "Yeah, I guess so."

Vanessa nodded. "Well, if you don't mind me asking, why are you all by yourself over here in the corner at your own party?"

Lil Joe shrugged. "I'm not real big on crowds. Besides, I'm not by myself anymore." He threw her a charming smile and she smiled back.

"Well, to tell you the truth, I'm not big on crowds either." She held up her bottle of beer. "I just came for the free beer."

Lil Joe laughed. He admired the way she made light of the situation. Tina never returned from using the bathroom, but neither Lil Joe nor Vanessa seemed to mind. They hit it off quite well and spent the next two and a half hours talking and getting to know one another. During that time, Lil Joe learned that Vanessa was a twenty-six year old third-generation Mexican American who was a single mother of a seven-year-old boy named Angel. She and her son lived only two blocks down from his mother's house. He also learned that Vanessa had just recently earned her real estate license and was working as a realtor for a local agency.

Lil Joe felt an instant connection with Vanessa. He found himself at ease in her presence, which he felt was a blessing considering that he wasn't particularly used to talking with beautiful women, or any women for that matter. Nevertheless, he felt comfortable in her company, and he definitely wanted to get to know her better.

When the party finally began to wind down and most of the guests began to leave, Vanessa looked at her wristwatch. "Wow, the time just flew by! I didn't realize it was so late."

"Yeah," Lil Joe said, "I guess it's true that time flies by when you're having fun."

Vanessa smiled. "Yes, it does. Well, I should be getting home. I have to get up early and do house chores tomorrow before Angel returns from his weekend with my parents."

Lil Joe nodded. "All right. Well, at least let me walk you home."

She said, "Okay, I'd like that."

"Well all right." Lil Joe stood up. "Just let me make a quick stop at the water park." He grinned. "I think I drank too much beer."

Vanessa laughed. "Okay, I'll wait right here for you."

On the way back from the bathroom, Lil Joe swung by the kitchen, where his mom and Tina were cleaning up. He kissed his mom on the cheek. "Thanks for the party, Mom."

She smiled. "Okay, mijo. Did you have fun?"

"Yeah, Ma, I did. Hey, uh, I'm gonna walk Vanessa home, so I'll be back in a while."

"Okay, mijo."

Tina grabbed her purse off the kitchen table. "Wait. Here, Joe," she said, handing him her house keys. "Just in case you get home late, that way you can let yourself in."

Lil Joe flushed as he realized what she was implying. He quickly put the key ring in his pocket. "Yeah, uh, thanks."

Both Tina and his mom giggled at his embarrassment. However, Lil Joe didn't stick around for more of their playful teasing. He went back to the living room, where he found Vanessa standing in front of a row of family pictures hanging on the wall. She was admiring an old childhood photo of Marco and him taken when he was just seven. She pointed to the picture. "Is that you and Marco?"

"Yeah," Lil Joe shyly replied.

"Oh!" she said in an adoring tone. "How cute!"

Lil Joe smiled. "Yeah, Marco was a good lookin' kid, he teased."

She turned around to face him wearing a tempting smile. "Yeah, well his brother was a cute kid too. Still is, as far as I can tell."

Lil Joe grinned and asked, "Are you all set to go?"

Vanessa held up her keys. "Yep, all set."

As they were about to walk out the front door, Lil Joe grabbed his coat off the arm of the couch and wrapped it around Vanessa's shoulders. "Thanks," she said with a sweet smile.

"No problem."

On the short walk to Vanessa's house, they made small talk, but as they got closer to her house, Lil Joe began to feel an unfamiliar tension growing in the air. He walked Vanessa up to her front porch and just as he was about to say goodnight and head home, she turned to face him and asked, "Hey, would you like to come in for another beer?"

Despite Tina's insinuations, the question caught him by surprise. "Uh, yeah, sure."

"Good," Vanessa said with a smile. After she unlocked her door and went in, she switched on the lights in the living room and Lil Joe shyly followed her in and closed the door. Vanessa put her keys on a small lamp stand next to the front door and pointed to a small sofa just a few feet away. "Go ahead and make yourself comfortable. I have to make a trip to the water park," she said with a smile. "I'll be back in a few minutes. Okay?"

Lil Joe nodded. "Okay." He took a seat on the sofa and looked around the house. It was identical to his mother's. The kitchen was off to the right of the living room, with the rest of the rooms in the back of the house down a narrow hall. Along the wall in front of the sofa was a large varnished TV hutch with several neatly placed pictures of a happy looking, dark haired little boy on it. Lil Joe assumed they were of Vanessa's son, Angel. Right next to the TV was a Play Station game box, which reminded Lil Joe of his childhood when he, Franky, and Jimmy played Atari games at Jimmy's grandparent's house. The memory caused a pang in Lil Joe's gut, but the feeling quickly faded when he saw Vanessa's smiling face appear from the shadows of the dimly lit hallway.

"Whew, do I feel better," she said as she disappeared into the kitchen. A few seconds later she reappeared carrying two bottles of Corona beer. Lil Joe noticed that she had changed into a pair of tiny grey sweat shorts and a white half t-shirt with the word "Hottie" printed across the front. She handed Lil Joe one of the bottles of beer and sat down on the sofa next to him with her legs curled under her butt.

"I like your shirt," Lil Joe said.

"Oh thanks. It's the shirt I usually sleep in." She pointed to his beer. "I hope you like Corona. It's all I have."

Lil Joe looked through the clear glass bottle at the yellow contents. Hmm, he thought, it can't taste any worse than Pruno. "No, this is fine, thanks." He pointed to the pictures on the hutch. "Is that your little boy?"

"Yeah, that's my Angel."

"He's a good lookin' kid. He takes after his mom."

Vanessa blushed. "Well, thanks. Hey, would you like to listen to some music or watch some TV or something?"

"Music would be cool. I haven't really been watching much TV lately. Too much drama about the war."

Vanessa leaned forward and retrieved a remote control from the glass coffee table in front of the sofa. "Are you against the war in Iraq?" she asked as she pointed the remote towards the CD player and pushed one of the buttons. Soon music from Sade filled the living room.

"I am. I think it's a shame that all those young kids are over there dying because of a few scandalous politicians and their crooked agendas."

Vanessa raised her brow. "Well said. My younger brother Michael was killed over there about four months ago."

"Aw, no!" Lil Joe said in surprise. "I'm sorry to hear that, Vanessa," he said with genuine sympathy.

"Yeah," she said and took a sip of her beer. "I was devastated at first, you know? But we all have to move on eventually. Right?"

Lil Joe nodded in agreement. "Yeah, I guess we do. Did he enlist for the college education?"

"Yeah, our parents couldn't afford to send him to college, so he joined the Army figuring it would be his only chance at getting a degree." She smiled. "He wanted to be a child psychologist." She paused and shook her head. "He was such a good kid too. He always tried hard in school and stayed out of trouble. He stayed out of the whole gang and drug scene. Humph! All that just to die over there in some desert for nothing!" She wiped her watery eyes with the back of her hand. "I'm sorry, Joe, I didn't mean to kill the mood by getting all girlie on you."

"No," Lil Joe said with sincerity, "you don't have to apologize for grieving. It's hard losing a loved one."

"Thanks. You're sweet." Then she quickly changed the subject. "You know, I have to admit I was a little nervous about meeting you at first because I didn't know what to expect. But now I'm glad Tina introduced us."

Lil Joe grinned. "Yeah, me too."

"Really? Because I thought that maybe you would think something was wrong with me for agreeing to meet a complete stranger who had just got out of prison."

Lil Joe laughed. "Well," he teased, "now that you mention it, that is pretty weird."

"Ah," Vanessa smacked her lips in response, "that's not funny." She smiled. "And for the record, Tina spoke very highly of you."

Good girl, Lil Joe thought. I'll have to thank Tina for that later.

"Besides," Vanessa continued, "being a single mother pretty much puts an end to your social life."

Lil Joe chuckled. "Well, it could be worse. You could be an ex-con!"

Vanessa laughed. "Yeah, I guess you got me there." She pointed to his beer bottle, noticing that it was almost empty. "Would you like another one?"

Lil Joe grinned. "Why, are you trying to get me drunk?"

"Yeah," Vanessa said with a flirtatious smile. "Maybe I am."

Lil Joe didn't know much about making moves on women, but he was getting the feeling that Vanessa was into him, so he decided to be up front with her. "Look, Vanessa, I don't wanna come off like a big ol' dork, but I'm really into you and I've been dying to kiss you all night."

She giggled at his use of the word "dork" and then took his empty beer bottle and set it next to hers on the coffee table. "Oh yeah?" she said as she leaned in close to him. "Then what are you waiting for?"

Lil Joe wasted no time making his move. He wrapped his arms around her, pulled her into his embrace, and kissed her. After several minutes of a heated makeout session, Vanessa pulled away from him. "Come on," she said, her eyes glazed with passion, "let's take this to the back." She took him by the hand and led him down the hallway into her bedroom where they continued to kiss while fumbling to undress each other.

Before Lil Joe knew it, he was stripped down to his boxer shorts and Vanessa was standing in front of him wearing only a white bra and matching thong panties. Lil Joe sat down on the end of the bed and pulled her forward by the hips, kissing her navel while he caressed her beautifully shaped buttocks. Her sex appeal drove him crazy with desire. Her body was shaped exactly the way he preferred; she was small in the waist, thick in the thighs, and round in the butt. Evidently she liked his muscular body as well because she couldn't keep her hands off him. "You're so gorgeous," he whispered and pulled her down to straddle him. He wanted so badly to take her, but he was hesitant to take her the way he wanted to. She felt so petite and fragile under his hands he feared that if he was too rough, he would end up breaking her little ass. After all, he had eighteen years of pent-up sexual energy to release, and he didn't want to hurt her.

Vanessa must have picked up on his thoughts because she pushed his back to her mattress and took total control. He soon realized how wrong he had been thinking that he would hurt her if he was too rough. To his utter amazement, she rocked his world all night long.

CHAPTER TWENTY-FOUR

EARLY THE NEXT MORNING, JUST BEFORE dawn, Lil Joe awoke in Vanessa's bed next to her half covered naked body, and as he lay there admiring her beautifully shaped curves, he had a hard time accepting what had happened as reality. All he could think about was how not even a week earlier he had awakened inside a cold prison cell after only dreaming of a night like the one he had just spent. Just then he caught her sweet scent and closed his eyes for a moment while he reminisced over the night before. He smiled at the memory of her sexual appetite. The girl sure does have endurance, he thought. Good thing I'm used to heavy workouts.

As dawn approached and the morning sunlight began to creep through the open blinds of her bedroom window, Lil Joe slowly got out of bed and dressed, wondering whether to wake her before leaving. She looked so beautiful and peaceful he didn't want to disturb her sleep, but he didn't want to leave without saying anything either. He decided he would just give her a quick kiss and let her know he was leaving, so after he was dressed, he walked over to the bed and stood there a moment caressing her body with his eyes. He was half tempted to crawl back in bed beside her, but instead he sat down next to her and leaned forward and gently kissed her on the forehead.

"Vanessa," he whispered.

She opened her eyes and smiled. "Hey," she said as she stretched her arms above her head and readjusted her position. "Are you leaving?" she asked in a soft whisper.

"Yeah, I should be getting home."

She drew in a deep breath through her nose and groaned with morning sleepiness. "Okay," she said in the same soft whisper. "If you want to, you can come by later tonight."

Lil Joe smiled and kissed her on the forehead again. "I would like that, but unfortunately I can't. Marco is off work tonight and he kinda wants to take me out for a brothers' night on the town."

Vanessa stuck out her bottom lip in a playful pouty manner. "Aw," he growled, "you're making things hard for me, girl. How about tomorrow night?"

She changed her pout into a smile and said, "Okay, I can live with that, but don't eat dinner, okay? Cause I'm gonna cook."

Lil Joe smiled. "Yeah? Sexy and a cook, huh? Okay then, I'll see you tomorrow night. What time should I show up?"

Vanessa sighed. "Well, I get off of work at three. How about 6 o'clock?"

"All right, I'll see you then."

"Oh, Joe, before I forget, Angel will be here tomorrow night and he can be a handful sometimes," she said with a frown.

"That's okay. I like kids." Then he leaned forward and kissed her on the lips. "Don't worry about it. The three of us will have a good time. Okay?"

She smiled. "Okay."

Lil Joe kissed her again and left for his mom's house. When he got there, no one was up and about yet so he quietly made his way to the bathroom and took a long shower. When he finally stepped out of the shower and began to dry off, he heard some early morning commotion going on outside the door. He instantly recognized the familiar baby gibberish of his niece. Hearing her cheerful early morning laughter put a smile on his face, so after he dressed he hurried off in search of her. He found her in the kitchen eating a bowl of oatmeal in her highchair next to Marco and Tina, who were enjoying a morning cup of coffee.

Lil Joe walked up behind Rebecca's highchair and planted a kiss on top of her head. "There's my little angel."

Marco looked up at him wearing a sly grin. "So, you made it back, huh? I was beginning to think maybe you had moved out on us already."

He and Tina chuckled, which sparked a giggle fit in Rebecca. Lil Joe leaned forward and gently tugged at her short brown pigtails. "Oh, that's funny, huh?" Then he kissed her again. She looked up at him with a big smile and giggled again.

"So," Tina said, "I guess I was right about you and Vanessa hitting it off, huh?"

Lil Joe smiled. "Yeah."

Marco grunted. "Hey, bro, you look like you had a long night. I guess I should of warned you about these Rialto girls." He looked at Tina. "They can be a handful, that's for sure."

Tina shook her head and wrinkled her nose at Marco in a teasing manner. "Well, hey, tonight's your guys' boys' night out, huh?" she said, changing the subject.

"Yep. I'm looking forward to it," Lil Joe said, looking at Marco.

"Well I'm glad. You guys have a lot to catch up on. But do me a favor, keep this one out of trouble," she said, pointing to Marco. "He has a wandering eye."

"Hey!" Marco protested. "That's okay, baby, as long as you know my heart don't wander," he said winking.

Tina laughed. "Yeah, yeah," she teased.

Lil Joe chuckled at their playfulness. "Hey, uh, Mom's still asleep?"

"Yeah," Tina answered, "she stayed up late cleaning up the house. But to tell the truth, I think maybe she was just doing that to wait up for you."

"Aw, man, I didn't even think about that. Did she wait up all night?"

"No, I heard her take a shower and go to bed about 3 o'clock."

Lil Joe felt bad hearing that his mom had stayed up all night waiting for him to come home. "Yeah, next time I'm gonna have to let her know not to wait up for me."

Tina smiled. "Next time? That's so cool. So you must really like her, huh?"

Lil Joe smiled. "Yeah, I do. Vanessa's a great girl. Oh, that reminds me." He pulled Tina's keys from his pocket and handed them to her. "Thanks, Tina."

"No problem."

"No, I mean thanks for everything."

Tina smiled. "It's my pleasure."

Lil Joe turned to Marco. "Well, hey, man, if I'm gonna be ready for tonight, I gotta get some rest, so I'll catch up with you later this afternoon. All right?"

Marco nodded. "All right, bro, I'll see you later."

Lil Joe kissed Rebecca one more time before heading to his bedroom to get some sleep. However, sleep didn't come easily for him. For the most part he just lay in bed thinking about Vanessa. So after a few hours of semi-rest, he decided to get up and sort through the boxes of junk his mom had scattered all over his room. It turned out to be an all day event, but he was glad to do it for his mom. He was still feeling guilty about her staying up all night waiting for him to come home. By the time he finished sorting out all the stuff and took another shower, it was already after 5 o'clock. Neither he nor Marco had eaten all day, so they decided to go out for pizza before going clubbing. To Lil Joe's surprise, Marco took him to an old pizza parlor they used to frequent a lot as kids, and seeing the place again brought back a lot of childhood memories for him. While he and Marco were eating their pizza, Lil Joe looked around, taking in the old familiar place. "This place hasn't changed much, has it?"

"No, not really," Marco said as he took a quick glance around the dimly lit restaurant. "I figured this place would bring back some memories for you." Marco pointed to a small room in the back of the parlor that was packed with kids. "Remember the arcade?"

"Yeah, we used to use those quarters that we rigged so we could play all day long."

Marco chuckled. "Yeah, man, it's amazing what a drill bit and some fishing line can do for a couple of kids with no money, huh?" They both chuckled at the memory. "So, hey, you and Vanessa, huh?"

"Yeah, bro, she's a good girl."

"Yeah, she's a little hottie too, ain't she?" Marco said.

"Whew!" Lil Joe shook his head. "You don't know the half of it."

"Did she tell you about her son?"

"Yeah, I saw a couple pictures of him too. He's a good lookin' kid."

Marco sighed. "Just wait until you meet him. He's a little monster."

Lil Joe laughed. "Well, he can't be any worse than you were when you were a kid."

Marco chuckled. "Yeah, I was kind of a hyper kid, wasn't I?"

"Shit, more like possessed."

Marco let out a belt of laughter. "Yeah, well things changed after you got locked up. Mom was kind of paranoid. I mean, she would overreact whenever I threw a tantrum or something. Did you know that she made me go see a shrink after you got locked up?"

Lil Joe laughed in disbelief. "Come on. Are you serious?"

"Yep, for three years, man. She was kinda freaked out about what you and Franky did, and I guess she wanted to make sure that I didn't do something like that. Shit, she practically locked me up in the house until I was almost out of high school."

"Wow!" Lil Joe said, absorbing what Marco was telling him. "I never really thought about how what I did affected you. It must of been kinda rough, huh?"

Marco frowned. "Yeah, man, it was a little crazy at times."

"I'm sure it was, bro, but hey, things turned out all right for you. Besides, Mom was just being a good mother. She was just lookin' out for you. Shit, I'd trade my life for yours any day. At least you didn't end up like me."

"Aw, come on, Joe," Marco protested, "you're doin' all right. You've just turned over a new leaf, man. You're gonna be all right."

Lil Joe smiled. "Yeah, well, it's good to know that you have faith in me." He decided to change the subject. "So what's up with Vanessa's ex? Is he still in the picture?"

"Nah. Why, you worried about him?"

Lil Joe chuckled. "No, it's just, you know they got a kid together, and I know sometimes those kinds of relationships can be difficult." He shrugged. "I just wanna know what I'm getting myself into."

Marco nodded. "It makes sense, but you don't gotta sweat that, man. The guy's a loser."

"Is that right? What's up with him?"

Marco sighed. "What isn't up with him?" He shook his head with a look of disgust on his face. "He's a dope fiend bro, and a fuckin' thief who steals from his own family to support his habits. And that's not even the worst part. He's also Tina's older brother."

Lil Joe was surprised by that last bit of information. "Aw, man, that's fucked up. What's his name?"

"Eddie. Eddie Cervantez."

Lil Joe nodded. "So I take it he's not a part of his son's life then, huh?"

"No, but it's probably better that way."

"Humph," Lil Joe grunted. "Yeah, I hear you."

"So hey, uh, I kinda got a surprise for you, man, but hey, it's not exactly something to get excited about. It's kind of a bittersweet surprise." He looked at his wristwatch. "We should probably get goin' before it gets dark."

Lil Joe raised a brow. "Get goin' where?"

Marco frowned. "Come on, bro, just trust me, okay? Come on, let's go!"

Lil Joe grinned. "Okay."

Marco then drove them a couple of blocks down the street and parked his Explorer along the curb at the side entrance to the Mountview Cemetery. Lil Joe searched the graveyard with his eyes and turned to Marco. "A cemetery, bro? This is your surprise?"

"Yeah, Joe." Marco sighed and stared his brother in the eye. "I did some inquiring, and made some phone calls, and I found out where Jimmy is buried."

Lil Joe sat silently for a moment while he shuffled his thoughts around. "Damn, Marco, I don't know what to say. I, uh, I kinda figured that the county had just cremated him."

"Yeah, well, as it turns out, somebody from his family read the papers and came forward to claim his body."

Lil Joe was aware that both of Jimmy's grandparents had died while he was still in the Youth Authority, so he wondered who it could have been that came forward to claim his body.

"I came down here earlier while you were resting," Marco said. "I wanted to check things out and make sure it was Jimmy's grave before I brought you down here." He pointed out of Lil Joe's window and into the graveyard. "You see that small grassy hill just beyond the walkway?"

"Yeah," Lil Joe replied.

"Well, he's right behind that hill in the front of the second lot."

Lil Joe nodded and stared off in the direction of Jimmy's grave. After a moment of silence, Marco spoke up. "Hey, Joe, we don't have to be here if you don't wanna be, man."

"Nah, bro," Lil Joe replied, "I'm cool, man. I was just thinking about how Jimmy ended up here."

Marco nodded. "I was gonna stay back and let you go by yourself, but if you want, I'll go with you."

"No, no thanks, I wanna go by myself."

"Okay, man, I'll wait for you right here."

Lil Joe opened the door and slowly stepped out of the Explorer. Then he turned back to Marco. "Hey, um, thanks, Marco."

Marco smiled sympathetically. "No problem."

Lil Joe nodded and closed the door, then made his way towards Jimmy's grave site. He found it fairly quickly and when he did, he was overcome by a variety of emotions. After reading Jimmy's name on the small plaque in the grass, his stomach tightened with sadness. "Damn, Jimmy," he whispered, "you ain't supposed to be there, man." He took a moment to regain his composure. Then he drew in a deep breath and chuckled. "I'm sorry, bro, I didn't mean to laugh. It's just I never pictured myself as being the kind of guy who talks to someone's grave. But hey, I imagine you can probably hear me, though." He looked around. "That is, if you're hangin' around here anywhere." Lil Joe smiled. "Shit, if that's the case, then you can probably see me too. But it's been a while since you last saw me. It probably took you a minute to figure out who this big ol' ugly lookin' Mexican is that's standing on your grave, huh?" He chuckled again.

"Yeah, man, I finally made it out, bro. But it's not exactly as great as I had imagined it. But hey, don't get me wrong. I'm enjoying being with my family. They've been great, man. It's just that I feel out of place, man. Nothing seems real, you know? I mean, everything seems like a dream that I'm gonna wake up from at any moment." Lil Joe chuckled sarcastically. "I guess I'm all fucked up, huh? I didn't realize how much prison had ruined me." He shook his head. "All that time on the inside I spent dreaming about being a free man and what it would be like living a normal life. But now, man, now that they've let me out of my cage . . . I don't even know what normal is, bro. I don't have a fucking clue. I think I can make things work, man, but I don't know."

Lil Joe drew in another deep breath, then exhaled slowly. "Disculpa [excuse me], bro, I didn't mean to come down here and lay out all of my problems on you. It's just that I can't talk to nobody else about this shit. They wouldn't understand, you know? Anyway, hey, I got my little baby niece out here. You probably met her before you . . . uh, before you moved on. She's a real sweetheart, man. Just being around her dulls the pain, you know? Marco has done real good for himself, bro. I'm proud of him. He's . . . uh, he's the one who found out you were here."

Lil Joe hung his head low for a moment and stood silently staring at Jimmy's grave while he reminisced about childhood memories when he, Franky, and Jimmy were together just being kids--laughing, horse playing, and enjoying their youth--a time before their lives took turns for the worse. "Damn, Jimmy, how did it all end up like this? I mean, I know nothing was ever perfect, but how did we end up here--you, Franky, me? What's it all about, man." Lil Joe let out a long sigh and said, "Tell me something, brother, does it get any better on the other side? Does this feeling of emptiness ever go away? Let me know, brother. Let me know that there's a reason for all of this, man, cause I'm not gettin' it, Jimmy."

Lil Joe let out a long sigh and stared off into the distance at the darkening sky while he gathered his thoughts. "Well, Jimmy, it's getting dark, and I got Marco waiting on me, so I'm gonna get goin' now. But hey, uh, I'll be stopping by every now and then to visit. All right?" Lil Joe clenched his jaw while he fought back the tears that had begun to well up in his eyes. "I'll see you, bro," he said and walked back to where Marco was parked.

When he hopped into the Explorer, Marco gave him a minute to his thoughts and then looked over and said with enthusiasm, "So, are you ready to go out and have some fun with your little brother!"

Lil Joe smiled. "Yeah, Marco, I've been lookin' forward to it for a long time."

Marco grinned. "Good, because I know just the place to go to kick start the night. It's a little strip joint downtown." He turned on the ignition and sparked up the engine. "I figured we could go watch some girlies get naked before we hit the club scene."

Lil Joe formed an image of the whole scene in his head. "All right, man, let's go!"

About ten minutes later, Marco parked in the small parking lot of a strip club called "Felines." As he and Lil Joe walked through the door and into an empty lounge, Lil Joe could hear the beat of loud music coming from behind a couple of doors on the other side of the lounge. A bulky, tattooed bouncer who stood in front of the double door that led into the main entertainment area greeted them with a "What's up?" and opened the door for them.

"Hey, how's it goin'?" Marco shot back as he and Lil Joe walked into the x-rated area of the club. Inside, Lil Joe's eyes lit up with amazement as he caught an eyeful of a couple of topless waitresses parading around the floor of the club serving drinks to a crowd of half drunk and excited men. Out of habit, Lil Joe began to look over the club in order to take in his surroundings. However, he was quickly sidetracked when a pretty, half-naked blonde waitress approached them. "Hey, fellas, what can I get you to drink?" she asked.

"Well, hi, sweetheart," Marco said. "I'll take a gin and tonic and . . . " both he and the pretty waitress looked to Lil Joe, who was trying his hardest not to stare at the blonde's young and perky bare breasts. "Uh, I'll take the same, thanks." Marco grinned at Lil Joe's boyish shyness and handed the waitress two fifty dollar bills. "Keep 'em comin'. Okay, sweetie? We'll be right over there." Marco pointed to a huge leather booth that surrounded the main stage where a tall, large breasted mulatto woman was in the middle of her routine.

"Okay, I'll have your drinks for you in just a minute," she said as she strutted off towards the bar.

Marco laughed and patted Lil Joe on the shoulder. "Come on, man, let's go have a seat and enjoy the view."

As they strolled over to the large booth, Lil Joe's eyes bounced around from one woman to another until finally Marco burst out in laughter. "You're just like a kid in a candy store, aren't you?"

Lil Joe smiled. "Yeah, man, this is a trip."

Marco chuckled again. "Yeah, I think my first time in one of these joints I must of looked something like you do right now."

As soon as they took seats in the booth, the pretty blonde dropped off their drinks. Marco tipped her five bucks and thanked her. She smiled at Lil Joe and walked back in the direction of the bar. "I think she likes you, Joe," Marco teased.

Lil Joe took a gulp of his drink and grimaced at the taste. "Yeah, she probably thinks I'm a pervert cause I can't keep my eyes off of her tits."

Marco laughed again. "I doubt that, bro. Look where we're at."

Lil Joe nodded. "Yeah, that's true. So, do you hang out at places like this a lot?"

"Shit, no," Marco said, "with work and Tina and the baby, I'm lucky if I have the spare time to sleep."

"Hmm," Lil Joe grunted.

Just then the tall mulatto exited the stage and soon after a pretty Latina wearing a Catholic school girl's uniform took to the stage. "Hot damn, Joe, look at that!" Marco blurted out. "Ouch!" He reached into his pants pocket and pulled out a large stack of folded singles and handed half to Lil Joe. "Here you go, man. When she comes this way, why don't you slide a few of these in her G-string."

Lil Joe chuckled. "Okay, thanks."

For the next couple of hours, Lil Joe and Marco drank and enjoyed each other's company while they watched numerous strippers perform their acts. Then Marco took a quick glance at his watch and said, "Hey, big brother, what do you say we go hit another scene?"

By then Lil Joe had developed quite a buzz from the gin, so he turned to Marco wearing a huge drunken grin. "Sure, bro, but what's wrong with this place?"

Marco laughed. "Nothin's wrong with this place, but if I don't get you outta here soon, you'll never wanna leave."

Lil Joe grunted. "That's probably true, so where to next?"

Marco rubbed his brow. "Aah, man, I know a lively little club in Rialto that I think you'll like."

Lil Joe nodded. "Okay, but are you all right to drive? Cause I'm a little buzzed already."

Marco smiled. "You just have a low tolerance for real alcohol, bro, but you'll get used to it in time. Come on, let's go!"

As they were heading for the door, the pretty blonde waitress came across them on her way to deliver drinks. "Oh, are you two leaving already?" she asked in a disappointed tone.

"Yeah," Lil Joe replied with a smile. He pointed to Marco. "He says if I stay any longer, I won't wanna leave."

The blonde smiled back at him. "Well, all right, but you came back again soon. Okay?" She gave him a wink and strutted off towards the giant booth.

Lil Joe watched her walk away and turned to Marco. "You know, I think you might be right about her. I might have to come check her out one of these days."

"That's right," Marco said with a chuckle, "you should do that, Joe."

As they stepped out of the club and into the clear dark night, Lil Joe drew in a deep breath of the cool, brisk night air and held it for a moment before exhaling. "Damn, Marco," he said, looking up at the night sky while he waited for Marco to unlock the Explorer doors, "do you know how many of my friends back in the joint would give the rest of their lives just to enjoy one night like this?"

Marco frowned and leaned his shoulder against the Explorer. "That's sad, bro, but I know it's a reality."

"Yeah," Lil Joe sighed, "locking a man in a cage for life has got to be some type of crime. You know, Marco, a lot of people don't know this, but a life sentence is far worse than the death penalty, man. You see, with the death penalty they kill your body quickly, but with a life sentence, they slowly kill your soul until finally you're no longer human."

Marco shook his head. "That's insane. You know, Joe, I can't even begin to understand what you've been through, man, but I want you to know that I'm here for you."

Lil Joe smiled. "My little brother has grown up to be one hell of a man. Come on, let's go hit that club you were talkin' about."

"Well all right," Marco said with excitement. "Let's do it then!"

They arrived at the crowded club some twenty minutes later and after finding a place to park and waiting in line for another forty-five minutes, they were finally back on track with their night of fun. As they stepped inside the club and made their way across the packed first floor towards the huge bar in the back, Lil Joe was awestruck as his eyes absorbed the whole scene. There were many seductively dressed women dancing in packs, music blasting loudly from all corners of the building, and a variety of different colored laser lights beaming in all directions. He had never seen anything like it, and Marco must have read it from his facial expression. When they finally reached the bar, he leaned in close to Lil Joe and shouted, "I know, it's a lot to take in if you're not used to it."

"Yeah!" Lil Joe nodded as he searched over the dance floor with his eyes, admiring all the women as they danced provocatively to the beat of the loud music.

Marco got the attention of one of the bartenders and ordered two shots of tequila. He handed one to Lil Joe. "Salud," he yelled.

"Salud," Lil Joe yelled back and downed the smooth liquid fire. Just then a cute, petite brunette with blue streaks in her shoulder length hair approached Lil Joe and without even saying anything grabbed him by the wrist and led him out onto the dance floor. He took a quick look back towards Marco, who shrugged his shoulders and grinned, then waved him off as if to say, Go ahead and enjoy yourself. So Lil Joe went with it. However, he was somewhat nervous because he didn't know how to dance. To his relief, there wasn't much dancing required on his part. Evidently the little vixen just wanted him to stand there while she rubbed her butt all over him. Lil Joe didn't mind, although when she turned around to face him and began grinding on one of his legs, he was grateful for the change because apparently he was quite sensitive to the other physical attention and feared that if he had to endure much more of the first position, he would have had an accident in his pants.

"Hey!" she leaned in close to him and asked, "what's your name?"

"Lil Joe," he yelled back. What's yours?

"Lil Joe, huh," she said with a wicked grin. "From what I felt a minute ago, there's nothing little about you!"

Lil Joe flushed and smiled.

"My name's Roxy," she said. "Nice to meet you."

"Likewise. Hey, Roxy, do you wanna go get a drink?"

She nodded. "Okay."

They walked off the dance floor together towards the bar where Marco stood nursing another drink. Lil Joe introduced Marco to Roxy. "Hey, Marco, this is Roxy. Roxy, this is my brother Marco."

Marco smiled at her. "Hi, Roxy, nice to meet you."

"You, too. I see handsome runs in the family."

Lil Joe and Marco smiled at her flirtatious comment. Lil Joe reached into his pocket and pulled out his money clip. "Say, Marco, you ready for another drink?"

"No, I'm cool with this one, Joe. Thanks."

Lil Joe turned to Roxy. "What would you like to drink?"

"I'll take a sex on the beach!" she said.

Lil Joe nodded. He was aware that some mixed drinks bore strange names, but he didn't exactly feel comfortable hollering out to the male bartender for a "sex on the beach" so he handed Marco two twenty dollar bills from his money clip and said in his ear, "Hey, bro, I don't know how much drinks cost. So could you order them? I'll take another tequila and she wants something called a sex on the beach."

Marco grinned. He knew what Lil Joe was up to. "You don't wanna order a girlie drink, huh?"

Lil Joe laughed. "Yeah, you caught me."

Marco shook his head. "Don't worry about it; I'll take care of it."

"Thanks, Marco."

After they got their drinks, Lil Joe and Roxy were engaging in small talk when one of Roxy's girlfriends approached and let Roxy know with a hand gesture that she was leaving. Roxy turned to Lil Joe and apologetically said, "Sorry, that's my ride. I gotta go. But wait." She hurried to her friend and quickly returned with a pen. "Here," she said as she took Lil Joe by the wrist and wrote a phone number on his forearm, "that's my number. Call me sometime so we can hook up." Then she leaned into him and kissed him on the cheek. "See ya!"

Marco whistled. "Man, you sure are getting a lot of play from the ladies tonight. They must smell fresh meat."

Lil Joe laughed at his brother's comment. "Yeah, well I suppose I got a lot of catchin' up to do."

Marco raised his glass. "Shit, I'll drink to that." Then he looked at his watch. "Damn, it's already after midnight. We should probably head home before we get too drunk. Besides, my little lady is probably waiting up for me."

Lil Joe smiled and patted Marco on the back. "Hey, all right, man, but hey," he said, looking around the crowded floor in search of the restroom, "do you think you can help me find the can? Cause I gotta piss before my bladder explodes."

Marco chuckled. "Sure, bro, I know where it is. Follow me."

After making a quick stop in the restroom, they called it a night and left for home. "So, tonight was fun, huh?" Marco asked on the drive home.

"Yeah, man," Lil Joe answered with a smile. "We're gonna have to do this again sometime."

Marco laughed. "Yeah, if I can ever get the time off of work again."

Lil Joe nodded. "I hear you, man. I've been noticing how many hours you work on a daily basis. It must be rough."

Marco sighed. "It is at times, but mostly because I'm away from Tina and Rebecca so much. How about you, Joe? What are your plans workwise?"

Lil Joe sighed. "I've been giving it some thought. I was hoping to land a job as a paralegal for a local private attorney or somethin', but I don't know," he said, shrugging. "I mean, I don't know how many people are willing to hire an ex-con, you know? But hey, I imagine I'll do whatever I have to."

Marco shook his head. "Well, I'm sure I can find you a job at the restaurant if that's something you would be interested in."

Lil Joe smiled. "Thanks, bro, but I wouldn't want to impose, man. I mean, hey, you got something good goin' on there, and you worked hard for it. You don't need your ex-con brother there fucking things up for you."

Marco wrinkled his brow in obvious discomfort. "Nah, man, it ain't like that. Don't even think like that, Joe. You know family always comes first."

Lil Joe smiled at his little brother's words and tried to ease his concerns. "I know, Marco. Hey, don't worry about it, all right? I tell you what, if nothing else comes through for me, then I'll take you up on your offer. Okay?"

Marco smiled, obviously satisfied with Lil Joe's response. "All right then. Sounds like a plan."

They arrived home a little after 1 o'clock and just as Marco had predicted, Tina was up watching a late night movie while waiting for them to get home. The events and lack of sleep over the past two days had finally caught up with Lil Joe, so after saying goodnight to Marco and Tina, he took a quick shower and went straight to sleep.

CHAPTER TWENTY-FIVE

THE NEXT MORNING LIL JOE AWOKE a little after 10 o'clock feeling refreshed and, to his surprise, hangover free. It had been a long time since he had slept that late, and he was grateful for the rest. After going through his morning wash up ritual, he went into the kitchen and found his mother making a fresh pot of coffee. "Hey, Ma, good morning," he said, giving her a kiss on the cheek.

"Good morning, mijo. Did you and Marco have fun last night?"

He smiled at the memory of the strip club. "Yeah, uh, we had a great time, Ma."

"That's good, mijo." She put her hand on his face and smiled at him with loving motherly eyes. "I'm so glad to have my two boys home with me."

Lil Joe smiled back. "I'm glad to be home, Mam_," he said and kissed her on the forehead.

Just then Marco came into the kitchen carrying Rebecca. Like always, she was all smiles and happiness. "Hey, Joe, what's up?" Marco greeted him.

"Aah," he sighed. "Not much, bro, just waking up. Where's Tina?"

Marco smiled. "Doin' the same. I got up early to feed Rebecca so she could sleep in."

Lil Joe nodded. "Hey, Marco, if you don't got any plans later, do you think you could drive me around on a couple of errands?"

Marco nodded. "Sure, no problem."

"Thanks, man. How's noon sound?"

"Noon's fine."

Lil Joe turned to his mom. "Hey, Mom, do you need us to pick up anything while we're out?"

She thought about it for a moment and said, "No, we have everything we need right now, but thank you."

"Okay, Mom."

After Lil Joe had a couple of cups of hot coffee in his system, he took another shower and he and Marco went out on a couple of errands. Lil Joe had Marco drive him to the bank first so he could make a withdrawal from the ATM and then to a Wal-Mart so he could buy a couple of Play Station games for Vanessa's son, Angel. He had a hard time deciding which games to get. "Hey, Marco, help me out here, man. I don't know which ones to get. What kind of games are appropriate for a seven-year-old boy?"

Marco shrugged. "I suppose something that's not too violent."

Lil Joe nodded. "Yeah, okay, that sounds cool. How about these two?" He picked two game cartridges off the display wall and read their names: "Sonic Heroes and Champions of Norrath?

Marco looked them over. "Yeah, those look fine."

Lil Joe looked them over again. "Yeah, I'll get these. Besides, if he don't like them or Vanessa don't, she can always trade them in for something different. Right?"

"Yeah, as long as they have the receipt."

Lil Joe shook his head. "Okay, fuck it, I'll go with these."

While the cashier was ringing up the games, Lil Joe said to Marco, "Hey, man, thanks for running me around today, bro. I appreciate it."

"Any time."

"Hey, uh, could we make one last stop at a liquor store on the way home? I wanna pick up a money order for Franky and a bottle of wine to bring to Vanessa's tonight."

"Sure, all right. So how is Franky anyway? I haven't heard anything about him since Mom visited him in the county jail."

Lil Joe shrugged. "I imagine he's doin' all right. The last time I heard from him was just before I paroled. He said that after I had time to settle down out here, I would be hearing from him."

"That's cool," Marco said. "Next time you write to him, tell him I send my regards."

On their way home after making a quick stop at a liquor store down the street from their mother's house, Lil Joe asked Marco, "Hey, bro, do you think you can teach me how to drive?"

Marco chuckled. "You mean right now?"

"No." Lil Joe let out a little chuckle of his own. "I mean in your spare time, like on your days off or somethin'"

Marco nodded. "Yeah, okay, sure. I'll teach you, Joe. It'll be fun."

Lil Joe chuckled again. "Yeah, well, we'll see if you still feel that way when I'm actually behind the wheel."

Marco laughed. "Well in that case, we'll have to practice in Mom's car."

"Yeah," Lil Joe said, laughing.

When they got home, Tina and their mom were ecstatic with the news of Rebecca speaking for the first time. "Oh, Marco, you should of heard her," Tina said adoringly.

"What did she say, babe?"

"She said Hi. Me and your mom were sitting here watching the novela [Spanish soap opera] on the TV and I was bouncing Rebecca on my knee when she started giggling and getting playful. So I looked down at her and said Hi, baby, and that's when she just blurted it out." Tina paused to smile down at Rebecca, who was sitting on her lap. "She said Hi," Tina said, mimicking Rebecca's baby voice.

Lil Joe's mother was sitting across the living room smiling proudly at her granddaughter. "Oh, mijo, I wish you could of heard her," she said to Marco.

"Yeah," Marco said, "me too." He scooped Rebecca up off Tina's lap and kissed her on the cheek. "That's my baby girl. You wanna say Hi to Daddy, sweetheart?" Rebecca giggled and put her finger in his nose. Marco laughed. "Well, I guess not, huh?"

Lil Joe smiled as he watched his brother interact with his daughter, and at that moment he realized just how fortunate Marco was. It made him wonder if he would ever be as fortunate as his brother and one day have a family of his own.

The rest of the afternoon, Lil Joe hung around the house and passed the time listening to Marco and Tina try to get Rebecca to speak again. Around 5 o'clock, he took a shower and got ready for his dinner date with Vanessa. After his shower, he walked out to the back yard to hang up his boxer shorts and socks on the clothesline. His mother was already hanging up some clothes she had just pulled out of the washing machine.

"Hey, Mom, is there room for my stuff?"

She smiled and pushed a sheet aside to make some room. "You know, mijo, you don't have to hand wash your clothes in the shower. The washing machine works just fine."

Lil Joe grinned. "I know, Ma. I'm sorry. I guess old habits die hard, huh?"

She smiled again and took his clothes and pinned them up on the line. "So, I hear you're going to Vanessa's tonight?"

"Yeah, I'm gettin' ready to head over there right now. Hey, Mom, uh, I got a letter that I wrote to Franky. I was wondering if you could send it out for me in the morning?"

"Sure, mijo, just put it on the lamp stand next to the couch and I'll make sure it goes out."

"Hey, thanks, Mom," he said and kissed her on the cheek. "I'll be home later tonight. Okay?"

"Okay, mijo."

After he finished getting ready for his night with Vanessa, Lil Joe grabbed the bottle of wine from the kitchen and the video games for Angel, put the letter for Franky on the lamp stand, and headed to Vanessa's house on foot. When he got there, her screen door was closed, but her front door was open. When he knocked, he heard Vanessa's voice holler out from somewhere in the house, "Joe, is that you? Come on in. I'm in the kitchen. I'll be right out."

"Okay," he hollered back. As he let himself into the house, he was immediately approached by a little dark haired boy he instantly recognized from the pictures as Angel. He introduced himself to the boy. "Hey, how's it goin'? I'm Joe."

The little boy smiled deviously, then walked up to Lil Joe and punched him in the stomach. "Hi, I'm Angel," the boy said with his chin up.

Vanessa had come out of the kitchen just in time to witness her son's greeting. "Angel!" she began to scold the boy, but Lil Joe shook his head and winked at her, letting her know it was okay. Then he grinned at the little boy and set the paper bag containing the video games and the bottle of wine on the table next to the door.

Then, with lightning speed, he snatched Angel off his feet and hung him upside down by the ankles. "Now let's see you try that again," he said in a joking tone.

The boy began giggling and squirming around, obviously enjoying being upside down. After a few seconds, Lil Joe set the boy on his feet and said, "Hi, Angel, it's nice to meet you, kiddo." The boy smiled. Then Lil Joe took the paper bag from the table and withdrew the two video games and handed them to Angel. "Do you have those ones yet?"

Angel shook his head. "Uh, uh."

"Well, you do now, kiddo, they're all yours."

"Cool!" Angel's face lit up with excitement as he turned to Vanessa and held up the games so she could see them. "Look, Mommy," he said excitedly. Then he turned back to Lil Joe and said, "Thanks. I'm gonna go play them right now!" He ran off in the direction of the television.

Lil Joe turned and looked at Vanessa, who was standing just outside the kitchen smiling at him in a way that captured his heart. He walked over and handed her the paper bag containing the bottle of wine and kissed her passionately on the lips. "Smile for me like that again, baby," he said while gazing into her soft brown eyes.

Vanessa gently bit her bottom lip while slowly shaking her head. "You're something of a charmer, aren't you?"

Lil Joe smiled. "Only when it comes naturally."

She smiled at him again and then turned her attention to the paper bag. "What's this?" she asked as she opened the bag and pulled out the bottle.

Lil Joe shrugged. "It's just some red wine. I wasn't sure what to bring, so Marco helped me pick that out."

"This will go great with what we're having!"

Lil Joe saw a bag of hamburger buns on the dinner table next to them and said, "Oh, hamburgers, huh?"

"What?" Vanessa looked confused and then laughed, realizing where he had gotten that idea. "No, silly, we're having chicken lasagna. Those buns are for Angel. He doesn't like lasagna so he's having a hamburger."

Lil Joe laughed at himself. "Sorry, I don't know that much about that kind of stuff. I've been eatin' prison food most of my life."

Vanessa smiled and Lil Joe took a moment to look her over, noticing for the first time that she had gotten all dolled up for their little in-house dinner date. She was wearing a sleek, short black dress that, to his delight, was clinging tightly to her desirable curves. Vanessa noticed he was gawking at her and shyly looked away, smiling. "Why are you staring at me like that?"

"Because you look so beautiful."

Vanessa blushed. "Thanks," she said in a soft, low tone. "And thank you for thinking of Angel with the gifts. That was real sweet of you."

"Don't mention it."

Vanessa sighed and clasped her hands together. "Well, dinner will be ready in about ten minutes, so if you wanna just hang out and make yourself comfortable until then."

"Well, can I help you with anything?"

Vanessa looked around at the dining area and into the kitchen. "No, everything is pretty much all set. Thanks."

"Well, okay then." Lil Joe cracked a boyish smile. "Then I'll go see if Angel will let me play the video games with him."

"Okay," she said with a smile, "I'll give you two boys a holler when everything is ready."

"Okay, sounds good," he said and kissed her before going to join Angel in the living room.

After they had eaten and Lil Joe had helped Vanessa clean up the dinner mess, he and Angel played a couple more rounds of wrestling on the Play Station. Then Vanessa put Angel to bed for the night. When she returned from tucking him in, Lil Joe noticed that she had changed into her tiny pair of grey sweat shorts and a white t-shirt, and he was instantly reminded of their night together. Vanessa joined him on the couch, where they spent the next hour or so relaxing and drinking wine while they talked. "So, Angel sure did take a liking to you, Joe. I'm a bit surprised. He usually acts like such a brat with people he's just met."

"Nah, he's a good kid. I like him even though he kicked my butt on that video wrestling game of his."

Vanessa laughed. "Yeah, he's good with his video games." She grabbed the remote control for the CD player off the coffee table and asked, "How about some music?"

Lil Joe nodded and she pushed the play button on the remote and put it back on the table. Soon the living room was filled with the smooth music of the Delfonics. "Hey, now," Lil Joe said, nodding his head to the music.

Vanessa smiled. "You like the Delfonics?"

"Oh, yeah, they're one of my favorite oldie groups."

"Me, too. How about that."

Lil Joe said with a sly smile, "A girl after my own heart."

Vanessa looked at him with smiling eyes and refilled both of their glasses from the half empty bottle of wine. "So, did you and Marco have fun clubbing last night?"

"You've been talking to Tina," he teased, "but yeah, I did have fun. It was pretty cool spending time with Marco."

"Yeah," she said in a soft, playful voice, "but I bet there were a lot of women hanging on the two of you, huh?"

Lil Joe fought back a smile. "No, not really."

Vanessa said unbelievingly, "Yeah, I bet."

Lil Joe smiled and chuckled. "Well, okay, maybe there were a couple, but there were none that I was interested in."

"Well that's good to hear," she said as she wedged herself between his legs and leaned back into his chest.

Lil Joe quickly gulped down his wine and then reached out and put the empty glass on the coffee table so he could wrap his arms around her and enjoy the warm feeling of having her body pressed against him. She began to gently run her fingers over his forearm, enticing him with her feminine touch. "Umm," she purred, "this is nice."

"Yeah," Lil Joe whispered as he brushed her hair to the side and kissed her softly behind the ear.

"Tell Me This Is a Dream" was playing on the CD player and all Lil Joe could think was how good it felt being there with her, and how much it felt like a dream. He nuzzled his face into the nape of her neck and gently rubbed his nose across her soft, sweet smelling flesh. Then he took in a deep breath and whispered into her ear, "God, I love the way you smell. It's so intoxicating." Vanessa purred again and then turned around and straddled him. They kissed and petted heavily for several minutes until Vanessa finally pulled away and rested her forehead on his.

"Stay with me tonight." Then she pulled back and looked into his eyes. "Will you?"

The first thought that popped into his head was what Angel would think if he woke up in the morning to find him still there. He drew in a deep breath and sighed. "I want to, baby, but maybe we should let Angel get used to seeing me around first."

"Oh," Vanessa sighed and set her soft gaze upon him. "I know that's the right thing to do, but I can't help myself. I want you here with me."

Lil Joe brushed her hair from her face and kissed her on the forehead. He could hardly believe that such a beautiful woman was saying those things to him. He looked into her soft, pleading eyes and had to muster up every ounce of will power he had. "Aw, Vanessa," he said, caressing her cheek with the back of his hand, "I gotta go before I give in."

She playfully pouted by sticking out her bottom lip and then reluctantly hopped off of him and walked him to the door. They stood there kissing for a minute before Lil Joe wished her goodnight and stepped out onto the front porch. Just as he was about to leave, Vanessa called out, "Hey, Joe!"

"Yeah."

"If we're going to be waiting for Angel to get used to you being around, then you're going to have to start coming by a lot."

Lil Joe smiled at her. "That's the plan," he said. Then he kissed her again and headed off home.

When he got there, his mother was up, sitting in the living room by herself watching TV. As soon as he walked through the front door, she greeted him with a smile. "Hi, mijo, how was your date?"

Lil Joe grinned, thinking that the question sounded like something she would have asked him as a teenager if he had been home at that age. "It was nice, Mom, thanks." He looked around. "Where is everyone?"

"Oh, Marco and Tina took Rebecca and went to bed a little while ago." Lil Joe nodded and his mom got up and turned the television off. "Well, mijo, I'm tired so I'm going to bed too. I was just waiting up for you to remind you that we have to go see your parole officer tomorrow."

Lil Joe raised his brow. "Man, I forgot all about that. I guess I've been having too much fun. So what time do you wanna leave tomorrow, Ma?"

Sometime before noon would be nice, mijo. That way we could get it over with.

Lil Joe smiled. "Okay, Mom, that sounds good. I'll be ready by 10 o'clock." He kissed her on the cheek and wished her goodnight. After his mother went to bed, he took a shower and called it a night. He wanted to wake up early and go for a good run before he headed to the parole office. He hadn't worked out since the day before he paroled, so he figured it was time to get back into a good workout routine. Besides, Vanessa had stirred him up quite a bit and he figured he could use the workout to burn off some of the unspent testosterone that she had built up inside him.

Come morning, Lil Joe was able to get an early start like he had planned. He arose before dawn and had washed up and was out the door for his run before 6 A.M. As he ran, he realized he was running along the old route that he, Franky, and Jimmy used to take to get around the neighborhood when they were kids. So he ended up taking a stroll down memory lane without even making a conscious decision to do so. He was glad he did. He couldn't make much sense of it at first, but when he passed by the old house where he and Franky had killed Robert so many years before, he realized that subconsciously he was trying to achieve some kind of closure and put the past behind him so that he could move on with his life.

Midway through his run, he came across an old abandoned apartment complex he remembered from his childhood. Back when he was a kid and the place was full of occupants, sometimes he, Franky, and Jimmy would sneak into the swimming pool area to check out the teenage girls who were sunbathing in their bikinis. He smiled at the memory of their horny pre-teen antics and chuckled to himself thinking that not a whole lot had changed since then; he was still just as hot blooded.

After he got home and showered, he and his mother went out to eat at a Pancake House near the parole office before his first weekly check-in with Mrs. Cummings. Then he accompanied his mother while she ran some personal errands.

For the next couple of weeks, his daily routine was pretty much the same. He spent time with his family and did a lot of work around the house to help out his mother. He also spent a lot of time with Vanessa and Angel. Then one day early in his second month as a free man, when he and Marco returned home from one of his driving lessons, he noticed that his mom had left a letter from Franky for him on the lamp stand. He immediately took it to his bedroom to read:

> March 2004
>
> Hey, bro, how's it going? I hope that all is well for you and the family. <u>Por favor</u> give my love to everyone. Well, I received your brief letter and the three hundred dollars you sent. Thanks, bro. So how are you enjoying life in the free world? I bet it's a hell of a change for you after spending most of your life in here. So do you have a pretty young woman to harass yet? I sure hope so. Otherwise, your ass don't deserve to be out there. <u>Puro pedo</u> [Just kidding]. Anyway, all is well for me considering where I am. I love the food here. I've always been curious to know what dog food tastes like and now I know! So hey, remember what I told you in my last letter about getting at you with someone to contact to help you get on your feet? Well, I have a couple of things stored at a friend's house for you. His name is Danny, and he lives in the Manor off of foothill. Here's

> his number--555-0131. He'll be expecting your call, so get at him soon. All right? And I know how you are with trusting people you just meet, but don't trip on Danny. He's trustworthy. You know I wouldn't say it if it wasn't true. All right then, bro, con mucho respeto y carino, siempre tu carnal [with much respect and love, always your brother], Franky.

Lil Joe read over Franky's letter twice just in case he had missed something the first time. But the only thing that stuck out was his friend Danny's phone number. He couldn't quite recall where he had seen it, but he knew he had seen it before. He was familiar with where the guy lived. The Manor was a small housing project on the border between San Bernardino and Rialto. It was where his grandmother had lived when he was a kid.

Lil Joe took Franky's letter into the living room and sat down on the couch. It was only a little after noon, and since no one else was in the living room at the time, he decided it was a good time to try and get hold of Franky's friend Danny. He picked up the phone and slowly dialed the number. After only two rings, a man's voice answered, "Yep."

"Yeah, hello," Lil Joe said.

"Yeah, who's this?"

"This is Joe. I'm calling to speak with Danny."

There was a slight pause, then the man on the other end excitedly said, "Oh, Joe, yeah, yeah, right. Franky's friend Joe. I've been waiting to hear from you. Yeah, this is Danny you're speaking to!"

Lil Joe chuckled, thinking that the guy sounded like he was drunk. "Yeah, hey, Danny. I just received your number today in a letter I got from Franky."

"Oh, hey, yeah, that's cool, man. I got a letter from Franky myself about a week ago letting me know you would be getting a hold of me soon." There was another slight pause, then Danny said, "Hey--uh--he did let you know that I had some things of his for you, right?"

"Yeah, he mentioned that in his letter," Lil Joe replied.

"Okay, good. Well shit--uh--I'm not particularly busy or anything at the moment, so if you'd like to swing by, you're more than welcome to."

Lil Joe thought things over for a moment. He didn't know exactly what it was that Danny was holding for him, so he didn't want to ask Marco to drive him to the guy's house not knowing what he would be involving him in. "Uh, hey, Danny, I don't really have a way to get over there to the Manor right now."

Danny cut in. "Ah, hey, don't worry about it. I can go pick you up. It's no problem."

"Yeah, cool," Lil Joe replied. He was a bit surprised by the guy's willingness to go out of his way for him, but still, he didn't know the guy and didn't want a stranger coming to his mother's house to pick him up. So he decided to have the guy pick him up at a nearby liquor store. "Hey, Danny, are you familiar with the Westside?"

"Yeah, sure."

"Okay, then, there's a little liquor store on "E" Street called the Seven Seas. It's right down the street from the San Bernardino High School. Do you know the area?"

"Yeah, I sure do."

"Okay, cool. How about we meet there in about half an hour?"

"All right then, Joe, I'll see you then. Oh, hey, I'll be driving a charcoal grey 67 Impala. That way you know what to keep an eye out for."

"Okay now, Danny. Thanks. I'll see you in a half an hour."

Lil Joe waited about ten minutes and then walked to the liquor store and waited for Danny to show up. He didn't have to wait very long. Danny drove up about ten minutes after he got there. At the time, Lil Joe was the only person standing in front of the store, so Danny spotted him right away. He pulled the Impala up right in front of Lil Joe and waved him over to the open window on the passenger's side. "Hey, you must be Joe," the beer-bellied, brown-haired man behind the wheel said.

"Yeah, that's me. You must be Danny."

"Sure am. Nice to meet ya, Joe."

"Likewise Danny."

"Well come on, hop in."

Lil Joe hopped in. "Nice ride," he said as he closed the door and looked around the inside of the Impala, admiring the detailed black leather interior.

"Yeah, thanks," Danny said as he adoringly caressed the shiny black dashboard with his hand. "She's my pride and joy."

Lil Joe grinned at the man's obvious love for his car. "So we're heading off to your place then, huh?"

"Yeah. So, Franky said you were locked up for eighteen years." He whistled. "That sure is a loooong time."

Lil Joe chucked at the man's cartoonish character. "Yeah, it's a little while."

Danny took his eyes off the road for a moment and glanced at Lil Joe. "It's a damn shame what happened with Jimmy and Franky. They were two of the best people I ever met."

Lil Joe picked up on the sincerity in Danny's voice and also saw it in his rough facial features. He nodded in agreement. "Yeah, me too." He could tell that Danny was at least in his mid-forties and he was a little curious to know how he had become friends with Franky and Jimmy. "So how did you end up meeting Franky and Jimmy anyway?"

"Oh, shit, it was under some pretty crazy circumstances, man. Jimmy was seeing my wife's niece Veronica, and well, my wife, Gina, is a registered nurse. So anyway, one night a couple of years back, Veronica brought Jimmy and Franky to our house. Jimmy was in pretty bad shape." He grimaced at the memory. "He had been shot and needed someone to tend to his wounds, and of course they couldn't take him to a hospital; the cops would of got involved for sure. So my wife took care of him and patched him up. Then the next day, Franky stopped by at our house and insisted that we accept an envelope full of money out of gratitude for us helping Jimmy." Danny shook his head and grinned. "He gave us ten grand, man, and it couldn't of come at a better time. Things were kind of rough, and I was out of work. I guess Veronica had mentioned that to Franky because he asked if I would be interested in doing small time odd jobs here and there for some extra cash." Danny shrugged. "So things went from there and I became good friends with both him and Jimmy."

Lil Joe nodded, thinking that Danny sounded like a stand up guy. "That's good, man. You sound like a real loyal friend, Danny. That's a quality hard to find in people these days."

Danny smiled at the compliment. "Thanks, man. So I bet you're wondering what it is that Franky left for you at my house, huh?"

Lil Joe grunted. "Yeah, a little bit."

"Well shit!" Danny said excitedly, "I think you're gonna like it. I put it together myself. But hey, I don't wanna ruin the surprise for you. You'll find out what it is soon enough."

A few minutes later, Danny pulled into the Manor and parked the Impala in a large driveway in front of the garage of an old green house. "Well, here we are," he said. They got out and Lil Joe followed Danny through the front door and directly into the kitchen just to the right of the door. Danny went straight to the refrigerator and took out two bottles of beer and handed one to Lil Joe. "Thanks," Lil Joe said as he unscrewed the cap and took a swig.

Danny did the same. "Aah, that's good stuff. Well shit, come on, let's show you what's behind door number two." He walked across the kitchen and opened the side door leading into the garage and switched the light on. Lil Joe followed him into the roomy garage and Danny pulled a key ring out of his pocket and handed it to Lil Joe. "Here you go, Joe." He pointed to a car covered with a large blue tarp. "There's your surprise, man!" he said with a broad grin. "Go ahead and uncover it. Check it out."

"A car?" said Lil Joe, a little taken aback by the unexpected surprise. He set his beer on the floor next to the car and hurriedly pulled off the tarp as if he were a kid unwrapping a Christmas gift. What he saw underneath the tarp left him speechless. He could hardly believe his eyes. It was a clean, cherried, shiny black 1965 Chevy Impala hardtop with chrome trim and matching fourteen-inch spoked rims. "Damn!" was all he managed to say.

Danny walked up next to him wearing a huge grin. "She sure is a looker, ain't she?"

Lil Joe nodded in agreement, still unable to put the right words together.

"Well, open it up and have a look inside. I detailed the inside with the same black leather interior as mine."

Lil Joe opened the door and hopped inside. He looked around in awe while feeling the interior. "You did all of this?"

"Yeah," Danny replied, smiling proudly. "I built this baby from the ground up. She was in poor shape when Franky and Jimmy first brought her to me, but I restored her in time," he said as he caressed the Impala's roof with his shirt sleeve.

Lil Joe shook his head. "Man, I don't know how to thank you for this."

"Oh, no, Joe." Danny waved it off. "It was my pleasure. I love rebuilding cars. Besides, Franky and Jimmy paid me quite handsomely for my work. So don't even worry about it, man." He pointed to the trunk. "Also, there's some things in the trunk that you might be interested in, but hey, uh, I got some things to take care of in the house, so I'll let you go through all of your stuff in private. I'll be right inside, so when you're all done, come on in and join me for another beer."

Lil Joe nodded. "Yeah, all right, thanks, Danny."

After Danny left, Lil Joe just sat in the front seat and daydreamed for a moment. The 1965 Chevy Impala was his absolute favorite car in the world. He remembered when he, Franky, and Jimmy were kids how they used to talk about what kind of car they would drive when they were all grown up. Lil Joe's car was, of course, the 1965 Chevy Impala, Franky's was the 1984 El Camino, and Jimmy's was the 1967 Chevy pickup truck. The childhood memory brought the pang in his stomach back to the surface. "Thanks, fellas," he muttered as he looked around inside the car in disbelief. He saw a piece of paper attached to the sun visor and pulled it down. It was the registration slip in Jimmy's name. He wondered if he would have to change the registration, but decided not to worry about it until later.

After putting the registration slip back where he found it, Lil Joe went to the back of the car and opened the trunk. With the exception of a cardboard box and a small two-gallon gas can, the trunk was empty. He pulled the box closer to him and opened it. Right away, he saw the black ten-millimeter Glock with a silencer attached to the threaded barrel lying on top of a neatly folded wool poncho. He removed the gun and set it aside and then took out the poncho and unfolded it. In the middle he discovered a large silver butterfly knife, two extra, loaded gun clips for the ten millimeter, a Zippo lighter, and an envelope full of cash.

"Damn, fellas," he muttered, "you sure did look out for a motherfucker." He made a mental note to make sure to thank Franky in his next letter. He set everything to the side except the envelope containing the money. He pulled the cash out of the envelope and counted it. There was four thousand dollars in large bills. He split the cash into two stacks of two thousand, folded one stack in half and put it in his pocket, and put the rest back into the envelope. He put everything else back into the box the way he had found it.

After he finished, he grabbed the envelope, closed the trunk, picked up his beer, and went back into the house. He walked through the kitchen and into the small living room, where he found Danny sitting on the couch nursing another beer. "Hey, there you are. You get everything straight?"

Lil Joe nodded. "Yeah, just about." He tossed the envelope onto the couch next to Danny. "For all your trouble," he said.

Danny picked up the envelope and peeked inside. "Oh, hey, man, you don't have to do this."

"Sure I do. It's the least I can do."

Danny frowned. "Man, thanks, Joe. I appreciate it."

Just then a familiar looking brunette with blue streaks in her hair walked through the front door. "Roxy," Danny greeted her. "Hi, sweetheart, this is a friend of mine--Joe. Joe, this is my daughter, Roxy."

Lil Joe grinned in embarrassment and Roxy smiled wickedly and said, "I know who he is, Dad. We met a while back at a club."

Danny chuckled. "Well, it's a small world."

Lil Joe turned to Roxy. "Hey, there, Roxy, how's it goin'?"

"I'm fine. How about yourself."

"I'm good."

Roxy looked at her dad. "So how do you two know each other?"

"This is Franky and Jimmy's friend," Danny explained. "Remember, I told you he would be stopping by."

"Oh, you came to get the car." She smacked her lips in disappointment. "I love that car."

Lil Joe smiled. "Yeah, I think that makes three of us."

Danny laughed and pointed to Roxy. "She practically watched me rebuild that whole car."

I sure did," Roxy said, smiling at Lil Joe flirtatiously. "You're a lucky man, Joe." Then she snatched his beer out of his hand and strutted off towards the back of the house, hollering over her shoulder, "I'm off to take a shower."

Lil Joe watched her as she walked off shaking her nicely shaped butt in her tight fitting Daisy Duke shorts and thought to himself, Damn, she sure is a sexy little thing. He turned to Danny wearing a grin. "She's a little wild, isn't she?"

Danny chuckled again. "Yeah, she takes after her mother that way, but she's a good girl."

Lil Joe nodded. "Oh, yeah, no doubt. So hey, uh, Danny, I have sort of a dilemma on my hands. I don't have a driver's license."

Danny cut in, "That's not a problem. I can drive your car to wherever you wanna take it, and Roxy can follow behind in my car."

"Yeah, I don't know, Danny. There's some pretty hot shit in that trunk. What if we got pulled over?"

Danny waved it off. "Nah, man. Look, in that case, you can ride with Roxy and I'll follow you guys. If for some reason I get pulled over, the cops won't have a reason to search the trunk. I'm not on parole or anything, and I have a valid driver's license. Don't sweat it, Joe, we're cool. As soon as Roxy gets outta the shower, we'll get on our way."

Lil Joe smiled. "All right, then, thanks, man. I really appreciate it."

While they waited for Roxy to get out of the shower, Danny pulled Lil Joe's Impala out of the garage and parked it in the driveway next to his car. While they sat in the front seat listening to the low hum of the sixty-five's engine, Lil Joe made up his mind to schedule the driving test as soon as possible. "Hey, Danny, what's under the hood of this thing anyway?"

"A .327. It's perfect for this car, man. I had a 65 with a .327 just like this one back when I was in my twenties. Man, it was a sweet ride, but unfortunately I wrapped it around a telephone pole."

Lil Joe chuckled. "Well shit, maybe I should drive this baby home after all," he joked.

Danny laughed. "Yeah, no shit, huh?"

Just then Roxy came out of the house and joined them. She squeezed herself into the passenger seat next to Lil Joe. "So you're gonna take her away, huh?" she said with a hint of disappointment in her voice.

"Yeah," he replied with a smile. "Do you think you could help me out with that?"

"Sure, what's up?"

"Well, your dad is gonna drive this car to my mom's place, and we were hoping that you would drive me home so your dad could follow us there." Roxy nodded. "Yeah, all right." She leaned across Lil Joe and held out her hand to Danny with a devious smile. "I need the keys to your car, Dad."

Danny gritted his teeth while he dug his keys out of his pocket and reluctantly handed them to Roxy. "Be nice to my car, baby."

"I will, Dad, I promise."

"Hey," Lil Joe cut in, "is there somethin' I should know about? You guys got me trippin' now," he teased. "She's not gonna drive us off a bridge or somethin' is she?"

Danny chuckled. "She just might, so you oughta say a prayer before gettin' in the car with her."

Roxy rolled her eyes. "Don't listen to him, Joe. He's only saying that because he thinks women don't know how to drive. But don't worry," she said with a wink, "you're in good hands."

Lil Joe smiled. "Well okay, then, I can't deny that. Let's do it."

When he and Roxy were alone in her dad's Impala, she looked at him with playfully accusing eyes. "Someone never called me," she said as she started the car.

Lil Joe grinned at her, thinking that if he wasn't already involved with Vanessa, he would be all over her. "Yeah, I know. I apologize for that. It's just that, uh, I'm seeing someone right now."

She looked at him in surprise. "Wow! I think you're the first guy I've met that's not eager to get a little action on the side."

Lil Joe thought about that for a moment before replying with a charming smile, "Yeah, well, I guess I'm just not eager to take on all of the problems that come with juggling women."

Roxy laughed. "I don't blame you. So where to?"

"Oh, uh, just drive towards San Bernardino High School and I'll let you know where to go from there."

Their short trip to Lil Joe's mother's house was uneventful, but the whole time Lil Joe kept glancing back to make sure that Danny wasn't being hassled by the cops. Roxy teased him about it every time. When they finally reached Lil Joe's mother's street, he had Roxy pull the car along the curb in front of the house while they waited for Danny to park the sixty-five across the street. After she cut the engine, Roxy turned to Lil Joe. "You know, Joe, if you ever feel like gettin' a little action on the side, or if things don't work out between you and whoever you're with right now, you come and see me. Okay? I promise I'll make things easy for you."

Lil Joe smiled at her straightforwardness. "Okay, Roxy, I'll definitely keep that in mind." After he'd gotten out, he poked his head back inside the car. "Thanks for the ride."

Roxy looked up at him with a sultry smile. "Oh, honey, I haven't given you a ride yet."

Lil Joe shook his head and let out a little chuckle, then made his way across the street to meet with Danny. As he approached, Danny tossed him the keys to his car and said, "She's all yours, man."

"Thanks, Danny. Thanks for everything, man. I really appreciate it."

"No problem, Joe. You know, anytime you wanna stop by or whatever, my door's always open for you."

Lil Joe nodded. "Likewise, man. If you ever need anything, you know where to find me."

"Well, all right, then," Danny said, extending his hand to Lil Joe, "I better get goin'. Take it easy, Joe."

Lil Joe shook his hand. "All right, Danny. You, too, man."

After Danny and Roxy left, Lil Joe retrieved the box from the trunk of the car and walked into his mother's backyard to an old tool shed. He stashed the box behind and under several other boxes and bags of miscellaneous gardening supplies that his mother no longer used. Then he went in through the back door. Searching through the house, Lil Joe found that everyone was gone except for Marco, who was taking a nap on the couch in the living room. Lil Joe kicked the couch to wake him up. "Hey, Marco, wake up, man. I wanna show you somethin'."

Marco woke up and slowly sat up yawning. "What's goin' on, Joe?"

"Come on outside, man. I want you to see somethin'."

"All right." Marco followed him out the front door, looking around curiously with his sleepy eyes. Lil Joe hurried across the street and stood in front of the Impala with his arms stretched out to his sides.

"So whatcha think, bro? Wanna take her for a spin?"

Marco's eyes widened with excitement. "Hell, yeah, man! Whose is it?"

"It's mine, man."

"Is that right? Where'd you get it?"

"It's a long story, man, but Franky and Jimmy had it stored away for me at a friend's house."

"Damn!" Marco said while he stood admiring the car.

Lil Joe handed him the keys. "Well, come on, man. Don't just stare at it. Let's go for a ride."

Marco looked at his watch. "Okay, man, let's do it, but I gotta be at work by five."

"All right, then we better get goin'."

They cruised around the Westside for a while until Marco had to return home to get ready for work.

CHAPTER TWENTY-SIX

LIL JOE STOOD IN THE SHOWER letting the hot water run over his body while his thoughts wandered. It was just two days from his three-month anniversary as a free man, and to his surprise he was adjusting quite rapidly to the outside world. He had just received his driver's license in the mail from the DMV and now he was preparing to take a trip to the Los Angeles zoo with Vanessa and Angel. Marco and Tina were bringing Rebecca along as well. They had planned the trip three weeks in advance so that Marco would take the time off and Lil Joe could clear the trip with his parole officer.

Lil Joe's mother had left for Palm Springs to visit with her sister yesterday. She and Lil Joe's aunt Josie always took one weekend every month to hit the tribal casinos in the Palm Springs area and spend some time together--just the two of them.

As Lil Joe turned the water off and stepped out of the shower, his thoughts drifted to his old friend Franky. Earlier in the week he had received a letter from him informing him that he had gotten caught up in a prison racial riot and was on his way to the S.H.U. for a couple of years. Lil Joe frowned and shook his head, knowing what kind of trials and tribulations lay ahead for his friend. He wasn't concerned about Franky's physical well being; he knew that he could survive the never ending violence on the inside. Surviving was the easy part. It was what surviving did to a man through time that concerned Lil Joe. It was the changes a man had to go through in order to survive the harsh and cruel conditions of hard time that concerned him. It wasn't easy for a man to distance himself from his own humanity and still manage to keep his sanity. It was perhaps the most cruel and harsh reality of life on the inside--one that Lil Joe was all too familiar with.

He shook off his thoughts when he heard a knock on the bathroom door followed by Tina's voice. "Joe, I'm sorry to rush you, but I have to pee!"

Lil Joe smiled. "Okay, I'll be right out." He quickly put on his boxer shorts and gathered his hygiene items and walked out to find Tina eagerly awaiting his departure. "Sorry I took so long, Tina."

"It's okay, sweetie," she said, rushing past him into the bathroom.

Lil Joe chuckled and made his way to his room to finish getting ready for their trip to the zoo. It was 7 o'clock. He had told Vanessa to be ready to go by 8 A.M. He smiled at the thought of her. He didn't know what to think about their relationship; he didn't even know if that's what it was; he had never been in a relationship before. All he knew was that ever since he got out of prison, he had spent most of his time either with her or thinking about her. His mother had teased him about his relationship with Vanessa, saying he was like a teenage boy in love with his high school sweetheart.

Lil Joe always grunted at the idea of him being in love. He wasn't even sure if falling in love was possible for a man like him. After all, loving someone meant trusting them, and prison had pretty much destroyed his ability to trust anyone. Whatever it was that he felt for Vanessa, she seemed to feel the same way about him, and he knew that their relationship was becoming serious. He decided not to give it too much thought just yet and to just let things ride.

Lil Joe drove over to Vanessa's house at five minutes before 8 o'clock and parked at the curb in front of her house. Marco parked his Explorer across the street and waited for Vanessa and Angel to come out and join Lil Joe. They had decided to take two cars so they wouldn't have to be cramped up in one. Lil Joe honked his horn once and a few moments later Vanessa came out followed by a happy, excited looking Angel. While Vanessa locked the door, Angel met Lil Joe at the car. "You ready to go see all the animals, Angel?"

"Yeah!" Angel energetically replied. "I wanna see the tigers!"

Lil Joe didn't know why, but that reminded him of a Scared Straight program that Tracy had going on while he was there in the hole. The guards would walk young kids from a juvenile detention program down the catwalk to look at all the "caged animals" doing time. Lil Joe shook away those thoughts when Vanessa walked towards him wearing her ever so tempting smile. As always, she looked beautiful. She wore a short, grey plaid skirt with a tight fitting black top and was carrying a black overnight bag. "Hey, baby" Lil Joe greeted her. He took the bag from her. "You look great," he said, then leaned in and kissed her smiling lips.

"Thanks," she answered, caressing his stomach with her hand.

Lil Joe put the overnight bag on the back seat next to where Angel was already seated and playing with his Nintendo Game Boy. Halfway to the zoo, he got bored and decided to playfully harass Lil Joe. "Hey, Joe, were you born in an earthquake?"

"No, I don't think so," Lil Joe replied, going along with the boy's banter.

"Then how do you explain that crack in your butt?" Angel said with a giggle.

"Angel!" Vanessa scolded the boy, wide eyed with disbelief.

Lil Joe chuckled and patted her on the leg. "It's all right, baby. It's a good question."

Vanessa smacked her lips and shook her head. "Don't encourage him."

"You know what, Angel," Lil Joe said, "I'm gonna have to ask my mom about that. Maybe I was born in an earthquake." He looked over at Vanessa and rubbed her leg. "What about you, babe?" he said with a wink. "Were you born in an earthquake."

Vanessa smiled and shook her head. Angel giggled again. "Yeah, Mom was born in a big earthquake!"

Lil Joe chuckled. "You better watch out, kiddo, she might decide to donate you to the zoo and put you in the monkey cage."

Angel laughed. "Yeah, the monkeys!"

Vanessa said, "He seems to like that idea."

Lil Joe chuckled again. "Yeah, he'd probably fit right in."

They reached the zoo a little after 10 o'clock and spent the entire day walking around and looking at all the animals. Both Angel and Rebecca seemed to really enjoy themselves and Lil Joe did as well. He hadn't been to the zoo since he was about Angel's age, so it was like seeing everything for the first time. The day went quite smoothly with the exception of one little incident with Rebecca. Midway through their tour, they had stopped at the petting area so the kids could pet some of the tame animals. As they were about to leave, Rebecca began to bawl out of control. Apparently she had become attached to some of the animals and didn't want to leave. Her crying was breaking Lil Joe's heart, so he stayed back with her a while longer while the rest of the group checked out the reptile area. Finally, about an hour after Lil Joe had taken her to meet back up with the others, she had cried herself to sleep and was quiet the rest of the day.

By the time they left the zoo, it was 4 o'clock, so after stopping at a local restaurant to have dinner and unwind, they checked into a downtown motel for the night. While they were getting ready to go to their rooms, Tina surprised Lil Joe and Vanessa by offering to take Angel into her and Marco's room for the night so they could enjoy some privacy. Lil Joe and Vanessa took her up on her offer and spent the night alone together in their room.

After showering together, they lay on one of the small beds together and talked for a while. "So, today was fun, huh?" Vanessa said.

"Yeah, it was. We should do something like this again real soon."

Vanessa lay flat on her stomach and turned to face him. "That would be nice, but expensive."

Lil Joe reached out and began to rub her naked butt. "Yeah. I guess it's time for me to start looking for a job."

"Have you decided what you wanna do?"

"Yeah. I suppose I'll do whatever I have to, you know? I mean, it's not like there are a lot of people out there willing to take a chance and hire an ex-con." Lil Joe snickered. "Too bad I can't do this for a living."

Vanessa giggled. "What? Rub my butt?"

"Yeah, it would be the best job in the world. I'd work long hours--overtime every day. Shit, I'd even bring my work home with me. I'd just be one big ol' workaholic."

Vanessa giggled again. "You're crazy, you know that?" she teased.

"Yeah, crazy about you, woman." He swatted her on the butt. "Come here," he said and pulled her into his arms. They made love through most of the night.

Early the next morning while Vanessa was taking a shower and Lil Joe was still sprawled out on the bed trying to shake off his early morning laziness, Angel let himself in and jumped onto the bed beside him. "Good morning," he greeted Lil Joe with energetic youth.

Lil Joe patted Angel's matted head of hair. "Hey there, monkey face, how's it goin'?"

Angel made a funny face. "I'm hungry."

"Me, too. As soon as your mom gets outta the shower, I'll jump in for a quick one and we'll go get somethin' to eat. All right?"

"Okay. Can we go to the Pancake House?"

"Sure, there should be one around here somewhere."

About an hour later Lil Joe, Vanessa and Angel met up with Marco, Tina, and Rebecca and they had breakfast in a local Pancake House before heading for home.

On the drive home, Lil Joe put on some music on the Impala's CD player and introduced Angel to the smooth sounding oldies by Brenton Wood, which Angel actually took a liking to. He especially liked the song "Oogum Boogum," mainly because of the peculiar lyrics. When they got within a couple of blocks of Vanessa's house, Lil Joe stopped in the middle of the street and turned to Angel, who was sitting in the back seat. "Hey, kiddo, do you wanna drive us the rest of the way home?"

The boy's eyes lit up with excitement. "Yeah!"

"Well come on up here and take the wheel."

Angel hurried and crawled into the front seat and onto Lil Joe's lap. He took the wheel in his tiny hands and turned to look at Vanessa. "Look, Mommy, I'm gonna drive!"

Vanessa smiled at him proudly. "That's right, honey. You be a big boy and drive Mama home."

"All right, Angel, you just grip the wheel tight and keep it steady. Keep us in the middle of the street. Okay?"

"Okay," Angel replied with nervous excitement.

Lil Joe gently stepped on the gas pedal until the car was moving fifteen miles an hour, and Angel steered them the rest of the way. As they pulled up in front of Vanessa's house, Lil Joe took the wheel and parked along the curb. As they got out and made their way to the front porch, Marco drove past and honked his horn to get their attention. Once he had it, he pointed to a primered Buick Regal that was approaching from the opposite direction. When Vanessa saw it, she looked disgusted. "Shit!" she cursed under her breath, "Eddie."

"Hey, no cussing, Mom," Angel scolded her as she hurried to unlock the front door.

"Okay, honey, go on inside." Vanessa looked at Lil Joe. "I'm gonna get him inside. I'll be back in a minute."

"Okay." Lil Joe wasn't sure if she wanted him to stick around or not, but he decided to hang out until she came back. While he waited, Eddie parked his car across the street and slowly walked across to the edge of Vanessa's front yard where Lil Joe was standing waiting. Lil Joe was a bit surprised by Eddie's appearance. He was a thin, medium height, grungy looking, lantern jawed man dressed in a pair of old, worn, dirty jeans and an equally dirty white t-shirt.

He stopped just a few feet short of where Lil Joe was standing and greeted him. "What's up, man?"

Lil Joe nodded. "All right now. What's up?"

Eddie's fidgety body language suggested that he was tweaked out on something. He appeared to be really nervous. Lil Joe figured that he was probably high on some sort of crank, and it made him uneasy. He knew that dope fiends could be unpredictable. "So you're seeing Vanessa, huh?" Eddie asked in a nonchalant manner.

"Yeah," Lil Joe replied with a halfhearted smile.

Eddie nodded toward the house. "How's the boy?"

"He's good," Lil Joe replied, feeling sorry for the guy having to ask a stranger how his own son was doing. "He's a great kid."

Eddie smiled with a sorrowful look in his eyes. "That's good to hear, man. He has a good mother."

Lil Joe nodded. "You know, it's none of my business, man, but your boy is still a young kid. It's not too late for you to be a part of his life." Lil Joe looked Eddie in the eye and asked, "Is chasing a needle really more important to you?"

Eddie stared back for a moment as if he were searching for the answer to the question in Lil Joe's gaze, then diverted his attention to an agitated looking Vanessa making her way down the steps of the front porch. She walked up next to Lil Joe and hugged his arm tightly, which answered his question as to whether or not she wanted him to stay there with her. "What are you doing here, Eddie?" she asked in a tone that matched the agitated look on her face. "I don't have any money," she spat, "so you can just leave. I don't have anything for you."

"Aw, come on, Vanessa," Eddie said, "don't be like that. I just wanna talk to you for a minute. In private, please." He looked at her with pleading eyes.

"No, Eddie. Just say what you came to say."

Eddie frowned. "I'm in trouble, Vanessa. I need help."

"Aah," Vanessa sighed, "you're always in trouble, Eddie." She shook her head. "I can't bail you out this time. Now I want you to leave."

Eddie ran his fingers through his greasy hair, appearing extremely stressed out. "Okay." He shook his head and let out a long sigh. "Okay." He looked at Lil Joe for a moment as if sizing him up for a confrontation. Lil Joe recognized the look and immediately tensed up in anticipation of a violent encounter. However, whatever it was that Eddie had in mind, he quickly decided against it and stormed off towards his car.

After Lil Joe and Vanessa watched Eddie angrily drive off, Vanessa turned to Lil Joe and buried her face in his chest. Lil Joe held her in his embrace for a moment while he gently caressed her back and tried to calm her nerves. After a few minutes, she lifted her head and looked up at him. "Will you stay here with me tonight? I don't wanna be alone."

Lil Joe saw that she was seriously upset. "I'll stay with you, baby. Don't worry about it."

Vanessa smiled, appearing to be a little more relaxed. "Thanks."

Then they went in and joined Angel, who was sitting on the living room floor in front of the TV hutch playing video games. For the rest of the day, they pretty much just lounged around the house while the day slowly crept by. Later on in the afternoon, Lil Joe made a quick trip to his mother's house for a quick shower and to change clothes before heading back to Vanessa's for the night. That night they ordered in pizza for dinner and spent the rest of their Sunday watching TV until Vanessa put Angel to bed at around 9 o'clock.

Throughout the whole day, Lil Joe and Vanessa had avoided talking about Eddie because of Angel's presence, but after Vanessa returned from putting him to bed, she was the first to bring up Eddie's name. She sat next to Lil Joe on the couch and hugged up close to him. "I'm sorry about the incident with Eddie today."

Lil Joe shrugged it off. "It's no big deal, but he sure did seem stressed out, didn't he?"

"Yeah," Vanessa said, shaking her head. "He's always like that. The only time he ever comes by is when he needs money. He just shows up out of nowhere, high on something, and asking for money." She sighed. "I'm so sick of it. He doesn't even care about his own son. All he cares about is how he's gonna get his next fix."

"That's a shame. It's sad to see someone lose himself like that."

"Yeah, it is. But that's not even the worst of it. He steals from us--from me and Angel. A few months ago, just before I met you, our house was broken into. I know it was Eddie who did it because the diamond necklace that my grandmother left me was the only thing taken. Everything in the house was untouched except my jewelry box, and out of all my jewelry, my grandmother's necklace was the only thing taken." She shook her head in disgust. "Eddie knew that that necklace was the most valuable thing I owned. We were still together when my grandmother passed away and left it to me. She left me a diamond ring too, but luckily for me, I was wearing it on the day of the break in. But after that day, I decided to store it in a safe deposit box at the bank."

Vanessa sighed again. "I probably sounded like a cold hearted bitch earlier when I talked to him the way I did, but I used to feel sorry for him and when he came by asking for money, I used to give it to him. But after the break in, I vowed never to feel sorry for him again." She shrugged. "I guess that sounds pretty cruel of me, doesn't it?"

"No, not at all. You have to look out for yours and Angel's best interests first, and you can't do that by allowing someone like Eddie to cause trouble in your lives."

Vanessa reached out and began rubbing his chest. "Well, I'm glad that you understand, because it's not my nature to just turn my back on someone in need. It's just that Eddie's too much for me to deal with."

Lil Joe nodded. "I know what you mean, but if you don't mind me asking, how did you get caught up with a guy like him anyway? I mean, I know I'm not exactly a saint myself, but I can't really picture you with a guy like that."

Vanessa sighed. "I know it seems weird, but he wasn't always like that. I've known him practically my whole life. We were actually high school sweethearts; we dated all through high school. By the end of my senior year, I was pregnant with Angel, and things just went downhill from there. I mean, I always knew that Eddie had messed around with drugs here and there, but it was just the small stuff, you know? Smoking weed and occasionally popping pills. But then after Angel was born, Eddie's drug habits progressively got worse and he started using some of the more hard core drugs until finally he became a full blown junkie." She paused for a moment to take a deep breath. "Anyway, once he was totally gone, I knew it was over so I just let him go and focused on raising Angel."

Lil Joe felt bad for her. Whenever she told him a story about an unfortunate part of her past, the pain in her eyes made him silently curse the world for causing her so much hurt. "Come here," he whispered and pulled her onto his lap and held her close while he gently caressed her shoulder and lost himself in his own thoughts. For the first time since he met her, he questioned their relationship, wondering if being a part of her life was a good idea. After all, even though he wasn't exactly like Eddie, he did have one thing in common with the junkie. He, too, had caused his loved ones a lot of pain and heartache. The idea of causing Vanessa any more pain in her life was unbearable, and the thought made him ask himself whether he was doing the right thing making himself a part of her and her son's lives. His doubts angered him, once again reminding him of how his time in prison had destroyed his chances of ever living a normal life. He was well aware of his inner demons, so he decided to give everything some serious thought later on when he had time to himself to think things over and put them in perspective. The last thing he wanted to do was make a selfish decision that he would end up regretting.

CHAPTER TWENTY-SEVEN

THE WEEK FLEW BY. LIL JOE spent every day applying for jobs as a paralegal with local, private practice law firms. Although he was more than qualified for the job, he had his doubts about any of the firms actually hiring him knowing he was an ex-con. He figured that more than likely he would end up working as a janitor for a fast food joint somewhere. The thought was repulsive and demeaning. However, he was determined to do what he had to as a man in order to make a life for himself in the free world.

On Friday afternoon, after returning home from a long day of job searching and running personal errands, Lil Joe caught Marco at home alone getting ready for work, so he decided to hang out with him until he had to leave for the restaurant. "Hey, bro, how's it goin'?" he greeted Marco as he walked into the living room "You're off to work early, huh?"

Marco sighed. "Yeah, I'm hosting a retirement party tonight in our private lounge, and I have to make sure that everything's good to go before the party starts."

Lil Joe frowned. "It sounds like you're in for a busy night."

"Yeah, pretty much. Oh, hey, before I forget, I got you something." Marco walked over to the coat rack next to the front door where his overcoat was hanging and reached into a pocket. He pulled out a cellular phone and handed it to Lil Joe. "Here you go, Joe, now you're all caught up with the rest of the twenty-first century."

Lil Joe took the little phone and smiled at his brother. "Thanks, man. How does it work?"

"Oh, here, let me show you. You see this button, you just push it and dial the number you wanna call and it'll put you through. The same goes for incoming calls. When your phone rings, you just push this button and you'll be able to talk with whoever's calling you."

"Do I push the same button to hang up?"

"Yeah."

"What's all this other stuff for?" Lil Joe asked.

"Those things are for text messages and other stuff like that. I'll show you how to use all of that stuff later. Okay?"

"All right, but . . . uh, what's my number?"

Marco chuckled. "Oh, yeah, sorry about that. Here." He pointed to the screen. "I programmed your number so it would show on the screen when it's on. See?" He pushed the on button and pointed to the small number that came on the screen.

Lil Joe nodded. "Okay, cool. Thanks again, Marco. I appreciate it."

Marco smiled. "No problem, man, and hey, you don't have to worry about the bill for a while. I've covered it for the next ninety days."

Lil Joe smiled at his brother's thoughtful generosity. "Thanks, bro. So where are Mom and Tina at anyway?"

"They took Rebecca to the pediatrician's office for some shots."

"Uh, oh, not the baby shots."

"Yeah. I'm glad I have to work." He looked at his watch. "Speaking of work, I better get goin'. So I'll see you later then."

"Okay, bro. Thanks again for the phone, man."

Marco shrugged. "De nada [no problem]." He grabbed his coat from the rack and headed to work.

After Marco left, Lil Joe sat on the couch and fiddled around with his cell phone in an attempt to learn how to operate it on his own. However, after failing to do so, he decided he would have Vanessa show him how to use all of its accessories later on when he met up with her after she got home from work. The thought of buying himself a cellular phone had never crossed Lil Joe's mind. He didn't feel it was necessary. In fact, everywhere he went, he saw people--even kids--attached to their cell phones, and he often wondered what they could possibly have to talk about throughout the entire day. But he had never really liked to talk on the phone because he thought it so impersonal. He preferred to talk to people face to face. Besides, he couldn't really picture himself walking around in public jibber-jabbing on a cell phone. It seemed a bit feminine to him. But now that Marco had bought him one, he decided to keep it and use it for emergencies or really important things.

Fiddling around with his cell phone made him think of Danny. He made a mental note to call him in the next week or so and see if he wanted to go out somewhere for a couple of beers. Since he had first met Danny, Lil Joe had kept in touch with him, and they had gone out on several occasions to have a few beers and shoot the breeze with each other. Lil Joe had managed not to pursue his interest in Danny's daughter, not only because of his involvement with Vanessa, but out of respect for Danny. He didn't feel it would be right for him to be screwing the daughter of someone he considered a friend.

Before Vanessa was due to return home, Lil Joe took a shower and prepared for his weekend alone with Vanessa. Earlier in the week she had made plans for her parents to pick up Angel from school that afternoon and keep him for the entire weekend. So he was looking forward to spending some quality alone time with her.

After waiting to give Vanessa some time to herself before he showed up, he headed over to her house. He felt it was just a common courtesy to give her some time and figured she would appreciate it. When he got there, he peeked in through the screen door and found her tidying up the living room while dancing to the sounds of The Dramatics blaring from her stereo speakers. He stood there for a moment smiling and admiring her joyful mood. Finally she turned and saw him standing there and blushed with embarrassment. "Hey, how long have you been standing there?" She walked over and turned the volume on the CD down.

"Long enough to be totally turned on," he replied as he opened the screen door and let himself in.

She greeted him with a tempting smile and a kiss, then playfully pushed him away. "Hold that thought," she teased. "We got all weekend, stud."

Lil Joe grunted and playfully smacked her across her rear end. "Well, I hope so, baby, cause I could use some good lovin'."

"Umm," she purred, "well we'll just have to take care of that then, won't we? But not right now. I got dinner on the stove."

"Sounds good. That way I can fuel up for later."

Vanessa laughed. "I see you have a one-track mind tonight."

"Yeah," Lil Joe confessed, "but you started it with your rump shakin'."

"Okay, fair enough."

They sat down on the couch and Lil Joe pulled his cell phone from his pocket and handed it to her. "Can you show me how to program this thing?"

Vanessa's eyes lit up. "Yes! About time. Now I can reach you at anytime during the day." She picked up her cell phone from the coffee table and began programming his phone number into it. "This is your number on the screen, right?"

"Uh, yeah."

Vanessa began to laugh and Lil Joe wrinkled his brow in confusion. "What's so funny?"

"Oh, I'm sorry, it's just that when I started programming your number into my phone, your expression was classic."

Lil Joe didn't realize he had made a funny face.

"Aw, poor baby," Vanessa teased, "you're hating this, aren't you? Well you better get used to it because that's what girlfriends do. They call their boyfriends and wanna talk for no particular reason at all. But don't worry, I promise not to call you all the time."

Lil Joe smiled and kissed her. "Okay, that's fine." He wasn't even thinking about the phone anymore. He was happily dwelling on her reference to them as boyfriend and girlfriend. Sure, it seemed like an adolescent thing to take heed of, but Vanessa was his first real girlfriend, and he cared about her. It was at that moment that Lil Joe realized how truly fortunate he was to have a woman like her in his corner. He knew that there was no way he could let her go; he was just going to have to bury his demons deep down in his soul and hope to God that they never surfaced.

Shortly after they ate dinner and Vanessa had shown him how to utilize all the features of his cell phone, they were relaxing on her couch when they heard the loud blare of a car horn right outside. When they went to see what the noise was about, they found it was Lil Joe's mother honking her horn. They hurried out to see what was the matter, and as soon as they approached the Regal, Lil Joe's mother started to explain.

"Mijo, Tina's in labor," she said, pointing to Tina in the passenger seat, who looked like she was very much in pain. "We're headed to St. Bernardines Hospital off of Highland." She pointed over her shoulder towards the back seat, where Rebecca was strapped into her car seat looking sleepy. "Vanessa, sweetie, would you watch Rebecca for us while we're at the hospital?"

Vanessa nodded. "Yeah, sure!"

"Okay, good." Lil Joe's mother stepped out of the car and reached into the back seat for Rebecca. After handing her to Vanessa, she pulled out a small, pink overnight bag and handed it to Lil Joe. "Vanessa, everything she'll need for the night is in there. She's had a long day, so she'll probably sleep through the night."

"Okay."

Lil Joe's mother said thanks to Vanessa and hoped back into the car. "Hey, mijo, we've already called Marco at work. He can get the rest of the night off, but his work is using his car for some sort of errand right now, so we need you to go pick him up and bring him to the hospital."

"Okay, Ma, I'll go pick him up right now."

As Lil Joe's mother put the Regal in gear and started to drive off, Vanessa waved to Tina. "Take it easy, Tina. I'll see you soon."

After his mom and Tina drove off, Lil Joe turned to Vanessa. "Well, this is a surprise, huh?"

"Yeah," she replied, gazing lovingly at Rebecca. She kissed her on the cheek. "Hi, sweetie, you're gonna be a big sister now. Whatcha think about that?"

Rebecca yawned and set her sights on Lil Joe. He laughed. "She doesn't seem that interested in becoming a big sister right now."

"Yeah, she's tired. Come on, honey, let's get you inside."

After he walked Vanessa and Rebecca into the house, Lil Joe kissed Vanessa and headed off to his mother's house to get his car and go pick up Marco. When he got to the restaurant, Marco was already standing just outside the entrance waiting for him. Lil Joe pulled up in front and Marco quickly hopped into the Impala. "Big night for you, bro," Lil Joe said with a smile as he headed towards the hospital.

Marco smiled. "Yeah, man, it sure is. I hope she gives me a son tonight, brother."

"Amen to that."

"You know how to get to the hospital, right?" Marco asked.

"Yeah, it's the one across the street from the cemetery, right?"

"Yeah, that's it."

Halfway to the hospital, Lil Joe's cell phone rang. Since Vanessa was the only one besides Marco who had his number, he knew it was her, so he pulled it out of his pocket to answer. "Hey, what's up, baby?"

A very frantic and hysterical Vanessa answered. "Oh, my God, Joe, something terrible has just happened." She began to sob loudly. "I tried to stop him. Oh, God, Joe, you have to come here quick!"

Lil Joe wrinkled his brow in concern, which in turn got Marco's attention. "What happened, bro? What's goin' on?"

"I don't know yet. Vanessa, baby, what happened. You tried to stop who from doing what?"

"Eddie!" she cried out, "He took her. He took Rebecca! He wore a mask, but I know it was him."

Lil Joe's heart sank down into his stomach. "We'll be right there." He turned the car around and began speeding toward Vanessa's house. "Joe!" Vanessa yelled into the phone, "what should I do? Should I call the police?"

"No! Don't do anything right now. I'll be right there. Okay? Just hang tight." He hung up and tossed the phone into Marco's lap. "Call Mom and tell her we're gonna be a little late."

Marco face was twisted. "What's goin' on, Joe?"

Lil Joe let out a powerful sigh. "Vanessa said that Eddie forced his way into her house and took Rebecca."

"What!" Marco yelled.

Lil Joe turned to look his brother in the eye. "Marco, I'm gonna take care of this. Don't worry."

"What? Don't worry! I'll kill that junkie motherfucker!"

Lil Joe gritted his teeth while Marco vented with confused anger. "What would that son of a bitch want with Rebecca?" he yelled. "How did this happen?"

Lil Joe was silently trying to figure out the answers to those questions, but Marco's ranting was keeping him from doing so. "All right, look, bro, get a hold of yourself and listen to me. Vanessa said that Eddie wore a mask, but she knew it was him. That's all I know. We'll find out everything in a minute. All right? For now just keep cool!"

Marco took a deep breath and shook his head, then picked up Lil Joe's cell phone from his lap. "I can't call Mom right now. Not like this."

Lil Joe nodded. "All right, but after we talk to Vanessa, you're gonna have to."

"All right," Marco agreed, still appearing confused and angry.

A few minutes later, Lil Joe pulled up and parked in front of Vanessa's house. She was standing on the front porch hugging her elbows and as Lil Joe and Marco came towards her, she hurried down the steps to meet them halfway. When she was under the streetlight and close enough to Lil Joe, he could see the swelling red bruise on the right side of her face. He clenched his jaw tight. "He hit you?"

Vanessa began to cry as she nodded her head in response and buried her face in his chest. He wrapped her arms around her and gently stroked her back while looking his brother in the eye. Marco's expression softened and he patted Vanessa on the shoulder. "It's okay, Vanessa, just tell us what happened."

Vanessa pulled her face away from Lil Joe's chest and wiped her tears with the back of her hands. "I'm so sorry. I tried to stop him, but I couldn't. Oh, God . . . " She stopped for a moment to take a deep breath. "I was just putting Rebecca down to sleep and all of a sudden he opened the screen door and ran into the house yelling, 'This is a robbery!' Then he pulled me by the elbow, drug me into my bedroom, and started rummaging through all my things." She shook her head. "That's how I knew it was him, because when he started going through my jewelry box, he was obviously looking for something specific. When he couldn't find it, he slipped up and yelled, 'Where is it?' That's when I knew it was Eddie and that he was looking for my grandmother's ring. I told him I knew it was him and that the ring wasn't here, and . . . "

Tears started to stream down her cheeks again, so Lil Joe hugged her and kissed her on the temple. "Is that when he took Rebecca?" She nodded. "And you tried to stop him and he hit you."

Vanessa nodded her head again and turned to Marco. "Oh, God, Marco, I'm so sorry. I swear I tried to stop him."

Marco reached out and gripped her shoulder. "I know you did, Vanessa," he said, looking down at her with soft eyes. He turned to Lil Joe. "So what's next?"

Lil Joe looked at Vanessa. "Do you know where he might of taken her?"

"No, I have no idea," she answered with an apologetic look.

Lil Joe looked back at Marco, whose face was riddled with worry. "Marco, stay here with Vanessa and call Mom. Try to explain what's goin' on the best you can."

"Where are you goin'?" Marco asked.

Lil Joe stared him in the eye. "I'm gonna find Rebecca and bring her home."

Vanessa looked worried. "But what about the police? Shouldn't I call them? I mean, we're talking about a missing child." She pointed to Marco. "Your daughter."

Lil Joe sighed. "Yeah, look, I can't be a part of that. So when the cops get here, I can't be here, and when they start asking questions, you can't mention me at all. I was never here, and I don't know anything about what happened." He paused and looked them both in the eye. "Do you understand what I'm saying."

Marco nodded. "Yeah, but I wanna go with you, Joe. It doesn't sit right with me just sitting around while you go off to find her."

Lil Joe's expression turned to stone. He looked Marco directly in the eye and said, "You know I can't let you do that, Marco. Just let me handle this thing my way, brother. You stay and take care of our family and let me take care of our family's problems."

Marco swallowed hard and nodded in understanding. He had quickly absorbed the meaning of Lil Joe's words. Unfortunately, so did Vanessa, and she began to cry out in a fit of hysteria, "Oh, no, Joe, no, you can't get yourself into any trouble. Please, just let the police take care of it. You don't have to be involved. I'll explain everything that happened. Just don't leave, not like this." She looked at him with soft, pleading eyes. "Please, Joe."

Her pleas were breaking his heart into pieces. He knew that there was nothing she or anybody else could say that would make him change his mind about what he planned to do. But she didn't know that, and it pained him deeply to know there was nothing he could say or do that would make her understand why he had to handle things his way. He turned to Marco. "Hey, bro, make sure that you guys don't let the cops know that you suspect Eddie of doin' this. At least not yet. You guys gotta give me time to find Eddie on my own."

Marco nodded. "Okay, I understand."

"Good." Then Lil Joe turned his attention back to Vanessa. He took her hands and looked into her sad brown eyes. "Look, don't worry about me. I'll be fine. I just don't trust cops to take care of anything. It's just who I am." He pulled her in close to him so that they were face to face. "Baby, everything's gonna be all right. Okay? Don't worry. I just wanna find Rebecca and get her home safely. That's all. Okay?" She nodded in understanding. However, the worrisome look in her gaze told Lil Joe she knew he wasn't being completely honest with her. He reached out and cupped her face in his hands, then kissed her softly on her forehead and said in a low whisper, "Vanessa, no woman has ever meant as much to a man as you do to me." He paused for a moment to stare into her eyes while he gathered his emotions. "But baby, you have to understand that I wouldn't be able to live with myself if I stopped being who I am as a man. Please understand that."

Then Lil Joe turned to Marco. "Marco," he said, placing a firm grip on his brother's shoulder, "I'll make sure she gets home safe. I swear my life on it." Then he turned and walked to his car without looking back. As he stepped in, he heard Vanessa whimper his name one last time before he closed the door and went on his way. As he drove away, his eyes welled up with tears of anger. Walking away from Vanessa was the hardest thing he'd ever had to do, and he silently swore to himself that he would make Eddie, or whoever else was responsible, pay a grave price for what they had done.

As he drove into his mother's driveway, he parked just outside the entrance to the back yard. Then he went out to the gardening shed to gather his weapons. After he had retrieved the ten millimeter and the silencer, along with an extra loaded clip and the butterfly knife, he went back to his car and screwed the silencer onto the gun. When he was finished, he called Danny on his cell phone. "Hello."

"Hey, Danny, it's me, Joe."

"Oh, hey, Joe, how's it goin', man?"

"Not too good, Danny. I have a problem."

"What's up, man?" Danny asked in a concerned tone.

"It's my baby niece. Some piece of shit dope fiend has kidnapped her, and I'm out to get her back."

"Fuck, man, that's terrible. How can I help, man? You know I'm here for you."

"Yeah, man, I know. That's why I called you. I need someone to take me around to all the city's dope spots, particularly junkie and hype hangouts. I figure those are the best places to look for this guy."

"Well, hey, I'm your man, Joe. Just come on over and we'll get right to business."

"That's right, Danny. I knew I could count on you. I'll be right over."

As Lil Joe backed out of the driveway and onto the street, he glanced over towards Vanessa's house and was surprised to see that the cops were already there. Although he would never go to the police for help, he didn't hold it against Vanessa and Marco for doing so. They were different from him. They were part of a society that went to the police for help. That was what they learned to do growing up. However, the society that Lil Joe had grown up in, and was accustomed to, saw law enforcement as a sworn enemy. He had grown not to trust anyone who wore a badge or represented any type of law enforcement. The laws of general society had no significance to people like him. His heart was his law, and he always did what his heart told him was right regardless of what consequences he would face for his actions. He was going to make things right according to the laws that were written in his heart, and the system could do with him whatever they felt compelled to do after he finished what he set out to do.

Lil Joe wasn't concerned with his own life at the moment. The only thing that mattered to him was Rebecca's safe return home and that he, personally, held the people responsible for her kidnapping accountable.

As he drove off in the opposite direction of Vanessa's house, Lil Joe realized that the classic rock station he had his car radio set on was playing the Rolling Stone's "Sympathy for the Devil." He scoffed as he listened to the old familiar lyrics. "Please to meet you, whoo, whoo, whoo, whoo. I hope you guessed my name."

He reached Danny's house in about ten minutes and Danny was already standing out in front smoking a cigarette. As soon as Lil Joe brought the Impala to a stop, Danny strolled over and let himself in. Lil Joe looked at the front of Danny's house and saw through the open front door that he had company. "Aw, hey, man, it looks like you have company in there. I didn't mean to intrude."

Danny frowned. "Nah, don't worry about it, Joe. You need help. Besides, those are just Gina's sisters. They came up from Indio to stay the weekend. Trust me, you did me a favor gettin' me away from all that yip yappin' in there."

Lil Joe chuckled. "Well, now I don't feel so bad. So, where to first?"

"Well, there's a spot on "F" and Baseline that we can start with. It's right next to a sex shop. Don't ask me how I know about it."

"Okay, I won't."

On the way, Lil Joe ran Danny down with everything that had transpired. When they arrived at their destination, Lil Joe pulled the sixty-five up along the curb in front of the sex shop, where he noticed quite a few hookers and several grungy looking dope fiends hanging around. However, it was too dark for him to get a good look at any of their faces.

Soon after he parked the Impala, a light complected black hooker wearing a blonde wig strolled over to the passenger side and rested her elbows on the window frame. "Hey, fellas, you guys lookin' for some company?"

Lil Joe pulled a wad of cash out of his pocket and pealed off two twenties, then reached across the seat and handed them to her. "No, honey, just information."

She looked curious and asked, "What kind of information? while stuffing the bills into her bra."

"We're lookin' for a junkie, a Mexican by the name of Eddie. Do you know him?"

The hooker rolled her eyes. "Yeah, I know him, but I ain't seen him around here in a few days. I think he's in trouble with someone and is trying to stay low." She looked Lil Joe in the eye. "I suppose you two are the ones he's hidin' from."

Lil Joe grunted while he processed the information. He figured that Eddie's being in trouble with someone might have something to do with his kidnapping Rebecca. "Hey, do you have any idea where he might be?"

The hooker bit her lip, looking as if she were contemplating whether or not to tell him what she knew. "Sure, you seem nice enough, and Eddie's an asshole anyway. You might wanna check out the Oasis Motel on Mount Vernon. I think I heard somethin' about him being holed up over there."

Lil Joe nodded his head. "All right," he said, pulling another twenty from his wad of bills. He handed it to Danny, who handed it to the hooker. "Thanks. I appreciate your help." Then he put the Impala in drive and headed toward the Oasis Motel. On the way there, he talked things over with Danny. "Hey, Danny, if I find him at the motel, I'm gonna drop you back off at home. I won't involve you any further."

Danny nodded. "I understand, Joe, and I respect your intentions, but you still might need my help later. So don't sweat it. I'm here for you, and I know that you would be there for me if I was in your shoes."

Lil Joe smiled, thinking back on a time when he had pretty much told Franky the same thing.

When they arrived at the motel, Lil Joe pulled up into the junkie infested parking lot and parked near one of the exits. Right away a crowd of hookers who were standing just a few feet away noticed him and one of them, a tall, slender Polynesian woman, broke away from the crowd and made her way over to Lil Joe's window. "Hey, baby, wanna get a room?"

Lil Joe shook his head, pulled fifty dollars from his stack of bills, and handed it to her. "Could you point me to Eddie's room?"

It was obvious that she knew exactly who he was referring to because her eyes widened with recognition at the mention of Eddie's name. She took the fifty dollars and slid it into the leg of one of her white leather, knee-high boots. Then she pointed to the door of a corner room directly across from where he was parked. "Thanks."

The hooker shrugged her shoulders. "No problem," she said and walked over to join her crowd.

Lil Joe pulled the ten millimeter from the front of his waistband and slid back the loading chamber. He turned to Danny, whose expression suggested that he was a little nervous about the gun. "Hey, Danny, I'm gonna go in and get him. If you can do me the favor and back the car up in front of his room and pop the trunk, I would appreciate it."

"Okay." Danny nodded, his eyes wide with excitement. "I'll take care of it."

"Thanks." As Lil Joe opened the door and put the pistol back in his waistband, he asked, "You ready?" and Danny nodded his head. "Okay, let's do this."

Lil Joe stepped out of the car and walked across the parking lot to Eddie's room. He checked the handle to see if the door was unlocked. It was. He quickly opened the door and stepped into the dim, filthy looking room to find Eddie perched up on the bed with his back resting against the wall. He didn't even flinch when Lil Joe barged into the room with gun in hand. He was in a deep heroin nod and probably didn't even realize that Lil Joe was standing there.

Lil Joe put the gun back into the front of his waistband and took a quick look around the room to see if Rebecca was there. She wasn't. Lil Joe walked over to the bed and started trying to get Eddie's attention. "Hey, Eddie!" he yelled and clapped his hands in front of the junkie's face. "Wake up. Snap out of it." Eddie barely managed to lift his head and mumble something incomprehensible, showing no signs of recognition as he set his half-slit gaze upon Lil Joe's face. Lil Joe shook his head. "You're just a stupid motherfucker, ain't you!" he said, frowning down at Eddie. "All right then, Eddie, I'll do all the work."

Lil Joe grabbed Eddie by the wrist and pulled him to the edge of the bed. Then he bent at the knees and slung Eddie's frail body over his shoulder. "All right, let's get you into the trunk, huh?" He opened the door and found his Impala backed up just a few feet away with the trunk wide open. He hurried to the car and flung Eddie's limp body into the trunk and curled him up next to the two-gallon gas can. Then he closed the lid and made his way back to the front of the car.

As he climbed back into the driver's seat and closed the door, Danny asked, "Did he give you any trouble?"

"Naw, the fuckin' dummy was in a heroin nod." He looked across the seat at Danny. "Thanks, man. I know what kind of risks you took coming out here with me tonight."

"Don't mention it, man. For what it's worth, I believe in what you're doin' here, Joe. A man has the right to protect his family from people like this idiot back there."

"Thanks, Danny. I appreciate that. Now let's get you home. You can't be around for what I'm about to do next."

Lil Joe drove Danny back to the Manor and dropped him off at home and thanked him again before driving off towards the old abandoned apartment complex near where Franky had lived as a kid. When he got there, he drove around to the back and parked in one of the old parking areas just a few feet away from a back entrance walkway that led into one of the apartment sections. He cut off the engine and went to the back of the car to get Eddie. When he lifted the lid, he saw that Eddie still appeared to be unaware of what was going on. "Come on, Eddie, wake up," he said as he reached into the trunk and grabbed the two-gallon gas can and set it down on the pavement. "We're about to go for a swim."

He pulled Eddie out of the trunk and flung his half limp body over his shoulder again. Then with his free hand he closed the trunk lid and squatted down to pick up the gas can. He walked through the narrow walkway and entered the vacant apartment section, walking straight to the middle of the quad where the empty swimming pool was, and then walked down the steps at the shallow end. The deep end of the pool was dimly lit by a reflection from one of the streetlights just beyond another walkway to the front entrance of the quad. He walked to the deep end of the pool and dumped Eddie's body onto the trash cluttered floor.

He stared at Eddie for a moment thinking about what he was about to do. Then he unscrewed the cap to the gas can and tossed it aside. "All right, Eddie, this is the point where you're gonna wake up and tell me where my niece is at," he said as he poured half the gasoline onto Eddie's face and upper body.

The burn and smell of the gas woke Eddie right up out of his nod. He sat up and began to cough and gag until finally he caught his breath and yelled out, "Hey, what the fuck, man!"

"Hey there, Eddie," Lil Joe greeted him. "You're just in time for the barbecue."

"What?" Eddie said, confused and trying to focus his eyes on Lil Joe. "Come on, man, what is this shit? Steve, is that you? Come on, man, I made up for what I did. I thought we were cool."

Lil Joe kicked Eddie hard in the rib cage. "You retarded motherfucker," Lil Joe yelled, "where's my niece?"

"What?" Eddie wiped his eyes and set his sights on Lil Joe just in time to see him pull his Zippo lighter from his pocket and strike a flame. He began to panic. "Oh, shit! No! No, man. Hey look, what do you wanna know?"

Lil Joe looked down at him. "Everything. Where's my niece?"

"All right, all right, I'll tell you everything."

Lil Joe shut the cap of the Zippo. "Okay, talk."

"I had no choice man, they were gonna kill me," Eddie explained. "Look, man, last week when I showed up at Vanessa's, I was really in big time trouble, man. I swear. Me and a buddy of mine pulled a jack move on a couple of small time dealers and got away with almost a key of junk, man. Except the guys we jacked turned out to be hooked up with a big shot named Steve Ochoa. When I found out that the shit we stole belonged to him, it was too late, man. Most of the stuff was already gone from partying and shit." He shook his head, then spit out some of the gasoline that had dripped down into his mouth. "That's when I went to Vanessa for help, but she wouldn't even listen to me. You heard her. You were there. I just needed some money, man. I figured if I could get enough to pay Steve back, it would be no harm, no foul. You know?"

"And you thought Vanessa had that kind of money?"

"Not all of it. I had some jewelry and stuff that I got from burglaries and shit like that. I just needed a few thousand maybe. My buddy was supposed to come up with the rest." He sighed. "But it didn't work out that way. After I left Vanessa's house that day, I found out that my buddy, Snake, had gone missing. I'm not stupid. I knew that meant that Steve had gotten hold of him. So I knew I had to think fast. Then

I remembered about Vanessa's diamond ring and I went to go get it, but . . . " he lowered his head. "When I couldn't find it, I panicked and I took the baby."

Lil Joe gritted his teeth. "Where is she, Eddie."

Eddie shook his head. "I know it was a low thing to do, but I had no choice."

Lil Joe kicked him again. "Fuck that, Eddie. Where is she?"

"All right, man," Eddie yelled, "just stop kickin' me! God, man!" He let out a low sob. "I'm really fucked this time." He sighed, shook his head, and explained. "Steve's baby sister Connie has her man. I heard a while back that she had tried to adopt a kid but got shot down." Lil Joe clenched his jaw tight, knowing exactly where Eddie was going with the story, but he let him continue. "I've known Connie since I was in high school, and I know that she can't have no kids, so, I figured she was my only way out of the mess I was in with her brother. So I went to her with the baby, knowing how badly she wanted one, and I begged her to take the kid and help me clear things with her brother. I told her that the baby was a teenage hooker's and that nobody would be lookin' for her. I could tell that she didn't believe me, but she took the baby and helped me clear things with Steve."

Lil Joe had heard enough. The story was making him sick to his stomach. "Where do I find Connie, Eddie?"

Eddie sighed, then ran his fingers through his gasoline soaked hair. "Aw, man, she took the baby and skipped town. You know, to lay low for a while."

Lil Joe began to boil over with rage and he kicked Eddie flat on his back, then stepped on his chest and began pouring more gasoline onto his face and upper body. "You fuckin' little rat! Where do I find her brother?" he demanded.

Eddie began gagging and coughing again from the gasoline, so he threw his arms over his face in an attempt to shield himself from the burning liquid. "Hey, man," he spat, "I don't know, I swear. Steve could be anywhere for all I know, man. Come on," Eddie pleaded, shaking with fear, "please, man, forgive me."

"Forgive you!" Lil Joe said with an acid tongue. "You kidnapped my niece--your own sister's daughter! And you traded her to pay off a fuckin' dope debt!"

Lil Joe knew that dope fiends as far gone as Eddie were licentious in nature and cared only about themselves and their disgusting habits. Eddie had proven that by his own actions. Lil Joe stood firmly with one foot still planted on Eddie's chest. He tossed the empty gas can to the side and stared into Eddie's frightened eyes for a moment. The image of Angel's smiling face popped into his mind and Lil Joe gritted his teeth, thinking of how much pain Eddie had caused for everyone. He took the Zippo out of his pocket and struck a flame. Then Eddie began to squirm underneath the weight of his foot with a terrified look on his face. "No, please!" he pleaded, but his pleas for mercy fell on deaf ears.

Lil Joe removed his foot from Eddie's chest and said, "Forgiveness is between you and your god, Eddie." Then he dropped the flaming Zippo onto Eddie's chest and walked back to the Impala. After pulling out of the abandoned apartment area and getting back on the road, Lil Joe called Danny on his cell phone. "Hey, Danny, I'm sorry to be calling so late, man, but it's just . . . "

Danny cut him off. "Nah, don't worry about it, Joe. I'm just in the garage hiding from my wife and her sisters. Besides, I've been kinda expecting you to call anyway. So, any good news about your niece?"

"I don't know. Do you know anything about a dealer named Steve Ochoa?"

"Aw, shit, is that low life involved in this? Yeah, I know who he is. He's a giant asshole surrounded by a whole shit load of turds."

Lil Joe grunted. "Yeah, go figure. Well, apparently he's my link to getting my niece back."

"Hmm," Danny grunted, "from what I know, this Steve cat has a real hard on for my Roxy. She's out right now, but let me give her a ring and have her come home and maybe we can figure out a way to get to this guy."

Lil Joe sighed. "I don't know, Danny. Are you sure you wanna get Roxy involved? Things could get ugly, man."

"Yeah, I know. Look, why don't you just come on over and the three of us can figure somethin' out together."

"All right, Danny, I'm on my way."

When Lil Joe reached Danny's house a few minutes later, Danny was standing in the open doorway of his brightly lit garage nursing a beer. After parking along the curb, Lil Joe walked up the driveway and joined him. Danny greeted him by handing him a can of beer and saying, "Roxy should be here soon. I just got off the phone with her."

"Thanks." Then he opened his can of beer and swallowed half of it.

"One of those nights you wish you could forget, huh?"

"Yeah, and there's still more to come."

Danny nodded. "You know, this Ochoa guy has quite a reputation around here."

"Yeah, I figured as much. Do you know if he's under anyone's wing."

Danny frowned and shook his head. "Nah, I seriously doubt it, not with the kind of crap him and his boys pull around here."

Lil Joe wrinkled his brow. "Like that, huh?"

"Yeah. Drive bys, home invasions, you name it."

Lil Joe smirked. "Sounds like a real hero."

Danny scoffed. "Yeah, a real fuckin' Robin Hood."

Just then a silver Honda Civic pulled up and Roxy stepped out and waved goodbye to the unseen driver as the car drove off. As Roxy strutted up the driveway towards the garage wearing a tight, black mini skirt and an equally tight, red tube top, she cheerfully greeted Lil Joe. "Hey, Joe, it's good to see you again."

"You too, Roxy," Lil Joe said and kissed her on the cheek.

She turned towards Danny. "What's goin' on, Dad. Why did you need me to come home?"

Danny looked at Lil Joe for a second and then turned his attention back to her. "Well, <u>mija</u>, we need your help with something. Is that <u>vato</u> Steve Ochoa still chasin' after you?"

Roxy rolled her eyes. "Yes, I just saw him at Olgas before I came home. Why?"

Danny looked at Lil Joe again and Lil Joe gave him a nod to go ahead and explain the situation to her. "Well, sweetie, Joe here has some business to take care of with Steve, and we need to find a way to get him away from all of his goons."

Roxy looked at Lil Joe with wonder in her eyes. "Business?"

Lil Joe cleared his throat. "Yeah, Roxy, the kind of business you probably shouldn't know anything about. But since I'm asking for your help, I think you have a right to know what's goin' on. Earlier tonight my baby niece was kidnapped, and as it turns out, this Steve Ochoa guy is my key to getting her back."

Roxy's eyes widened with sorrow. "Oh, God, how terrible. Of course I'll help you, Joe. What do you want me to do?"

Danny cut in. "Well, honey, since you said you saw him at the club earlier, I think our best bet is to have you go back down there and hit on him and somehow talk him into leaving with you alone. Maybe have him drive you to a nearby motel or somethin' where we could be waiting." He looked at Lil Joe. "What do you think?"

Lil Joe nodded. "I like the idea, but it's up to her. I won't ask her to do anything she's not comfortable with."

Roxy shook her head. "No, I'm game. Let's do it!"

Lil Joe smiled for the first time since learning of Rebecca's abduction. "I'm forever in your debt, Roxy." Then he looked at Danny. "I owe the both of you more than I can ever repay."

Danny patted him on the back. "No, Joe, you're a good man; you don't owe us anything."

Lil Joe smiled again. "Okay, so how do you guys wanna do this?"

Roxy looked at both of them. "Why don't you guys drop me back at Olgas and then head over to the Motel Six on Foothill and wait for me to show up with him. I'll have him there within an hour," she said with a wink, "because I'm good."

Lil Joe couldn't help but laugh. He really liked Roxy's character. She was one of a kind.

After dropping Roxy back at the nightclub, Lil Joe drove to the Motel Six just like they had planned and parked at the back of the parking lot. Then he and Danny waited for Roxy to show up with Ochoa.

"Do you think she can pull it off, Danny?"

"Yeah, she'll pull it off. I got faith in my girl."

Lil Joe chuckled. "She sure did seem sure of herself. Anyway, uh, hey, man, I can't thank you enough for all of your help. This whole night has just been fuckin' insane, man. But it would of been a lot worse if it wasn't for you."

"Shit, Joe, I'm trippin' out on how calm you've been about all of this. I can't even imagine what's been goin' through your head all night."

Lil Joe thought about that for a moment. "Shit, everything has happened so fast I haven't had much time to think about it, which is probably a good thing. If I start to think about what I walked away from tonight, I'll probably go crazy."

Danny shook his head, frowning. "It's a damn shame, you having to throw everything away because of cowards like Ochoa and that other asshole junkie."

"Yeah, I hear you, Danny, but I suppose any man in my situation would be willing to sacrifice everything for his family."

"Not every man. Don't sell yourself short. Only a chosen few have that kind of strength."

Lil Joe's heart filled with pride. Hearing those words from a man he respected meant a lot to him. "Thanks, man, that means a lot coming from you."

Just then their attention was diverted to a black Cadillac Escalade that pulled into the lot and parked near the check-in entrance. Soon afterwards, Roxy hopped out of the car and stood next to it while a tall, slender, dark haired man got out and walked into the office. Lil Joe grinned with satisfaction. Roxy had come through for him. He turned to Danny. "Are you ready?"

Danny frowned and nodded. "Hell, yeah."

"All right. Look, we'll wait for them to go into their room and then I'll go in after them and make sure that Roxy gets out okay. After Roxy's outta the room, you take my car and head home. I'll take everything from there." Lil Joe put his phone in his pocket and handed Danny the keys to the Impala. "Give it to Roxy; she deserves it."

Danny stared Lil Joe in the face for a moment before saying, "It's been a pleasure, Joe. I don't know what will become of all this, but you'll always have a loyal friend here whenever you need me."

Lil Joe nodded and then looked in the direction of the motel office when he caught some movement out of the corner of his eye. Steve and Roxy were heading to their room. Lil Joe and Danny watched as they stopped in front of the door of a room just three doors away from the office. After they had both gone in and closed the door, Lil Joe hopped out of the Impala and said, "Show time!" Then he quickly made his way across the parking lot to the room, stopping in front of the door to pull the ten millimeter out from his waistband. He knocked three times on the door and then stood to the side out of sight of the room's window and waited. A few seconds later the door opened and a half-naked Roxy poked her head out. Lil Joe waved her to the side and stormed into the room, pointing the pistol directly at Ochoa's face.

"What the fuck is this?" a very confused and angry looking Steve Ochoa said as he got up from the bed wearing only a pair of black silk boxers.

"Shut up, stupid!" Lil Joe said. Then he turned his attention to Roxy. "Roxy, get your stuff and go out to the parking lot. Your dad's waitin' for you."

"Okay." Roxy began to dress and gather her things while Lil Joe silently stared down Ochoa and waited for her to leave.

Ochoa turned his angry scowl towards Roxy as she was about to leave. "You bitch," he yelled, you set me up!"

Roxy turned to him wearing a wicked grin. "Ha! We'll see who's the bitch when the night's over, Steve!" Then she winked at Lil Joe and walked out of the room, closing the door behind her.

"Sit down on the bed," Lil Joe commanded.

Ochoa stubbornly refused, saying, "Look, man, I don't know who the fuck you think you are, but . . . "

Lil Joe didn't let him finish. Instead he dropped the silenced gun barrel down to Ochoa's leg and shot him at close range just above his right kneecap. "Aah, fuck!" Ochoa hollered out in agony, falling to the mattress clutching his wounded leg.

"Shut up and listen, you fuckin' idiot," Lil Joe spat as he stood towering over the frightened man. He looked into Ochoa's hazel eyes and saw that the man's aggressive attitude had been replaced with fear and uncertainty.

"All right, man, what do you want?" he whimpered in pain.

"Earlier tonight a dope fiend named Eddie kidnapped my baby niece and gave her to your sister Connie in exchange for his own life for robbing one of your pushers. I want my niece back."

Ochoa shook his head and cursed. "That rat son of a bitch. I knew I shoulda killed him when I had the chance!"

Lil Joe stared Ochoa in the eye and smiled coldly. "I'm afraid it's too late for that, Steveo; maybe in the next life."

Ochoa gritted his teeth. "Why should I help you? Obviously you're gonna kill me or you wouldn't of shot me."

Lil Joe shrugged. "Maybe you're right, but you're gonna help me anyway because if you don't, I'm gonna hunt down your sister just like I did you and I'll kill her too. In fact, if you don't help me, I'll make it my life's mission to hunt down your entire family and wipe them all off the fuckin' planet!" He stood over Ochoa in silence for a moment allowing time for what he had just said to sink into his mind. "I'm not into killing women, Steveo. Neither am I inclined to take vengeance on people who have nothing to do with the cause of my anger, but whether or not I do is completely up to you."

Ochoa stared hard at Lil Joe for a moment while he digested everything he'd said to him. Then he sighed and chuckled sarcastically, realizing that he had come to the end of his road. "Who are you anyway? I should at least know who it is that's gonna send me on my way."

Lil Joe grunted. "I'm nobody, Steveo. Besides, that's not what's important. You have a choice to make. So what's it gonna be?"

Ochoa smirked and shook his head in disbelief. "All right, what do you want me to do?"

Lil Joe reached into his pocket and pulled out his phone. He tossed it onto the bed next to where Ochoa sat, bleeding. "Call your sister and tell her to listen very carefully to what you're about to say."

Ochoa nodded in acknowledgment, picked up the phone, and slowly dialed his sister's number. A few seconds later she answered and he began to give her instructions. "Hello, Connie. Yeah, it's me. Yeah, look, I need you to listen very carefully to what I'm about to tell you. Okay?"

He looked up at Lil Joe and waited to be told what to say next. "Tell her that she has to return the baby to her parents, and that she won't be in any trouble if she does. Tell her there's no cops involved and to do exactly what you say."

After Ochoa relayed the message word for word, he looked up at Lil Joe. "All right, she's on board, but she wants to know what's goin' on."

Lil Joe stuck out his free hand. "Give me the phone." Ochoa reluctantly handed it to him and Lil Joe said, "Hello, Connie?"

"Yes, who's this?"

"Never mind that. That baby girl you got is my brother's daughter, so here's the deal. I'm gonna give you a number to contact. Then exactly five minutes after we're through talking, you're gonna call that number and ask for Vanessa."

"Vanessa?" Connie repeated.

"Yes, Vanessa. She's gonna give you her address and directions to her home. Then you're gonna get in your car and drive my niece back home to her parents. Do we have an understanding?"

Lil Joe heard her sigh. Then she replied, "Yes, but it might take me a while to get there because I'm in Highland."

"That's fine. We're not going anywhere."

There was suspicious concern in Connie's voice. "Is everything okay with my brother? Because I swear we didn't know about the baby. We thought a teenage hooker had abandoned her. That's what we were told."

Lil Joe didn't bother calling her on her lie. He just wanted to get Rebecca home safe. "Your brother's fine," he lied. "After you return my niece to her parents, I'll have my people tell you where to find your brother. But this is a one-for-one exchange. Do you understand? He goes nowhere until my niece is safe at home."

Lil Joe saw Ochoa smirk at that.

"Yeah, I understand," Connie answered. "What's the number?"

"555-0204. Do you got that?"

"Yes."

"Okay, good. Remember, five minutes."

Lil Joe then called Vanessa. She answered after the second ring.

"Vanessa, it's me. Are the cops still there?"

"Joe." She sounded relieved. "Where are you?"

"Vanessa, never mind that, just listen. Are the cops still there?"

"No, they just took Marco to the hospital to be with Tina and your mom, but they said that some people from the F.B.I. would be coming over in a couple of hours to work the case from here. But Joe, shouldn't I tell them about Eddie?"

"Don't worry about Eddie. Vanessa, look mija, I need you to listen carefully. All right?"

"Uh, huh."

"I found Rebecca."

"Oh, my God! You did?" she said with a mixture of excitement and relief. "Where is she? Is she okay?"

"Yeah, she's fine, but listen, I don't have much time. In a few minutes you're gonna get a phone call from a woman named Connie. She has Rebecca. I've instructed her to call you and get directions to your place. But don't give her your address. Instead, have her meet you at the corner market where there'll be other people. Once you have Rebecca, call my cell phone and let me know that you have her. But Vanessa . . . "

"Yes, I'm listening."

"Good. Look, if for some reason she doesn't bring Rebecca or something else goes not according to plan, I want you to call me right away, and as soon as I answer, I want you to say, Hello, Jimmy, is that you? You got that?"

"Yeah," Vanessa replied, sounding a bit worried. "But should I be expecting some kind of trouble from this lady?"

Lil Joe sighed. "No, I don't think so, but you never know what to expect from anyone."

"Okay." Vanessa lowered her voice to a soft whisper. "Joe, when are you coming back?"

Lil Joe felt an instant pang in his gut. He didn't know what to tell her. "Vanessa, we'll talk when this is all over, but for now I have to go. Connie will be trying to get through to you soon. As soon as you get off the phone with her, call Marco and let him know what's going on. Okay?"

"Okay."

"Also, when Rebecca's safely with you, tell Connie that her brother's at the Motel Six in Rialto off of Foothill, Room Number 4. But only tell her that if everything goes as planned. Can you remember all of that?"

"Yes. I'm writing everything down."

"Good girl. All right, baby, you gotta hang up now."

"Okay," she said in a saddened tone. "Bye."

After he got off the phone with Vanessa, Lil Joe sat in the motel room with Ochoa and waited. The time seemed to slowly creep by, giving both Lil Joe and Ochoa plenty of time to think. Ochoa seemed to have forgotten all about the pain in his leg and he sat silently on the bloody bed appearing to be deep in thought. Lil Joe assumed that the reality of his situation had sunk in and he was trying to come to terms with his suspected fate.

Lil Joe was thinking somewhere along those lines himself, and he found it odd that he was standing silently in the small motel room staring across at a man he was about to kill and wondering what would become of his own life after the fact. Once again he found himself in a predicament where he had pretty much accomplished what he had set out to do, but he had no plans for what to do next. He knew that he had to run; that much was obvious. But the question of where was the dilemma. His thoughts were suddenly interrupted by the ringing of his cell phone. As he pushed the on button and lifted the phone to his ear, he met the gaze of Ochoa's grief stricken face. "Hello."

"Joe, it's me!" a very happy and relieved Vanessa said. "She's home, Joe, she's here with me! Marco and your mom are already on their way here. Oh, God, Joe, I'm so happy. Did you know that Marco hadn't even told Tina what had happened yet? He didn't want to upset her while she was in labor. But now . . . oh, Joe, I'm so relieved!" She sounded as though she were crying, but Lil Joe knew that her tears were tears of overwhelming joy and relief.

"That's great, baby!" He tried to sound enthusiastic, but it was hard. Of course, he was happy and relieved to know that his niece was back home safe and sound, but his mood was also gloomy because of the bitter sweetness of the moment. "So I assume that Connie's on her way here now."

"Yeah. Joe, she was real apologetic and extremely frightened." She paused for a moment. "Joe, could you please come home now? I want you here with me."

Lil Joe's heart sank down into his stomach. She really had no idea what kind of situation he was in. "I know, baby, I'll be on my way soon, but I gotta go now. Okay?"

"Okay."

He pushed the off button and tossed the phone to the motel floor. There was so much that he wanted to tell her, but he just didn't have it in him to come up with the right words. He hoped that he would have the chance to properly say goodbye to her later, but at the moment he had to focus on the task at hand. He took a few seconds to prepare himself for what he was about to do.

"Well, Steveo, your sister did the right thing and I'm a man of my word. I won't hurt her or anyone else in your family."

Ochoa gave a halfhearted smile, nodded, and said, "Get it over with ese, I'm tired of waiting already."

Lil Joe grunted. "All right then." He put the pistol into the front of his waistband and pulled the large butterfly knife out of his pocket and flipped out its blade. Ochoa's eyes widened with surprise for a brief moment before Lil Joe stepped up to him and buried the six-inch blade in his chest. A few minutes later, after positioning Ochoa's body on the bed with his back against the wall, Lil Joe took the keys to his Escalade and walked out, leaving the door open just a crack. He got into the car and moved it to the back of the parking lot facing the gruesome motel room and waited for Ochoa's sister to show up. He wanted to witness her discovering her brother's bloody corpse. He knew that it was cruel of him to want to see her reaction, but he felt that he deserved to see her suffer for her part in causing his family grief and sorrow.

He could just as easily made her suffer the same fate as Eddie and her brother, but that wasn't his style. He doubted that he could bring himself to kill a woman and he felt satisfied with what he had chosen for her punishment for her role in Rebecca's abduction. Not only was she going to have to live with the guilt of her brother's death on her conscience for the rest of her life, she was also going to have to live with the haunting image of her brother's death, and it wasn't pretty. After killing Ochoa with the knife blow to his heart, Lil Joe had cut Ochoa's body from neck to navel, opening his entire torso and releasing his intestines into a disgusting pile of bloody flesh.

Lil Joe wondered if Vanessa would still feel the same about him if she knew the kind of things he was capable of doing when enraged. He doubted it. Sometimes he even questioned his own monstrous capabilities and wondered if anyone could truly love such a being. His thoughts automatically put him back into the cold and numbing state of mind that he was accustomed to.

A few minutes later, a woman driving a dark colored sedan pulled into the parking lot and parked where the Escalade had previously been. A moment later, Lil Joe watched as the thin, medium height brunette got out of the car and wearily approached the slightly open door to Room Number 4. Lil Joe then started the Escalade's engine and soon afterwards the brunette ran out of the motel room toward the check-in office screaming in horror. The dark, pudgy clerk heard her screams and came running out to see what was going on. Lil Joe pulled the Escalade out of its dark parking space and slowly drove past the check-in office staring at the faces of the confused clerk and Ochoa's horrified sister. As he did, Connie recognized her brother's Escalade and began screaming and pointing at it as Lil Joe pulled out of the parking lot.

Almost halfway to his mother's house, Lil Joe noticed that a San Bernardino Police Department cruiser had pulled up behind him and begun to tail him. Although he wanted to believe it was just a coincidence, his gut told him it wasn't. As the wheels of his mind began turning, trying to figure out how it was possible that the police could already be on to him, his thoughts instantly went to modern technology. He had forgotten about the tracking devices that many new model cars had in them. If Connie had called the police immediately and given them the proper information about her brother's car, the police would have had no problem tracking him down.

"Fuck!" he cursed at his own carelessness in overlooking that scenario. Well, he thought, maybe it's just a coincidence. However, as he drove on in nervous anticipation, his fears of being prematurely apprehended became a reality. Just as he was about to turn off the main street and head the remaining two blocks to his mother's house, another cruiser pulled in directly behind the one that was already following him. Then the sirens began to sound as a warning for him to pull over. "Fuck you!" he muttered as he pulled onto a side street just a block away from his mother's house.

As he continued on his course, Lil Joe pretty much abandoned his earlier idea of running. Now all he wanted to do was see his family safe and together at home one last time before being hauled back to prison. He looked at the clock on the dashboard. It was 2:46 A.M..

He wondered if his family was even home, or if they had gone back to the hospital to be with Tina. As he pulled up in front of his mother's house and brought the Escalade to a stop in the middle of the street, he saw that his mother's tan Buick Regal was parked in the driveway alongside the house.

When he looked into the rearview mirror, he saw that the two police cruisers had pulled in behind him and were positioned in such a way as to block him from going back the way he had just come. Then out of nowhere, Lil Joe saw two more police cruisers come barreling down the street and come to a screeching halt just a few yards in front of the Escalade. Despite the situation, Lil Joe chuckled and muttered to himself, "I see you boys ain't bullshittin', huh?" He looked over to the passenger's seat where he had put the ten millimeter earlier while he waited for Connie to show up at the motel and began considering whether or not to hold court right then and there.

Then suddenly, out of the corner of his eye, he saw his mother's front porch light flicker on, and soon after his mother, Marco, and Vanessa stepped out onto the front porch looking weary and confused. Lil Joe stared at them for a moment. Marco was holding Rebecca in his arms and to Lil Joe's surprise, she was looking in the direction of the Escalade wearing one of her huge, angelic smiles. At that moment Lil Joe decided that he would just surrender. He couldn't hold court and go out in a blaze of gun smoke with his family standing there watching. It wouldn't be right of him to make them witness such a thing.

Just then, one of the cops got on the bullhorn and began to give him instructions. "Driver, turn off the vehicle's engine and slowly toss the keys out of the driver's side window!"

Lil Joe looked out of the windshield towards the four uniformed cops who had taken protective cover behind their open car doors and were pointing their firearms in his direction. He let out a long sigh, then complied with the instructions. After he had tossed the keys out of the window, the cop on the bullhorn yelled out more instructions. "Driver, place your left hand out of the driver's side window! Then using your right hand, slowly open the door and step out of the vehicle with both of your hands above your head!"

Lil Joe took another quick glance in the direction of his mother's front porch, then gritted his teeth and complied. After he stepped out of the Escalade, the cops closed in on him from both sides with their guns drawn yelling, "Get face down on the ground! Get face down on the ground!"

Soon after that, Lil Joe sat handcuffed in the back of one of the cruisers staring towards the Escalade while two of the officers searched it. During that time, a couple of plain clothes detectives showed up and after talking with the officers who were first on the scene, the male and female duo began talking with Vanessa and his mother. Lil Joe couldn't hear what they were talking about, but he could tell that his mother was trying to get the female detective to let her go over to the cruiser so she could talk to him. Unfortunately, the detective wouldn't allow her to do that.

Lil Joe sat in the back of the cruiser for another ten minutes before two male uniformed officers hopped into the cruiser and drove him off to the same Westside police precinct that he had been taken to some eighteen years earlier. As he sat in an interrogation cell by himself waiting to be interrogated by detectives, the only thing Lil Joe could think about was the expression on Vanessa's face as she watched the cops drive him off in the police cruiser. It was the same dreaded, hurtful, and confused expression that his mother had worn on her face back when she visited him at the police station as a kid. It was an expression he had hoped never to have to see on a loved one's face again.

CHAPTER TWENTY-EIGHT

ALMOST A YEAR LATER, LIL JOE sat in his cell in the hole at the Tehachapi Reception Center for the Department of Corrections waiting to be called out for his scheduled visit with his mother. Since his arrest, she had come to see him every other weekend, both at the county jail and at the reception center, but the upcoming visit would be the last. He had been informed Friday that he would be transferred back to the Pelican Bay S.H.U. the following week. His journey was close to its end. His whole life had basically come full circle. He was still a young man, but his life was over.

After being found guilty of two counts of first degree murder, the trial jury sentenced Lil Joe to two life terms without the possibility of parole. His trial hadn't even lasted three days. After the jury learned of all the physical evidence that linked him to both Eddie's and Ochoa's murders, along with the testimony of Ochoa's sister Connie, it was pretty much a done deal. Lil Joe hadn't even bothered to take the stand on his own behalf, not that it would have mattered anyway. There was nothing he could have said in his defense that would have changed the outcome of his trial. Besides, even though Connie had gotten on the witness stand and lied about the involvement of her and her brother in Rebecca's abduction, Lil Joe wasn't about to get on the stand and rat on her. Plus, she was pretty convincing with her story of how Eddie had dropped Rebecca off at her house claiming that he was babysitting for his sister and asking her to watch Rebecca while he ran some errands.

So it really didn't matter whether or not he told his side of the story. He knew how the system worked. The word of a convicted murderer didn't stand a chance in hell up against the word of a sweet and innocent appearing young woman. Nonetheless, he had done what he felt was right, and he wasn't surprised by the consequences. They were what they were.

He was a bit surprised at how quickly the cops had discovered Eddie's charred body. According to the court transcripts, just two days after he had been arrested for Ochoa's murder, a homeless wino had stumbled upon Eddie's remains and notified the police. After that, it didn't take long for the police forensic lab to identify the body as Eddie's, and soon after they did, Lil Joe was charged with the additional murder.

When Lil Joe was escorted to the visiting area and placed in a small visiting cell, his mother's smiling face awaited him on the other side of the glass. After the escort guards unhandcuffed him through the door slot and left, Lil Joe sat down on the small wooden stool and spoke into the screen divider. "Hello, Ma, how are you?"

"I'm fine, mijo. How are you?"

He shrugged. "I'm catching the chain back up to the Bay soon."

"Oh." His mother frowned. "When?"

"Sometime next week."

His mother made a sad face. "So this will be our last visit for a while, huh?"

Lil Joe smiled. "Yeah, Ma, but that's okay. I'll write to you at least once a week."

"Me too. I heard from your dad the other day. He said that he had just sent you a letter. He wants to visit you too."

Lil Joe smiled sorrowfully. He had wanted so badly to see his father while he was on the outside, but had never gotten the chance. He had written to his dad shortly after he was arrested and tried to explain everything that had happened the best that he could. To his relief, his father was as understanding and supportive as he had always been.

"I would like to see him too, Ma. It's been a real long time."

His mother nodded. "Oh, before I forget, mijo, Tina told me to tell you that she and Marco are going to have some pictures of Rebecca and baby Fabian developed real soon and to be expecting some in the mail."

Lil Joe smiled at the mention of his niece and newborn nephew. "Okay, thanks, Mom. But hey, tell Tina to send them to the Pelican Bay address. That way I'll get them right away."

"Okay, mijo, I will."

Lil Joe's thoughts drifted to Tina. Even after everything that had taken place between him and her brother, Eddie, she still treated him with the same loving kindness that she had since the day they met. She had even written to him while he was in the county jail and let him know that even though she was sad that her brother was dead, she held no ill feelings towards him for killing Eddie. And that she was forever grateful to him for getting Rebecca back for her and Marco. Tina was a remarkable woman in his book.

Thinking of Tina automatically reminded Lil Joe of Vanessa, and suddenly he was overcome with sadness. They hadn't had any type of communication since the night of his arrest. His mother recognized the sad look on his face and asked, "What's wrong, mijo?"

"Aw, nothin', Mom. I was just thinking about somethin'."

"You were thinking about Vanessa, huh?"

"Yeah. How is she?"

"I'm not sure, mijo. I mean, I'm sure she's fine, but ever since Marco and Tina moved out, I haven't really heard anything about her. You still love her, don't you, mijo?"

"I guess so, if that's what you wanna call it. I still think about her every day."

"Why don't you write to her? Maybe she's ready to talk about everything."

"Yeah, I don't know, Mom. Maybe I should just leave things as they are."

His thoughts drifted to something that the district attorney had said at trial during his closing statement to the jury. He had referred to Lil Joe as a violent psychopath who should never have been let out of prison to begin with. Although Lil Joe didn't agree with the first part, he did often wonder if things would have been better for everyone had he never been released from prison. When he thought about it, all that he seemed to have accomplished by getting out was hurting the people he loved. "Mam_, I'm sorry for all the pain I've caused you. All of my life, all you've ever done is love and care for me, and all I've ever done in return is cause you heartache. I don't deserve the love that you give me."

His mother wrinkled her brow and looked at him with soft, loving eyes. "No, mijo, don't think like that. I love you, and I'm proud of you. Don't ever think anything different!"

Lil Joe took a deep breath and smiled at his mother. "I love you too, Mam_, but I just wish that I could of had a different life--one that you could look upon and smile about instead of one that makes you sad when you think about it."

She shook her head and sighed heavily. "Mijo, I'll admit that things have been hard for me at times when it came to you, but you know what, I'm very proud of the man you've become. I don't care what society, or anyone else, may think about you. I know your true heart and your good intentions, and no matter what, I want you to always know that in your mother's eyes, you're a great son and an honorable man."

Lil Joe was choked up with emotion. Hearing his mother say those things to him lifted a weight off his shoulders that he had been carrying around for many years. At the end of their visit, Lil Joe went back to his cell feeling more at peace with himself than he had since he was a child.

CHAPTER TWENTY-NINE

SOMETIME DURING THE NIGHT WHILE LYING on his bunk looking back on his life, Lil Joe fell asleep thinking about everything that had occurred in his life and wondering what his purpose in life had been. The more he thought about it, the more he saw that the only thing left for him to do was to wither away and die.

Early the next morning, Lil Joe awoke in the S.H.U. to the old familiar echo of flushing toilets and running water in sinks. But he arose in good spirits, having dreamt of fond memories of times spent with Vanessa.

As he kicked the sheet off and sat up in his bunk, he smiled as he reminisced about his first night with Vanessa and how beautiful she had looked lying beside him the following morning. As unmerciful as his fate may have been, at least he would always have his memories of her.

Lil Joe shook away his thoughts and got up to begin his early morning wash and clean up ritual. Just as he was finishing up, he heard a knock on his cell wall coming from his next door neighbor, followed by a vaguely familiar voice. "Hey, Cell 102!"

"Yeah!" Lil Joe answered.

"Hey, man, what's your name?"

"My name's Lil Joe de Verdugo."

"Aw, shit, man. Is that you, Lil Joe? Hey, man, it's me, Franky!"

Lil Joe grunted. "I'll be damned," he muttered. "Ain't that something."